Second to Nun

Bad Habit Book Club Book #3

Lissa Sharpe

www.smartypantsromance.com

Copyright

Chapter 1
Nina

"Surprise!"

I freeze like a deer caught in the headlights. Actually, a deer probably has slightly better instincts. Sometimes they keep running, don't they? Or they stop in their tracks and stare the car down, hoping they can intimidate the driver in to swerving away.

I don't do either of those things. When I open a door to a darkened apartment, hear someone shouting at me, and my instincts tell me that I'm about to be murdered, I don't run away or bravely stand my ground.

I close my eyes and wait to die.

"Nina?"

Recognizing Helen's voice, I open my eyes again. She approaches me from the darkened inner room, smiling apologetically, her eyes filled with concern. "You poor thing!" Over her shoulder, she calls out, "I told you this was a bad idea!" To me again, "Matilda really wanted this to be a surprise party. Blame her for everything."

"Matilda's here?" I ask, confused but happy at this development. Now *that* is a nice surprise—finding out that a friend who's recently moved away is back for a visit. Getting yelled at as you walk into a darkened room? Not so much.

Matilda bounds toward me from out of the shadows, beaming, arms outstretched. "Nina!" She envelops me in one of her too-tight, but completely heartfelt, hugs. "Surprise parties are fun! It was fun, wasn't it?"

When she pulls back, waiting expectantly for my response, her smile is so big it transforms her entire face. She hardly looks like the dour, cynical woman she was almost a year ago before she met her now husband. Back then, she wasn't one for physical affection, even with her closest friends. Now she's offering out hugs like candy at a parade, even if she hasn't totally gotten the hang of them yet.

I don't want to make her feel bad about her obvious excitement over the idea of a surprise party, so I just nod as enthusiastically as I can. "So fun," I agree.

Appeased, Matilda grins. Then her expression narrows with irritation as she pivots to look back over her shoulder. "Turn the lights on already! She obviously knows we're here now. The surprise is over!"

Ah, there's the friend I know. I love all the changes I've seen in my friend since she met Kimo, but sometimes I do miss her old brusque, curt self. Seeing glimpses like this let me know the old Matilda is still buried somewhere underneath all those happy smiles. I want her to be happy, of course, but it's good to know she can still be counted on to lead the survivors if there's ever a zombie apocalypse.

Various lights around the room turn on, revealing the other attendees of what, I suppose, is my going-away party: Thad, Helen's fiancé, who looks glum about the fact that he has somehow been talked into wearing a party hat. (Honestly, I have some questions about how that was accomplished.) Kimo, Matilda's husband, who is his usual big happy ball of energy, punctuated by his own paper hat and party horn that he blows enthusiastically. And Grady, who gives me an apologetic shrug, like *What are you gonna do?* since he totally could have warned me about this whole surprise-party thing but obviously didn't.

I give him my best death glare, even though I've been told it's more *cute* than *fear inspiring*. I guess when you're five foot nothing, pretty much everything you do is considered cute. Reaching for something on a high shelf? Cute! Riding a bike? Cute! Shouting in irritation at a broken parking meter? Cute! It's a bit frustrating sometimes to be treated like a doll when you're a full-grown woman, but I've gotten used to it. Mostly.

This eclectic group of people make up my very best friends in the entire world. Most of us have very little in common, except for the big thing we have in common—Matilda, Helen, and I are all former nuns, and Grady is an ex-priest. We each served for different amounts of time and at different levels of intensity. Matilda belonged to the most austere order, the Poor Clares; Helen was technically a sister, never a full-fledged nun; and I was only ever a postulant. Grady was a priest for the longest amount of time and is the one who most recently left his order.

So despite being different ages and coming from different backgrounds, there's a common language we speak, a common experience that no one else can really understand unless they've lived through it. It's bonded the four of us forever, no matter how our lives change.

And there have been some big changes over the past couple years: Helen falling in love with her bounty hunter, Thad, and getting engaged; Matilda marrying Kimo and moving to Hawai'i with him and his family; and Grady finally teaching me how to ride a bicycle. Okay, that last one might not sound quite as life-changing, but it's really helped me get around downtown Chicago much faster.

"Peke!" Kimo greets me, coming forward for a hug. He's so tall that it's always somewhat comical to attempt to find a non-awkward way to fit our bodies together. We manage by me going up on my tiptoes and him hunching over.

"Peke?" Helen repeats.

"Kinda like shorty," I tell her. It's the nickname Kimo started calling me around Thanksgiving. I was supposed to go out and visit him and Matilda and the kids for a week in Hawai'i—they'd bought the plane tickets for me and everything— but at the last minute, I couldn't find my passport or driver's license. I was absolutely crushed to be missing the visit, and I was so embarrassed to have wasted their money; but they surprised me by buying last-minute tickets to come see me instead. Flying five people (including Matilda, his mother, his niece and nephew, and himself) the week of Thanksgiving and buying the tickets with less than twenty-four hours' notice must have been enormously expensive, but they'd insisted they wanted to be with me for the holiday. And they had been, whenever I wasn't helping my aunt and uncle with whatever they needed.

So while normally I wouldn't *love* someone calling me a name based off my height, or lack thereof, I know it comes from a place of affection. Plus the size difference between Kimo and me really is hard to ignore. And Kimo's so good-hearted that he could probably find a way to call you "poop face" that would sound endearing.

I smile at the man in question as he wraps an arm around Matilda. "You two didn't have to come all the way out here for this!" I say, although I'm so thankful they did. Aside from some video chats, I haven't seen the two of them since Thanksgiving, so about six months ago now. We all make the best of things, using our group chats (one with the guys and one without) to regularly keep in touch, but there's a noticeable hole in our friend group without them around. I like it best when we're all together.

"Nonsense. Of course we did!" Matilda ushers us forward so we can join Thad and Grady in the living room. The couples arrange themselves around their respective partners, and I take a seat next to Grady on the "singles" couch. I don't think anyone pairs us this way intentionally; it's just the natural pattern we fall into whenever we all manage to be in the same place at the same time.

"We had to see you off for your big adventure!" Helen agrees.

"How long are you going to be gone, anyway?" Kimo wants to know.

"I think it's supposed to take about eight weeks." I hope my smile doesn't slip too much at the prospect. I'll be traveling with my aunt, uncle, and cousins to a town called Green Valley in the mountains of Tennessee so my cousin Harmony can participate on a reality dating show called *Mountain Man*. It's a pretty big departure for my serious, church-going aunt and uncle, but Harmony has managed to persuade them that she can use the show to launch her career as an Instagram pastor and "help spread the glory of Christ."

In my humble opinion, I have a hard time imagining God using reality television or Instagram to spread the good news. But no one asked my opinion on it. They never do.

"Eight whole weeks?" Matilda protests, sounding put out, even though (again) she doesn't live here anymore and thus likely wouldn't see me in all that time, anyway. "Why? You're not going to be on the show, are you?"

"No!" I repress a shudder at the thought—all the lights and cameras and attention focused on me. No, thank you. That's Harmony's forte, not mine. I'm not really a spotlight kind of person. I prefer to lurk in the background. That word always has a negative connotation—*lurk*—but I'm not sure why. It isn't only scary things that prefer to stay hidden in the shadows. "I'm just going along to help with the kids."

My uncle and aunt have eight children. The two oldest have already gotten married and moved out of the house; Harmony, the oldest one living at home, is twenty-two, a few years younger than me. Charity and Honor, the next oldest kids, are off at college and a mission trip, respectively, but that still leaves the three youngest siblings who need extra help sometimes. Plus there's the cooking, the cleaning, the laundry, and all the other household tasks that I'm in charge of.

"Helping with the kids" is the umbrella term that's been used to cover everything I do for my family since I was a child myself. I know it sounds like a lot. Okay, maybe it doesn't just *sound like* a lot—it *is* a lot. It's a full-time job that I've never been paid for. And if I'm being honest, sometimes I do resent it. There are other things I used to dream about doing with my life. But at the end of the day, when your family needs help, you help your family. Especially when you owe them so very much.

The room falls silent, and I can tell everyone is trying to exchange glances without me noticing that they're exchanging glances. I give them a moment to get it out of their systems, staring down at my lap. I'm used to this—all the meaningful looks that I'm not supposed to see.

Grady nudges me with his elbow. "Help me with some drinks, yeah?" He makes a show of looking around the room. "Beer? Wine? What's everyone having . . . ?"

As soon as we're in the kitchen, I smile at him gratefully. "Is it just me, or have they gotten even *less* subtle in the past few months?"

"Less chances to practice, I expect," Grady returns easily. "With Matilda and Kimo living so far away now and all. Harder to exchange weighted looks over Zoom."

As he gathers all the drinks, he glances at me sidelong. "You're all right though?"

I like the way he checks in on me. He doesn't try to talk around his concern, like I won't notice, but he also doesn't tell me what I should be feeling about a situation. He gives me the chance to ask for help if I need it, then lets it go if I don't.

Because of that, I feel freer to talk to him than I do my other friends. I know they mean well, but sometimes they treat me like I'm so delicate I start to *feel* that way around them, too. Not with Grady, though. He's become the big brother I never knew I wanted or needed.

I shrug in answer to his question. "It doesn't make a huge difference to me, whether I'm stuck in a house in Tennessee or in Illinois."

Stuck is maybe putting it too strongly. I don't want to sound ungrateful. My uncle and aunt have done a lot for me over the years. My parents died when I was seven—a car accident. We didn't live near any family, so for three months I was under the custody of child protective services, moved from foster family to foster family. To be honest, I can't remember much from that time. I know, of course, that I was devastated about losing my parents, but I think the shock was so intense that it's like there's Bubble Wrap around those memories. I can't get too close to them without popping something painful, so I usually just leave them alone.

Suffice it to say, there weren't a lot of people clamoring to adopt an emotionally traumatized, practically mute little kid. Except for Uncle Aaron and Aunt Hope. They took me in when nobody else wanted me. And they took me *back* after I made a mess out of everything. It's only fair that they expect some things in return, like keeping up with the daily grind of a house full to bursting with people. Of course, all of that stuff wears on you over time, especially if you have other part-time jobs you do to pay rent, but that's just life, isn't it? Real life, anyway. Not the stuff out of fairy tales.

I'm not being totally honest, though, about it not making a difference where I go with my family. At least here in Chicago, I have my book club group, even if our numbers have been dwindling lately. I have Tuesday night Pizookies with my friends (including Matilda over Zoom), and when my temp jobs are located in the city, I meet up regularly with Grady for lunch.

In Tennessee? I'll have nobody.

Selfish, I chastise myself. That's the second sin I'll have to write in my sin journal tonight. Being selfish and lying.

Grady looks pretend thoughtful as he strokes his face. "You know, there's a pub expo coming up in Knoxville. I was thinking I might drive down there and check it out. Turns out it's not too far of a drive from Green Valley—if you'd like a visit from a grouchy ol' fella."

He's trying his best not to smile, so I do it for him, launching myself at him and hugging him. "That'd be all right," I agree.

Carrying Helen's glass of wine and two bottled beers for Thad and Kimo, I head back down the hallway toward the living room. Grady sent me on ahead since he's making a more complicated mocktail for Matilda and me; Matilda is trying to get pregnant, so she's not drinking at the moment, and though I'm allowed the occasional indulgence of a glass of alcohol, I'd rather use my splurging for the week on some of the delicious brownies Helen made.

Before I can reach the living room, though, I catch a fragment of the conversation that's been going on in my absence. ". . . of course I'm worried! Those people are awful to her."

It's Matilda speaking—as usual, at ever too slightly loud a pitch for the size of the room—and I glean pretty quickly that the "her" in question is me. "Those people" must be my aunt and uncle. I guess it shouldn't come as too much of a surprise that my friends discuss my family situation when I'm not around, but I've never actually overheard what they say. Despite myself, I'm curious.

"Don't work yourself up, Mattie." Kimo's soothing voice is less piercing and therefore more difficult to hear. "But yeah, those people are definitely buttheads. Should we offer to let her stay with us again?"

"We've tried that, too." Helen, now. "I don't know if she wants to go to Tennessee, or if they just aren't giving her an option."

"I've run their backgrounds." Thad is quietest of all, which is inconvenient since I'm most interested in hearing how that disclosure is going to continue. I take another tentative step closer, hoping the floorboards don't betray me. "No arrests for the uncle or aunt, but something is fishy. They've moved around too frequently."

Every two to three years, for most of the time I've lived with them. When I was seven, they were in North Carolina. Down to Georgia at age ten. Then Arkansas, Oklahoma, and Texas. They were in Ohio while I was in the convent, then spent one year in Pennsylvania. Illinois is the longest they've stayed in one place, going on four years now. Maybe that's why I've been so unfazed by the sudden relocation to Tennessee. A part of me has been waiting to pack our bags and start everything all over again, even as I desperately hoped this would be the time we stayed put. Chicago is the first place that's really felt like home to me. It's the first place I've had friends. It's the first place I've had *anything* outside of my uncle's church.

"Maybe that's normal for her uncle's line of work?" Helen suggests, though she sounds uncertain. "I'm not sure how it works with the evangelicals."

I realize I'm not sure, either, despite having lived with my uncle for all these years. I always assumed it was normal, how often we moved around from place to place, how frequently the name of my uncle's church changed as he started a new congregation. The rules and practices have always remained the same, though; I figured it wasn't too unusual to rebrand in each new place. Now, hearing the way they're talking about it? I'm not so certain.

It seems like no one else knows, either, since a moment of silence briefly falls, only to be punctured by Matilda. "They're creeps! I'm sorry, but it isn't right how they keep her on that leash. We all know it isn't right."

"I understand, babe, but what can we do? Aside from being there for her, if and when she needs us. Until then, we have to trust her. She *is* an adult, after all."

I expect a sharp retort from Matilda, but instead it's Helen who gives an aggrieved sigh. "It's just . . . sometimes she feels *so* innocent. Our little fairy-tale princess . . ."

This isn't the first time I've overheard my friends call me a fairy-tale princess. Because I love them, and I know they love me, I know this isn't a criticism. I know what they mean when they call me that. They mean that I'm pretty and quiet and a little sad.

That last part is important, even if they don't realize it. Calling someone a fairy-tale princess is probably meant to be a compliment but only if you haven't really been paying attention to fairy tales. The princess might get her happily ever after in the end, but only after a lot of pain. Misunderstandings. Loss. Heartbreak.

People always talk about fairy tales like they're these idealized fantasies. A fairy-tale romance is supposed to be one that feels too good to be true. But anyone who's read fairy tales knows they're bleak. Grim. Full of pain and sorrow.

A love that could overcome that is extremely rare. And it doesn't come easy or cheap. So, of course it's the thing everybody would wish for—a love that could bloom out of so much ugliness and endure through so many thorns.

I don't have too much longer before I'm either discovered by the living-room group or by Grady coming up behind me with the other drinks. Still, I take just a moment to press my eyes shut and inhale deeply through my nose. That word has hounded my steps for a long time now. *Innocent.* It always amazes me that this is how my friends see me, when I know the truth about myself to be very far from that.

I'm not so innocent. And definitely not as naive as they all think.

Chapter 2
Nina

I've done some things I'm not proud of in my life.

I've lied to my aunt and uncle, several times. Mostly through the sin of omission, not outright fabrication, but still. A lie is a lie. *The Lord detests lying lips.* And yet I do it so frequently. Here are just some of the things I've lied about:

Sometimes I crave sugar so bad that I sneak into the pantry when everyone else is asleep and take a handful of sugar cubes to bring up to my room. I don't do it too often, but whenever I do, I don't write about it in my weekly food journal. (*Gluttony.*)

I keep a stash of fashion magazines in my room. They're usually just the old ones that the library would otherwise throw away. Helen saves some for me, and I slip them into my piano sheet music so Aunt Hope won't see me bringing them into the house. I like to look at the way the clothes are made and try to figure out what pattern I would use or what type of material something is made of. (*Worldliness.*)

I keep leftover scraps from the clothes I make for my family and practice making some of the outfits I see in my magazines. They always turn out strange because the fabric is mishmashed and not quite right, but sometimes, I'm proud of how well they look. (*Pride.*) I daydream about sequins and fabric and thread the way Harmony dreams about makeup. (*Envy. Greed.*)

It irritates me that Aunt Hope changed her name from Esperanza to be more white passing. I hate that she dyes her hair a lighter brown and uses special creams so her skin won't get as tan. I hate it even more that Uncle Aaron still always uses her as his example of how the Lord loves *all* people, even if they committed "the terrible sin of being born brown." He's never said that in so many words, of course, but sometimes I feel like that's the underlying truth no one is saying out loud. I hate that I think that way, and I hate that I can't stop. (*Judge not, lest ye shall be judged.*)

I stained the carpet once with cranberry juice and blamed it on Isaiah, when he was still too young to speak up for himself. (*Dishonesty.*)

I don't defend my aunt and uncle to my friends because sometimes I agree with them. Sometimes I think my aunt and uncle are too overbearing. Sometimes I resent all the rules they make me follow and all the things I've had to give up to make them happy. (*Ingratitude.*)

This last one might be one of my worst sins, because deep down I know my uncle and aunt are right to treat me the way they do. I'm a sinful person. My judgment might seem right to me, but I've made mistakes before—big mistakes. Mistakes that will follow me for the rest of my life.

So even though I chafe against my uncle's rules, even though I sometimes wish I could live a normal life, I know this is what's best. I've stumbled too many times to be left on my own.

I'm not someone whose judgment can be trusted.

I'm going to tell you a story now, and I'm going to tell it *as* a story. A fairy tale. Not because I imagine myself as being as brave or strong or resilient as any of my favorite fairy-tale characters. But because sometimes it's easier to remember the things that have happened to me if I can think of them almost like they were happening to someone else. If I can reimagine them as the kind of tale that might have a happy ending, if someone else were writing it.

The Orphan Girl and the Thief
Part One

Second to Nun

When the Orphan Girl was eighteen, she made the biggest mistake of her life.

She can't talk about it. Still. Ever. That isn't what *this* story is about.

But it was the reason she was sent to a convent to take her vows—even though doing so would mean following the same religion that her relatives had once told her was so wicked and false. Anyone who would take her off their hands turned out to be not so very wicked after all.

The Orphan Girl was surprised to find that convent life wasn't much of an adjustment after living in her uncle's house. She was told to be silent. She lived a life of prayer and scripture study and service. The nuns called her by her new religious name given to her as a postulant, Agnes, which also wasn't so different, since she was used to being whatever someone else wanted her to be.

About six months into the Orphan Girl's postulancy, Sister Theresa recruited her, along with a few nuns and a handful of other postulants and novices, to serve at the local prison, ministering to anyone who was seeking Christ through Bible study and prayer.

That was where she met the Thief.

The Orphan Girl didn't notice the Thief at first. She tried not to look too closely at any of the men during worship. It wasn't because they were prisoners—after all, Christ had said to do good to those who were *even the least of these my brethren.*

It was because they were *men.* The Orphan Girl had a hard time trusting men. There were also too many memories of Uncle Aaron, keeping the family under his thumb. They could never challenge him, they could never raise their voices to him.

Then there were the memories she wouldn't let herself think about, memories of the biggest mistake she'd ever made.

Men were dangerous, you see.

So the Orphan Girl always kept her eyes down on her Bible. At the end of each meeting, it was her job to gather up all the handouts that had been left behind.

On her third visit to the prison, the Orphan Girl noticed that someone had made a detailed drawing on one of the printouts. When she examined it more closely, she saw it wasn't just any drawing.

It was a sketch of *her.*

Someone had drawn her from the shoulders up, wearing her black tunic, her head, neck, and hair covered by her coif. Her expression was serene and downcast, only the faintest hint of light showing in her eyes.

The drawing didn't take any liberties. It didn't capture anything that couldn't have been easily observed by any one of the men. It shouldn't have felt as deeply personal as it did. But the fact that someone had observed her so closely rattled the Orphan Girl. Whoever the prisoner was who had drawn this, he was a skilled artist. He'd only used what appeared to be a basic pencil, but she recognized her own expression, the slight tilt to her head, the way she tucked her chin slightly under. Her long, naturally dark lashes and the curve of her mouth. The shadows from the light overhead, playing out across her features.

The Orphan Girl threw the picture away. She always regretted that afterward, but in the moment, she worried it would be vain to keep it.

When they met with the prisoners the next week, though, the Orphan Girl circumspectly cast her eyes around the room as Sister Theresa took everyone through a reading of Psalms. Everyone was looking down at their printouts of the verses.

One pair of eyes, though, was focused on her.

The Orphan Girl had never seen eyes like those before, and she hadn't since. They were pale sage green, with just the slightest hint of hazel in them. And they were watching her so closely, as if tracing every faint shift of her expression.

The Thief's face was beautiful—there was no other way to describe it. The Orphan Girl had never thought of a man as being beautiful before, but he was. His dark blond hair was buzzed down almost to the scalp, which only intensified the symmetry of his face—his strong jaw and sculpted nose. He had a tattoo of what looked like a dragon climbing up his neck from underneath the collar of his shirt, which should have made him look dangerous, maybe a little scary; but this roughness was contrasted sharply with his lips, surprisingly full for a man's, plush and soft looking.

When their gazes met, the Orphan Girl felt like someone had turned on all the lights in her body. She quickly looked away, back down at the Bible, her hands shaking under the table.

She didn't dare look up again for the rest of the meeting. But afterward, when the Orphan Girl went to gather the handouts, she saw another sketched version of herself waiting. This time, she was looking up and straight ahead. The way the

Thief had drawn her, it was as though her dark eyes were staring straight off the page, gazing out at her. And at him, as he'd drawn her.

The Orphan Girl felt a complicated series of emotions in response. A thrill at being singled out, at being *seen*. Followed by an immediate sense of shame, because she was so susceptible to vanity. Then worry, because vanity could be a very slippery slope into far worse sin, as she'd learned once before. Then guilt, because she ought to tell someone what was happening. Then more guilt, because she didn't *want* to say anything, because she knew that then it would stop. No more drawings, no more Thief.

So the Orphan Girl didn't say anything. (*Lying by omission.*)

That silence opened a door between her and the Thief, and in the weeks that followed, the sketches kept coming. Sometimes he would write her messages— short little notes, mostly, that could have been for anyone, but she knew they were for her.

My name is Cass.

I like your smile.

Your eyes are incredible.

I could draw your face for the rest of my life and never get bored.

The Orphan Girl started to pay more attention to the Thief in their weekly meetings, doing so as subtly as she could, so no one else would notice. She tried not to let *him* notice, either, but whenever he caught her watching, he would smile at the Orphan Girl, and it would send her heart into a gallop.

Made you look, he'd write to her when that happened.

But the Orphan Girl noticed things about the Thief, too, that he probably would have been just as surprised to learn. The way the other men interacted with him, and the guards, too. They sometimes teased him about being so good-looking. The Orphan Girl guessed that's where his name probably came from—Cass, short for Cassanova, because he was so charming. She worried that meant he had lots of women writing to him, visiting him, maybe even waiting for him on the outside. He must have noticed that, too, because one day he wrote her a simple message:

I only have eyes for you.

On that day, he only drew the Orphan Girl's eyes, nothing else, staring out from the page. There was such an intense expression in them, a mixture of hope, of worry, of longing, of fear. She didn't know how he managed to capture all of those feelings in nothing but a pair of eyes, but she saw them all there. She saw exactly how he saw *her*.

These silent exchanges of details and shared looks and scattered words went on for weeks and weeks. It all added up to a bunch of nothings, but it began to feel like everything to the Orphan Girl. It was the only thing she had to look forward to all week long. It was the only time she felt like she wasn't invisible.

No, that wasn't entirely right. Her whole life, people had commented on what a pretty girl she was, then what a beautiful woman, but that kind of praise had always made her feel uncomfortable. She didn't want most people to notice her or single her out. It felt like they only did so because they wanted to take something from her.

With the Thief, though, it didn't feel that way. It felt like he was giving her something by noticing all those little things about her.

It was the first time the Orphan Girl wanted to be seen.

Chapter 3
Nina

"We're in Tennessee!" Harmony hollers, rolling down the fifteen-passenger-van window so she can stick out her head and howl like she's a she-wolf. "Land of whiskey and country singers and . . . trees!"

My eyes dart up to Uncle Aaron as I wait for his response. From where I'm sitting in the back of the car, I can only see the back of his golden-blond head and part of his profile; I can't see the exact expression in his pale blue eyes. The sunlight streaming through the driver's window glints off the platinum of his Cartier watch; he's in slacks and a button-up shirt, even though we've just been driving all day. *You never know who might be watching,* he reminded us before we left the roadside hotel that morning.

For a moment, it feels like everyone in the car is holding their breath, waiting to see how Uncle Aaron will react to Harmony's joyous howling. After a moment, he just huffs a little and shakes his head, like *Oh, well. That's just Harmony.*

And that *is* just Harmony. She's always been this way, from the time she was a young girl. Fiercely and unapologetically herself. You would think with seven siblings, she might disappear in a sea of children, especially being stuck in the middle. Instead, Harmony seems to have taken her inauspicious birth order placement as a challenge to stand out in every way possible. Her height helps make that possible, since she's the tallest girl in her family by a few inches, and her food journal is kept just as strictly as mine, so she's slim with an athletic frame. Her signature color is pink, and she's always wearing it on at least one piece of her outfit; today she's in a ruffly pink T-shirt, jeans, and white sneakers with laces that match her top.

She's a bright, beaming ray in Uncle Aaron's dour house, and even though he's always quick to squash his other children under his thumb when they try to assert any independence, Harmony's always seemed to have immunity somehow.

I honestly can't think of any of her siblings even being bold enough to attempt what Harmony's managed to pull off with this trip. Not only has she convinced Uncle Aaron and Aunt Hope to pick up and move to a different state for almost two months, she's also somehow gotten their blessing to appear on a TV show. A *reality dating competition* TV show. With lumberjacks. I think? I'm not entirely sure what the show's about, since this will be its first season—not that we would have been allowed to watch it if it were already airing, anyway.

Aunt Hope turns in her seat. "Harmony Anne, shut that window before you destroy all of our eardrums. Or ruin your blowout."

Knowing my cousin, I've no doubt it's the second part of that statement, and not the first, that persuades her to hurriedly roll up the window. (That's right—we're old-school in this fifteen-passenger van. No fancy automatic windows for us!) With a sigh, Harmony falls back against her seat. "Green Valley, I think I'm in love!"

She's not the only one. In all the moving we've done around the United States, I don't know if I've ever seen a place quite this beautiful. We had to drive through Great Smoky Mountains National Park—hundreds of miles of lush forest, majestic mountains, and leaf-covered paths that disappeared into endless stretches of trees—to get to this amazingly quaint little valley, nestled in between mountains—a cozy, homey, magical town with shops and cafes and bearded men galore.

It almost feels like . . . well, it almost feels like a fairy tale.

The nice kind. Not the kind with toes getting chopped off or whatnot. Although sometimes, they are all one and the same . . .

"We're staying at a place called the Donner Lodge," Harmony gushes, like she can't believe it's all happening to her. That's part of Harmony's charm, too—she becomes so genuinely excited every time she gets her way. "It's where that lady I love from Instagram—the banana cake queen, Jennifer Winston—makes her famous, award-winning banana cake. I can't wait to try it."

"Instagram?" Uncle Aaron repeats.

His tone makes my spine stiffen and my armpits break out in vicarious nervous sweat, but Harmony just laughs it off. "I only go on there to post Bible verses and find recipes, Daddy. That's how I know about the banana cake . . ."

Liar, liar, pants on fire, I could say if I wanted to get Harmony in trouble. And/or if I were twelve. Just the other day she was showing me all the profiles of the men she thought might be part of the show, even though the producers are keeping all of that hush-hush. That hasn't stopped Harmony from putting her detective skills to good use.

"He's single, good-looking, lives in the Green Valley area, and he works at a gym, which everyone knows means he can take eight weeks off work to film." She explained her deductive reasoning to me before clicking on one of the photos. "And just look at his abs! *Yum* . . ."

Just like I keep my box of secret fashion magazines, Harmony has collected pictures of handsome men over the years—movie stars and musicians and whatnot—so she can . . . gaze upon their strong chins and hard bodies, I guess? I don't blame Harmony for having her own secret vice, but I've personally never been able to get that excited about someone just by looking at a picture of them. Attraction for me is less about the way a person looks and more about who that person is—their likes and their mannerisms and the way they talk and move. You can't tell any of that from a picture.

But Harmony sure likes looking—and it isn't banana cake recipes she spends most of her time scrolling through on Instagram. I raise my eyebrows at her, and she just giggles, completely unrepentant. "Mmm, I can't wait to try some banana cake on this trip," she says, waggling her eyebrows at me, and I can't help but laugh with her, shaking my head.

Harmony gushes her way through the hotel check-in, rhapsodizing about how glamorous the Lodge is and how sweet it was of the producers to put all of us up in a suite and how she can't *believe* she gets her own room, etcetera, etcetera. I love Harmony, but sometimes she's a bit much. I've tuned her out by the time I finish putting away everyone's luggage into their respective rooms.

Note—I *won't* be getting my own room. I'll be sharing with my two younger female cousins, who are fifteen and sixteen. It was decided that my thirteen-year-old cousin, Isaiah, needs the other single room to himself, because . . . testosterone, I guess? I do get my own bed, though, since Felicity and Merit will be sharing the bunk beds.

I think. Surely they wouldn't put me in a bunk bed, right . . . ?

Harmony's been swanning through the suite, exclaiming about everything she comes across, so at first I don't register her "Hey, what's this?" But she must've not got the response she hoped to receive, since a moment later, she asks again, louder, "Hey, what's this?"

I exchange a quick glance with my cousin Merit—the there-she-goes-again look that my introverted young cousin and I have bonded over throughout the years—before we begrudgingly go to see what all the fuss is about. I've learned from experience that until Harmony gets the attention she's seeking, she will *keep* seeking.

"What is it, Harm?" I ask obligingly as I find her in an empty room in the suite.

To be fair, it *is* a strange room. It looks too small to be a bedroom, but too big to be a closet—plus it has a window. Aunt Hope pops her head in the doorway and frowns. "Storage?" she guesses. "We can put all of our luggage in here to keep it out from underfoot."

"Or," Harmony interjects quickly, "Nina could stay in here!"

I look at her in surprise, then panic, wondering what she's up to. It's already been decided: I'm sharing a room with the twins. I shake my head at Aunt Hope to show her this wasn't my idea. "It's fine. I don't mind sharing—"

"But Nina gets up so early to make breakfast, and sometimes she's up late doing the laundry or tidying up," Harmony reminds her mother. "And Felicity is such a light sleeper . . ."

I can see Aunt Hope weighing the options in her mind. Uncle Aaron was the one who determined I should stay with the younger girls, and she never speaks out in opposition to him. But we all know what Felicity is like when her sleep is interrupted. (Proverbs 21:19—look it up.)

"I'll speak to Father about it," Aunt Hope says, giving me a firm look, as if this was all my idea. "Don't get your hopes up."

After she leaves, and Merit goes in search of something to eat, Harmony looks over at me with her trademark mischievous grin. "Don't ever say I never did anything nice for you."

I want to remind her that I didn't ask for this—and that if Uncle Aaron gets irritated by the request, I'm the one who will take the blame. But Harmony looks so excited, and it *would* be nice to have my own space away from the twins. "You are incorrigible," I tell her.

She brightens. "What does that mean? Does it mean I'm pretty?"

I roll my eyes, although I can't totally squash my smile. "Yes. That's exactly what it means."

Before too long, there's a knock at the door, interrupting our unpacking. We all poke our heads out of our respective rooms and go into the common room to see who it might be.

As soon as the man sweeps into the room, I know he is the showbiz type—not just because he's unusually trim and handsome, with almost blindingly white teeth, but also because he's wearing salmon-colored pants and glasses that seem to be purely ornamental. "Welcome, Miller family!"

We all look to Uncle Aaron to see what his reaction will be. I've heard him give sermons before about "effeminate manhood," and I have a feeling that we'll all be getting an earful later about the producer's "pink" pants.

But for now, to the producer's face, Uncle Aaron smiles his trademark, golden-boy smile. Even though he's in his fifties, you can still see traces of the high school quarterback who became a successful salesman who became an even more successful pastor. That smile of his makes you feel like he's your best friend, like you're the most interesting person in the room.

Not that I would know from experience; he's never used it on me. But I've seen the effect it has on other people.

"Thank you so much." He shakes the producer's hand earnestly, sandwiching it between both of his palms. "We feel so blessed that y'all have welcomed us with such open hearts."

The producer looks a little disoriented, receiving so much intense focus from Uncle Aaron. *Dazzled* is what people usually say after meeting him, like they've just brushed up against a celebrity. "Of course! I'm Lyle, and I'll be happy to help you all with whatever you need."

His tone is perfectly friendly, but he pulls away from what Harmony jokingly calls Uncle Aaron's "triple-decker handshake," taking a careful step back as he turns to face the rest of us. There's nothing rude about what he just did, but he didn't seem to have fallen for the full Uncle Aaron effect like most people do. I see Uncle Aaron register this, and I swallow as I watch the way his jaw sets ever so slightly.

Then for some reason, Lyle's eyes zero in on me, and they widen a notch. "Harmony. My God. They told me you were beautiful, but I didn't know you were so stunning." He glances back at his assistant, who seems to be writing down everything he says religiously. "Tell makeup they won't have to do much to make this one camera-ready."

My face floods with heat—both because of Lyle's gushing, and because I'm aware of Uncle Aaron's gaze on me. "Oh, no, I'm not—"

"I'm Harmony!" Harmony chimes in, entering the room with a good-natured flourish. "And I got chosen for my charm, not my looks, thank you very much!"

She's being self-deprecating. Harmony *is* beautiful. She's the wholesome, bubbly, sunny girl next door. People just tend to fuss over my looks because I'm so out of place with the rest of my family. My cousins all inherited my uncle's height and paler skin, and almost all of my female cousins have dyed their hair blonder to mask the naturally dark hair they inherited from Aunt Hope. As a result, with my dark brown hair, olive-toned skin, and dark eyes, plus my small and compact frame, I'm the odd one out in every family photo.

Lyle moves on easily to Harmony as the lead he should be fussing over. "Of course you're Harmony! How does the Miller family manage to produce so many beauties?"

It's a diplomatic way to save face and also include my younger cousins in the compliment. So there's no reason for Uncle Aaron to clear his throat. "*She* isn't a Miller," he says, jerking his chin at me. "She's a Delgado."

The mood in the room instantly becomes strained. I keep my gaze trained on the floor so I won't have to see anyone's face or how they react to what he just said. Technically he's right, of course. I'm not a Miller. I have a different surname.

Uncle Aaron didn't say anything untrue or even especially unkind—but it still stings, because I know what he's really saying. *She's not one of us.*

"Riiight," Lyle says after a moment, his voice falsely bright. It's the voice you use when you've accidentally stepped into another family's mess and you don't know how to get yourself out of it. "Well, like I said before, I'm Lyle Mortimer, and I'm the producer who's been assigned to guide Harmony through the turbulence of reality television."

He's trying his best to inject some positivity back into the room, and Harmony joins him with an exuberant squeal. "I can't wait!" She throws back her head and poses dramatically. "I'm ready for my close-up, Mr. DeMille!"

Lyle furrows his brow ever so slightly, evidently confused by the reference. "It's Mr. Mortimer—but please, call me Lyle."

Harmony's face tinges with pink. She was quoting the classic Hollywood movie *Sunset Boulevard;* actually, to be technical, she was misquoting it, but it hardly seems like the time to tell her that. Uncle Aaron and Aunt Hope have always highly regulated what we are allowed to watch in their house, but almost anything made before 1960 is fair game, so we've watched a lot of classic films over the years. Sometimes it's hard to remember that not everyone else is as familiar with them nowadays.

"We'll need to grab Harmony for an hour or so to do a meet and greet with the other Mountainettes," Lyle continues, "but Miller family and . . . uh, others . . . please feel free to let me know at any point if you need anything to make your stay more comfortable."

Lyle has just dropped a bombshell, although he probably doesn't realize it. I look at Harmony, only to see her face pale. "I'm sorry, did you just say *other* Mountainettes?" She does her best to keep smiling. "I thought I was *the* Mountainette."

"That *was* the original plan," Lyle agrees, "but then Sienna and Raquel realized they didn't want to get sued by *The Bachelorette,* so we're shaking things up a bit and have multiple Mountainettes dating multiple Mountain Men. Fun, right?" Seeming to sense that he's ruffled Harmony's feathers with this news, Lyle presses on. "You know Sienna Diaz and Raquel Ezra, our executive producers and movie stars extraordinaire?"

Despite her reservations, Harmony can't help but beam at the name drop of two of the world's biggest movie stars. Even *I've* heard those names before, though I've never seen any of their films, since I don't get to see too many movies that aren't G-rated. "Of course I do!" she gushes, then sees the look on Uncle Aaron's face and quickly amends, "I mean, not *that* well, but I've heard of them. I don't watch anything that isn't uplifting to the Lord. Naturally."

Lyle looks back and forth between Harmony and Uncle Aaron, seeming to fully register just what a land mine he's walked into. "Riiight," he says again. "Well, let's get you down to that meet and greet, Harmony . . ."

As he passes by me, Lyle's gaze locks onto me speculatively. "You know, if a situation arises where one of the Mountainettes needs to back out . . ."

"She's not interested," Harmony interjects quickly, before I've even had a chance to process the implied offer. And with that, she tugs Lyle out the door, his assistant scrambling after them.

Harmony's right. I wouldn't be interested in becoming a Mountainette. I know she's only trying to protect me and make sure I'm not forced into a situation where I wouldn't be comfortable.

But sometimes . . . sometimes, I think it might be nice to get to speak up for myself.

Chapter 4
Wes

I don't hear Morrie as he approaches. The sound of a lone car traveling up a long, secluded gravel driveway is usually noticeable, but I have my noise-canceling headphones on, and I'm focusing on notching my arrow and aiming it toward my homemade target. I'm also blasting John Powell's instrumental score to *How to Train Your Dragon*, getting swept up in the vaulting strings and epic drums that carry me far, far away from my property in rural Michigan and into a land of fantasy.

Movie scores have always been my favorite thing to listen to. They make me feel like I'm living in a different world, one that's full of action and adventure and honor and sweeping, epic love stories. When I listen to *this* score, I feel like I've stepped into a different time, like I'm a Viking who gets to ride dragons. With nothing but open, rolling green fields around me, I almost feel like it could be true.

How badass is that?

The moment is ruined as soon as Morrie taps me on the shoulder. Like any dignified man of the law who daydreams about being a dragon-riding Viking, I shout in terror over the rousing beats of "This Is Berk" and swing my notched bow and arrow around so that it's level with Morrie's trim, regulated chest.

I know that's a weird way to describe someone's torso, but everything about Morrie is orderly and well maintained, from his Caesar cut to his pressed slacks to his fitted black tee. The only personality showing in his outfit are his Nike Undefeated Jordans, which he keeps impeccably clean, there's not so much as even a smudge of dirt on them. He seriously loves the sneakers in his collection; I've heard him talking to them before. It's . . . unsettling.

Morrie just glares at me through his glasses. Me brandishing an antique weapon at him has happened one too many times for him to be as terrified as he probably should be when someone points an arrow at his vital organs. The look on his face would better be described as exasperated.

He doesn't even try talking to me, just motions impatiently to my headphones. Sheepishly, I lower my bow with one hand and use the other to push them off.

"Let me guess—*Pirates of the Caribbean* or some of that other 'film music' you're always listening to?" he asks, not bothering to hide his disapproval.

Glancing down at my bow, I scoff. "Don't be ridiculous. The pirates in that movie don't shoot arrows." Lowering my equipment carefully to the ground, I move to take off my bracer. "It is a great score, though. Better for swordplay or rope climbing, I think."

Morrie just shakes his head at me. "How could I have made such a *ridiculous* mistake?"

I know he's mocking my life choices to my face, but I don't take it personally. Not everyone appreciates a good timpani like I do. A rousing string section. Ooh, or a bagpipe. Damn, I love me a good bagpipe. Name an instrument that gets your heart pounding faster. I'll wait.

Morrie continues shaking his head at me. Again, I don't take it personally. I know I've been a disappointment to him ever since we were assigned as partners, about six years ago now, right after I was recruited to the FBI at age twenty-three. He thought he'd be getting a cool wingman to drink beers and watch college football with in his downtime. Instead he got . . . me. The guy more likely to invite him to my D&D campaign and gift him home-brewed mead for Christmas.

"Is this really the best use of your time?" he asks. I'm not sure why Morrie always feels the need to act like he's my father instead of my peer when he's a whopping four months older than me, but I'm half convinced the man was born with the personality of a forty-year-old insurance salesman. "You should be prepping, going over the case files, practicing the challenges . . ."

To be totally honest, I tune him out after that. Morrie can be a nice guy. Sometimes. Well, that one time, really, three years ago. He and I just have very different approaches to our FBI work. He's made it his entire personality, living and breathing work twenty-four seven; and when I'm off the clock, I run as far away from it as I can possibly get.

Don't get me wrong, I'm so grateful to be doing what I do. Getting to help people and make a difference is my life's ambition. But the long, grueling hours, the seemingly endless travel, the mental gymnastics and pressure of dealing with life-and-death situations . . . it can wear on a person. When I'm not working, I want to enjoy my life. Doing these so-called "nerdy" or "waste-of-time" activities helps me to re-center myself and feel like I'm not just a cog in the FBI machine.

Unfortunately, I can't quite tune out the last part of what he says: ". . . unless you're just planning to coast by on your looks again?"

Ah, yes, the usual sore point between us. I think my healthy work-life balance has made me a better FBI agent who has thus gotten lots of amazing career opportunities. But Morrie has decided the only reason I'm assigned so many missions is because of . . . well, because of my face.

I'm pretty immune to Morrie's digs, but that one always annoys me. Look, I'm not naive, and I'm not blind. I know I'm traditionally handsome, with my sandy blond hair, green eyes, and jawline that could double as a grindstone for my swords. When most people look at me, they probably imagine a certain personality that usually goes along with this particular set of facial features combined with an athletic build. But . . . why? Why should the fact that I'm fit and handsome mean that I don't like role-playing games? Or that I shouldn't have a full Jon Snow costume in my closet that, yes, I've worn to plenty of conventions?

I know Morrie thinks I'm a dork, but frankly, if he knew the kind of attention even a moderately attractive man could get dressed like Jon Snow at a fantasy convention . . . Well, I'm pretty sure he'd be singing a different tune.

For the record, that's not why I do it. I just love fantasy. Not only because of the dragons or the dire wolves or the magical powers or whatnot—though, let's be real, those parts are fucking awesome. What I love are the epic battles of good versus evil. I love the struggles to stay honorable in a corrupt world. And yeah, I'm not too manly to admit, I love the epic love stories that prove love can conquer all. When Arwen and Aragorn met again after the Battle of the Pelennor Fields? Come on—I cried, you cried, we all cried. We're not animals.

I shrug off Morrie's negativity, pulling my phone out of my back pocket and flipping to my saved videos. "Trust me, I've been putting my time to good use."

I show him the most recent video I've completed, which is an edited compilation of me doing various events from the traditional Scottish Highland games, including shot put, hammer throw, and tossing the caber. The title to the video reads "Highland Gaming like Jamie Fraser" (aka, my man from *Outlander*), and the music I've chosen to accompany the sequences is—you guessed it—a bagpipe jam from an awesome group called Tartanic that I first saw performing at a local Renaissance faire.

Is there any part of me who thinks Morrie will enjoy watching this video? Not really. But honestly, something about his persistent disappointment in me is endlessly entertaining.

Morrie scrunches up his face at what he's seeing, as if he finds it physically distasteful to watch a man in his athletic prime throw a wooden beam that's three times his height up into the air. (Come on, man. No one's buying it. That shit's *awesome*.) "What the hell is this?" he demands.

"It's *GeekOut*," I remind him. Seeing his blank face, I roll my eyes. "I've been sending you these videos for weeks. I'm doing a TikTok workout series for geeks. 'Swordfight Like Jack Sparrow,' 'Shoot a Crossbow Like Daryl Dixon,' 'Fire a Rifle Like Mal Reynolds.'" Yeah, I dabble in some sci-fi, too.

Morrie stares at me, aghast. "You've been posting your face online?"

"Of course not." I let him see how affronted I am at the suggestion. Scrolling through a few of the older videos, I show him the final product. "I use a filter." My go-to is the one that gives me a black mask like Zorro (sick, right?), but I admit I've sometimes caved to peer pressure and gone with whatever was trendy, like the puppy face or Batman. Hey, sometimes you gotta give the people what they want.

As irritated as I am at Morrie's implied suggestion that I'm not doing my due diligence, I begrudgingly understand the concern. In my line of work, it's best for my face not to be too visible. I've gone undercover in all kinds of disguises and in all kinds of situations. No, I'm no Sydney Bristow in bright-colored wigs. Most stuff is pretty dull, truth be told—it's just blending in and listening. But when I have had to infiltrate a group, you'd be surprised how much even slightly altering your appearance can change the way people perceive you. Yes, all you "how can no one tell Clark Kent isn't Superman?" haters—you'd honestly be amazed by how much changing the way you comb your hair and adding something like a pair of glasses can change the way people perceive you. The fake accents and color contacts can help, too.

But since I'm about to go undercover yet again, I can't risk my dumb mug being plastered all over the Internet, even if I am using a burner account with no trace of my actual identity on it.

This case will be the most high-profile one I've ever worked on; it might even be the last because of how highly visible it's going to be. I'm about to go on a reality show competition as one of the contestants. The show is called *Mountain Man*, and it's being filmed in some Podunk town in the middle of Tennessee.

If our target hadn't been otherwise so reclusive and avoidant about bringing people into his inner circle, I doubt the bureau would have agreed to let one of their agents go undercover in such a spectacularly public way. The fact that I've been given this assignment just shows how important it is that Aaron Miller is stopped. And if it means making myself a spectacularly public figure in the process, well, I'm willing to do so for my country. For the victims who have already suffered so much.

Do I want to go on a dating show? As Wes—hell no. That's the last thing I'd ever willingly put myself through. I could barely even watch the episodes of the comp shows I was sent as part of my training. And before you get your hackles up, it's not because the shows focus on love. I'm a big fan of love. *True* love. "As you wish" kind of love, where you would fight pirates and brave the fire swamp to be with your ladylove. The cheesy, wooden nonsense that you see on these reality dating TV shows? No, thanks. I want a real connection or nothing. If I'm not burning with passion, I'd rather be alone.

Luckily, it isn't Wes going on this show. I mean, it's my body, sure, but I'll be playing a part. Nate R. *He's* the one who'll be going on *Mountain Man*, not me. Everything I say or do will be what Nate R. would say or do, and Wes will just keep quiet for a while. I know it might be confusing if you haven't been through it, but I have to compartmentalize, just like I do every time I go undercover. There's the character I'm playing, and then there's the real me, and the twain shall never meet.

Tonight, Morrie will spend the night here, then we'll drive from my place down to Green Valley over the next day and a half. By the time we get there, I'll no longer be Wesley "Wes" Ackerman from Michigan; I'll be Nathan "Nate"

Russell from Small Town, Tennessee. I've been working on my "yes, ma'ams" and Southern drawl to try to get into the spirit of things.

I've also been working on my Nate R. persona. As Morrie has hammered into me many, many times, Nate R. is not into anything "humiliatingly infantile," like shooting crossbows or learning whip tricks. Nate R. is a former frat brother, a good Christian boy, and a passionate fan of college football.

Nate R. sounds a little boring, honestly. You can see why I had to spend the day trying to escape into a Viking fantasy world.

"You need to put all of your extracurriculars on hold for now," Morrie reminds me yet again, then needlessly tacks on, "maybe forever. Nate R. doesn't waste his time with emasculating fantasy fandoms and"—he shudders—"role-playing games."

I have to bite my tongue. This is an old fight between us. To be fair, Morrie isn't bad people overall—he just has some very antiquated views on what masculinity means. He's confided in me that he grew up in a family of athletes, and there was a lot of pressure put on him and his siblings to excel at sports so they could qualify for college scholarships.

I didn't grow up in that environment, though. I have sisters. My oldest sister played volleyball, my middle sister swam competitively, and I dabbled in T-ball and soccer, mostly to be social; but that was just what we did on the weekends— the athletic culture didn't rule our lives. We spent a lot of time playing make-believe, fighting goblins, building forts, climbing trees. And I have no idea why any of that is considered less "tough" or "manly" than wearing a costume to look like your favorite athlete and chasing a ball around a field.

But I've hashed this out too many times—with Morrie and with other "macho" men I've encountered throughout my life—for me to think I have any real chance of changing anyone's mind. So I just roll my eyes and treat this like playful banter, hoping he won't see that even though it's an old wound, it can still sting. "Emasculating? Sure. Find me a manlier man than Gareth of Orkney. Madmartigan. Geralt of Rivia."

Morrie just blinks back at me. "I obviously don't know who any of those people are, but that's exactly the kind of nonsense I'm talking about. I don't want to hear any of that fantasy shit while you're undercover, Wes. I mean it!"

He might be coming from a place of sad, sheltered, toxic masculinity, but he isn't entirely wrong. I do need to compartmentalize. Letting Wes leak through when

I'm undercover puts the entire mission in jeopardy. With a sigh, I relent. "Fine. Fine. I'll be Nate Russell for the next two months. Watcher of football and drinker of beer."

"That's right." Morrie nods, looking more reassured. "Have you been practicing any of those challenges I sent you?"

To ensure that I can stay on the show long enough to achieve my mission, the FBI has had to inform the executive producers of who I really am. After some reluctant back-and-forth on their end, they sent ahead a list of some of the challenges the Mountain Men will be completing on the show to make sure I can do them competently enough that it makes sense for me to stick around.

Winning the weekly competitions is important, but not as important as ingratiating myself with the women contestants, the Mountainettes. They're the ones who will ultimately decide which Mountain Men move through to the next week. So really, all that alpha-male nonsense I was supposed to practice—like tackle football, weight lifting, etcetera—is ultimately unimportant if the ladies decide they like me. And, well . . . come on. Sandy blond hair. Green eyes. Chiseled jaw.

I smirk at Morrie. "It's gonna be fine."

He frowns, clearly not loving that answer. "What does that mean, 'it's gonna be fine'? It's gonna be fine, as in you practiced all of the challenges so you'll definitely make it through—thank you, Morrie, for all your careful preparation? Or some other kind of 'it's gonna be fine'?"

He's really going to make me say it, isn't he? Sighing, I shrug. "Look, what can I say? It's not gonna be a problem, man. The Mountainettes will put me through, whether I can split a log or win a lip-sync battle or not."

Morrie folds his arms skeptically. "And, why is that, exactly?"

Wasn't he the one saying it just a few minutes ago? I got the face, the bod. No problem. I gesture to myself. "Come on, man. This show is being filmed in the middle-of-nowhere Tennessee. I'm gonna be competing against a bunch of Appalachian bumpkins. I got this in the bag . . ."

Reader, I do not have this in the bag. *This* has escaped from the bag. It's loose on the city, attacking the townsfolk.

What the hell is in the water in Green Valley, Tennessee? I've never seen so many incredibly good-looking people in such a small area before. The whole town has, like, three restaurants, but on every street corner is some huge, ripped dude with a beard. I gawk out my window as we drive down Main Street. "What the hell?" I stammer when I'm able to finally find my voice.

Morrie is eating all of this up, by the way. He's been pointing out every Greek god in flannel he can see. "Wow, look at that guy over there. Is that a classic car he's driving? Oh, wait, look at that guy who's coming out of the library. Is that Adonis a librarian . . . ? No, no, wait, did you just see that guy in the park ranger uniform? *Damn*, if I do say so myself!"

"Shut up," I grumble, slouching down low into my seat.

Still laughing, Morrie shakes his head. "Got this in the bag, huh? You might as well put a bag over your face, if you're standing next to *that* guy . . ."

"Hey!" I'm surprised to find that I'm genuinely wounded by the insult. My face has always been my moneymaker. From the time I was in high school, my classic good looks let me charm my way out of most situations, no matter how hairy they got.

But driving through Green Valley, for the first time, it's occurred to me that it might not be enough. Who am I, without the face? Just some nerd with a Medjai tattoo (just like Rick O'Connell's in *The Mummy*) in a discreet location that I would prefer not to disclose at this present moment.

Morrie tsks at me sympathetically, but in a way that is completely condescending. "There, there, Wesley. I'm just messing with you. You'll probably still be the prettiest boy at the ball—just not the tallest, the most ripped, the most masculine—"

"You can stop listing things now," I interrupt him grouchily. "Come on. Let's get to the rental ASAP."

"Why?"

I let out a long, irritated sigh through my nostrils. "So I can practice chopping firewood . . ."

As Morrie laughs some more at my expense, I tune him out, staring morosely out the window. I'll give Green Valley this much—it's a beautiful place. Nothing will ever come close to Michigan in my eyes, since that's home, but being surrounded by the Great Smoky Mountains on basically all sides does lend a certain charm.

Not to mention the number of abnormally beautiful people in such a small radius. I mean, the woman walking down the street is an absolute knockout, even if she is dressed like a—

The ending to that thought draws me up short. *A nun.*

I had an intense run-in with a nun a few years back, when I was deep undercover on one of my jobs. There's no way the woman we passed on the street just now was her, though. I try to muster a laugh at the sheer absurdity of the idea. Right. A nun just casually wandering down the street of a very small, sequestered town in the Appalachian Mountains. I'm positive it was only someone who looked vaguely like her. After all, I only saw her briefly as we drove past, in profile, walking in the opposite direction.

It wasn't her, I tell myself.

"You okay, Ackerman?" Morrie asks, jarring me from my thoughts.

I shake my head to clear it. "Yeah. Just thought I saw a ghost, that's all . . ."

Chapter 5
Nina

The Orphan Girl and the Thief
Part 2

The Orphan Girl continued to visit the prison regularly, and each time she learned something new about the Thief. She learned that he had a dimple in his left cheek when he smiled; she learned that he would roll his pencil through his fingers when he was idle; she learned that he would wink at her if he caught her trying to steal a glance his way.

One day when the Orphan Girl arrived for Bible study, the Thief was nowhere to be found. She felt her heart sink, but quickly reprimanded herself for feeling that way. The nuns didn't come to the prison to flirt or be gazed upon. They came to bring people to Christ. The Orphan Girl realized the Thief's absence must be God's way of reminding her that she had been going down a dangerous path, and she resolved to do better.

The week before, Sister Theresa challenged the prisoners to memorize a scripture verse from an approved list, and today she broke the nuns off into small groups with the men to listen to them recite. The Orphan Girl was paired with Sister Catherine and a prisoner named Rodney, who stumbled through his proverb.

As Sister Catherine gently corrected him, the Orphan Girl's mind wandered. Where was the Thief? Why hadn't he come to Bible study? Was something wrong? Or had he just grown bored of the game they were playing?

The Orphan Girl was jolted from her thoughts as the door opened and a guard escorted the Thief into the room. The Orphan Girl's body became instantly alert at the sight of him. When his gaze began to sweep across the group, she made herself look away so he wouldn't catch her staring.

"Sorry I'm late, Sister Theresa." The Thief sweet-talked the matronly woman shamelessly, and even without looking, the Orphan Girl could perfectly imagine his smile, the one that made his far-too-distracting dimple stand out. "You know, seeing your face is the best part of my week."

Despite herself, the Orphan Girl looked up at those words and found the Thief giving her a brief, meaningful glance. He had the exact smile she'd been imagining—the cheeky scamp in trouble with the teacher—but who could have the heart to scold *that* face?

Sister Theresa could, as it turned out. "We're halfway through our recitations," she barked at him, unimpressed. "You'll have to catch up."

"Yes, ma'am."

"Sister Agnes!" called Sister Theresa.

The Orphan Girl's entire body froze as she realized Sister Theresa was calling to her, and why. She had no choice but to look up; it took all of her willpower to do so, and to not freeze in place. Trembling, she raised her gaze to see Sister Theresa briskly gesturing her into the conversation with the Thief.

The Orphan Girl felt his eyes on her but didn't look at him as she rose woodenly to her feet and crossed the room. "Yes, Sister Theresa?"

"Go over the verse with this young man." To the Thief, sternly, "We don't have much time left, so get straight to it."

"Yes, ma'am."

The Orphan Girl still didn't look at the Thief as she walked over to a free set of chairs. She felt him, though—felt his gaze on her, felt the warmth of his body closer to hers than it had ever been before. In her peripheral vision, she saw him take the seat across from her, and only then did she manage to summon up enough courage to meet his gaze.

Mistake. That was a mistake. An electrical charge went off through her entire body the moment their eyes made contact. And based on his slow, deliberate swallow, the Thief felt it, too.

"Sister Agnes," he acknowledged her quietly, shifting forward slightly in his seat. That current charging the air between them rippled with his every movement. She felt it pulsing between them, alive and dangerous. "Is that your real name? Agnes?"

He shouldn't be asking her that. Sister Theresa had sternly informed all of the nuns they were only meant to go over the Bible verses with the prisoners, not discuss anything personal. Still, with the Thief right across from her, just an inch or two separating their legs, his eyes so striking up close, such a vivid, pale green—the Orphan Girl found herself shaking her head. "No. It's—" She pressed her lips together to stop herself from going any further, from telling him her real name. *Nina.* No matter how much she might want to hear that name on his lips.

She slid her gaze away from his and put on her most businesslike tone, trying to diffuse some of the charge between them. "Are you ready?"

The Thief shifted again, his knee brushing up against hers. Both of their bodies were fully covered—his with an orange prison jumpsuit, and hers with a black postulant jumper. Even so, the Orphan Girl felt that touch through her entire body. Shivering, she jerked her leg away, doggedly keeping her gaze downcast. She was trying so very hard to be good, to honor the path she had taken; she didn't understand why this was happening to her. Her body had never responded to anyone like this before. Not to the boys she'd known in church growing up, definitely not . . . her big mistake. She'd thought perhaps God was sparing her from a life of sin by removing the temptation.

If that had been the case, it was no longer true. The Orphan Girl's heart was racing. Her body felt flushed and restless. His nearness, his touch, the intensity of his eyes, the sound of his voice—they roused her into awareness, awakening what had long been silent.

She couldn't look at him. There were too many emotions charging through her. She was sure none of them were holy or good.

He surprised her by nudging her with his knee again, this time a much more deliberate gesture, and clearing his throat. "Okay, here goes. 'Surely I am too stupid to be a man.'"

The Orphan Girl didn't mean to laugh, but he'd startled it out of her. She quickly clamped down her mouth to silence the sound, her eyes darting up to his. She found his clear green eyes sparkling at her with mischief, and it made him look younger, boyish, so horribly endearing that she didn't know if she would ever recover from it. "I feel like that probably applies to most of my gender."

He was trying to make her laugh. That should make her cross with him, not pleased. The Orphan Girl did her best to hold his gaze and to bite back her smile, but it was difficult, especially when she saw the pleased grin on his face at having gotten a reaction out of her, his smile so wide it made the dimple pop in his cheek.

"That wasn't one of the approved verses," she reminded him, in what she hoped was her sternest voice.

The faintest flicker of a smile pulled at his lips. "It wasn't? I must have gotten mixed up. Let's see . . ." He pretended to consider it for a moment. "'You have stolen my heart, my sister, my bride. You have stolen my heart with one glance of your eyes.'"

This time, the Orphan Girl couldn't seem to find the will to tear her eyes away. They snagged on his lips as he spoke those loaded, heavy words, and she felt something opening and blooming in her, her body coaxed into life.

It likely goes without saying that *that* wasn't one of the approved Bible verses, either. Nothing from the Song of Songs would be. But this time, the Orphan Girl didn't bother to correct him. She and the Thief stared at one another across the thin but indivisible space between them, her heart hammering in her chest as she wondered if he knew just what he had awakened in her.

Chapter 6
Nina

Everyone keeps talking about how nice it is to finally get a vacation. To be totally honest, it hasn't felt like much of a vacation for me so far. While my family spent the morning exploring some of the local hiking trails, I stored everyone's suitcases for them and organized a grocery pickup so there will be plenty of food around for my cousins to eat. (And believe me, preteens and teenagers can *eat*.) Then I had to help everyone get ready for the "family package" video we're going to film. For each Mountainette, the producers are putting together a short video of her with her family to show her background and where she came from. Even though the video will only be about two minutes long, we spent all afternoon getting ready. I had to help the twins straighten then curl their hair, then spend more time finding Isaiah a suitable replacement for his dress shirt after he spilled orange juice all over the front.

All of that sounds like a lot of whining, I know. If I'm thinking positively and with a heart full of gratitude, I'm sure there are perks to being here in Green Valley. Like . . . at least I won't have to clean the church building for the next eight weeks. That will definitely feel like a vacation for me!

There was very little time left to get myself ready for the family package, but that doesn't matter so much. I'm sure I'll only be in the background anyway. I'm not planning on wearing anything special—just one of my long floral skirts, a button-up dress shirt, and my best, softest cardigan. I'm sure that's not exactly what the producers mean by being "TV ready," but it's what I have available.

If it were up to me, I'd probably wear something different. I've been really into A-line silhouettes lately, so maybe I'd do something with that pattern. A simple material, since that shows up best on camera—and a bold color, maybe, with minimal print. High heels, to give my silhouette some length. A shade of lipstick that doesn't match with my dress but doesn't clash, either.

But that's all just wishful thinking. I haven't bought a brand-new outfit since . . . maybe since I was eight? Everything has been secondhand since then, hand-me-downs from my cousins or thrift-store bargain finds.

Envy. I cut off that train of thought quickly. I'm happy and I'm healthy and I'm fed and I have shelter. Anything else is just icing on the cake of life.

When Lyle arrives at the suite, he brings the same boisterous energy from yesterday. "Millers!" he calls enthusiastically as he enters the sitting area. He meets my gaze and gives a slight nod. "And Delgado."

People don't usually single me out when I'm with my family. I'm usually just the shadow in the room, the one they pretend not to notice, unless I'm serving food or drinks. Maybe because I crave attention and praise—at least, according to many of the sin accounts given to me by my aunt at the end of each month—I can't help but like Lyle, even though I know he's going to rub my uncle the wrong way. Between his innate cheerfulness and his penchant for pastels, it's a real toss-up for what's going to get Uncle Aaron's goat more.

"Aren't we all looking snazzy?" Lyle asks, and Uncle Aaron doesn't bother to hide his grimace at the word.

Lyle quickly walks us through the filming process—how we'll be shooting in various locations around Green Valley, how we should pretend we don't notice the cameras unless we're being directly interviewed. How they'll set up separate times for filming those one-on-one interviews, which are called "confessionals," even though we might not film them until long after we shoot the outdoor sequences. It will all depend on what the producers decide they need to develop the narrative.

I can't help but find it all fascinating, even though it's obvious all of the showbiz lingo is grating on Uncle Aaron's nerves. He's no stranger to lights and cameras, since he often broadcasts his sermons and has to deal with all of the production elements that go along with that. But Uncle Aaron also has an innate dislike of anything to do with "Hollywood." That's his catch-all term, meaning anything ranging from show business to progressive social politics. "Hollywood's at it again," he might grumble to himself if he sees a commercial with strong sexual undertones, or even something as benign as a same-sex couple holding hands.

I truly, sincerely hope that Lyle and Uncle Aaron don't get too much one-on-one time together. I have a feeling that would not go well for anybody.

Finally, it's time for us to head out. "All right, Millers!" Lyle encourages us. "I know you have a big crew, so it might be easiest if we all just caravan. I'll lead and you can follow—"

We all stand up. I brush my hands over my skirt, wishing the floral print wasn't quite so big. It's going to look terrible on camera. Not that my tight braid or over-sized dress shirt will look much better. *Vanity*, I remind myself. Today isn't about me. It's about Harmony.

I move to follow my cousins out of the room when Uncle Aaron gives me a little shake of his head, almost like an afterthought. "Not you, Antonina."

My stomach clenches, anticipating the blow a second too late, before I feel a familiar queasy sensation, like I've been spun around in circles too many times and can't properly orient myself. This isn't the first time Uncle Aaron has humil-iated me in front of a group of people, but somehow it always takes me by surprise. Somehow I always trick myself into thinking, *This time will be the last time*. That it won't happen again.

"It will just be too confusing to explain the family dynamics," Uncle Aaron says calmly, without any trace of rancor in his voice, but without any suggestion that he can be budged on this issue, either. "And this is Harmony's big day."

I wince, even though I immediately understand what he means. Aunt Hope is darker than the others, but with her dyed blonde hair, she can pass for maybe being European, or just really tan. There is no question that I'm Hispanic and that I don't fit in with everyone else. Having me in the mix on television would mean we'd either have to take time out of Harmony's story to explain who I am, or invite lots of questions online. Either way would take the attention away from Harmony and put it onto me—the very thing that Uncle Aaron is always chal-lenging me not to do.

I never intentionally try to take attention away from Harmony, or anyone else for that matter. I never want anyone to notice me if I can help it. But even without meaning to, even without trying to, it seems like I'm always doing something to make myself the center of attention, and therefore even *more* of a burden on my family than I already am.

So I understand why Uncle Aaron is telling me to stay behind. I just wish he would have told me *before*, not in front of everyone like this.

Aunt Hope is the first to recover from the surprise of Uncle Aaron's announcement, but there's a long enough pause that I know she hadn't been informed of this decision beforehand either. "All right, let's go. Everyone in their usual seats in the van—"

"I'm sorry," Lyle interrupts, his head swiveling around to take in what's happening in the room. "Is there a reason Antonina can't come along?"

The edge in his voice tells me that he suspects enough to get to at least the surface-level truth of the answer—that I don't look like the rest of my family— and that this is *not* an answer he likes or approves of.

It's surprising to have an almost stranger try to stick up for me, and if I'm being honest, gratifying, too—but also terribly, terribly worrying, since I see the way Uncle Aaron's eyes narrow. The rest of his expression stays the same, but there's a definite squint to his eyes now. That's never a good sign. He won't take his anger out on Lyle because he's a stranger, but later on there will be repercussions —probably for me, since I'm the one Lyle was defending, even though I didn't ask for it.

To be clear, Uncle Aaron would never hit me or do anything physical to punish me. Even when I was a kid, I didn't get spanked for misbehaving, not like his own children. His punishments are more creative. They're designed to embarrass me, to pull me down when he feels like I'm getting too high. To remind me of my place.

I know Lyle means well, but I really, really wish he hadn't said anything at all.

"Why don't you worry about your show," Uncle Aaron says in that quiet but authoritative voice of his, "and let me worry about my family?" He is smiling his handsome movie-star smile, but his eyes are cold.

Lyle clearly does not realize who he's dealing with. "Why don't *you*—" he starts, in a way that does *not* feel like the rest of the sentence is going to progress positively.

I quickly intervene. "I don't mind! Really. I don't want to be on camera." I meet Lyle's gaze, trying to show him how sincere I am. My skirt would clash, after all. And I don't want to take anything from Harmony, ever. "*Really*. But thank you."

A long, awkward pause follows. Then Uncle Aaron moves toward the door, a clear indication the conversation is over. Everyone else follows after.

Harmony lingers behind the others, casting me a regretful look. "I'm sorry, Nina. Maybe he'll let you come out tomorrow and you can watch the first part of the filming?"

"Maybe," I echo back with a smile, even though I highly doubt that will happen. Harmony probably doubts it, too, but she's as powerless as I am to get Uncle Aaron to change his mind when he's already set in his ways.

"Be right out!" Lyle calls after her. When everyone has left the room, he turns to me and gives me a long, searching look. "Blink twice if you're in danger."

How dramatic! I can't help but laugh. "I'm fine. Uncle Aaron is just stubborn sometimes." I gesture around the suite. "I'll be fine here. I never get time alone."

That much is true. I'm in a beautiful suite in a beautiful hotel. What a blessing to get the entire space to myself. I might even be able to choose something *I* want to watch on television!

Lyle looks at me doubtfully. "Listen, I don't want to overstep, but I'm not from LA. My family's from Oklahoma. Okay? So I know the whole megachurch pastor vibe. And believe me, I get not fitting in." He gestures down to his pastel blue pants and matching ascot. "My brother and dad are both part of the rodeo." He shudders visibly. "The *rodeo*. And the only bull I've ever ridden is—" Something about my expression seems to make him reconsider finishing that sentence. He clears his throat. "Anyway, the point is, I know what it means to need to escape some uncomfortable family dynamics. If you need me, call me."

He slides a card into my palm, then on second thought fishes something else out of his pocket—his car keys.

It takes me too long to realize what he's offering me. I draw my hand back instinctively. "Oh, no, I can't drive your car."

"Go explore the town," he insists. "*Get out of this hotel room.* Buy a drink, if you like! But don't sit in here like some sad little mouse, or I'll corrode with guilt."

I . . . don't know what to say. In all the years I've lived with him, my uncle has never let me drive his car. I had to learn how to drive the fifteen-passenger van so I could help do the grocery shopping and take my younger cousins to tutoring and youth worship, of course, but my uncle's Hummer? Never in a million years.

And yet Lyle, who's basically a stranger, offered his keys to me in less than a couple days of knowing me.

His generosity is incredibly sweet—in an entirely overwhelming way that makes me worry I might break out into hives. "I can't." No use pretending the reason is anything other than what he suspects it is, I guess, since he just saw everything. "If Uncle Aaron found out . . ."

"Uncle Aaron won't find out." Lyle pulls out his phone. "Here. Put in your number and I'll text you when we're on the way back." His eyebrows arch theatrically at me as a new thought seems to strike him. "They let you have a phone, don't they?"

It's not an entirely unfounded question based off what he's seen, but I still can't help but laugh at the drama of it all. I know Uncle Aaron is strict, but it's not like I'm a prisoner. Emotions can get heightened sometimes, and sure, I wish I had more freedom, but overall things are fine. "Yes, I have a phone." I roll my eyes a little just to show him he doesn't have to be as worried as he clearly is.

But somehow, I find myself giving him my number and reluctantly taking his keys. Not because I need to escape. It just seems so important to Lyle that I get out, I feel like I have to do it, so he knows things aren't as bad here as he seems to think they are. "Thank you." A new thought strikes me. "But how will you get to the filming?"

He grimaces. "I guess I'll be catching a ride in the van." With another visible shudder, he puts back on his Hollywood-producer megasmile, then turns and charges toward the hallway. "Oh, Millers . . . !"

At first, I don't intend to really use Lyle's car. I plan to just stay in the hotel room and pretend I went out when he comes back. But then the cleaning staff comes in and starts acting cagey about having me in the suite, and I feel too awkward just sitting down in the lobby by myself, so I figure, a little drive into town wouldn't hurt.

That's how I wind up driving *an electric car* for the first time in my life. Luckily the streets of Green Valley aren't too busy, because I'm freaking out behind the wheel of this thing. It feels *expensive*. And it's so quiet! I keep thinking the engine has cut out and start frantically hitting the brakes, only to realize the car is just a soft purr instead of the loud roar I'm accustomed to.

Oh, heavens. I'm going to crash this thing. I'm going to have to spend the rest of my life paying off my debt. *Again.* I don't know how much a car like this costs, but I bet it's a lot. I'm sure I resemble an octogenarian, sitting as close to the steering wheel as I can get, hands in the ten and two position, driving about fifteen miles under the speed limit. I've gotten a few honks—okay, a *lot* of honks. I finally put on my hazards and hope that people will just go around me.

When I make it to the town library, I decide that's as good a place as any to park and rethink my life choices. Or, you know, sit for a few minutes, then drive slowly back to the hotel. At least then I can truthfully tell Lyle I used his car and left the hotel, as he urged me to do.

After a few minutes pass, though, and my heart rate returns to a normal, nonlethal level, I decide it isn't the *worst* idea to explore the town some more. On foot, though. Lyle will be so proud of me. And so would Helen and Thad and Matilda and Kimo and Grady, if they were here. That resolves me to do it. I've spent my whole life surrounding myself with friends who are much braver than me, hoping at least a little of their courage will rub off on me.

Harmony's always worn her WWJD (What Would Jesus Do) bracelet proudly. If I could, I'd get one that said WWHTMK&GD. (What Would Helen, Thad, Matilda, Kimo, and Grady Do.) Maybe now, I'll add an L to that grouping, too, for Lyle.

Be brave, I try to encourage myself, but even to me, my own inner voice isn't all that persuasive. Instead, I try to summon Matilda's voice, and it comes briskly and easily: *Stop being such a big scaredy-pants. Go do something for once!*

Hard to argue with that. So, I force myself to wander.

Not too far from the library is a cute little diner called Daisy's Nut House. I consider my options. I'm trying to push myself today, but I don't know if I feel quite courageous enough to sit down at a booth and eat by myself. Maybe if I had a book with me . . . ? But since I don't, I wonder if it would satisfy my inner Matilda for me to go in and order something to go? I listen for any harsh, faintly Russian reprimand. Receiving none, I decide that's as good as a go-ahead, and I make my way determinedly to the diner's entrance.

I'm surprised to find how packed it is, especially for a relatively early weekday afternoon. Good thing I'm not hoping to get a table. All the various groups of people make me nervous, even though none of them seem to be paying attention to me. I'm worried they'll look up and just know, somehow, that I'm not meant to be here.

As I deliberate backing out of the door, Matilda's voice berates me. *They're just people, for goodness' sake! Who cares what they think? I'm sure most of them are idiots anyway.*

Wow. A little harsh. These people all seem really nice to me. But weirdly, even though I know it's only my own brain telling me a maybe-exaggerated version of what my most intimidating friend might say, it does bring me comfort. None of these people know me. No one even seems to have noticed I'm here. Who cares what any of them think?

Taking in a deep breath, I propel myself forward toward the counter, where some of the baked items are on display in a glass case. My stomach instinctively grumbles. Uncle Aaron always insists we start the day with oatmeal—just oatmeal, no cinnamon or brown sugar or cream. But on holidays we get to add some fruit! Throughout the week, we each receive a sugar allotment that we're not allowed to exceed, so I've gotten very good at carefully rationing out my food so I can splurge on Pizookies every Tuesday night with my friends.

But despite myself, the items in the bakery are calling to me. Brownies. Cookies. Pastries. And pie! So much pie. There's one called a Derby pie that literally has my mouth salivating at the sight of it. Pecans, chocolate, a buttery crust, and it comes with a dollop of homemade cream on top. *Yum.*

"Can I help you, hon?" asks a pretty older woman behind the counter.

I speak without thinking. "I'd like a slice of the Derby pie, please."

"Sure thing."

Almost immediately, guilt sets in. My send-off with my friends was only a few days ago, so eating a slice of this pie will definitely send me over my sugar allotment. But my fear of Uncle Aaron's disappointment is at war with my people-pleasing anxiety over calling after the woman and telling her I've changed my mind. She's already cut out a hefty slice and set it out on a nice plate. It would be so rude to tell her to put it back.

Now, I don't have to guess what Matilda might say in this situation—I've already heard it from her too many times before: *Who cares what your uncle thinks? Why is it any of his business, anyway?*

I never know what to say to her, because honestly, I'm not sure what answer I could give. It's a truth I've been warring against for a long time now. Ever since I left my postulancy. I know on some level that all of my uncle's rules serve a purpose, and that he's only trying to help us live a better, worthier life. But sometimes sugar and all the other things we're meant to abstain from don't seem like they're so evil. Sometimes, I remember what it was like to have sugar. Sometimes I think about how good sugar made me feel.

My indecision must show on my face, because the woman hesitates before handing the plate to me. "Are you worried about allergies or something?" she asks gently. "I can tell you what's in it. It was made fresh here, just this morning."

She's given me an easy out. I can just pretend to be allergic to one of the ingredients. No harm, no foul. But suddenly, even without the help of my inner Matilda, a new stubbornness takes hold in me. "No, that's all right. I'll take it."

After I pay for the pie, I realize that she's given me a plate instead of a takeaway box, which means that despite my earlier plans to eat the pie on the curb at the library (I wouldn't dare risk getting crumbs all over Lyle's car!), I'll have to either get a table here or ask her to re-box it.

I've already reached my limit of daring today, though, and it really would be too much trouble to ask her to put the slice in a takeaway container. My heart racing, I glance around the room, trying to find the most tucked away, obscure table possible. To my dismay, I see that all the booths are taken. Maybe I can just stand in the corner and hope I don't spill anything . . . ?

"You can come sit with us!" a cheerful voice interrupts my spiraling.

I blink in surprise to see two beautiful and stylish women sitting at one of those booths that wraps three-quarters of the way around the table, so there's plenty of space to sit. Even so, I hesitate. They're probably only being nice and don't actually want me to sit with them.

"That's okay," I say, smiling back. "Thank you for the offer."

"It's the best you're gonna get," the same woman says to me, with a friendly smile. She's a gorgeous, curvaceous woman, in her late thirties / early forties, who has a no-fuss look about her, even though it's obvious she takes very good care of herself. Her clothes are simple but stylish, obviously well-made, but practical, too. "Unless you want to take that empty seat at the counter, but I have to warn you, Cletus Winston thinks that's his seat and he will make you move if he comes in and finds you there."

"Oh." I falter, looking to the other woman for guidance. She's strikingly beautiful but I'd guess a few years younger than the first woman. Her clothing also looks elegant and expensive, with slightly bolder cuts and prints.

When she smiles at me, her face is friendly but sympathetic. I'm used to that look. No matter where I go, something about me seems to broadcast how awkward and out of place I am. I try not to take it too personally when I see other people realize it, but it still doesn't feel great, becoming someone's pet project. "Join us," she echoes. "I've been dying to try that pie. You can tell us how good it is."

They're both smiling at me so broadly, and they're both so extraordinarily beautiful, that I have no choice but to take the seat being offered. "Thank you," I tell them. "I promise I won't be long."

"Take your time," the classically stylish woman encourages me. "And don't mind us drooling as we watch you eat."

"I'm Rae, by the way," the striking woman tells me.

The first woman tells me her name, too, but at that exact moment someone comes in and triggers the bell over the door, so I don't hear it clearly. Weirdly, they're looking at me expectantly now, like maybe I'm supposed to know who they are? They do both look vaguely familiar, but between the busy diner and the extra sugar and the invitation to sit with strangers, I'm feeling extra slow today. "Nina," I tell them.

They exchange a quick look while trying not to let me notice they're exchanging a look. *Oh, brother, here we go again.* I feel like everything I do and say is pretty normal. Why does everyone always act like I'm announcing that I'm an alien queen from the pancake planet?

Instead of focusing on them, I dig into my first bite of pie, bracing myself for the rush of sweetness and flavor as I put it into my mouth, not quite fully ready for just how rich and delicious it will be. "Oh," I moan without meaning to.

What a weird thing to do! Bleating like I'm a sheep that's just been led out to pasture. Embarrassed, I glance up at the two ladies, but luckily, they seem to find my odd noises amusing and not mortifying. "My kind of girl," the first woman encourages. "A pie that good should be savored."

"I don't recognize you from around here," Rae adds. "Are you one of ours?"

I blink back at her, not understanding. "One of yours?"

"Are you here for the show?"

All at once, everything clicks into place for me. That's where I recognize these two women from. Raquel "Rae" Ezra and Sienna Diaz. The executive producers of *Mountain Man*. Two of the most famous actresses in the world, and I couldn't place them because I was too dazzled by pie. I feel like an idiot.

But even more worrying than that is the knowledge that Uncle Aaron is not going to like this. I wasn't even allowed to film the family package because he was afraid I would try to steal Harmony's shine. So instead I went into town and shared a table with two of the producers of the show. None of it was intentional, of course, but I'm sure Uncle Aaron won't see it that way.

"No," I manage finally, wondering how I can politely extract myself from the situation. "My cousin is one of the Mountainettes. Harmony Miller?"

"Oh, right! She seems like such a sweetheart from her audition tapes." Sienna smiles encouragingly, as if she senses my sudden shift in mood and wants to reassure me. "We're meeting all the women this evening for cocktails."

"Hmm." I use another bite of pie as a reason not to commit to more conversation. Not that it's a hardship. It's really good pie.

"You didn't want to be on TV?" Rae asks. "You have the face for it."

"Absolutely adorable," Sienna agrees.

I feel my skin heating. "Oh. Thank you. No. That's more Harmony's thing."

"Oh. So what's your thing?"

I'm not sure why these two women are so interested in me. Most likely they feel sorry for me. I wish I could tell them that it's okay, I know I'm nothing special. I've made peace with that. I'm the person in the back of the family pictures, if I make it into them at all. I don't have much of interest to say. I'm not charming or vivacious or funny. I'm happiest at home, alone, lost in one of my fashion magazines.

I should have stayed back at the hotel.

You should have, but your vanity got in the way. Now it's Uncle Aaron's voice in my head, sounding stern and disapproving. *You were upset that you didn't get to tag along for the family package, so you decided to make a spectacle of yourself in town.*

Swallowing, I realize that too long of a pause has followed Sienna's question, and now both women are looking slightly worried behind their smiles. I should say something, then find a reason to politely excuse myself. Without overthinking it too much, I tell the truth. "I like design. Sewing. Clothing. Costumes."

I brace myself for them to look at me like I'm an idiot. My own wardrobe is hardly what anyone would call fashionable. But my interest in clothing has never been about how any piece would look on me. I like seeing how clothing can transform other people, make them into their best, most beautiful and confident selves.

To my surprise, they both seem interested, not dismissive. I'm sure they're only being polite, but it still feels nice not to have someone roll their eyes when you tell them about your dream.

Sienna leans forward. "It's funny you should say that. We've been looking for a few extra interns to help out with our wardrobe department."

"We have?" Rae asks—then, exchanging a glance with Sienna, she quickly corrects herself. "We have! That's right. I forgot about that."

She might be a great actress on screen, but her delivery in person is less than convincing. Still, I can't help the jolt of excitement that rushes through me. They're offering me the chance to work in a wardrobe department? For a television show? I think of all the costumes, the fabric, the buttons. The sequins! I bet there'll be a lot of sequins for a show like this. I might not look like it, but I'm someone who appreciates a little shimmer and shine.

As soon as my hope starts to build, though, I instinctively squash it back down. They aren't offering me the position because I've demonstrated any skill or talent. It's because they feel sorry for me. It's exactly the kind of charity that Uncle Aaron is always warning me against taking. *Remember it has to come from somewhere*, he'll tell me darkly, *and it has to be taken away from somebody else.*

Oblivious to my dark turn of thoughts, Sienna continues, "Since you're going to be around for the filming anyway, you might as well get some experience out of it, right?"

I look back and forth between them, torn. I can tell that what they're offering comes from such a kind place. And they're both so persuasively beautiful, it's hard to even comprehend the idea of turning them down. Truthfully, I don't want to turn them down. This is a once-in-a-lifetime opportunity, and they're just handing it to me out of the kindness of their hearts.

But it's not just about what I want. Sometimes I have to put the family first. It feels like I only ever put my family first, but apparently it's still not enough. "I don't know . . ."

Sienna leans forward, arresting me with her beautiful, dark eyes. "Nina, can I be totally honest with you? You would be doing us a favor if you agreed to this."

"I . . . would?" I look between them again. Doing a favor for someone is much harder to turn down than accepting a favor from them. I've had it programmed into me to avoid taking at all costs, but it's never worked the other way. I've always, always been expected to give.

Seeming to sense she's hooked me, Sienna continues, "The studio has saddled us with one of their executives to oversee the filming, and honestly, it's made everything into a fight. We had such an incredible vision of this empowering dating show where women were going to get to call the shots."

"All the dresses were going to have pockets," Rae laments, with real wistfulness in her voice.

"Perry is sucking all the joy out of the show and trying to turn it into another dumb reality show where the girls are in bikinis the whole time and the men are macho caricatures." Intense irritations rolls off Sienna in waves. She takes in a breath, trying to calm herself. "And since he's not only a killer of joy but also a cheapskate, he's told us that we are strictly, absolutely not allowed to hire anyone new." Her eyes gleam now as she looks at me.

I look dubiously at the two women. I might need to re-evaluate my opinion of them. They might not be angels; they might be demons. Beautiful, well-dressed she-demons. "You want to hire me out of spite?"

"Sienna makes most of her best decisions out of spite," Rae says sagely, as if that makes any sense, which it definitely doesn't.

But my discomfort must show, because her face softens. "All jokes aside, it's just a little way to prove that this is still *our* show, not his. Haven't you ever wanted to push back and remind someone that you're in charge?"

The idea feels wild and heady and frightening in a way I don't want to look at too closely. *Yes*, is what I want to say. *I know exactly what you mean.*

"No," I lie, but it doesn't sound entirely convincing, even to me. Maybe it's time for just a smidge more honesty. "I just don't think it's a good idea. My uncle really wouldn't like it if I distracted from Harmony's experience in any way."

Sienna waves my concern away like it's nonsense. "You'll be behind the scenes! No one will even see you on camera."

"And don't worry about your uncle," Rae adds, with a mischievous gleam in her eyes. "Sienna and I can be very persuasive . . ."

I don't doubt that's true, since they somehow persuaded me to sit, eat pie with them, and confide my life's ambitions in under five minutes—but they also don't know my uncle. Or the shame I've put my family through, more than once.

The intention is kind, but I chalk up their offer to just one of the many disappointments in life—the dreams you hope will come true, before a crushing dose of reality wakes you.

Chapter 7
Wes

Listen, I don't mean to brag, but I've never exactly had trouble in the dating department. I'm six feet tall, gainfully employed, physically fit, and apparently something of a pretty boy. No need to pretend that I've struggled to get attention.

Finding a connection? That can be trickier, especially when your hobbies are a bit "weird" and "off-putting to women" (according to Morrie). But who doesn't struggle to find the one in this day and age, when we're so connected and yet never been more disconnected from each other?

But I digress. All of that bragging about my sexy *lewks* is to say I'm not someone with an inferiority complex by any stretch of the imagination—so when I say my fellow *Mountain Man* contestants make me feel like a hobbit, I'm not being down on myself. I'm an above-average-looking guy.

These men? These are Greek gods.

I don't think anyone else on this show is under six three. And they're all built like they do nothing but juggle car tires all day. There's some body diversity, which is a pleasant surprise; so not all the men are totally ripped, but they're all *big*, strong, burly, barrel-chested types.

That's when it hits me—I'm part of the body diversity, too. I'm the token little guy.

At first I tell myself, no problem! I'm a friendly dude. I can skate by on my charm, easy. I've done it before—hell, I've done it undercover in prison. Reality TV should be a walk in the park in comparison to that, right?

Wrong. These handsome, brawny gods are frickin' dreamboats in the personality department, too. This is honestly the most interesting, coolest group of men I've ever talked to before. Jerome, from North Carolina, runs a nonprofit for kids who are color-blind. Nicky, from Virginia, is from a legacy firefighting family that goes all the way back to the nineteenth century. Denver, from, well, Denver, is studying to be an archaeologist and is training to be one of a handful of people left in the world who can read a dead language.

And myself? I am Nate Russell from Tennessee. Personality ambiguous. I've come up with a few token hobbies and habits, but when I was putting together my cover story, I was trying to find ways to blend in as much as possible, not stand out. Even the fact that I'm one of two Nates on the show (hence, why I have to go by Nate R.) was designed so I wouldn't make too many waves.

I can't exactly give Nate all of my actual hobbies and personality traits, either, since (a) I like to keep a firm line between my undercover persona and my actual life, and (b) I've been warned in no uncertain terms from Morrie that I must never, ever tell people about how much I love bagpipes.

But I'm probably blowing things out of proportion. Maybe these guys aren't as impressive as I think. Or maybe they are, but I fit in just fine with them. Maybe any inferiority on my part is all just in my head.

This hope is almost immediately dashed as I take in the look on Morrie's face after the meet and greet with the other men. He's posing undercover as my producer, so he got to witness firsthand just how much of a loser I am compared to pretty much every other guy on the show.

When we're finally alone together, he winces at me. "Do you have any secret skills?" Before I can get too excited, he adds, "Something actually impressive, like being able to bench-press one of the Mountainettes, not, like, swallowing a sword."

What's cooler than swallowing a sword, I ask you? But, admittedly, as this skill has never gotten anyone a girlfriend in the history of the world, I can see Morrie's point. Frustrated, I rake a hand through my hair. "What are we gonna do?"

This is about more than just my ego, after all. I *need* to stay on *Mountain Man* for as long as possible so I can get close to one of the Mountainettes. Harmony

Miller, daughter of Aaron Miller. This entire undercover mission hinges on that. But why would Harmony choose me when I'm the only guy who isn't built like Thor and whose undercover personality could best be described as "elevator music, but a person"?

Morrie sighs. "I think it's time we visit the executive producers."

It's pretty much a last-resort strategy. Morrie and I have never admitted as much out loud to each other, but I'm almost positive it's a mutual feeling.

We're scared of the executive producers.

Sienna Diaz more than Raquel Ezra, I think. She's frighteningly direct and will say things out loud that most people would be way too chickenshit to vocalize. Though, Raquel has that intense stare that makes it feel like she can see right through you, so honestly, it's a toss-up. It also doesn't help that they're both stunningly gorgeous. And they always smell so good. I'm not sure why, but that makes them even more terrifying.

A couple years ago, I spent three months undercover in prison, and somehow I feel more unsure of myself now, knocking on the door to their office, than I did then. "Come in!" a voice calls from inside.

Morrie and I exchange a glance. I wonder if he'd let me hold his hand . . . ?

Kidding. Mostly.

Drawing in a bracing breath, Morrie lurches ahead of me and pushes open the door. "Ms. Diaz. Ms. Ezra. We were wondering if we could have a moment of your time?"

This is ridiculous. We're both employees of the Federal Bureau of Investigation, for goodness' sake, but Morrie's voice cracks like he's going through puberty, and my hands are legitimately shaking. I smile my broadest smile to cover it up. "Just a tiny moment. Half a moment, really."

Raquel and Sienna exchange amused looks, like they're used to men turning into babbling idiots in their presence. "Half a moment," Raquel agrees, looking pointedly down at her watch. "Aren't you supposed to be at a photoshoot soon?"

They're both looking at me now. I don't make direct eye contact, for fear I might turn to stone. "About that . . ." I do my best to sound like a polished professional and not trip over my words. "I met the other men just now, and I couldn't help but notice they're all . . ." I search for the right word.

"Panty-melting?" Sienna supplies.

Probably not the phrasing I would have gone for, but she's not wrong. And, as if she's well aware that she's not wrong, Sienna smiles knowingly at Raquel. "We have a real eye for sexy."

"And they're so interesting," Raquel adds. "Everyone is so cultured and smart and wonderful. We're really happy with our group."

"Yeah," I agree. "That's kind of the problem."

One of Raquel's eyebrows arches. She is completely stone-faced. Yep, she's definitely the scarier of the two. "Problem?"

Sienna lets out an aggravated sigh. "We are up to our necks with problems, boys. Between the studio sending in a lackey with the personality of a paper towel to babysit us to a wardrobe department intern's creepy uncle demanding that he get to do product placement on the show, we have filled our weekly quota of problems." She lets that sink in a moment before giving us each a meaningful glare in turn. "So this had better be something important. Or ideally, something really, really easy to fix."

I look to Morrie for help. He wipes his palms on his trousers before gesturing toward me with a thumb. "Unfortunately, we've realized that 'Nate' is rather bland compared to the rest of the cast."

Raquel and Sienna react with surprise at the word choice, checking my reaction, but I'm too aware of the issue to be offended. I shrug. "A little on the tame side," I agree.

"Like . . . beige wallpaper," Morrie continues.

I frown at him. "They get it, Morrie." Still feeling the collective gaze of beautiful executive producers on me, I turn back to the two women and hastily add, "Not *me*, me. My undercover character. *I* can juggle knives. So."

My comment just hangs in the air for a long, uncomfortable moment. Then Sienna clears her throat. "Okay. I'm struggling to see how this is a problem. For us, anyway."

"He's short, too," Morrie chimes in. "I mean, not relatively speaking, in most contexts. But when you stand him next to those guys, he looks like Peter Pan."

Peter Pan? "I'm not *that* much shorter," I object.

"Like a tiny, little boy who never got to grow up," Morrie continues, just rubbing that salt right in my open wound.

Raquel holds up a hand, cutting both of us off. "Let me make sure I understand. What you're saying is we chose a cast of men who are too interesting and too tall."

I check with Morrie. We both nod at that assessment.

"For a reality show that we're hoping will be a massive success," Raquel continues. "Because if it's a massive success, we can use the proceeds to fund our studio's projects—even the ones with women and LGBTQ and BIPOC writers and directors that might not get greenlit anywhere else."

"What were we thinking?" Sienna deadpans.

I shake my head. Clearly, this isn't coming out right. "Obviously you want the show to do well. And you chose great! But since it *is* a competition, and I do need to stay on the show long enough to complete my important *federal* business —" I really emphasize the word "federal" to remind them just how official this is.

Nonetheless, Sienna looks decidedly unimpressed as she holds up a hand. "Let me cut you off there, boys. We've been very compliant with the FBI's request to put a special agent on the show. But this is a show about women's empowerment. About *consent*. So let me be extremely clear—we will not be forcing any of our contestants to choose to keep you on. If they send you home, we will not be intervening. We want our Mountainettes to have a real shot at romance. At *love*. Now, I'm sorry if you're feeling intimidated by the sheer awesomeness of the other men around you. But I encourage you to use this as a learning opportunity. When will men finally understand that it's not size that matters—whether it be height or length or girth? A man who's confident in himself, who asks questions, who really listens to the answers is far more appealing than the tallest, hottest dude with the hugest schlong."

I clear my throat. "For the record, I'm not worried about my dick size." Lies. I'm totally intimidated. Those other men are *huge*. That's gotta translate to other places too, right?

Sienna rolls her eyes at Raquel. "Do you think he heard anything that I just said?"

"Confidence," I repeat back, to show I was paying attention, "asking questions. Being a good listener. I can do all of that. Totally."

Raquel gets a far-off, contemplative look on her face. "A really long tongue doesn't hurt, either."

Huh? I move my tongue around in my mouth, wondering if it's considered long or short or average. It's, frankly, something I've never considered before. Great. Now I'm going to have one more thing to overanalyze and spiral about.

Sienna checks her watch pointedly. "Aren't you going to be late for the promo shoot . . . ?"

"Ma'am. Yes, ma'ams." For some reason, Morrie and I back out of the room, like we're peasants leaving the presence of two queens.

Once we're in the hallway again, we look at each other, no longer bothering to hide our dismay.

"Do you think any of that stuff about confidence and being a good listener is true?" I wonder out loud. "Is that really what women care about?"

Morrie doesn't even have to think about that. "Of course not."

"Shit," I say.

"Shit," Morrie agrees.

Chapter 8
Nina

I can't believe it. I can't believe I'm actually in a television production wardrobe department, sorting through costumes for upcoming challenges and dates for the heroes and heroines of the show.

I wouldn't exactly say this is my childhood dream job. My dream job would be to be the dressmaker for a beautiful lady going to a Regency-era ball. Or for a medieval queen! Oh, gosh. The fabric. The colors! In my dream job, there probably wouldn't be so much flannel or . . . banana hammocks? Oh, boy. I can already tell Uncle Aaron *really* isn't going to love that date when it airs on live television . . .

But to be in a room absolutely stuffed full of hats and shoes and clothes—to see the sketches of costume plans for what looks like an upcoming masquerade ball . . . wow. Weirdly, I've never given too much thought to what Heaven might look like, but I think it might be this room. We're only on the bottom floor of the Donner Lodge, in one of the conference rooms, so it's not like I've even gone very far from the room I've been holed up in for most of my time in Green Valley. But still. I'm here by myself, without Uncle Aaron or Aunt Hope or any of the kids. I'm working on a job with costumes, not running errands or helping with chores. I'd braced myself to be trapped this entire trip, and instead by some miracle, I've been set free—even if it's only for a few weeks.

Somehow, Rae Ezra and Sienna Diaz pulled it off. Somehow they convinced Uncle Aaron to let me work here. I was so sure he would say no. I was waiting for him to come out with that familiar, reproachful look—the one that I'd think borderlines on disdain if I didn't know he only holds me to such a high standard for my own good.

When it came down to it, though, Uncle Aaron didn't say *anything* to me about it, good or bad. I didn't know what the final verdict was until the next morning when Lyle came to get Harmony for her photoshoot and motioned for me to follow after them with a wink. "Come on, Thumbelina. You're with me today."

And now I'm here, on a television set. Holding . . . a spray bottle?

"It's full of glycerin and water," Deja tells me as we make our way to the preshow photoshoot for the Mountain Men. "It'll make them look sorta sweaty, but in a hot, manly way."

Deja is one of the longtime stylists for the network, and she is *beautiful*. She has dark skin and wavy hair that reaches to her shoulders. With her dark eyes and incredible bone structure, she looks completely glamorous even without wearing any makeup. Her clothes are nondescript dark colors, but they're fitted well to her body, which gives her an elegant, timeless, Audrey Hepburn aesthetic.

My job today is to make sure the men stay glistening throughout the photoshoot. I'm happy to do whatever the producers want me to as long as it gets me out of doing Bible study with my younger cousins upstairs. Although admittedly, part of me hopes that at some point in working for the wardrobe department, I'll move on to something more ambitious, but it *is* only my first day. And I'm so thankful to be here! Honestly, what an experience. I can't wait to tell Helen and Matilda all about it.

When we reach the set (!), which has been prepared for the photoshoot with all the Mountain Men, the photographer and his assistants are finishing getting the lighting just right. Most of the men are already dressed, although a few are still being adjusted by some of the other stylists. The attention to detail is incredible, honestly. The stylists take their time with each man, rolling a sleeve up, then back down partway, finding the exact right position on each Mountain Man's forearm for maximum impact.

And I have to admit, I'm a little dazzled. I'm not usually one to take so much note of people's looks, but these men are almost a different species of handsome, they're so tall and broad and chiseled. Even though on its own, their handsomeness doesn't *do* much for me in terms of "getting my engine revving," as Matilda might say, on a purely aesthetic level, I can appreciate it. I would love to make costumes for some of them. Sleek-lined suits, maybe, specially tailored for their extra-tall frames . . .

"Glisten Girl!" one of the stylists calls out.

Oh! That's me. Heart pounding, I hurry forward. I want—*need*—to do a good job today. I need the stylists to want me to come back, and to learn my name so I don't have to answer to "Glisten Girl" anymore. I want Sienna and Rae to not regret making that phone call. I want my uncle to have no reason to keep me back in the hotel suite.

"Neck, upper chest, arms," the stylist, whose name I think is Amber, tells me seriously. "Don't spray on the clothes. Or the face. We want them to look healthy and glowing, not damp and sweaty."

I nod vigorously to show I understand. "Got it."

I move up and down the row of men. They seem to hardly notice me, distracted by all the lights and busyness in the room. Which is absolutely fine by me. I don't need any of these flannelled gods to pay me any mind. I wouldn't know what to do with that kind of attention, anyway.

Judging by the bits and pieces of conversation floating around, it seems like most of the men have just arrived in Green Valley in the last day or so and are meeting each other for the first time. Some of the men are local, but from what I gather, all come from places close to big mountain ranges—the Cascades, the Rockies, and so forth. Most of the men are making small talk, and some have already fallen into an easy rhythm of teasing each other. A few seem very quiet and withdrawn, and I can't blame them much. I'd absolutely whither under these many lights, a camera, so many people watching.

I smile to myself as I think of Harmony, off doing the Mountainettes photoshoot at a different location. (They want the heroes and heroines to meet for the first time on camera, naturally.) I bet wherever she is, she's eating all of this up.

I'm so caught up in my task that at first I don't really register his face. That jaw. Those lips. He's looking away from me, talking to the man next to him, wearing an easy smile. My mind slows. *I know him*, I think, and my mind runs over the possibilities. He's older. His hair has grown out. But more than that, I never thought I'd be seeing him here of all places. Not in a million years.

Cass.

When the recognition finally clicks into place, I freeze. At just that moment, as if he can sense the weight of my attention, his eyes slide over to me. Away, then back again, snagging. I see him go through the same process, the same stutter as his mind tries to place me so far out of context from where he would have known me. I see the wrinkle in his brow, the shock that shudders through his eyes.

Breathe, Nina, I tell myself. Something that usually comes so naturally now becomes an effort to accomplish. My entire body feels like it's locked up, frozen with shock. My brain, too. But not my heart—it's the only thing still functioning, albeit at higher-than-usual capacity as it pounds away in my chest. Two years. It's been sleeping for two years, and now, finally, it's been woken up.

It's probably only the briefest of moments that we stare at each other. It feels longer. Much, much longer. His lips part, like he's going to say something.

No. I can't let him. I don't know why, exactly, but I know I can't hear what he has to say. It won't be good, I'm sure, whatever it is. He'll ruin it, all of those memories we had together. And I've treasured them for so long now. Treasured *him.* He's been the one bright spot I've carried with me all this time. The dream I've nurtured quietly, gently; the one thing I've let myself keep just for me. I can't let anyone take that away, not even him.

So before he can speak, I turn and abruptly move on to the next man, gambling on the fact that Cass won't call after me, make a scene. He doesn't, but I can feel his eyes on me as I spritz the man next to him, then the man after that.

Oh my word. Oh my word. Oh my word.

Cass is here. Cass is *here.* I was so sure I'd never see him again, and now he's here. He knows the real reason why I had to leave the postulancy. He knows, because he was there. And . . . participating.

"Are you okay?" Deja asks me when I rejoin her after I've finished glistenizing the long line of men. "You look sorta clammy. Did you spritz yourself?"

I try my best to smile, even though I think I may be sick. "Maybe by accident."

But I know it's not an accident, none of it is. I'm being punished. I did a bad thing a long time ago, and it's only a matter of time before everyone finds out.

Chapter 9
Nina

The Orphan Girl and the Thief
Part 3

The Orphan Girl and the Thief continued to meet once a week, almost never actually touching or speaking, just looking, but having so many conversations within those stolen glances. In his sketches, tucked into folded sheets of paper for only her to find, the Orphan Girl saw herself through his eyes. She saw versions of herself that were pensive, some that were smiling. Some where she looked kind. Some where she looked sad. Some where she looked brave.

That last one he must have just imagined, since the Orphan Girl had never been brave a day of her life; but still, it was flattering to see.

They passed a few months this way, though it felt like much longer. The Orphan Girl knew she was playing with fire. She knew she ought to tell somebody about what was happening, confess, repent. Only . . . she didn't feel guilty. She knew, as well, that if she told somebody, these encounters would come to an end, and more than anything, she did not want that to happen. Sometimes the thought of seeing the Thief was the only thing that brought her joy all week.

So how could it be sinful? How could it be wrong? In the many quiet hours she spent pondering over it and praying, the Orphan Girl began to wonder if God hadn't placed the Thief into her life intentionally. Not as a test or a trial, but as a solace. She had felt so alone for so very long. And now? She was noticed. She was seen. She was treasured.

I'm falling in love with you, the Thief wrote on one of those crumpled-up pieces of paper, left behind for her to find. She kept that one, even though it was risky. She would not have parted with it for all the world.

That night, the Orphan Girl asked God for a favor. If the Thief was meant to be in her life, please, could He provide a way for her to speak to him, alone?

She had been so trained to not want anything for herself that even this small act felt monumental. She waited, and hoped, and wondered if she was foolish for asking for such a thing.

Then the night before the sisters were supposed to go on their usual visit to the prison, several of the nuns came down with food poisoning. It was only a mild case, but they would be in no position to visit the prison the next day. Only the Orphan Girl and Sister Catherine had been spared.

The Orphan Girl felt sorry, of course, that everyone had gotten sick, but she couldn't help feeling like this was a sign.

In the back of her head, though, she heard Uncle Aaron's voice, reminding her that to receive the answer to her prayers, others had to suffer. She was always taking, taking, taking, even when she didn't mean to. She was a selfish, sinful girl.

And still, she did not tell anyone. Still, she hoped against hope that her prayers were coming true.

The Orphan Girl worried all morning that Sister Theresa would tell them they couldn't go on their own; but when no word came, the Orphan Girl and Sister Catherine decided they would still perform their ministry.

Don't be foolish, the Orphan Girl ordered herself on the bus ride to the prison. This was not a sign from God. She would still be in a room full of prisoners, with Sister Catherine by her side. There was no guarantee she would get to speak to the Thief alone.

Then to her surprise, only the Thief and one of the prison guards was in the meeting room when they arrived. The Thief rose to his feet at the sight of the Orphan Girl, their gazes colliding.

"Where is everyone?" Sister Catherine asked.

The Thief shrugged, not taking his eyes from the Orphan Girl. "They didn't feel like coming today."

The Orphan Girl thought that was strange, but she was too distracted by her proximity to the Thief, with so few people between them, to pay it much mind.

"If we'd known, we wouldn't have trekked all the way out here," Sister Catherine groused. She was one of the older sisters, and she had a bad knee.

The Orphan Girl helped her find a seat and made sure she was comfortable, aware of the Thief's gaze on her the whole time. She realized it would be up to her to run the meeting that day, since Sister Catherine usually napped through most of the prayer sessions.

She took her seat, and the Thief did, too. They gazed at one another.

"Let's turn to Peter, chapter four," the Orphan Girl said, trying to keep her voice from trembling.

She and the Thief took turns reading the chapter back and forth, verse by verse. Sure enough, by the second reading, Sister Catherine was already drifting off. Still, the Orphan Girl carried on, knowing that she might stir, or the guard in the doorway might start to pay attention. This could be her best opportunity to have an important conversation with the Thief.

So she made sure that she was the one reading aloud once they got to verse eight: "And above all things, have fervent love for one another, for love will cover a multitude of sins."

She paused and forced herself to meet the Thief's gaze, to check whether he'd understood. What she saw in his eyes made her shiver. What she saw in his eyes made her burn.

A loud, piercing shriek cut through the building. The Orphan Girl jumped. Her first, irrational thought was that God was calling out her sin—but she quickly realized it was an alarm. The lights in the room were flashing with warning.

The guard bolted into action, one hand moving to his gun, the other pulling his radio to his mouth. Through the garbled voice on the other end, the Orphan Girl could make out the words *prison riot*.

When the Orphan Girl looked back to the Thief, she saw guilt flicker across his expression. He'd known this was going to happen. The other prisoners must have known, too, which was why they hadn't come to Bible study. But the Thief had still chosen to attend. Why?

The Orphan Girl thought maybe she knew why, but she didn't want to give that idea too much hope. It wouldn't hurt as badly when the Thief grew tired of her or disappointed her in some other way, if she didn't hope too much for something else.

Her attention was drawn back to the guard, who was having a hushed but frantic conversation over his radio. Somewhere, not too far off, she could hear shouts and the sounds of destruction. Clamoring. Shouting. Screaming.

Suffering, Uncle Aaron's voice reminded the Orphan Girl. *This is what you asked for.*

The Orphan Girl looked to the Thief, but for once he wasn't looking back at her. He was watching the guard, too. "Go," he told him. "Lock us in. I'll keep them safe."

Indecision played out across the guard's face. Frantic calls for backup coming over his radio seemed to make up the guard's mind. "Don't let anyone in until you get the all clear," he instructed the Thief briskly.

He left them there, locking the door behind him. As the Thief moved to barricade the door with some desks, the Orphan Girl's mind was whirring. She didn't understand what was happening. The guard shouldn't be leaving a prisoner on his own with two civilians, should he? And why had he and the Thief exchanged such a long, deliberate look?

Sister Catherine stirred, squinting up at the flashing lights overhead. "What's going on?"

"There's a prison riot," the Orphan Girl informed her quietly, trying not to let her panic bleed into her voice.

Sister Catherine blinked. "Ah." Unfazed, she put her head back down on the desk and, to the Orphan Girl's astonishment, went back to sleep.

When she turned back, the Thief had finished stacking desks in front of the door. They faced each other, no barriers between them now, and (almost) nobody else in the room.

There were so many questions the Orphan Girl wanted to ask. So many things she wanted to say.

Instead, what she blurted out was, "Why would the guard leave us alone with you?"

A strange, conflicted look flashed across the Thief's face. He blinked it away, meeting her gaze earnestly. "I'm not going to hurt you."

"I know," the Orphan Girl returned quickly, and meant it.

They gazed at each other for a long moment, until more shouts sounded from nearby, followed by what sounded like scattered gunfire.

The Orphan Girl gasped in surprise. The Thief closed the distance between them, pulling her under the conference table with him. "What about Sister Catherine?" the Orphan Girl asked.

"I think if anyone manages to break in, they'll assume she's dead," the Thief returned, and they both laughed at the ridiculousness of the situation.

It was only then the Orphan Girl realized how close they were to one another. The Thief had positioned them so his back was up against one of the table's thick legs, his body between hers and the doorway. She was half in his lap, pressed flush against him, their faces only a few inches apart. She felt the moment he registered this, too, in the way that his heart began hammering against hers.

"Agnes," he murmured. The way he said the name sounded so reverent. She wished it was really hers.

She thought he might kiss her; but then there were more shouts, sounding very near the door. The Orphan Girl jumped, and the Thief tightened his hold on her with one arm. His other hand came up to cup the back of her head protectively, like she was precious. "You're safe," he told her. "I'll keep you safe, I swear."

Somehow, she believed him. The Orphan Girl couldn't remember the last time she'd felt the security of knowing someone was looking after her. She ought to be terrified; but how could she be, wrapped in the Thief's arms, her ear pressed to his chest, listening to the steady thrumming of his heart?

She was the one to turn her face up to him. *She* was the one who broke her vows, seeking the warmth of his lips with her own. Later, the Orphan Girl would remind herself of this, remind herself of how weak and sinful she was. But in that moment, it didn't feel wrong. He was so gentle, so reverent with her, as he cradled her face in his hands and stroked her chin with his thumb. She lost herself in his touch, yes, but she found herself there, too, her heart and her spirit and her body in perfect, vivid harmony together, lost in his patient, reverent embrace.

They kissed. They only kissed. But that was enough to mean she could not continue being a postulant. The Orphan Girl might have done many, many things wrong, but she couldn't live a lie. She couldn't pretend her vows hadn't been broken. She couldn't pretend to be the same girl she'd been when she walked into the prison that morning.

Even as she was kissing the Thief, she knew it, but in that moment, she couldn't bring herself to care. This would be the end of their story, of course. He was in prison, and she would have no other choice but to go back to her family. There was just no other way this story could go. But they could have this for now, this one stolen moment of time, just for them.

That was what she told herself. But when it came time to leave, it was still agony. She couldn't bring herself to tell him she wouldn't be coming back. Even though he had never truly been hers, she felt the loss so keenly. And even though an ending with the two of them together could have never been, she knew a part of her would always be longing for it. Her heart was his now. That was all there was to it.

That's the thing about thieves, though. They take what doesn't belong to them, and even if they give it back, it no longer feels like it's yours anymore.

Chapter 10
Wes

Shit. Shiiiiiiiiiiiiiiit. *Shit.*

The rest of the photoshoot, I'm half out of my head. My face is smiling, I'm tilting my head and moving my limbs as instructed by the photographer, but my mind is miles away. Or, more accurately, years away. It's Sister Agnes. She's here, somehow. I don't understand it. I can't wrap my mind around it.

I tell myself not to look at her, but in every break between shots, my eyes find her in the room. I don't have to search for her. My body is aware of her in ways I don't totally understand. There's attraction, sure, but I've been attracted to plenty of women before. It's something more visceral than that, this recognition, this *cognizance* of her, like she is some part of me that's been missing. A phantom limb, reminding me of its existence in the most inconvenient ways.

The last time I saw her, I was in prison, pretending to be someone else but somehow still falling desperately in love with her. It wasn't my first undercover mission, but it was the first time I'd been left in such a high-stakes environment on my own. At the time, I'd been so sure that I would be able to stay focused, get what information I needed quickly, and be extracted within a month.

Then I met Agnes. Agnes, with those incredible dark eyes and that shy smile. Agnes, who always held herself so carefully, so still, who looked like she had an infinite universe of secrets she kept locked inside of her. She was so beautiful, even in the shapeless clothes, with her hair mostly covered. But that wasn't why I was drawn to her. It was because she looked like someone who was in the middle of her own story. I don't know how else to describe it. She was clearly a heroine in the making, but it was like she hadn't yet realized her own power.

What was supposed to be a month of undercover work bled into two, then longer. I needed more time. Not on the case, mind you; Big Tom, who I'd gone into prison to befriend and retrieve information from, already trusted me like a son. I could have asked him anything, but I didn't, because I wanted the excuse to spend more time with her.

On the day of the prison riot, I should have been at Big Tom's side, sealing my place as his confidant. Instead, all I could think about was what would happen to Agnes if someone found her in the library on her own. So I went to Bible study, even though everyone else stayed behind to be in place for what was about to go down. When the chaos started, I held her in my arms and promised to protect her. I kissed her, and felt the warmth of her small, soft body against mine. I cracked open that day, knowing I had lost something I would never get back.

And I never saw her again. She never did come back to the prison. Never sent a letter, never gave me any explanation. Once I was extracted, I tried to look her up, but the convent wouldn't release her information, and I had nothing to go off but a first name. Agnes. I told myself then that I had to move on, that I wasn't going to see her again, that she clearly didn't want to see me. She was a ghost now. Nothing more than a memory.

Except here she is. Looking at me with big, terrified eyes, like I'm the one who left her without so much as a word. Like I'm the one who broke *her* heart.

So many strings were pulled to get me on *Mountain Man* so I could get close to Harmony Miller, and by extension, Aaron Miller. I have to stay focused; I can't allow for even the smallest distraction.

And yet, even knowing all of that . . . I see Sister Agnes and my heart clenches. I can't look away. When her eyes meet mine, it's earth-shattering.

So. Yeah.

Shit.

The photoshoot stretches on for what feels like an eternity. God, how many pictures do they need, anyway? When I'm not zeroing in on Agnes, wherever she is in the room, I'm trying to make meaningful eye contact with Morrie to let him know there's a problem. Alas, Morrie has discovered the craft services table and is happily noshing away at finger sandwiches, completely oblivious to my distress. The man does love a good finger food.

Finally, the production staff calls for a break. One of the producers instructs us to eat, grab some water, and use the restroom while they pull a few of the men aside for one-on-one interviews.

Luckily, I'm not among the chosen few. As the other men amble over toward craft services, I find Agnes in the crowd. She's carrying a tub full of the prop sunglasses and hats they had us wear for some of the "silly" poses, and is heading toward the back corridor.

This is it—my chance. After ascertaining that no one is paying attention to me, I follow after her. The bathrooms are on the other side of the building, but I figure I'll just claim I got turned around if anyone acts suspicious. I really ought to tell Morrie before I duck out of the room, but he's busy yucking it up with one of the other producers, and I might not get another shot to be with Agnes alone before she can blow my cover.

Up ahead of me, I spot her down the hallway, just about to turn the corner and disappear out of sight. "Agnes!" I call out to her.

Agnes's entire back stiffens. Even without seeing her face, I read the indecision playing out in the set of her shoulders, the lines of her body. I can just imagine her internal dialogue. Can she play it off, pretend she didn't hear me and still make her escape?

"You obviously heard me," I inform her dryly. "Come on. We need to talk."

Agnes doesn't turn around, but she doesn't leave, either. I make short work of the distance between us, circling around her so that we're face-to-face.

No matter how hard I try to brace myself, it still feels like a punch to the jaw with brass knuckles when our gazes finally meet. *Those eyes.*

Despite everything, I think I'm doing a pretty good job of keeping my expression schooled. She isn't doing quite so well. Her face is pale, her hands gripping tightly to the tub of props. Her eyes dart over my face rapidly before dropping downward, like she can't bear to look at me. She's terrified.

I swallow back the hurt of that, welcoming in the anger, instead. Way easier to cope with that emotion. What right does she have, to act like I've hurt *her* in some way, when she was the one to abandon me without so much as a goodbye?

"Not happy to see me, I guess." I don't bother to hide the snark from my tone. I always turn into a sarcastic bastard when I'm hurt. What other chance did I have, growing up idolizing Han Solo?

Agnes's eyes dart up to mine, then away again. She shifts, like she's thinking of running for it. "What are you doing here?"

"What am *I* doing here?" *Ma'am, the audacity.* "What are *you* doing here? Last time I checked, television shows don't hire nuns for their wardrobe department."

"I'm not a postulant. Not anymore. Not since we . . ." A flush works its way up to Agnes's cheeks that might be distracting if I weren't so pissed off.

Okay, it's still distracting. I can't help but remember the last time I saw her face this rosy, the way she pressed her lips to mine, her small hands smoothing over my chest—and *that* pisses me off even more. "Made out in prison?" I finished for her, my voice nonchalant. "I guessed you must've left the convent, since I never heard from you again."

Agnes glances around the hallway, like she's worried one of the invisible people around us will hear her dirty little secret. Her flushed skin darkens. "It was . . . complicated."

I shrug, like it *isn't* the very memory that still haunts me when I wake up early in the morning in the throes of an anxiety spiral. Realizing that Agnes wasn't coming back to the Bible study. Knowing I would never see her again. "Buyer's remorse. I get it. It happens. A letter would have been nice, but . . ." I shrug again, which probably is overselling my insouciance. But hey, she still isn't looking at me, so what does it hurt? Aside from my heart, that is.

I'm about to call her out for her lack of eye contact when all of a sudden, her gaze snaps back up to mine. It's another sucker punch, straight to the jaw. I can see she's been steeling herself up to this moment by the way she sets her mouth and raises her chin.

"Why does the call sheet list you as Nate Russell?" she asks me.

Whoops.

That's all I can think of. Because yeah, when I chased Sister Agnes down this hallway, I guess I didn't fully plan out the conversation—how she might find it strange that the ex-con she'd met in prison was suddenly sporting a radically different look and going by a completely different name. Probably should have thought that one through a little more.

"Uh . . ." I stall, eloquently.

She takes a step toward me, and I instinctively back up. Which is ridiculous since she's five foot nothing and probably weighs about a hundred pounds wet, but . . . damn. Those *eyes*. "And why, when I tried to look up an inmate named Cass to write you a letter, did the prison have no record of you?" Her dark eyes search mine. "Who are you?"

This is really not a conversation for the hallway. Now *I'm* the one paranoid about all the people who might overhear us—or come wandering into the middle of a discussion that requires high-security clearance. I make a quick assessment of the corridor, spotting what appears to be a utility closet. Without pausing to think, I take the tub out of her hands, set it on the floor, then pull her after me into the room.

As soon as we're shut up together in the confined space, I realize my two mistakes. The first, I overestimated the size of the closet. It's small enough that we're going to basically have to spend the entire time trying to consciously *not* be pressed together.

The second is that I've touched Sister Agnes's hand to pull her into the room with me, and her skin is ridiculously soft and smooth and warm. She smells good, too, dammit. Like rose petals.

Releasing her quickly, I curse out my dumb self internally. I really should have debriefed with Morrie before attempting this conversation, but here we are. I don't know if I'll get another chance at this before Agnes tells someone that I'm going by a fake name. Sienna and Raquel are already aware of the situation, but we asked them to withhold that information from anyone else unless absolutely necessary. That means none of the other producers, crew, or production staff know. So if Agnes mentions something to someone else in the wardrobe department, and the rumor gets around . . . sure, Raquel and Sienna might be able to intervene, but that won't squash the intrigue over why I'm lying about my identity. And I very much need to be able to fly under the radar if I have any chance at getting into Aaron Miller's inner circle.

If I'd talked it through with Morrie, I might've been able to think of some plausible excuse to give Agnes as to why I'm going by a new name. Why my former name wasn't in the prison system. Why my neck tattoo has completely disappeared.

But the combined factors of having no time to prepare and unexpectedly seeing the nun I used to love in secret? It's all thrown me for a loop. So I just blurt the first thing that comes to mind, which happens to be the truth.

"My name isn't Nate Russell. And it was never Cass Demonte." Fun fact— everyone in prison thought "Cass" was short for Cassanova, but in the background I'd put together for my character, it was short for Cassian, like Cassian Andor from *Rogue One*. Morrie had no idea I snuck that one in there.

But I digress. Steeling myself, I take a deep breath. "It's Wes Ackerman. I'm an undercover FBI agent."

Chapter 11
Nina

For longer than I would care to admit, I just stare at Cass. Nate. Wes. Whatever his name is. Once again, in the face of what should be a fight-or-flight response, I completely freeze. I have no idea how to process everything he's just told me. Not only is his name different, but he's also just completely rewritten all my memories of him.

Every exchanged glance, every shared moment between us, starts to warp into something unrecognizable. He wasn't really a prisoner? I guess that makes sense why the guard would have been willing to leave me behind with him during the riot. But I have a harder time reconciling the rest of it. There is no Cass. Cass is dead, for all intents and purposes. He never even existed. This man, this Wes, is all that's left of him. But who even is he? Why did he spend so much time drawing me, writing me notes, memorizing naughty Bible verses? Was it all just part of his undercover mission? Was any of that real?

My memories of Cass have always been complicated. But now they've been decimated. Was he leading me on the whole time? And for what—a distraction? Out of boredom? Or was it just to see if he could? The memories of our time together continue to taunt me. Cass drawing me. Cass smiling at me across the table. Cass seeing me—*me*, Nina, not Agnes.

But now those same images don't flood me with warmth. They are barbs that cut and burrow and sting. My one happy, perfect memory turned out to be nothing. Empty. Cass is dead. Cass never even existed.

I want to throw up. I want to scream. I want to cry. But just like always, the feelings are frozen inside of me. In the face of emotional danger, I can't fly or fight. I freeze, and all I can do is stare at him, willing my eyes not to flood with tears.

The Wes standing in front of me now furrows his brow with concern, some of his snarkiness from earlier dissolving. "Hey, are you okay? You look like rigor mortis just set in."

Maybe not *all* of the snarkiness. I blink back at him, drawing in a breath to steady myself. "Undercover FBI?" I echo weakly.

It barely scratches the surface of what I'm feeling, but it is at least a part of my confusion that I'd like to have resolved.

"I was on a mission to gain the confidence of one of the other guys in the Bible study group," he informs me. "You remember Big Tom?"

I can say with all honesty that I do not—although, by the name alone, he seems like a hard guy to forget. But I guess I was pretty preoccupied at the time, what with falling in love with someone who didn't actually exist and breaking my vows and bringing shame upon my family and all.

"Anyway," Wes continues, correctly interpreting my silence for a no, "it all went to seed after you, and I . . ." He gestures between us awkwardly. "I got pulled from the case. Almost lost my job."

"Hmm." I try to sympathize, but it's difficult under the circumstances. "Well, I *did* lose my vocation, so."

Wes at least has the good grace to grimace. "Right."

In a roundabout way, though, I guess I have my answer. Kissing me wasn't part of his mission if he'd been pulled from the case for it. So could that mean . . . the rest of it was real, too?

Even through my thick fog of confusion, learning who Cass, who *Wes*, really is, it's impossible to deny the pull I still feel toward him. Impossible to keep my eyes from darting to his full, soft lips, to keep myself from remembering how they felt on my neck, the shell of my ear, my—

"And now?" I prompt, both to divert my train of thought and because I feel I deserve an answer. "You're undercover again—on a television show?"

The question makes Wes cagey. His face shutters off. "I'm not really at liberty to discuss."

He sounds so official and serious, so unlike himself—or the *himself* I thought I'd known—that I have to stifle a laugh. Wes catches it, though, and despite himself, his face twitches, like he, too, is fighting back some mirth at the preposterousness of the situation we find ourselves in. "Come on, now, Agnes. I'm a serious federal type. I can't just go around spilling all my secrets."

His tone is playful, and a smile tugs at the edge of his lips. He always had such a nice smile. I avert my gaze, smoothing my hair behind my ears. "It's Nina. Short for Antonina. Agnes was my religious name."

"Huh." Wes says it like he's going to have a hard time wrapping his brain around this new information. Well, welcome to the club, buddy. "Which do you prefer— Antonina or Nina?"

The question throws me. I can't remember the last time someone asked me that. Uncle Aaron always calls me Antonina, and most everyone else in my family has followed suit, except for Harmony. So I answer to that name readily. But with my parents, then my friends, it's always been Nina. I can't imagine my friends calling me by my full name, no more than I can picture Uncle Aaron calling me by my nickname. "I . . . don't know," I answer stupidly.

His face furrows, but before he can probe any deeper, I hastily change the subject. "Am I in danger being here? On set? My family's here, too, staying at the Donner Lodge."

As soon as I say it, I realize how selfish I've been, staring at Wes's lips and thrumming at his nearness. If the FBI is investigating someone involved with the show, my entire family might be in harm's way.

He places a reassuring hand on my shoulder. "Relax. You're safe. The person we're investigating has a history of white-collar crime, allegedly. No history of violence, nothing that will put anyone in physical jeopardy. Just don't give out your bank account information to a charming stranger, okay?"

I try to feel reassured by Wes's response, but I'm a little too distracted by his hand on my shoulder. The warmth of his skin seeping through the thin cotton of my blouse. How many years have I castigated myself for my weakness in kissing him? Suddenly I'm not entirely convinced I wouldn't do the exact same thing right now if he asked me to. If he slid his hand on my shoulder a little lower, used the other to grip me by the waist and pull me close . . .

No. Nope. No. *Nina, get ahold of yourself.* I'm really not usually like this. I never was the teenage girl with crushes. I barely noticed the boys around me, and usually I wished they wouldn't notice me so much. Even when I could acknowledge a person was good-looking, it was purely on a superficial level. Their attractiveness had no pull over me. I liked to read about relationships in stories, but only when I could sense a true emotional connection between the characters. The lure of the physical body on its own didn't make much sense to me. I didn't understand the weakness of the flesh that Uncle Aaron was always preaching about over the pulpit, the hormones that were meant to make people lose their common sense and make terrible decisions.

Instead I went through life wondering what all the fuss was about. I'd thought I was immune, but maybe my hormones were just more selective. When I met Wes, it was like I'd been a seed packed in cold, frozen earth, and suddenly it was spring. That's how it felt being near him. Like I was feeling the sun for the first time.

And he still has that same pull, that same power over me. I feel it everywhere all at once—his nearness, his touch, his eyes on me. My heart racing. My skin flushing.

Sucking in a deep breath, I step away from him. Away from temptation. "I should get back to work. They'll be wondering where I am."

A lie. No one even knows my name yet; I think they're all confused why Sienna and Rae made them hire someone new at the last minute, especially when that someone has no experience and no visible fashion sense. But *he* doesn't need to know that.

I'm free from his touch for about two seconds before his hand snags out, catching me. "Wait."

His warm fingers close around my wrist, locking me in place, almost like he thinks I might run away. I'm not running, though. I couldn't run, even if I wanted to. I'm frozen in place again. The rest of my body has disappeared, and there is only the feeling of his skin on my skin, the surprising strength of his long, lean fingers, the subtle roughness of the calluses on his fingertips. There is only the sight of the veins cording up the back of his hand and into his forearm, his skin a pale gold against my dark olive.

His grip shifts so his thumb moves over the pulse point on my wrist, rubbing slowly over that soft, vulnerable patch of skin. It's such a small motion—he may not even realize what he's doing—but it wakes up the rest of my body again, sending currents of electricity running through my veins, spreading outward from where he's touching me until my whole body is alert in a way it hasn't been for . . . years. In a way it hasn't been since him.

Stupid girl. I'm actually holding my breath, hoping he'll tell me that he feels it, too. That he couldn't forget me, either. That it was real between us, all the important parts.

Wes clears his throat, dropping my hand. "I hope it goes without saying that what we've discussed here is confidential. It would jeopardize the case if you told anyone."

I blink. Right. "Right," I say out loud, nodding too vigorously to show I understand. "I won't say anything to anyone." I pull my hand up against my chest like it's wounded, even though my heart is what feels the sting. "I really do have to get back to work."

And I run away before I do something far, far worse.

Chapter 12
Wes

I think my conversation with Nina went pretty well, all things considered. As well as blowing your cover to the woman who broke your heart and jeopardized your career *can* go, that is.

Okay, scratch that. That's my wounded ego talking, not how I really feel. What happened after Agnes—*Nina*—wasn't her fault. *I* was the one who made the choice not to go to the prison riot that day, not to be at Big Tom's side, not to solidify my place as his number-two guy. Afterward, there was a noticeable change in Tom's demeanor toward me, and my handler deemed it necessary to extricate me before Big Tom could (violently) eject me himself. I could have gotten the information I needed from him weeks before; but instead, I'd dragged out my time in prison and was left with nothing.

I wasn't fired for that, although maybe I should have been. And even though it wasn't Nina's fault that I failed the mission, it feels like a bad omen to be seeing her here now, during my riskiest undercover assignment yet. I have a track record of not being able to see a case clearly when she's involved. Hell, I have a track record of not being able to see anything or anyone else in the fucking room when she's involved.

Unfortunately, Morrie seems to be of the same opinion when I rendezvous with him in his room after the photoshoot and tell him what happened. "You did *what?*" he hisses, the vein in his forehead coming out like it always does when he's pissed. Usually at me. It's such a frequent occurrence that I've even given the vein its own nickname—Achilles. You know, 'cause of all the rage and stuff. (Yeah, I read epic poems on occasion. I'm cultured. Don't let my commemorative *House of the Dragon* dinner plates fool you.)

"What choice did I have?" I protest. "She recognized me. She knew I was going by a fake name, and the last time she saw me, I was in prison with a neck tattoo that's mysteriously disappeared. It was either tell her the truth or try to go the long-lost-secret-twin route, which almost never works."

"I'm going to have to report this to the ASAC." Morrie paces the length of the room, running a hand over his face. "She's going to pull you from the case."

"No, she won't," I say with a certainty I don't feel, because, yeah, she might. But she *shouldn't*, and I need Morrie to see that, so he can help me convince the assistant special agent in charge. "I've already met all the other contestants. I'm in the cast photoshoot. If they pull me now, it'll be hella suspicious and we'll lose this route to Aaron Miller. At least this way we have a possibility of achieving our objective."

Morrie pretends to pull out an invisible pad of paper and mimes writing on it with a pen. It's a really annoying bit he does that for some reason he thinks is funny. For the record, it is not. I sigh. "What are you doing?"

"Writing down that genius speech you just gave me. 'Hella suspicious.' I can't wait to report that back to Agent Decker."

"Ha ha." I pick up one of the pillows off the bed and toss it at him. He ducks, because his reflexes are amazing, even if his mime skills could use some work; the pillow hits the wall behind him, sliding to the floor. "I'm not wrong, though," I persist. "You have to convince her."

Retrieving the pillow, Morrie squishes it in his hands like a giant stress ball, his face pensive. "You think this girl can be trusted?"

I think of Nina, her blouse buttoned almost all the way up to her chin. Her big, beautiful, guileless eyes. The way her face always seems to catch the light, no matter where she's standing in the room. I swallow. "She was training to be a nun the last time I saw her. So, yeah. I'd say she's pretty salt of the earth."

Morrie contorts the pillow some more. Poor thing. It's never gonna go back to its original shape now. "She'd have to be vetted. Registered. Debriefed. On a need-to-know basis, but still. I suppose having a CI in the wardrobe department *could* be useful."

He's coming around to the idea of Nina being a confidential informant. I can smell it. Doing my best to keep my tone nonchalant, I offer, "I could help with bringing her onboard. She knows me. Trusts me."

As soon as I say the words, I can't help but wince, remembering the way she completely froze up when I told her Cass had never been real, that all of it was a lie. It wasn't, of course—not all of it, not to me. But her feelings on the subject were clear when I'd touched her wrist and she'd flinched like I was causing her physical pain. I swallow again. "Kind of."

Morrie narrows his eyes at me. "No. Your only goal while you're here is to do such a fucking fantastic job convincing Harmony Miller that you're head over heels in love with her that she has no choice but to take you home to her creepy preacher daddy." He straightens a little, smirking to himself. "You leave the pretty little ex-nun to me."

Morrie's the closest thing I have to a best friend. Hell, a brother. So the flash of blind rage I feel at his insinuation takes me by surprise. I clench and unclench my fists, my jaw, basically anything in my body that can clench. (I'll let you connect those dots yourself.) I draw in a deep, steadying breath and try my best to look unfazed.

I must not be very convincing, because Morrie arches an eyebrow at me. "You okay, Ackerman?"

"Gr-r-r-r-eat," I say, drawing it out Tony the Tiger–style for some inexplicable reason. "Yabba dabba doo."

"What?" a baffled Morrie asks.

"Better get going," I say in lieu answering, picking up the discarded trapper hat that was part of my photoshoot costume off the bed. "Got some bonding to do with some lumber-giants. Someone already threw out the nickname Short Stack within the first five minutes of meeting me. So, gonna be a fun experience—great for my ego."

I beeline for the door, hoping to escape before Morrie can question me too closely.

Luckily, he doesn't call after me, but I can't as easily outrun my own churning thoughts. I pick apart each memory of Agnes, then each nuance of my interaction with Nina today, her eyes on a relentless loop in my mind. No one has ever had this much effect on me, not before or since Nina, and not in the interim between. I somehow forgot what it was like, this pull she has on me. The way my thoughts, my energy, my focus, all get drawn toward her, so I lose sight of everything else.

I already jeopardized one mission for her, only to be abandoned without a note, a goodbye, anything. I can't, I *won't*, let myself do that again.

Chapter 13
Nina

Last week, I was worried about being stuck in the hotel—cleaning and laundering, tutoring my cousins, and knitting for my aunt's African Relief Society—for the entire eight weeks of our stay in Green Valley. Now, I'm part of the wardrobe department for a reality series, and I'm also an informant for the FBI.

Life can be strange sometimes.

My new handler, Morrie, made contact with me the day after my conversation with Cass and brought me on board. Sorry, not Cass—Wes. I'm still wrapping my head around that one. Anyway, after giving me a special burner phone for all our communications, Morrie explained that the FBI may or may not use me for information. Apparently they're still in the process of running my background check, so for now, nothing can be explained to me about the case, but the FBI might have questions for me based on anything I might observe. In the meantime, Morrie reminded me that under no circumstances am I to tell anyone Wes is an undercover agent, so help me God. (That last part may have even been verbatim.)

I wish I could fully explain to Morrie how few people there are for me to tell anything to. Everyone in my family pretty much treats me like I'm part of the furniture. If I were suddenly to announce at dinner that I was working with the FBI, I'm pretty sure they'd just keep talking over me like I hadn't spoken at all.

To be fair, I don't usually have very much to say that's interesting.

The thought depresses me, so I turn my mind to my friends. *WWHTMKG&LD*. If anyone from my book club were here, I guess I might be in some danger of spilling the beans, although even then, I'm pretty good at keeping a secret.

I've had a lot of practice, after all.

As I ready each of the carefully selected beanies the men will be wearing for their first scene today, I entertain myself by musing over which of my friends would make the best confidant, *if* I were going to tell someone about the FBI being on set, which I most definitely will not.

Matilda would be the absolute worst person to tell, I decide. I love her with all my heart, but she is not someone who can keep her opinions to herself. She would out Wes within minutes, then probably give him unsolicited advice about what he was doing wrong in the investigation—and she'd probably be right.

Helen is no better at keeping secrets. Even though she would try to keep the information to herself, she would probably inadvertently give it all away, because her face reveals everything she's feeling, all the time.

Kimo? No. Just, no. I love him to pieces, but what a trainwreck that would be.

Thad could probably be trusted to keep the secret to himself, but based off conversations I've had with him in the past, I suspect he has strong opinions about law enforcement officers, all the different types. In his job as a bounty hunter, he's had run-ins with everyone from the Boy Scouts to the CIA. I've never heard him talk about the FBI specifically, but if he dislikes them as a rule, he might not be as cooperative as Morrie and Wes would want him to be. No one makes Thad do what he doesn't want to do—except Helen.

Grady, I decide, smiling to myself. Grady would be the best person to confide in, if I were going to tell somebody, which I'm definitely not. Grady is an escape room in human form. He is a puzzle. A mystery. He might even be keeping more secrets than me.

"Nina."

Hearing my name is startling enough. Hearing my name murmured in Wes's voice right next to my ear sends my heart racing and my limbs flailing. I knock a bunch of the beanies off the table. Embarrassed, I whirl around to face him, only for my heart to take off at a gallop anew at the sight of him.

The other day for the photoshoot, the men were dressed up like lumberjacks, but highly stylized, almost cartoonish versions of lumberjacks, to play into the stereotype of the mountain man. They looked good, but a little ridiculous, in a fun, extra-cheesy way.

Today the goal was for the men to dress like actual rugged mountain men, emphasis on the sex appeal.

As I slowly look Wes up and down from top to bottom, all I can say is, Deja and her team have really outdone themselves. If the men are supposed to be walking embodiments of a sexual fantasy, the wardrobe department has nailed it. Wes is already a good-looking man, but right now he is . . . wow.

Boots. Dark, snug-fit jeans. A flannel shirt rolled up to the elbows and unbuttoned down the front to reveal a generous glimpse of chest underneath. The garishly bright red flannel all the men were wearing in the photoshoot has been switched out for a much more muted pattern with blues and blacks and dark red. Even though I know firsthand that the shirts have been distressed by a team of wardrobe consultants (including yours truly) to make them look more authentically lived-in, the effect is . . . good. Very, very good. If I didn't know better, I'd think he was really a mysterious, sexy woodsman who just happened to wander down the mountain and onto set.

I must be acting like a real weirdo, because when I finally stop ogling Wes and meet his gaze, his brow is furrowed in concern. "You okay? I didn't mean to startle you."

Ah, right. Because I turned into a human windmill, knocked a bunch of hats everywhere, and then spent two completely silent minutes just staring at his body. Those veins on his forearms.

"Hats," I say stupidly, squatting down to pick up the beanies.

Wes drops down with me, helping to gather them up. I am incredibly aware of my body, his body, and their proximity to each other. The heat emanating off him. The almost brush of our hands as we reach for the same hat, only to both jerk away like we've been burned. I try to steal another sly peek at him, but find him already looking back at me. A jolt of warmth passes through me.

I feel hot and bothered. He looks *concerned*. That's an embarrassing combination.

"Listen," he says quietly, "I know Morrie talked to you. If all of this is too much, you don't need to get involved."

Oh. *That.* He thinks I'm being weird because he's in the FBI, not because he's got just the right amount of stubble on his face or because the color combination on his shirt makes his eyes look super green.

On the one hand, it's much less embarrassing for me if he thinks I'm knocking things off tables because I'm intimidated by the investigation. On the other hand . . . I don't want to be uninvolved. I'm surprised, honestly, to find how much I want to be involved. This is by far the most exciting thing that's ever happened to me—well, except for that time I was in the middle of a prison riot. Wes was there then, too, come to think of it.

I stammer, trying to come up with a plausible excuse for why I am so jumpy. "No, I want to help! I do. You just startled me, that's all." I dare a quick glance over my shoulder to make sure no one else is paying too much attention. "How will I be helping, exactly?"

Wes glances around, too, before responding. "After your clearance comes through, we'll mostly ask you for information about our person of interest. Day-to-day activities. Habits, preferences, things like that."

Oh. I'm half relieved, half disappointed. I thought being an FBI informant would be much more proactive—rifling through the suspect's belongings, hacking into computers, beating up bad guys who are trying to destroy the world. Come to think of it, I think I'm just imagining scenarios from *Kim Possible*.

The way Wes describes it, I'm not going to be in any danger whatsoever. It'll be like I'm the FBI's official gossip. Which is fine, I just thought that maybe . . .

If you were more involved, you'd get to spend more time with Wes. As soon as the thought crosses my mind, I reproach myself for it. How stupid can one person be? Wes is being as professional with me as possible, because this is his job. But a part of me keeps expecting *Cass* to be somewhere in there—the guy who couldn't keep his eyes off me, who drew me like I was the most beautiful woman in the world. Who kissed me like . . .

Stop it, Nina. That wasn't Wes. Or maybe it was, that part of it, but not all of it? I think? The whole identity of Cass was just a part he was playing, as much as Nate R. is a role he's taking on for the show. The truth is, I have no idea who this man is, not really, and I need to stop hoping for anything more. I need to officially and completely move on.

It's just like Grady always says—"You'll never plow a field by turnin' it over in your mind." And okay, I know that doesn't exactly apply here, because in this case the field shouldn't be plowed . . . Wait, am I the field? No. What I mean to say is, I need to stop going in circles, stuck on an endless loop of thinking about Wes and Cass and wishing they were the same. Wishing won't make it so.

The entire war that just played out in my head must have also played out on my face because when I blink back at Wes, he's looking at me with clear concern. "Where'd you go just now?"

I obviously am not going to tell him that. "I was just thinking. About my friend. My friend Grady. Back in Chicago."

The gentleness on Wes's face immediately hardens. "Ah."

Ah? What ah? Why ah? He rises back up to his feet and I follow after him, confused, clutching the beanies I gathered in my hands. He drops the rest on the table, but does so with just a little too much force, sending the remaining pile scattering onto the floor.

"Shit," he says, dropping down to gather them.

A few of the other contestants are turning to look now. "Now, I'll take care of it," I whisper to him, motioning for him to leave.

He seems caught up in a wave of frustration, though, and continues to bunch up and toss the beanies onto the table like they've done something to personally offend him. His movements are so erratic and jerky that half the beanies he tosses on the table end up overshooting and falling back off again.

Finally, with a frustrated harrumphing noise, he stands and kicks one of the beanies lying on the floor. He just stands there, hands clenched. "I should get back," he says abruptly, then pivots and stalks over to rejoin the other contestants.

Chapter 14
Nina

Once all the men's costumes have been sorted, Deja invites me to watch them film the "meet-cute," the scene in which the Mountainettes will meet all the Mountain Men for the first time.

"Technically," Deja tells me, "we'll be there in case anything goes wrong with wardrobe, but really, it's just fun to see all the hormonal chaos."

Deja has worked on other reality dating shows, so I'll take her word for it. Although I'm intrigued to see the contestants interact with each other, I also feel a little sick to my stomach. And not just because I'll be watching Wes flirt with a bunch of women. I'm also vicariously nervous for all the Mountainettes. I can't help but imagine myself as one of them, how anxious I would be meeting so many big, imposing men, with all the lights on me, the cameras tracking my every move.

All of the men have seemed nice enough in my brief interactions with them, but I know if I were in the show, I'd worry they were only talking to me because a producer was making them. My anxiety would insist that no matter how pleasant they were being, they'd be wishing they could talk to one of the other Mountainettes instead of me.

I voice a carefully pared-down version of this concern to Deja. "It would be so hard to try to juggle so many men at once."

"Two tops," Deja agrees, nodding sagely. "Three gets complicated. Four is just plain messy."

Something about her tone makes me think I better not ask any follow-up questions. I'm relieved when I see various producers positioning the Mountainettes into place in front of the log cabin being used for shooting. "Cabin" is a bit misleading, since the structure is huge, easily big enough to house all the Mountain Men who make it past the first round. Although it's more rustic than the Lodge, where my family is staying, it has all the basics the men will need, along with an absolutely breathtaking view of the Smoky Mountains.

The Mountainettes have all been styled in different colors of cute flannels, with beanies to match their chosen shade. Jeans and boots complete the ensemble. I see Harmony was assigned pink, which should thrill her. Pink is her signature color, after all.

I notice, with a pang I try my best to squash, that each Mountainette looks beautiful, polished, and confident. "They look so pretty," I tell Deja, trying my best to smile. "You all did a great job."

There. See how magnanimous I am? You would never guess I'm about to watch them all flirt with the only man I've ever loved. (*Envy*.) But I'm fine with it. It's fine! (*Dishonesty*.)

Deja points to where the road comes around the bend. "That's where the men will be arriving. Production found four old DeKalb Lumberjack trucks, the kind from the 1950s, and refurbished them. Each one will carry in eight men."

So that will be thirty-two men total, all competing for four Mountainettes. Sounds complicated. "How many will they eliminate this week?" I ask her.

"Each woman will get to choose six men she wants to keep on for this first round. Every week, one more will be eliminated, until each woman only has one man left—or decides to leave the show single."

I must be a horrible person, because my immediate, unfiltered hope is that Wes gets cut in the first round. That he decides to go back to wherever it is he really comes from. That way, I won't have to watch him flirt with anyone.

Then again, if he leaves in the first round, I'll probably never see him again. My dumb heart can't decide which prospect would be worse.

Deja and I are positioned across the dirt driveway from the Mountainettes, where we'll be able to see the Mountain Men arrive but stay out of the shot.

Between the cast and the production crew, there are so many people on set, I don't expect Harmony to take any notice of me. To my surprise, she spots me right away and gives me a happy wave, motioning excitedly to her hat. *Pink!* she mouths.

I give her a double thumbs-up to show how happy I am for her.

Her attention is drawn away by Lyle, who seems to be giving her some last-minute instructions, so I let my gaze drift around the group gathered to watch the filming. I never realized there would be so many people on film sets. I recognize Lyle, of course, and Sienna and Raquel, though all of them look far too busy for me to approach. Everyone seems occupied and determined, focused on whatever their job is on set.

Everyone but Morrie. I've been put under firm instruction not to acknowledge him in person unless strictly necessary, so I'm surprised to find that he's staring at me intently, looking back and forth between Harmony and me with a furrowed brow.

My attention is snagged away by Deja, who nudges me and points toward the first truck rounding the bend. The Mountainettes snap to attention as the cameras start rolling, trying to capture their reactions to the first group of men. As the vehicle approaches, I see the Mountain Men are thrumming with excitement, buoyed by the adventure and the cameras and the pretty women waiting for them.

I scan their faces and am relieved that I don't see Wes yet, then annoyed at myself for feeling relieved. Before either emotion can get too carried away, my attention gets snagged by Morrie again. He's still staring at me.

Weird. Though his eyes are fixed on me, I avert my gaze, feeling too awkward and self-conscious to look back and have him catch me watching him in return. (Someone help me make that make sense, please.) Even so, I see him gesturing at me—jerking his head to the side, indicating I should join him.

Frowning, I look at Deja, trying to come up with a good excuse to leave her. "I'm just going to . . ."

I trail off when I realize she's too busy watching the filming to care about what I do.

After sneaking over to Morrie, I look at him questioningly, but he jerks his head at me again. "Don't look at me. Stand a few feet in front of me. Face forward."

Without thinking, I do as he commands, even though it's an extremely strange way to behave. If anyone notices us, we'll look far more guilty than if we just have a regular conversation with each other. "What's going on?" I whisper back to him. Well, I think I'm whispering to him, anyway. It's possible he's already walked off, since my back is turned to him.

"You know Harmony Miller?" he asks.

Wherever I thought this conversation was going, this wasn't it. "Y-yes," I stammer, stupidly.

Morrie's voice sounds grim. "We need to talk . . ."

Chapter 15
Nina

Five Reasons Why I Should Have Suspected Uncle Aaron, but Didn't:

1. We moved every few years, right as Uncle Aaron's church was really starting to take off, just as the money was really starting to roll in. That was the life of a missionary, Uncle Aaron always claimed. We could never stay put for long. But then, we never kept in contact with the people we left behind, either.
2. The name of the church changed everywhere we went. To reflect God's new purpose for him, was Uncle Aaron's excuse.
3. Uncle Aaron was firm about controlling any mentions of him on social media. If a parishioner tagged him in a photo or caption, the post was removed quickly after his lawyers got in touch. Uncle Aaron preferred to have control over his image, he said; it mattered more to him than others, because he was a representative of God.
4. Despite Uncle Aaron talking a lot about the vow of poverty he'd taken, there'd always been money. A big house. Nice clothes and watches and shoes and jewelry. Lavish vacations. The Lord has blessed us, Uncle Aaron always said.
5. Uncle Aaron isn't a kind person. He claims to be a follower of Christ, but Christ was kind and compassionate. Uncle Aaron is shrewd and spiteful. He is not forgiving. He does not turn the other cheek. He is a

cruel, cruel man, and even though I'm surprised to find out he's under FBI investigation, it's not a shock, not really. I know more than anyone that he is not who he pretends to be.

The Orphan Girl and the Man with Two Faces

When the Orphan Girl first arrived at her aunt's house, she thought it was an answer to her prayers. Aunt Hope looked so much like her mother, the Orphan Girl assumed she would have a heart like her, too. The house was big, beautiful, and filled with cousins, whom she hoped would become like her siblings, and her uncle was important and charming and made a big fuss when she arrived. There was a film crew at the house, recording her arrival and asking lots of questions, most of them to Uncle Aaron.

"In this tragedy, we've been blessed by a great gift from God," Uncle Aaron told them, "a chance to expand our family and to demonstrate what it is to live a charitable Christian life."

The Orphan Girl realized that *she* was the great gift Uncle Aaron was referencing. She'd been so sad and so frightened when her parents died, but it seemed that everything would be all right now. She'd found her happy ending.

For the first few weeks, the Orphan Girl did feel like a great gift. She was a novelty to her cousins, who all fought over whose turn it was to play with her. If they made her play *their* games and follow *their* rules, the Orphan Girl didn't mind, because it was so nice to be included. If they made a point to remind her the toys belonged to *them*, she told herself not to care, because it was only the truth.

At church, Uncle Aaron would talk about her from the pulpit, and in the same breath he would preach about charity and how it must start in the home. The Orphan Girl tried not to notice that she didn't sound so much like a gift anymore, but more like a burden—not something to be treasured, but something to be borne. She told herself she was being ungrateful.

But as the family grew accustomed to the newness of her and settled into their routine, the Orphan Girl noticed some changes. They were subtle at first, so subtle she could tell herself she was imagining things. But soon they became difficult to ignore.

The Orphan Girl didn't eat dinner with the family. Dinnertime, she was told by Aunt Hope, was for family only. The Orphan Girl had thought she *was* family, but apparently not in the same way as everyone else. She ate in the kitchen, sometimes with the housekeeper, sometimes on her own.

When the other children finished with their independent study, they got to play. They had so much time to play they could complain about being bored. Not the Orphan Girl. When she wasn't studying, she was helping around the house or minding the younger children. The Orphan Girl didn't know what it was like to be bored, because she always had something to do. Sometimes she daydreamed about what it would be like if she could just have an hour to herself, uninterrupted.

As the year came to a close, the whole family was excited for Christmas. There was going to be a big service at church, followed by a feast. All the children would be getting new clothes. Their lists for Christmas presents grew every day, as they thought of more and more things they wanted.

The Orphan Girl wasn't sure what her place was in all of these Christmas traditions her cousins took for granted. She didn't want to impose. She had been given so much already. So she felt guilty for wanting a new pretty dress, too, and for envying the new toys and books and treats her cousins were going to receive. She hoped she would be included in some way, but she worried this was one of those times when she wasn't really family.

So she was surprised one day when Aunt Hope called her into her bedroom. "You haven't given me your list yet," she told the Orphan Girl. "We're almost out of time."

The Orphan Girl couldn't help it—she burst into tears. She hadn't realized what being included in Christmas meant to her, truly, until Aunt Hope asked her. It wasn't only about getting presents. It was about understanding that this was really her home after all.

Aunt Hope looked at her in astonishment, not understanding. "There's no need to cry," she chastised her. "Just get it to me by tomorrow."

That night, the Orphan Girl carefully crafted her list. She thought about the types of things she'd heard her cousins asking for. She didn't want to be too presumptuous and ask for anything too expensive. She didn't want her list to be too long. She remembered that Miriam had asked for some new hair bows, so she asked for those; and Harmony had asked for a doll, so she wrote that down; and her other cousins had asked for things like books and sketch pads and colored pencils, so she added those things, too.

On Christmas morning, the children excitedly took the presents from underneath the tree and passed them to whom they belonged to. The Orphan Girl helped, and she was too busy doing so to notice that none of the presents had her name on them. But when all the presents had been distributed, the Orphan Girl saw there were none in her pile.

She froze, uncertain how to react. Uncertain what it meant. Why had Aunt Hope asked her for a list if they'd never planned on giving her any gifts?

Don't be ungrateful, she told herself, over and over. Her new mantra.

Her cousins were too excited about opening their own presents to notice. Before they could tear into the wrapping, though, Uncle Aaron raised his hand. Everyone in the room fell silent, waiting dutifully.

"Before we begin, I want each of you to take one of your gifts. Choose any gift." He waited until his children had done so. "Now give it to Nina."

The Orphan Girl froze. Her cousins, usually so quick to heed their father, froze, too.

"Give it to Nina," her uncle urged. "Too late to change your present. Hand her whichever one you picked up."

He didn't have to shout or say it too sternly. In the months the Orphan Girl had been living with them, she'd already learned that her uncle could say more with a silence, and hide more with a smile, than most people could by ranting and raving at the top of their lungs.

Her cousins obeyed, even though the Orphan Girl could see in their expressions how much they resented doing so. *I didn't choose this*, she wanted to tell them. *This isn't what I want.*

But she knew Uncle Aaron wanted her to remain silent. He was trying to make a point, and he was using her to do so. "Open them," he ordered her.

With everyone watching, the Orphan Girl opened each of the gifts she'd been given. Many of the items were things she'd asked for, but she could not muster up any excitement for them, knowing they hadn't been meant for her and that she'd only received them by taking them from someone else. The silent resentment of her cousins pressed down on her.

When she finished opening the last present, Uncle Aaron spoke to his children. "Remember that there are sacrifices for living a Christlike life. You have been called to serve and to give. What do we always say about charity?"

"It begins in the home," her cousins grumbled back.

Then Uncle Aaron looked straight at the Orphan Girl. "And remember to show gratitude where it is owed. Remember where everything you have comes from."

He did not need to say it directly for the Orphan Girl to understand, even at such a young age. Everything came from her family. She was not owed Christmas presents, or new dresses to wear to church, or anything else. She only received what they were willing to give her—and every time she was given something by them, she was taking something away from them, too.

After that, the Orphan Girl was not surprised to learn she had not been made a new dress, and that she would stay home while the rest of the family went to the special Christmas service and party. There were some things that were just for family, after all.

And she'd already taken so much.

Chapter 16
Wes

Being part of a TV show is a lot of sitting around and waiting, I've discovered. As we idle at the Donner Lodge to be transported over to the cabin where most of the filming will take place, I shoot the shit with the other guys. We play cards. I stare off into space. It's a bit of a letdown, honestly, to see how the sausage is made.

But as we're loaded into the trucks and nearing the cabin, the mood shifts. Despite myself, I get carried away by the urgency and energy of the show. There are lights everywhere. Cameras surround us that we're supposed to pretend not to notice.

Wes Ackerman finds this to be extremely weird. But not Nate Russell. Nate R. played football in high school and college to packed stadiums. He's used to lights and cameras and attention. So I do my best to smile as I bump over dirt roads in the back of a vintage logging truck, surrounded by seven other men in matching flannel outfits. Easy. Not weird at all.

Most of the other guys are joking and laughing with one another, but I notice that Everett, who's sitting next to me, has gone quiet. Nervous, most likely. I nudge him lightly with my elbow. "Hey. It's gonna be okay. It's only a TV show."

For them. For me, it's an undercover operation to take down a hardened embezzler who's ruined dozens of lives. Relatively speaking, I'd say he has it pretty easy.

Everett shakes his head. "I'm not nervous. Just trying to remember my poem."

"Poem?" I echo, confused.

"Yeah, for the meet-cute moment with the Mountainettes. I'm gonna recite a poem."

Huh. I look over to Nicky, hoping to see that Everett is talking nonsense, but Nicky nods. "Nice. I'm gonna do a rap with all of their names—hopefully none of them has one crazy-hard to rhyme with." He shudders. "Like Mildred."

That sounds like an oddly specific problem. I want to reassure him it isn't likely, but his face looks haunted, like he's having 'Nam-style flashbacks to an impromptu rap session gone terribly wrong, so I leave that one alone.

A few others, those sitting close enough to hear the conversation over the rumble of the truck down the road, chime in with their meet-cute ideas. Themed knock-knock jokes. Backflips. Break-dancing.

Uh-oh.

I nod along like nothing about this discussion is surprising or alarming to me because I am totally prepared. Internally, I am panicking like Jaskier in the middle of a battlefield. This seems like the sort of thing Morrie should have warned me about.

Then again, now that I think about it, I vaguely remember something in his notes about the first meeting with the Mountainettes. I assumed it would be more shaking hands, exchanging names, less bursting into spontaneous song.

Joke's on me, I guess.

As quickly as possible, I run through my talents that could potentially be put to use in a situation like this. Most of them need a prop. Swords, whips, rope drums. I don't suppose anyone on set has a crossbow . . . ? Unlikely.

I could quote Inigo Montoya's entire monologue to the six-fingered man. But somehow, that's never been as impressive to women as I feel like it should be.

I got nothing. Absolutely nothing. Unless . . .

I scan the area as the truck approaches the cabin, searching for anything that I could use for my intended purpose. Pine cones? Not flashy enough. Stones? Too small—I bet they won't show up properly on camera. Axes? Too dangerous, even for me.

As I see the row of beautiful Mountainettes awaiting us, I feel the rustle of nervous energy from the men around me. This should be the point where I start to panic—but instead, I hone in on the women's shoes, an array of brightly colored boots matching the color-coded outfit of the woman wearing them.

Huh. I do some quick mental configurations. I can work with that.

With that settled, what I *should* be doing while I wait my turn to go is take the opportunity to surreptitiously study Harmony Miller, my target. I should be watching the way she responds to the other men who do their meet-cutes before me so I can tailor my approach and make myself as appealing to her as possible. And I do. Mostly.

But my eyes keep wandering over to the side of the road where the production crew is watching the filming. I could pretend I don't know who I'm looking for, but I do.

It takes me a few tries to find Nina, likely because she's so small and unassuming. Everything about her, from the lack of makeup to the muted colors to the high-buttoned cardigans and ankle-length skirts, seems designed to keep people from noticing her, but it's always done the opposite for me. Anyone who has to try that hard to dim the way they naturally shine must be pretty spectacular. I wondered when I first knew her, and I still wonder now, who convinced her she had to fight so hard to stay hidden.

As if she can feel my gaze on her, Nina looks up. Our eyes meet across the sea of bodies. The world around me quiets, stills, and something in me centers and realigns.

Dammit. Goddammit. Not again. Not now. But if I'm being honest with myself, I've never really forgotten her. If I'm being honest with myself, she's the face I always draw, the heroine of every book I read.

"Nate R.," one of the producers calls. "You're up."

With Herculean effort, I wrench my gaze away from Nina, giving myself a shake as I rise to my feet and cross the truck bed. The other men still waiting their turn pat me as I go by. "Good luck, man!" a few murmur.

I force myself to smile broadly. Time to be Nate R. Charming, unflappable, care-free Nate R.

Easier said than done, with hot, bright lights blazing down on me, cameras tracking my every move, and four women watching me critically as I approach, not to mention the audience of about a hundred crew members.

"Ladies," I call in greeting to the Mountainettes, in a voice that only vaguely sounds like my own. "I'm Nate from Tennessee, and I'm so excited to have y'all here in my home. Welcome to the Agriculture and Commerce State!" Really wish you had a better state motto, Tennessee, but we play the cards we're dealt. "By the way, you're all looking beautiful tonight. I love the flannel, love the boots. In fact, would each of you be willing to loan me one of your boots?"

The Mountainettes look at each other in surprise. A couple of them giggle. I make meaningful eye contact with Harmony Miller and let my smile widen a bit, as if I really, really like what I see. "I promise I'll take good care of them."

Harmony looks intrigued, which is a good sign. I will myself to focus all my energy into that, into her.

After a moment's hesitation, she peels off one of her bright pink boots and hands it over to me. From each of the other contestants, I get yellow, green, and blue boots, too. I gather the shoes, then step back into place. "Thanks so much. You see"—I hold the four boots pressed together in my hands, testing out their weight —"I'm here for love. And I know it's a bit of a gamble, going on a dating show and competing with a bunch of other men. How can you find love, real, lasting love, when you're juggling a bunch of relationships?"

I toss the first boot up into the air, then quickly follow with the other three, falling into an easy rhythm of juggling all four together. Some of the women let out appreciative cries at the spectacle. I can't tell if Harmony is one of them, but I hone my focus toward her, even as I keep my eyes on the shoes. "I know there are a lot of us men to choose from tonight, and I'm sure all of us are a great catch." I catch the pink boot first, quickly tucking it underneath my arm before catching the others in turn. "But at the end of the day, we're all looking for one person to love." I hand the blue boot to its owner, the green, then the yellow, before turning, finally to Harmony. "And if the shoe fits . . ."

I hold her gaze meaningfully as I move to hand back her pink boot, just like I did with the three others. Her lips twitch with a smile, clearly pleased at the attention. But before she can take the boot back from me, I drop dramatically down to my knees, holding the boot for her so she can slip it back on, Cinderella–style. "Milady."

Morrie's probably going to give me shit for the "milady," since that definitely reads more as Wes than Nate R., but old habits die hard. Harmony looks deeply flattered to have been singled out, so who cares if some of my nerdiness trickled through?

As I'm ushered off by one of the producers, I look back over my shoulder to give Harmony a wink. She smiles and the other girls nudge her, clearly catching on that I've singled her out. Maybe it would be smarter to ingratiate myself to the other Mountainettes, too, but with all the other male contestants looking like a mix of Ajax and the Rock, I want to stake my claim on Harmony and go in guns a-blazing. I don't have the luxury of being timid or wishy-washy, not if I want a shot at getting close to Harmony so I can, by extension, get close to Aaron Miller.

The moment I'm off camera and away from the lights, I cast my gaze back at the production crew, trying to find Nina. With a sinking heart, I realize she's gone.

And why would she stay? Just to watch me shamelessly flirt with a bunch of other women—and one woman in particular?

This is going to get complicated, quickly. I run a hand through my hair, feeling queasy. It's more than possible that Nina doesn't feel anything for me anymore. It's been two years since we've seen each other, after all, and she ended up having to leave her nun training for me. Plus, the other day she was name-dropping her "friend" from back at home. Grady something or other, which for the record, is a totally stupid name. *He's* probably tall. Whatever. I don't care.

Maybe it's even possible that Nina *never* felt for me what I feel for her.

But I don't think so. I could be completely fooling myself, but when I look at her, and when she looks at me, and suddenly it's like the rest of the world disappears, like our two souls are finding each other, like I've always known her—that can't be just my imagination.

And . . . I've signed up for seven more weeks of trying to keep my eyes and my mind and my hands off her while I intentionally pursue somebody else.

Gorramit.

Morrie appears at my side, his face unusually sober as he claps a hand on my shoulder. "Listen, Ackerman, we have a problem." He lowers his voice so no one can overhear us. "It's Nina."

Whoa. How did he know I've been struggling to keep my mind off her all night?

Morrie's joked around before about being able to read me like a book, but now I'm wondering if he actually can. I watch him warily. "What do you mean?"

"She's Harmony Miller's cousin. Aaron Miller's niece."

Chapter 17
Nina

When I get back to the hotel after a long day on set, I'm relieved to find that my family (sans Harmony, of course) all seem to be asleep. The hotel suite is dark and silent. Even though I've been daydreaming about an actual meal that isn't off the craft table and a warm, soothing bubble bath all day, I don't want to risk waking anyone up.

I can't have a conversation with any of my family members right now, not when I'm still reeling from the revelation about Uncle Aaron. Is it true? Does Aunt Hope know? What about all of my cousins? What will happen to them if Uncle Aaron gets arrested?

So instead of the soothing, relaxing night I've been hoping for, I forage in the kitchen as quietly as I can and manage to grab some cheese, crackers, and grapes. That will have to do. My closet/room doesn't have its own en suite, so I decide to wake up early and try to shower and get out of the hotel before anyone else wakes up.

Well, earli*er*. I'm always an early riser, but I've been getting up well before my usual start time on this trip to take care of some of the things I can't do throughout the day since I'm working on the show—packing lunches for my younger cousins, prepping dinners Aunt Hope can cook on short notice if she gets one of her headaches. Luckily the hotel has a laundry and cleaning service, or I don't think Uncle Aaron would have ever agreed to let me work for someone else full time. Even if he *is* benefiting from it; Harmony told me he negotiated with Sienna and Rae to let him do a short sermon on the show.

The thought makes me queasy, knowing now that Uncle Aaron has been embezzling from his congregations. Allegedly. I certainly don't want to give him more opportunity to widen his net of people to prey on.

As I shut the refrigerator door, I jump at the sight of Uncle Aaron standing on the other side of it. I don't know if he moves like a ninja or if I was just so caught up in my own thoughts that I didn't notice the sound of his approach. I'm so startled I end up dropping the crackers and cheese and grapes all over the floor.

Instinctively, I bend down to clean up the mess. My heart races in my chest, and I half hope that Uncle Aaron will just get whatever he came to get out of the kitchen and leave again. Instead when I glance up, I find him watching me with narrowed eyes.

My mouth runs dry. My palms break out in sweat. I'm always nervous around Uncle Aaron; even though I almost never have anything to actually feel guilty about, I always worry that I've done something bad without realizing it. Like when you're driving and you see a cop, and you know you aren't speeding or breaking any laws, but you start to worry that maybe the speed limit changed without you realizing it, or that your taillight is out.

And now my anxiety is even worse than usual, because I *do* have something to feel guilty about. Kind of. Do I? Uncle Aaron is the one who broke the law. Allegedly. But I'll be the one who's lying to him and my entire family over the next few weeks. Which is worse? Earlier today, I thought it was definitely his behavior, but now standing underneath his piercing blue gaze, I'm no longer so sure.

Uncle Aaron remains silent until I've finished gathering up my mess. "Are you right with the Lord, Antonina?"

This is a common question from Uncle Aaron. It's his way of saying, *I suspect you're up to no good, so if you are, you better confess it.* But in a much more polite, passive-aggressive way.

Normally this question results in me spewing out every tiny indiscretion I can think of, just to make sure I'm not doing anything to anger God. But tonight for the first time it strikes me that it isn't God who's judging me. It's Uncle Aaron. And frankly, he's living in a glass house right now (allegedly) and should not be throwing any stones.

Second to Nun

I lower my gaze but bite back the instinctive spill of words threatening to come tumbling out of my mouth. Instead, I say quietly, "Yes, Uncle."

A long silence follows. I know he's waiting for me to break. My entire body tenses, from my neck to my fingers to the muscles in my calves, as I fight against my ingrained response.

After another long beat, Uncle Aaron makes a sniffing, dismissive sound with his nose. He doesn't say anything else to me, just fills up the glass of water he came to get, then leaves silently.

I think I might pee my pants if I let my body relax too quickly. But I also feel weirdly . . . free. I was so sure that Uncle Aaron would take a look at me and realize I was guilty, that he'd be able to know what I was up to without me even saying a word. So many times, it's felt like he's been able to read my mind—to know I was trying to meet up with my friends when I said I was going to be doing something else, or if I spent too long looking at the *Vogue* website to see what the newest fashions were supposed to be.

But tonight, even if Uncle Aaron suspected something wasn't quite right with me, he didn't actually *know* anything. And I didn't have to tell him anything I didn't want to.

Because Uncle Aaron isn't God. And I don't have to answer to him.

Back in my room, I change into my pajamas, then binge on cheese and morosely contemplate the events of the day. I should have known. Shouldn't I? If I weren't as sheltered or naive. But then again, whose fault is it that I don't interact with more people, that I have to rely on my family for my survival? Uncle Aaron has arranged my life in such a way to make me be codependent, even while reminding me at every turn of how much of a burden I am.

It was Helen and Matilda who first clued me into the fact that something wasn't quite right with the way my family treats me. I would drop things casually into conversation and see the way they reacted. I got good at pretending not to notice, because I didn't want to acknowledge anything was wrong. I didn't want to examine what their responses might mean. Of course Uncle Aaron and Aunt Hope have asked a lot of me. They have so many responsibilities, so much good work they are doing in the service of the Lord. How ungrateful would I have to be not to be willing to help out?

But it isn't "helping out." Serving my family, catering to their every need, is a full-time job that I never get paid for. I cook. I clean. I mind the younger children. I run errands. I mend clothing. I do whatever is asked of me. But it's never really asked of me; it's always expected, always required.

I've been slowly realizing these truths over the last few years. It's not like Morrie's revelation about Uncle Aaron's potentially criminal behavior suddenly made me see everything in a new light. It's more like I've been watching these truths take shape over months and months, but what he told me finally clicked everything into place.

The revelation about Uncle Aaron should be the thing I'm most preoccupied with. To be fair, I'd say it takes up the vast majority of my mental space. But if I'm being honest, my mind keeps snagging on the other piece of what Morrie told me tonight, and what I saw firsthand.

Wes won't just be competing on a reality dating show. He's there for the express purpose of dating my cousin, Harmony. I know it will all be in the service of investigating my uncle, but what if Harmony develops real feelings for him? I've seen her fall fast, and I've seen her fall hard. I know there will be other contestants in the mix, too, but Wes has been studying her online, figuring out what she likes, what she'll respond to. She doesn't deserve to be led on that way, regardless of whether or not it's Wes doing it.

But . . . it *is* Wes doing it. I know he's not Cass now. I know he isn't the same person I fell in love with back in my postulant days. But he has the same smile. And sometimes when he looks at me . . . it's hard to remember that he was probably pretending with me just as much as he will be with Harmony.

And now I'm going to be on set, with a front-row seat, watching the only man I ever thought I loved pretend to love my cousin. Maybe actually falling in love with my cousin. Isn't that what the entire show is designed for—to make two strangers fall head over heels in love?

I don't know what thought is worse—that Wes will just be leading Harmony on the entire time, playing with her emotions. Or that he might start to care about her, not just as Nate R., but as *Wes*.

Oh, God. Panic starts to well up in my chest. *Deep breaths, Nina,* I remind myself. *Everything will be as it should be.*

The idea is nice, but believing it is easier said than done. Trying to find some way to distract myself, I pull out my phone. I hope one of my friends might have messaged me, but they've gone silent ever since I came to Green Valley. There's not even anything new in the group chat.

Oh, well. I'm sure they're busy. And maybe it's my turn to reach out to them anyway. I pull up the group thread, but I don't have anything to say—or at least, not anything I'm allowed so say. Instead, I scroll through a bunch of GIFs, trying to find just the right one.

I know it's stupid, but I really, really love GIFs. Uncle Aaron and Aunt Hope gave me my phone so they could get in contact with me when they need me to run errands, and they gave me strict instructions it should be used for *only* that purpose. It's one of Aunt Hope's older phones that she didn't need any more once she got the newest upgrade. It's pretty old now and has a lot of weird glitches, and the only app I'm allowed to have, aside from the basic stuff that comes with the phone, is for library books. Aunt Hope monitors that pretty closely, too, to make sure I'm not reading anything too worldly. I mostly check out classics and Christian literature, and sometimes I can get approval for my book club books so long as they don't have covers that are too inflammatory or racy.

Even though there isn't a lot to do on my phone, it's a source of comfort for me. It feels like one of the only things that's really mine. I follow Uncle Aaron and Aunt Hope's rules so I can keep it, but without the apps there isn't really much to do on it . . . except look at GIFs. They're the only bright, colorful, fun, happy thing on my phone. I know they're frivolous and I shouldn't spend so much time looking at them, but seeing them helps me feel more settled.

I choose the happiest one I can find—a bunch of balloons drifting through a park on a sunny day—and send it off to my friends. Too late, I realize that it's probably meant to be a birthday GIF, and it isn't anyone's birthday. Oh, well. Hopefully one of my friends will see it and it will brighten their day, just for a moment, and let them know I'm okay.

I'm just about to put away my phone when a loud trilling sound startles me. At first, I think it must be coming from my phone, but I'm still holding it in my hands, and it's completely silent.

The burner phone! I realize, scrambling for it. Okay, so maybe it's totally paranoid to think that Uncle Aaron or Aunt Hope can (a) hear my phone through the wall and (b) have my ringtones memorized, but if anyone is capable of it, it would be them.

I find the burner phone hidden deep in my suitcase and answer it quickly to shut it up. "Hello?" I whisper.

There's a pause. Then a deep, familiar voice comes through. "Nina?"

It's Wes. My heart takes off at a gallop. I'm already holding on to the phone tightly with one hand, but I use the other to hold it even more firmly in place. In case of what, I'm not sure, but it feels important to anchor him here as close to me as possible. "Yes."

Reality catches up to me pretty quickly. He's obviously not calling me on an FBI-issued phone just to chat. There must be something wrong. "Is Harmony okay?" I ask.

"She's fine, I just . . ." A pause. "I heard about your conversation with Morrie and . . . I wanted to make sure you're okay."

We are silent, the moment stretching out taut between us. I'm holding my breath. It sounds like he might be holding his, too.

"Officially," he tags on a moment later. "In terms of the case. I mean."

Oh. I let one of my hands drop, angling the receiver a little away from my mouth now. "I'm fine. It's fine." It's not, but this isn't really a conversation I want to have over the phone, especially with someone who only cares about how useful I'll be as an informant. "I can't really talk now."

"Okay. Sure. Morrie can debrief with you tomorr—"

It isn't very nice of me, but I hang up before he can finish talking. There's only so much battering a heart can take in one day, after all.

Chapter 18
Nina

The next morning, I'm late for work because Isaiah spills orange juice on his shirt and Aunt Hope panics about the stain. Isaiah has approximately twenty other shirts he's brought on this trip, but for some reason Aunt Hope determines that *this* particular shirt must be saved at all costs. And because I've been the one doing all the laundry in the household for the last fifteen years, my services are suddenly deemed indispensable, even if it might mean I'll lose my job for being late.

As I rinse out the juice with cold water in the suite sink and then apply dish soap to the stained area, I try to practice patience. Aunt Hope has decided this shirt is important for some reason, even if it doesn't seem all that important to me. Even if, as I've gently reminded her many times, the Lodge has a laundry service on-site. Even if anyone could google how to get an orange juice stain out of a shirt, so I'm not sure why it has to be me.

Only . . . my job in the wardrobe department is important to me, too. I know that part of belonging to a family means compromising, but why does it always feel like I'm the one giving up what I want? Sacrificing my time, my energy, my needs, for the sake of everybody else's?

At least Uncle Aaron stays in his room, working on . . . whatever it is he does when he locks himself away to escape all the family drama. I couldn't possibly dare to think such rebellious thoughts in his presence. Somehow, he would look at me and just *know*.

After finishing up at the sink, I run the shirt down to the laundry service before sprinting to the ground floor of the Lodge, where the wardrobe department is currently being hosted in one of the conference rooms. I'm almost half an hour late. Hopefully I still have a job. If not . . . my life will go back to the way it's always been.

The thought sends such an unexpected surge of panic through me that I have to lean up against the wall to keep from falling over. Another few seconds of precious time, wasted. *Happy thoughts, Nina. Happy thoughts.*

Puppies. Ice cream. My friends. The *Vogue* September issue that Helen always smuggles to me once the library takes it off display. That slice of Derby pie I ate the other day at Daisy's Nut House, that I've been dreaming about ever since.

Gathering myself, I run the rest of the way to the conference room.

Deja all but accosts me as I walk through the door. "Nina! There you are. Thank God! We have twenty-four mountain men who need red boxer briefs and chest contouring."

I was so prepared to be fired that my brain takes longer than it probably should to process what she just told me. "So they're going to be . . . ?"

"Practically naked." Deja gives a wolfish grin and waggles her eyebrows theatrically. "Don't say this job doesn't come with any perks."

This might be a good time to laugh along and pretend I'm totally unfazed by the prospect of a bunch of half-naked men. But thinking of Uncle Aaron hearing about this sends my stomach roiling. "Is there a reason they'll be almost naked?" I ask, trying not to sound like the wet blanket I totally am. "Isn't that . . . I don't know, a little exploitative?"

Deja shrugs. "Maybe. But Sienna and Rae have this whole thing about the importance of the female gaze and using it as a critique of the oversexualization of women in media. I wouldn't recommend asking them about it—seriously, that'll be at least an hour of your life that you'll never get back." She waves her hand. "And anyway, it's for charity. The men will be doing a photoshoot for a calendar, with the proceeds going toward helping women's shelters. So, you know, soft-core porn for a good cause, and all."

I try to smile back, but I'm having some mixed feelings. Uncle Aaron will definitely not be happy if he finds out Harmony was on set with a bunch of men in their underwear. If I tell him about it, he'll want Harmony to quit the show, and she'll be furious with me for snitching. But if I don't tell him about it and he doesn't find out until the episode airs, he'll punish me for keeping it a secret.

Well, maybe by then he'll be in prison. The thought, flippant and hardly recognizable as my own, comes into my mind unexpectedly. Guilt floods through me, but the more I think about it . . . He'll only go to prison if he's committed the crime, right? So why should *I* feel guilty about that?

I don't know. But I still do. Kind of. Sort of. Maybe?

Before I can dwell on it for too long, Deja loads me up with an armful of bright red underpants. "Come on. Let's go teach a bunch of ripped dudes how to tastefully tuck in their schlongs . . ."

When we arrive in our production truck at the log cabin, I see some of the men blinking blearily and drinking coffee outside. I instinctively scan the faces for Wes but don't spot him yet. Even though it's creeping up on ten o'clock, some of the men are clearly still struggling to wake up; shooting lasted until early this morning, since the first Axing Ceremony had the most men to sort through. Thirty-two men have now been narrowed down to twenty-four, which is still an absurd number of men I'm about to see in their underpants.

Deja pulls out her phone and uses it to emit a loud audio clip of an air horn. "Wake up, mountain men!" she shouts through cupped hands to amplify her voice. "It's time to get naked!"

After that, the truck is swarmed with men. Deja and I climb into the bed to better distribute the costume pieces. All the men will be wearing red underpants, matching red socks, and boots, but production has also chosen some of the men to have extras—suspenders, beanies, lumberjack caps, etcetera. As the two dozen men gather around the truck, I unsuccessfully attempt to stop myself from searching again for Wes in the crowd. We're not supposed to know each other. I'm not supposed to give him any extra attention. And yet—

As soon as I spot him, standing a few feet away, I find that he's already been watching me. Our eyes meet. It feels like sticking my fork into a toaster, but in a way that isn't entirely unpleasant. My eyes skitter away, and I use all of my willpower not to look back again.

"Listen up, boys," Deja calls, completely unflustered by being surrounded by so many beautiful men. She might be one of my new heroes. (*WWHTMKGL&DD?*) "Here's how today is going to work . . ."

To my relief, it seems like all the contestants are genuinely psyched to do the photoshoot, and no one is being coerced into doing something that will make them feel uncomfortable. I sigh at the invisible weight being lifted from my shoulders. That's one less thing to worry about.

No sooner has the thought crossed my mind than movement out of the corner of my eye draws my attention. I glance over just as one of the men—Steve, I think his name is?—whips off his shirt, then starts on his pajama pants.

I hastily look away, only to see most of the other men following suit. Shirts are being shucked off left and right. Sweatpants, too. Even . . . underpants?! I quickly turn my eyes heavenward. Holy guacamole. I was so worried the men might feel pressured to get naked that I didn't consider the alternative—that they might be willing and eager to strip off all their clothes.

How long will it take before they put on the red underwear? It's going to be very difficult to do my job today if I can't stop looking at the sky.

Do not look at Wes, I warn myself sternly.

I mean, it doesn't matter now, but I've definitely daydreamed about what Cass looked like underneath that prison uniform. Wes isn't Cass, though. They might have the same body, but that's it. And bodies have always been the least inter-esting thing about a person to me. It was who I thought Cass was that drew me most to him, not his beautiful face and lean, muscular body. *Wes's* beautiful face and lean muscular body. Also, I want to respect his privacy. After all . . . after all, how would *I* feel if I were peeling off my clothes, knowing Wes was watching me?

The thought sends a hot, heavy current streaking down my lower belly.

I look. I don't mean to! My eyes just keep finding him naturally of their own accord. This time, he's facing away, his backside completely bare. I swallow as I follow the path of muscles down the slope of his broad shoulders and tapered waist and the perfect bubble crescent of his—

Lord in Heaven. (*Lust. Lust. Lust!*)

Deja nudges me with her elbow and I'm so surprised I have to bite back a yelp. She just grins. "Perks of working in the wardrobe department, huh?" Her eyes track something going on out of my field of vision, and she bites her lip in obvious appreciation.

I cast my gaze up to the sky again. "Mm-hmm . . ."

Chapter 19
Wes

In all the many, many times I imagined myself being half naked with Nina, I can't say this is exactly what I had in mind. Ideally, there were fewer other men involved in my fantasy, as in zero other men. Not so many lumberjack caps.

But the craft services table? That can stay.

There's something about being in nothing but my underwear that makes me much more aware of Nina's presence. I have to stop myself several times from openly staring at her as she goes about her business. To distract myself, I strike up a conversation with some of the other guys. I learn that Everett is really into bird calling and that Scott can complete a thousand-piece puzzle in under two hours.

I give little bits of myself, slightly amended or skewed, to Nate R.'s personality so he'll ring more true, and so I won't feel so much like I'm lying to everybody I talk to. I push down the pang of guilt I feel anyway, because no matter how many times I go undercover, I forget how much this part sucks.

What I don't do is follow Nina with my eyes as she moves around, helping contestants with the various extra bits of their costumes. I don't do that! I *do* catch myself flexing my muscles compulsively, because I am basically naked, surrounded by dudes who look like they were carved by Michelangelo. I'm, weirdly, getting the butt workout of a lifetime with all this clenching and unclenching, so that's an unexpected perk.

Am I aware of where Nina is in proximity to me at all times? Sure. Nothing wrong with that. I'm just keeping tabs on my informant. Making sure she's safe. Am I also aware of how some of the other contestants are responding to her? Do I notice the way Oliver straightens and thrusts out his chest whenever she passes by him, or the way Lee seems to lose his train of thought when he looks directly into her beautiful big dark eyes?

Clearly, yes.

I'm only human. I can't help myself. But I don't tuck Nina under my arm like a football and run off into the forest, so. There's that.

"Nate R.?" the other wardrobe assistant calls—I think her name is Deja.

I snap to attention, turning away from the small group of guys I've been shooting the shit with. "Over here!"

She jogs over, carrying a plain box in her hands. "Sorry, still learning everyone's names."

I know that's probably code for *Most of you won't stick around long enough for me to bother learning your name*, but I smile good-naturedly nonetheless. "No problem. What can I do for you?"

"Sienna and Rae watched the footage from the first night and decided you're the funny guy," Deja tells me.

I furrow my brow. "The funny guy?"

Deja waves a hand. "You know—on shows like these there's always different guys. The smart guy. The aloof guy. The sweetheart guy. The heartthrob guy." Seeming to realize she probably shouldn't have said that last one—and thereby let me know that I'm definitely not in *that* category—she rushes to add on, over enthusiastically, "And the funny guy!"

Great. The petty part of me wants to insist that in almost every other group of guys, I've always been the heartthrob guy. My prison nickname was Cassanova, for goodness' sake! But I definitely can't say that, and so I do my best to smile through my grimace. "Awesome."

"Anyway, they thought it would be hilarious if you had an add-on to your costume." Deja opens the box, showing me what's inside. "Fun, right?"

It's a coonskin cap. You know, with the furry top and the raccoon tail trailing down the back, like something Davy Crockett might wear. "So fun," I manage finally.

Oh, Raquel and Sienna are clearly messing with me. Maybe they even hate me. Maybe they want me to be so humiliated that I remove myself from the show. Possibly even the planet.

But even if it weren't my job to roll with whatever punches come my way, to stay undercover for as long as possible, I wouldn't want to give either woman the satisfaction of seeing me crawl away with my tail between my legs. Instead, I'll wear the cap proudly on the top of my head. They want me to be the funny guy? I'll give them a funny guy.

I'm pulled out of my dramatic resolution when Deja randomly pokes me in the stomach. "Hey!" I protest, flinching away and putting a protective hand up. No one pokes funny guy in the tum-tum!

"Sorry." Deja doesn't sound all that sorry—liar, liar, pants on fire. "Your skin tone isn't going to read well on camera. All your definition is gonna get washed out."

Hi, Salt, have you met my good friend, Open Wound? Apparently, I'm funny, pasty, and not as muscularly defined as the other guys. Got it. Maybe I should pull up my bank account info so Deja can find some more ways to take digs at me. "Okay?"

"Nina will help you out with this. Nina!"

Before I can fully brace myself, Deja waves Nina over to my side. I clench all of my muscles reflexively, torn between dreading how I'm about to be humiliated but also excited to be near her in any capacity. *Oh, you glutton for punishment, you.*

Nina approaches, not quite making eye contact with me, a flush already creeping into her cheeks. Maybe that flush can be attributed to her being around so many hunky dudes in their underwear, but I see it in the brief moment our gazes connect. That flush is for *me*.

"Nate needs some help with his abs," Deja tells her. "You know what to do?"

Nina nods, which makes me wonder just how many other men's abs she's been handling today, but I quickly push the thought aside, because I feel like it might make me go on a one-man journey to Spiral Town, and I do not have time for that today.

Reassured, Deja hurries off, undoubtedly to humiliate one of the other guys, leaving me alone with Nina. Well, let me take that back. We're not *alone*. We're surrounded by a bunch of guys and the production crew as they set up the first shot they're going to do.

But any time I get to stand this close to Nina, look into her eyes, talk to her, it feels like it's just the two of us.

For a moment, we just gaze at each other. I know I can't let this drag out for too long, but I give myself thirty seconds to drink her in. She's wearing a white cardigan today. She looks so beautiful in white. Like an angel. Her beautiful dark hair is braided, and I would give anything, *anything*, just to reach out and touch the soft ends.

Okay, officially time to snap out of it. I draw in a breath. "Sorry you have to, uh, paint my abs." God, I'm stupid. How did I ever get hired by the FBI? "Do you need me to clench or is it better if I just let loose?"

Nina can't quite make eye contact with me. Another flush begins climbing her neck, and it sends an unexpected flare of heat surging through me. "Uh, clenching is better, if you can." Focusing in on my torso, she bites her lip.

Knowing Nina, she is not doing this to turn me on. But try telling that to the Dread Pirate Roberts. (Yes, I call my cock the Dread Pirate Roberts, and no, I won't be answering any further questions about that.) Things are about to take a very weird turn on set if I can't diffuse some of the tension between us.

Thinking quickly, I theatrically spread my arms and legs wide. "My body is your canvas. Paint me like one of your French girls, Nina."

She smiles, one of her sweet, reluctant Nina smiles—the kind that feels special because it's so hard to earn. "Don't distract me," she scolds, but her eyes are sparkling. "Otherwise your abs will look like a Picasso painting."

"Wouldn't be the first time." But I obediently shut up, clenching and waiting for her to do her thing.

Makeup and brushes in hand, Nina leans forward so she can begin contouring my abs.

Let me say that again, louder for the people in the back—Nina's hands and face move in close proximity to my abs, which happen to be located very near another part of my anatomy that is *very* excited by the prospect of these hands and that mouth getting closer to it.

Second to Nun

While I'm practically naked.

With only a teeny, tiny pair of red underwear to cover up any awareness I feel about this scenario.

Dammit, Dread Pirate Roberts! Be cool!

Think of the queen! I urge myself. It's something my dad used to tell me to do if I started to get, ahem, inconveniently excited. He was talking about Queen Elizabeth, of course, because imagining a grandmotherly figure is supposed to kill your libido. But I can't help but think of *my* queen, Daenerys Targaryen, Mother of Dragons, and then I think of Nina wearing one of Daenerys's outfits, and that definitely isn't helping my situation at all.

Then, by a pure stroke of luck, something happens that completely deflates any possibility of sexual tension. Oblivious to my distress, Nina dips one of her brushes into some dark brown makeup and begins dabbing it onto my torso. The soft brush tickles my skin.

And I giggle like a schoolgirl.

To be clear, I don't usually sound like Hello Kitty when I laugh. It must be a combination of my nerves and Nina's nearness and the whole situation with the underpants. But the sound that comes out of me is not remotely masculine or cool.

We both freeze. Nina looks up at me. I look down at her. I realize this could be the moment I become overcome with awkwardness, because of my wounded masculinity, and get weird and snippy and drive her away.

Instead, I waggle my eyebrows at her.

My eyebrows are independent forces of their own, so I'm not worried about anyone nearby seeing this and thinking I'm flirting. There's nothing sexy about what I'm doing with my face. I know I look absolutely ridiculous, and I lean into it, hard. "There's more where that came from, honey britches," I promise her. "I'm ticklish as hell."

It's Nina's turn to giggle. She's doing her best to muffle the sound, pressing her lips together tight and inhaling through her nose. I don't want her to hold it in, though. I want to hear her laugh. So even though it doesn't take long for me to get used to the sensation of the bristles, I continue to ham it up. Every time she puts her brush on my skin I squeal theatrically. I giggle, manfully. I contract then expand my stomach to make it roll like a beach wave. (Jealous?)

This whole spectacle isn't just about covering up my embarrassment now. For the first time, it strikes me that I've never heard Nina laugh out loud. I've seen her smile, but even then it seems like she often tries to subdue her reaction—pressing her lips together, hiding her emotion. On the few occasions I've gotten a laugh from her, she's kept it silent, her shoulders shaking, mouth covered, but no sound coming out.

That isn't by accident. Someone—and I have a few educated guesses who—has made Nina feel like she shouldn't make noise. Take up space. Express joy.

Bullshit. Not on my watch.

Despite my best efforts, though, Nina continues to hold in her laugh until she's finally done sculpting my sweet, sweet abs. As she steps back to check her work, I glance down, too, and am impressed by my own musculature. Damn. If I'd known it was this easy to get ripped, I would have given up on *GeekOut* a long time ago and just spent my mornings reading graphic novels and eating potato chips.

"Hold on," I tell her. "It still needs something."

I quickly squat and pick up the coonskin cap off the ground. Pulling it down firmly onto my head, I strike a muscle man pose and resume rolling my stomach. "What do you think?"

A sharp, loud squawk erupts from Nina's throat. It sounds like when you've let your car sit for too long and you try to get the engine going again—the protesting, whirring sound of a machine left idle too long. Nina claps a hand over her mouth, her eyes darting up to me in horror.

But there's no need. I'm grinning like a kid on Christmas morning. I got her to laugh, really laugh, and make a goofy noise doing it.

Maybe I *am* Funny Guy?

Turns out, I don't hate it.

With color in her cheeks, Nina packs up her supplies. "I better see if Deja needs anything . . ."

After one last lingering, charged look at me, she leaves.

I try not to make it too obvious that I'm totally staring after her.

A moment later, I feel a presence at my side. Morrie. He clears his throat. "So, you remember you're Nate Russell, right?" he says quietly, not looking at me.

I, too, continue to stare straight ahead. "Uh-huh."

"And your sole focus is on Harmony Miller, and nobody else, correct?"

"Yep."

"And you shouldn't be wasting your energy flirting with or even thinking about anyone else, especially not one of our informants?"

Even though I already know what Morrie is saying is true, the reality of our situation still sits in my throat like a weight. I give a slight jerk of a nod. "Mm-hmm."

"Good." It sounds so firm, so final, the way Morrie says it. So who can blame my heart for clenching up, just a little? For missing something that was never mine to have.

Chapter 20
Nina

When I arrive on set the next morning, I worry about what Deja will ask me to do next. Groom the men's chest hair? Rub them down with grease so they can fight each other in a mud pit? Stuff socks into their pants to make their bulges look bigger on camera?

I'm joking, kind of. I'm so, so grateful to have this job, to get the chance to work with all the pretty clothes and to escape from my uncle and aunt's hotel suite. To do something that's *mine*, even if it's as simple as fixing a zipper or distressing flannel shirts. (So many flannel shirts!)

Instead, to my surprise, it's Lyle who's waiting for me down in the conference room instead of Deja. "You're coming with me, dollface," he says, taking me by the shoulders and guiding me out of the room before I've even fully stepped inside.

"But," I protest, "the flannel! Deja!"

It's more my surprise at this sudden change of plans that has me protesting than an actual desire to go back into the conference room. There's nothing wrong with the conference room. It's a nice conference room! But aside from trips to set and my one adventure into town, I have spent most of my time inside the Lodge.

So I don't drag my feet *too* much as Lyle leads me out of the hotel and toward his car, parked at the curb. "Get in, loser. We're going to make a TV show."

Oh. *Ow.* That stings! I thought Lyle and I were becoming friends, so why did he just call me a loser?

My dismay must show on my face, because Lyle's expression immediately morphs into one of contrition. "Oh my God! I'm sorry, Nina. It's a quote! A famous quote. From a super popular movie. *Mean Girls?* Well, not the part about making a TV show . . . The point is, I was just making a funny." He gives me a quick, tense squeeze. "Come on. I cleared it with Deja. I need your help on a side project today."

The side project turns out to be driving around one of the most beautiful lakes I've ever seen. Apparently it's called Bandit Lake, and it's one of the most highly sought-after places to live in Green Valley—though you can't buy the property, only inherit it, according to Lyle.

Gazing out my window at the breathtaking bright blue water, surrounded by lush green trees, I can see why it's such a highly coveted spot. I don't know if I've ever seen anything quite as beautiful before. Imagine living in a place like this, no one there to bother you. Just you and the trees and the water.

I also have zero idea what this scenic drive has to do with my job. Raising an eyebrow, I glance over at Lyle. "Are there costumes out here or something . . . ?"

"We're scouting locations for one of the events the guys are going to do next week. Think inflatable unicorns. That's all I can say right now." Lyle's voice has its usual cheery intonation, but I notice he doesn't quite look at me while he's responding.

"But I'm not a producer," I press. "I'm supposed to be helping Deja with the costumes."

I know I shouldn't be complaining. And I'm not! It's amazing to get out into Green Valley and see some of the beautiful sights. But I can't help but feel like Lyle is hiding something from me. I've helped to raise a bunch of my cousins, after all. I know when someone is being selective with their version of the truth.

Lyle sighs. "So . . . don't panic, and don't spiral about this, but the other executive producer is on set today." His normally affable expression sours dramatically. "Perry."

The pieces still aren't quite connecting for me. "Okay . . . ?"

"Sienna and Rae may not have been totally transparent about hiring you. And he may or may not have decided that he's going to fire you to save some of the budget costs."

My heart plummets. I'm getting fired today? No wonder Lyle is driving me out into the forest. This is just like that scene from *The Fox and the Hound*, and I'm the fox. Okay, that's ridiculous; I'm pretty sure Lyle won't actually abandon me in the woods. (Right?) But he probably brought me out here to soften the blow.

And it is a blow. I feel it land on me like someone's hit me in the ribs, hard. As much as I sometimes felt trapped inside the conference room, that experience was nowhere near as bad as being trapped in the suite with my family. Cooking and cleaning and meal prepping and doing whatever other odd job they want me to do. Nothing that's for me. It's all for them.

When I glance back at Lyle, his expression looks like he's torn between sympathy and trying desperately hard not to laugh. "Nina. Darling. I'm not firing you. I'm hiding you from the guy who's trying to fire you."

He says all of that like it's supposed to make any sense. "But can't he still fire me if I'm not there?"

Lyle laughs and shakes his head. "That is the beauty and the chaos of Perry. He has the attention span of a goldfish. No, worse than a goldfish—a Gen Z who was raised by an iPad." Clearly still seeing my confusion, he elaborates, "Perry likes to throw his weight around, remind Sienna and Rae that he can make decisions. Some of them have been very detrimental to the vision our two queens have for the show—the fantastically meta take on reality dating shows that embraces everything bonkers and empowers our Mountainettes in the process. Perry just wants it to be another hookup show with a bunch of influencers making out and having threesomes in hot tubs."

Again, my face must show my exact thoughts about *both* those scenarios because Lyle holds up a hand. "Don't worry, that's not going to happen. Most of us producers on the show are Hollywood veterans at this point. We know how to give the runaround to studio guys who think they have an amazing idea that would actually be an absolute dumpster fire. You have to occasionally give in to him on the little things so he thinks he's winning, then save your real fight for the stuff that really matters."

It makes sense, kind of. I've never put it in so many words, but don't I do the same thing with Uncle Aaron and Aunt Hope? If I don't push back on things like my clothes and my chores and my food journal, then I get Tuesday night

Pizookies with my friends. I give in on little things to get what's most important to me.

But spelling it all out like that makes me realize just how infantilizing the whole process is. Why should Rae and Sienna have to pretend to change their vision for the show just because some guy from the studio thinks he's a reality TV genius?

Why should *I* have to wait to get permission from my uncle and aunt to spend time with my friends? I'm twenty-five years old. I'm an adult in every sense of the word. I can vote. I can buy alcohol. I can rent a car! I've always just assumed my uncle and aunt must be right about everything because Uncle Aaron claims to be so close to God. But Uncle Aaron is a liar.

So why should I have to listen to him?

It's an earth-shattering thought, one that I'm afraid to poke at too hard because I can already sense the consequences will be life-changing. And to be honest, I don't know if I'm totally ready for that yet.

Instead, my thoughts circle back to what Lyle has been explaining to me. "So," I say slowly, "shouldn't you sacrifice *me*? Let Perry fire me, so you can save your pull for when it really matters?"

Lyle gives me some serious side-eye. "Didn't I already warn you not to be a martyr?" Shaking his head, he fixes his eyes back on the road. "Besides, you are something that really matters. To me and Sienna and Rae. And Deja too. We all want you here."

The answer makes me soften. Dear Lyle. I feel like he's adopted me ever since I got to Green Valley and he insisted I go into town that first day instead of staying cooped up in the hotel suite. Now, he's become my ride to work when I want to go straight to set instead of staying at the Lodge. The rides to set are usually the best part of my day. We sing along to Disney songs and Broadway musicals. He tells me about his dreams to someday be a famous film director, and we gush about which Met Gala outfits are our favorites. He's become an insta-friend, and someone I am so, so grateful for.

I know what I'm getting out of my friendship with him. He's fun and witty and helps pull me out of my turtle shell. But I have no idea what he and the others are getting out of keeping me around.

"Why?" I'm not fishing for compliments here. I'm genuinely perplexed. It's not that I think I'm a terrible person or anything—well, not most of the time anyway —it's more that I always feel like I'm wholly forgettable. So why is this group of strangers willing to stick their necks out so far to keep me around?

"Because we like you, doofus." Lyle winks at me. "Don't worry about Perry. He gets distracted easily by shiny things. He'll forget you even existed by next week . . ."

We drive in silence for a while, just enjoying the serene beauty of the lake and the majestic forest surrounding it. It's obvious we're no longer scouting any filming locations, we're just enjoying the view, but I'm not complaining. The music is good, and the company is even better. We've both been singing at the top of our lungs to *The Sound of Music*, music up, windows down, and my heart feels full and happy in the absolute best way.

But as much as I love the film, *The Sound of Music* is a loaded musical for any ex-nun. Julie Andrews had it so easy once she left the convent. Well, aside from the Nazis, I mean. She found her captain and her new family, and it only really took a song or two for them to realize how amazing she was.

I can't help but think of my own time returning from the convent. The long, angry silences from my uncle and aunt. The whispers from my cousins. The stares from the congregation at church. I always felt like I had to work extra hard to get any scraps of love or attention, and after leaving my order, it got so much worse. My whole life became a penance for something I wasn't even sure I regretted doing.

Kissing Cass. Which I guess was actually kissing *Wes*. It's weird; I still can't fully see them as the same person. Somehow it feels like Cass is still out there, doodling in prison and daydreaming about me. Okay, that sounds bad. I don't want him to be still trapped in prison. Maybe just on an island somewhere with no women, still pining for me. Is that so much to ask?

Wes feels like an entirely different person from Cass in so many ways. He's definitely not as dreamy and romantic. But he's funnier. So much funnier. My sides were aching from laughing the other day on set when I was . . . painting his body while he was standing there in his underwear.

I try not to go back to that memory too much, really. It feels skeevy, picturing all the guys in their underpants. But truthfully, it's not all the guys I'm picturing. Just one guy. I can glisten the other men's chests and contour their abs, and I feel absolutely nothing. But when I am that close to Wes, feeling his warmth, his presence, almost close enough to touch . . .

Lust, I remind myself. It's just lust! I hear the disapproving voice of my uncle in my mind, warning me that it's a sin—and one that, apparently, I'm especially susceptible to.

But at the same time, that word feels wrong. Because lust isn't what I was feeling for Wes on set. I wasn't ogling his torso or arms or any of the rest of his body because they were hot, sexy man parts. They *were* hot, sexy man parts, to be clear, but for me, it was mainly because they were Wes's. I could see another pair of hands that looked exactly the same but would do nothing for me because they belonged to somebody else. But as *Wes's* hands, they became irresistible. The allure was not in divorcing the body from the person, trying to take away his worth as an individual; the person imbued the body with worth. The body meant something to me because it was Wes's.

So is that still sinful?

I decide to ask Lyle, because apparently he likes me and wants to keep me around, so why not jump into the deep pool of conversations about morality? "Do you think lust is a sin?"

Completely unfazed by the question, Lyle grins back at me. "Only if you're doing it right."

I laugh in surprise, reminding myself yet again that not everyone comes from my super religious family or has the same strict outlook on life. And sex, mainly. There's a whole demographic of people who celebrate sexuality and don't treat it as something shameful.

Must be nice.

I should probably just drop it there, but I'm too curious, and the topic is weighing too heavily on my mind. "What if you're devaluing someone by only seeing them as a body, or . . . you hurt someone who gets caught in the cross fire?" I think back to my biggest mistake, the one I've spent most of my adult life atoning for, and I swallow heavily.

"What if," Lyle counters, "I like driving my car. I like that it's a nice car and runs smoothly and gets me where I need to go. It's possible I *could* hurt people with my car if I drive recklessly or don't pay attention, but I don't. I'm careful with my car. So why shouldn't I enjoy it?"

Whoa. I sit back in my seat, impressed. The look on Lyle's face tells me that he knows he's wowed me, and I can't help but laugh at how pleased he is with himself. "Okay. I see your point." It can't be that easy though, can it? I search for another loophole. "But what about—"

"Let me ask you this, before you ask that question," Lyle interrupts, kindly but firmly. "Is the question you're about to ask me what *you* think, or is it what your uncle has made you believe you should think?"

Again, whoa. I stare at Lyle, flabbergasted. "Are you a mind reader?"

He grins, keeping his eyes on the road. "No, but I grew up Catholic. *Very* Catholic." He waves his hand at me. "I know it's not quite the same with your uncle's church—"

"I was a nun for about a year," I blurt, mostly so he won't feel the need to try to explain to me the differences in belief systems. And, yes, I was a postulant, not a full-fledged nun, but it's just easier to explain it this way to laypeople.

Lyle's eyes widen as he looks over at me. "Shit, really?" He throws back his head in a loud, cackling laugh. "You are the most interesting, random little pixie, aren't you? Please don't tell me you've also worked for the CIA."

He has no idea how close to home he just hit with that joke. "Not yet," I demure.

"Anyway," Lyle reins the conversation back in. "My point being, there were some great things about growing up religious. I loved the sense of community, the feeling of belonging to something important. But I hated the judgment, the double standards, the hypocrisy."

I nod in understanding.

"So what do you do with those conflicting feelings?" Lyle continues. "Do you just throw out all the good stuff about your faith, just because it wasn't perfect? But then, how can you go back to it when parts of it were truly harmful?"

I don't know the answer. It's something I've struggled with, too, ever since I left the convent. Living under Uncle Aaron's roof, I had no choice but to go back to a life that revolved around church—*his* church, to be more specific. There are parts of it that resonate with me, and parts that have sometimes made me feel uncomfortable. There were also aspects to being a postulant that I enjoyed, times that I felt genuinely moved by the spirit, and others where I felt shamed or disconnected. "What did *you* do?" I ask, curious to see if Lyle has some answers.

"Construction, destruction, and reconstruction," he tells me, as if this is something I should already know.

I furrow my brow at him in confusion. "What?"

"Construction, destruction, and reconstruction," he repeats, then rolls his eyes self-effacingly. "My hairstylist told me about this guy on TikTok, who I guess heard about it on some podcast, so take what I'm saying with a grain of salt, but the idea is basically this: When you're a kid, your beliefs are influenced by your family, your teachers, your religious leaders. That's the construction phase of your faith. The structure is probably pretty simple, but it's steady enough to see you through for a while.

"At some point in your life, though, you start to notice some problems. Leaks in the roof or cracks in the foundation. Things that make you question that original construction and its ability to weather the storms in life. That's the destruction phase of your faith.

"After that, some people just abandon the building, and that's fine. Some people's buildings have more problems than others. But if you see potential in the building, you might want to go back and fix some of the problems. Get rid of what wasn't working, but keep what's good and sustainable. Rebuild as needed. That's the reconstruction phase."

I take a minute, absorbing the ideas. "So you're saying . . . I don't have to keep the leaky roof, just because that's what was built for me?"

Lyle grins. "Nope. You can build your own roof, out of whatever material you want to use."

"I can build my own roof," I echo quietly, letting that seed take root. What would that even look like, I wonder? What roof would I choose for myself, if I could choose anything? What beliefs would I hold closest to my heart? Smiling at Lyle, I shake my head. "Wow, your hairstylist's TikTok guy's podcaster was really onto something."

He nods sagely. "It's all about finding the right algorithm," he agrees, winking at me as we pull up to the Lodge.

As he turns his gaze forward again, something catches his eye. "Oh. My. God," he says, but before I can see what he's looking at, the car's front wheel hits the curb, and we go jolting forward.

Lyle quickly steers the car back down onto the street. "Are you okay?" he asks me sheepishly.

"I'm fine." I'm more frazzled than beaten up, although we did hit the curb pretty hard. I wonder what distracted Lyle so much . . . ? After following his gaze to the front of the hotel, I'm too excited to worry about a minor case of whiplash.

Before I'm even fully unbuckled, I'm already opening the car door and climbing out. "Grady!" I call, rushing forward and launching myself into his arms.

Chapter 21
Nina

In all the hubbub of everything that's been going on—what with being reunited with my long-lost love and getting a job on a reality TV show and all—I'd totally forgotten that Grady had promised he'd come down to visit me. When I pull back, Grady is grinning, looking just as happy to see me as I am to see him.

He takes me by the shoulders and gives me an appraising once-over. "You doin' all right?" he asks.

I nod enthusiastically. "I'm so glad to see you! You have no idea." And I mean it. I've been so lucky to have met incredible people here—Lyle and Deja and Sienna and Rae—but there's nothing quite like having a good, close friend by your side. Someone you don't have to explain yourself to or put on any front to impress. Someone who gets you and loves you, warts and all. Especially with how frazzled I've been with Wes coming back into my life, having Grady's calm, anchoring presence feels like a balm to my soul.

Behind me, someone clears his throat theatrically. "Eh-hem."

I look back to see Lyle standing just behind me. He's left the car parked at the curb, and if I'm not mistaken, it looks like he's also brushed his hair. And is that a mint I smell on his breath?

He smiles, blushing, at Grady, extending his hand. "Hi, I'm Lyle. And you must be . . . ?" He looks expectantly at Grady, waiting for him to answer. "Nina's boyfriend?"

Grady laughs and shakes his head. "Nah. More like an unofficial older brother."

The excitement on Lyle's face at this news is far too easy to read. I laugh to myself. Grady *is* a very good-looking man, but unfortunately I think Lyle is barking up the wrong tree.

Lyle turns his gaze back to me and raises his eyebrows a bit. "Where have you been hiding him, hmm, Wild Card?"

"Grady's my friend from back in Chicago." I look back at Grady and give his arm a squeeze. "And I'm so, so, so, so happy that you're here. Why didn't you text me?"

"I've *been* texting you," Grady says, "and I didn't get any response, which made me wonder if . . ." He glances over at Lyle, and I realize that he doesn't want to say anything about my family situation in front of him.

Lyle picks up on the subtext anyway, though, and gives a commiserating grimace. "Ah, yes, say no more. Creepy, controlling uncle—I'm totally up to speed." Looking into Grady's eyes, his grimace softens out into a woozy grin. "Actually, scratch that. Please keep talking. Say whatever you'd like. Read the phone book, for all I care. I'm just happy to listen."

Laughing, I shake my head at Lyle, though my mind is puzzling over what happened to Grady's texts. "When were you messaging me?" I ask him.

"Over the past few days," he replies. "And some when I was on the way down today."

Lyle continues to moon at Grady, apparently unconcerned by this mystery. "You came all this way just to see our little Nina and make sure she was okay? What a good friend you are . . ." If there was a sound to accompany the heart-eyes emoji, it would be Lyle's voice right now.

"Err, thanks," Grady says, with an awkward laugh.

I only half hear them since I'm busy scrolling through my phone. I frown as I see that there are, in fact, texts from Grady, but for some reason, I was never notified about them, even though it shows they've been read. I shake my head. Maybe there's some strange glitch happening with my phone? I know that Deja said we have some weird stuff going on with the limited service out at the cabin. That must be it.

I smile up at Grady, putting my phone away. Whatever might have happened with the texts, I'm just glad he's here and that I get to see him.

"Are you here for a while?" Lyle asks, still not taking his eyes off Grady.

Lyle had informed me on the way here that he'd need to drop me off quickly because he needed to return to set. That all seems to have been forgotten now that he's conversing with my handsome Irish friend.

Stifling a laugh, I look to see what Grady's response will be.

"Unfortunately no," Grady returns. "I'm only here for the day. Just passing through on my way to the Bar and Pub Expo up in Knoxville."

Disappointment floods through me, but I tamp it down. It was so nice of Grady to go out of his way just to stop in and see me. I won't be greedy and ask for more.

"Are you done with work for the day?" Grady asks me. "Do you have some free time?"

I wince, shaking my head at him. "No. I wish I'd known you were coming. But I've already missed so much work this morning . . ."

Grady sighs and runs a hand through his hair. I can see the effect this has on Lyle, since—let's be honest—Grady has incredible hair. It's dark and curly and just the right length to always look a bit windblown. "Ah, shame." He gives me an unconvincing smile. "But I understand, work comes first."

Lyle manages to shake himself from the hair-induced stupor to give me a pointed look. "Don't be ridiculous. Take a few hours to go visit with your friend. I'm sure Deja wouldn't mind if you make up the work another day. And anyway, it'll keep you out of Perry's way if he's still on the warpath." A sudden thought seems to strike him, and he looks between Grady and me hopefully. "Unless . . . why don't you bring Irish McHandsomeson here to the set?"

I look at Lyle in surprise. "Isn't it supposed to be a closed set?"

"Usually, yes," he hedges, "but today we are filming an on-the-town date, and we always need good-looking extras." He glances at Grady to gauge his interest level. "Are you an actor, by chance? You totally could be, for the record."

Grady and I exchange a look. This is always the awkward part—when we have to decide just how much to reveal to a layperson about our previous vocations. If you haven't lived a consecrated life, it's hard to understand just what it entails, and people can have some very strange reactions. At the same time, it feels uncomfortable lying about a huge part of your past that still shapes so much of your present.

I see the indecision weigh out on Grady's face for a moment before he admits, "I'm between jobs at the moment, deciding what to do with my life." A hesitation before he adds, "I was a priest up until about a year ago."

Lyle brings a fist up to his mouth and bites down on it, hard. "Hmm," he says in a strangled tone that is probably him doing his best not to overreact.

Remember how I said people can have strange responses to learning about our former religious lives? Yeah. That's one of them.

To his credit, Lyle recovers quickly, or at least makes his best attempt to do so. "Well. If you're still undecided, I happen to be pretty connected in the Hollywood scene. You could come out for a visit sometime. Anytime, really. See if you have any interest in acting or production. I'm sure an ex-priest would be quite a novelty, even in an industry that's seen pretty much everything."

Grady nods, his expression impressively blank. "I will, yeah."

Lyle's face lights up at that. I don't have the heart to tell him that I've been friends with Grady long enough now to know that that's basically the Irish way of saying "not a chance."

And anyway, being on set is not exactly my idea of a good time. Aside from all the lights and cameras and the fuss, the thought of Uncle Aaron hearing about me appearing on camera and stealing Harmony's spotlight makes me feel queasy. I know I've decided not to care so much about what he thinks anymore, but I've spent years and years of living my life based off his rules and whims. That's going to take more than a few days to get over completely.

"I don't think it's such a good idea," I hedge.

Lyle looks at me, assessing my face in a way that makes me feel like he already knows me way too well. "Come on, Wild Card. Deconstruct a bit, huh?"

The look on his face lets me know that he gets it. And I believe he really does, based off some of the experiences he's shared with me. The other day he told me about the first time he wore pink sunglasses out in public and how he was so terrified to let anyone see him, he sat in his car for thirty minutes before he was brave enough to get out. In Oklahoma, with his conservative family, it would have been such a big deal to walk down the street wearing something like that. But in LA, nobody even noticed or cared.

It's amazing how much our own perspectives can shape the way we think the world sees us. How one person's pink sunglasses could be another person's . . . well, pink sunglasses. They're so benign, it's hard to imagine anyone taking offense to them.

Maybe it's the same thing I'm doing right now, turning down a chance to be on a TV show because Uncle Aaron might not like it. No, scratch that. Uncle Aaron definitely won't like it but . . . who cares? I won't be hurting anybody. I'll just be in a crowd of faces. I might not even make it into the final cut of the episode.

Taking in a deep breath, I look to Grady. "Wanna be on TV with me?"

Grady glances back and forth between Lyle and me, seeming to recognize something important has just shifted. Then he smiles. "Sure. Why not? As long as we can have a proper catch-up . . ."

Chapter 22
Wes

A new day, a new humiliation devised at the maniacal hands of Sienna Diaz and Raquel Ezra. I'm currently standing in the warm sun, under blazing film lights, talking with the other guys and trying to pretend like I'm psyched to be here because I'm so into Harmony.

Once we're all in formation and the director cues us in, the show's host, Chet Hodgkins, beams his megawatt smile at the camera. A former NFL tight end turned TV announcer, he's the kind of person for whom it feels like you need to use their full name, every time—more a product than a person. *Chet Hodgkins*. "We're back. Mountain Men, how did you enjoy your modeling gig yesterday?"

Some of the guys really ham it up for the camera, I've noticed. Guys who seem to have nothing to say in between shots suddenly become Mr. Personality once they get a shot at screen time. I guess these shows always have people who are only in it to get famous. Then again, I'm lying about my entire identity, so I guess I'm in no place to judge.

The thought curdles in my stomach, but I do my best to smile and be easy, care-free Nate R. "Awesome," I echo along with some of the other guys.

Chet Hodgkins grins back at us. His teeth are *so* white—it's a bit uncanny, but it must look good on camera. "That's great, guys. I'm sure we all know how important it is to give to charity. And don't worry, I've asked and yes, you can keep the red underwear from the photoshoot yesterday." Pause for laughter. "If you could use one word to describe the shoot, what would it be?"

"Humiliating," one guy calls out, but his voice sounds good-natured, and the rest of us laugh.

I don't particularly want to draw attention to myself, but I remember I'm supposed to be the "funny guy," and I really do need to get my head in the game. So I look straight at the camera and wink. "Liberating."

That earns some more laughter, and Chet Hodgkins shakes his head at the camera, still grinning. "We have all kinds here, don't we?" He claps his hands together, signaling a more serious shift. "Well, the day is still young, and the Mountainettes are eager to make the most of it. Ladies, why don't you join us now?"

The four Mountainettes walk into the shot, arms linked together. They were present yesterday throughout the shoot, watching us get our pictures taken and interacting with us through staged bits when the camera was rolling. I saw Harmony in passing, but aside from one short conversation about my coonskin cap, we didn't get a chance to speak much. Maybe that means she's already become more interested in one of the other guys.

The thought shouldn't fill me with so much hope.

Once the Mountainettes are lined up next to Chet Hodgkins, he beams broadly at the camera. "It's time for the Mountainettes to get to know their Mountain Men better. For the rest of the day, each Mountainette will choose the Mountain Man contestant of her choice to go on a date—just the two of them."

At this news, I feel the guys shifting around me, all of them eager to be singled out—whether for more screen time or more time with one of the women, it's hard to say. I'm probably the only guy standing here hoping I won't be picked.

Chet Hodgkins slightly angles his body toward the Mountainettes, while still keeping his face mostly turned toward the camera. "Allison, let's start with you . . ."

I zone out slightly as Allison gives an obviously rehearsed speech and then chooses one of her contestants. This will be the first prolonged one-on-one time the Mountain Men will be getting with the Mountainettes. Whoever gets to spend this time with a Mountainette will probably be the first to start really building a bond with her. I should be frothing at the mouth for this opportunity with Harmony.

So why do I wince as Harmony steps forward to take her turn?

Dumb question. I know why.

My eyes instinctively search for Nina in the crowd, but she isn't here. She hasn't been here all morning. I try not to think about what that could mean—if Aaron Miller has somehow discovered she's being onboarded as an informant for the FBI. Who knows how desperate he could become if he finds out he's under investigation. How dangerous. If he's prevented her from leaving, or hurt her in any way . . .

Stop it, brain, I tell myself firmly. It's hard for me not to catastrophize when I'm undercover. There are just too many things that could go wrong at any given point in a case. Adding a civilian into the mix makes things that much more volatile. And when that civilian is *Nina,* sweet, lovely Nina, with her reluctant smiles and those dark, expressive eyes . . . I'm going to have to work twice as hard to stay focused on the mission.

"Gentlemen, I really appreciate you putting yourselves out there yesterday," Harmony begins, sweeping her gaze over each of her six remaining contestants in turn. "As most of you know by now, giving back to the community is one of my core values, and I was so impressed to see how willing all of you were."

I fight to keep my face blank, despite feeling a twinge of instinctive dislike. Listen, I also think helping people is important, but in my experience? When you have to go around announcing to everyone how charitable you are, you're usually doing it for yourself, and not for other people.

I'm probably being ungenerous, though. Most likely, Harmony was encouraged to say something like that by one of her producers. And why shouldn't she take the opportunity to establish her brand and try to go after her dreams?

"But I think it's obvious that one of you put his dignity on the line more than the others," Harmony continues with a laugh. "And that willingness to go above and beyond really impressed me. So today, I'd like to take Nate R. on my date."

Nate R.

Holy shit, that's me.

I almost don't manage to curb my look of dismay, but at the last minute, I transform it into one of surprise, instead. "Even with the coonskin cap?" I ask, earning some more laughter from the other contestants.

"You can leave that one back at the cabin," Harmony quips.

She reaches out her hand to me, so I take it, joining her as we wait for the last two Mountainettes to reveal their picks. All the while, my mind is racing. This is good. This is good! This is exactly what Morrie and I have been planning. When I steal a glance over at him, I see him holding up double thumbs-ups, grinning wildly.

I wish I could muster the same enthusiasm. And it's not because of Nina. Well, not *only* because of Nina. In all the times I've had to pretend to be somebody else, I've never had to pretend to be falling in love with somebody. As an abstract concept, it felt like something I could do, to achieve the necessary end goal of gaining Aaron Miller's trust. But now, with Harmony standing right beside me, her hand in mine, I don't know how I'm possibly going to be able to pull this off.

When I trained to become an undercover agent, I was warned that it's easy to lose yourself. Most human beings are naturally empathetic. There's a reason why laughter is contagious; if someone else laughs, our instinct is to laugh with them. If we see someone hurt, we feel sorry for them. We seek connection with other people, and we do that by feeling what they feel, intuitively responding to what emotion is shown to us.

So when you go undercover and someone is kind to you, laughs at your jokes, confides in you, it's incredibly difficult to remain neutral to them. Even if you go in with the mindset that all of your interactions are pretend, that they aren't real to *you*, the fact that they're real to someone else makes it hard not to get sucked in. Try as you might to remain removed, emotions always get involved. Always.

Earlier in my career, I thought taking on physically dangerous tasks, like going undercover for a drug cartel, would be the most difficult part of my job. But it's really the emotionally dangerous missions that can fuck you up. Like befriending someone. Integrating yourself into their family. Growing to genuinely like and care about them.

I'm not worried that I'll fall in love with Harmony. My heart is otherwise preoccupied. But what am I supposed to do if she starts falling in love with *me*?

As if she can read my thoughts, Harmony turns to me now, smiling. The cameras are still rolling, but this isn't a moment that's been orchestrated by the show. It's just a small exchange between the two of us. "Are you excited?" she whispers.

Hearing the nervousness in her voice, the hopeful hitch, my heart clutches painfully in my chest. *Wrong.* This is wrong. I do my best to smile. "Can't wait," I murmur back.

The producers give the four Mountain Men who were selected for one-on-one dates a short amount of time to change and get ready. We're herded back to our respective rooms. To get a better sense of "who we really are" (ha), we're meant to wear our own clothes from home on these one-on-one dates, so there's no one from the wardrobe department to help us get ready.

As I go through the motions of getting dressed, my mind is spiraling. I don't know if I can do this. I don't fucking know if I can do this.

When I step outside the room, Morrie is waiting for me in the hallway. I can see by the grin on his face that he's ready to give me shit, as usual. But when he catches sight of my expression, he sobers immediately. "You need the recording?" he asks me.

"I need the recording," I confirm grimly.

This isn't my first time going undercover with Morrie. We always have an escape hatch in case things start to get too real once I'm deep undercover, if I lose sight of what it is I'm trying to do. I've never had to use it so early before.

Morrie takes me back into the room and locks the door. Without saying a word, he hands over his phone. I pull up the file and listen to the recording he has saved there.

The voice is a woman's. Mabel Winthrop. I can hear the strain of emotion as she struggles to tell her story matter-of-factly. "My husband, William Winthrop, was a deacon in the Church of Light. The senior pastor was Aaron Miller . . ."

I listen as Mabel recounts how her husband was taken in by Aaron's charm, by his pretend kindness, by his enthusiasm for William and the work they would be doing together. She describes the complete trust that Aaron put into William, and says that William happily reciprocated, believing that Aaron had been called by God, and that together, they would do great things.

Unfortunately the tale quickly takes a dark turn as Mabel tells how William began to have some doubts. He made some financial discoveries in the church records that he asked Aaron about, believing there must have been some mistake. Not too long after that, Aaron and his family left town. And William was left behind with a paper trail of bank statements, deposits that he never knew about, withdrawals that were made under his name but that he never authorized.

All of it added up to an embezzlement charge that not only landed William in prison, but lost him his church, his congregation, and his community.

"That life was everything to William," Mabel states. "He worked so hard. He truly believed that he was doing God's work. He would have done anything for Aaron, and in return, Aaron betrayed him. He framed him. He humiliated him. He broke him. He—"

Her voice breaks off as she begins crying.

By now, of course, I've listened to this recording so many times I already know how it's going to end. It doesn't make it any easier to hear.

Not long after his imprisonment, William found a way to die by suicide in prison. Mabel was left behind with their three young children. As if that sorrow wasn't enough, Mabel was ostracized from her church community, who still believed that her husband had committed these terrible crimes against them.

"Those people were our family," Mabel tells us in a choked voice. "And then we were nothing to them."

I stop the recording, breathing heavily, as I try to regain control of my emotions. This is what I'm here for. This is what I can't lose sight of.

William Winthrop was just one of the many people betrayed, framed, humiliated, and broken by Aaron Miller. And if I can't find a way to stop him, he'll just keep doing this again, and again, and again.

There has to be proof. He's smart but he's not invincible. Everyone makes mistakes. Even Aaron Miller.

I just have to find a way to prove it.

I look up to see Morrie watching me, his face grim. "You good?" he asks.

For once there's no trace of anything sarcastic or snarky in his voice. As much as he gives me shit, Morrie is in this undercover operation with me. He's been trained to help me through it, and to pull me out when it seems like I might be getting in too deep. He also knows exactly what I need to hear to keep my head in the game.

I finally manage to nod back at him. "I'm good." And I am. Or at least, I will be.

Morrie gives me an awkward pat on the back. He's not much of an affectionate guy, but I know he means well. "Come on, Gandalf," he says with forced enthusiasm, making a halfhearted fist pump.

"Gandalf?" I repeat quizzically.

"Yeah, he's, like, a cool wizard or something. You're into that stuff, right?" Morrie shrugs. "I thought it'd be inspirational."

I scoff. "Gandalf would never go undercover. He's too high-profile." I consider it. "I guess maybe Bilbo might be the closest thing to an undercover agent that Tolkien writes? Since he misrepresents himself to Golem and Smaug to get the information he needs." Shaking my head, I pat his back sympathetically. "But nice try."

Morrie rolls his eyes at me, and I'm relieved to see we're falling back into our usual pattern. "How will I ever live down my shame at getting that wrong," he deadpans.

I shrug, grateful for the return to normalcy. "We all have our cross to bear . . ."

Chapter 23
Wes

As we pull up to the filming location, the production site is already mostly set up. I don't see Harmony yet, but most of the crew, the cameras, and the sound equipment seem to be in place. Some locals are crowding around the fringes, trying to catch a peek of what's going on with the filming. A few people are seated at the tables outside, but I think they must be extras, not locals, since they haven't been cordoned off from the set.

The first part of our date, Morrie explains to me, will be at a place called the Donner Bakery. "Hopefully not named after the Donner Party," I quip. "I'm human-flesh intolerant, so that would be a hard pass for me."

Morrie just shakes his head. "Please don't make that joke on camera."

Yeah, that wasn't really my best work. "Noted."

Morrie nods toward the bakery. "Right now Harmony's inside talking to the owner, who's apparently famous online—the Banana Cake Queen?"

Never heard of her. But banana cake sounds delicious right about now. Hopefully I'll get to eat some.

"Afterward," Morrie continues, "Harmony will come out to get you. We'll film you talking and flirting for a bit. Then Harmony will take you inside to buy a pastry. They'll probably make you do something cheesy, like order an éclair and eat it *Lady and the Tramp*–style, but that's showbiz, baby."

The "baby" is so out of character that, seemingly by mutual agreement, Morrie and I both pretend it never happened.

The date he outlined sounds simple enough. Well, not the sharing the éclair part—that just sounds messy, frankly. But the rest of it, I think I can handle just fine.

Morrie positions me near the glass windows at the front of the bakery, where I'll remain until Harmony comes out to get me. "Wait here. I have to verify details about the musical number tomorrow."

"The musical number?" That sounds ominous. "They're not gonna make me do something stupid, are they?"

The look on Morrie's face tells me all I need to know. "Just remember you're serving your country."

This can't be good . . .

While Morrie talks with some of the other producers, I wait. Then wait some more. Then, for a fun change of pace, I do some more waiting.

After a while, out of sheer boredom, I begin people watching. I look at some of the Green Valley locals gathered around to watch the filming. No surprise—they're all extremely good-looking. Geez, what is with this town?

When I run out of onlookers to observe, I start squinting through the window to see what I can glean about the inside of the bakery. It's one of those floor-to-ceiling windows that's slightly tinted, so it's probably easier for the people inside to see me than it is for me to see them. Nevertheless, I manage to spot Harmony standing at the counter with her back turned toward me. Behind the counter and facing me is a pretty woman with long brown hair and violet eyes. Violet? Nah, that must be a trick of the light coming through the windowpane. No one really has that eye color in real life.

I move on, eyeballing some of the desserts in the case, then some of the extras seated inside at the tables. I see the producer who's always rocking bright colors —I think his name is Lyle?—eyeballing some of the cannoli hungrily. Same, brother.

Just when I'm about to find something new to study, I stop, doing a double take.

Is that . . . ? No. My eyes must be playing tricks on me again. Or maybe it's just my own loopy brain, showing me who I want to see.

Because it looks like Nina is sitting at one of the tables. And right next to her is one of the handsomest men I've ever seen.

I'm not going to defend my masculinity. I feel no need to do so. I'm a heterosexual man who's 98 percent into women, but I can recognize a good-looking man when I see one. For the record, that remaining 2 percent is for if I ever get stranded on a desert island with Henry Cavill with no hope of rescue, because come on, I'm straight but I'm not blind.

Luckily, the man sitting next to Nina is not Henry Cavill, but he's still uncomfortably handsome. He's got dark, tousled hair that looks like an angel just ran her fingers through it, a jaw so strong it could chip ice, and eyes so dark . . . okay, I'm running out of metaphors, but his eyes are all dark and smoldering, but also softened by the crinkles around the corners. And he's smiling at Nina like she's the most adorable thing he's ever seen.

I don't like it.

I don't like it at all.

I mean, listen, she's single. I'm single. We can't be together. I know that. But at the same time, I don't want any guy to ever look at her or talk to her again. And I don't think that's too much to ask, is it?

No. *No, Wesley*. It's fine. It's fine! I'm fine. I'm here to woo the shit out of Harmony, and if Nina wants to flirt with some handsome extra, then that is A-OK with me. I find it a little strange that she's not back at the wardrobe department, doing wardrobe things. I mean, I thought that was her job. She's only been working there for, like, a week, and she's already blowing it off to sit at a table with an extremely handsome man? That doesn't sound like my Nina. Mine, as in, my person that I know, not *mine* mine. She belongs to herself. Not to me. And not to *this* guy, either, whoever the hell he is. Probably a model. Or a serial killer. Or both.

I realize that at the angle I'm standing at, I can't quite make out what's going on with his hands. Hers are clasped on the table, but his are nowhere to be seen. I start to run through all kinds of horrible scenarios of where his hands might be. I mean, nothing crazy, they're in a public place in broad daylight being recorded for television, for goodness' sake. I'm not out of my mind. But what if he's, like, touching her knee, or something?

Trying to angle my head just right while also trying not to make it super obvious what I'm doing, I must miscalculate how close the glass is to my face, because the next thing I know I'm feeling a sharp pain, hearing a THUD, and losing my balance, falling to my ass on the ground.

Huh. Dazed, I shake my head. Maybe no one saw that?

The collective gasp from the locals who are watching the filming puts that thought immediately to rest. Sheepishly, I rub my head. Maybe no one *inside* saw that?

But when I look up, I see everyone staring back at me—the extras at the tables, the workers in the shop, the pretty lady with the purple eyes. Harmony. The extremely handsome man. And, yes, Nina.

Well . . . shit.

Chapter 24
Nina

"Poor fella," Grady says, watching with a sympathetic wince on his face as several people from the production crew surround Wes to make sure his head is all right.

I had my back to the glass-smacking incident and didn't see what happened, but I heard the thunk. It was a loud thunk. I'm actually not sure how Wes managed to hit his head? Did he walk into the window, or something? The glass *is* extremely clean. Or it was, before he left an imprint of his cheek on it.

I don't have long to ponder the thought, though, since Harmony clocks what happened and rushes outside. "Nate!" The door closes, so I can't fully make out what she's saying, but I see her squat down in front of Wes. She coos and touches his forehead, brushing back his hair, and he laughs winsomely.

I tell myself to look away. I *want* to look away. But it's like when you accidentally type in a weird word combo and you pull up a GIF you were *not* expecting, one of the NSFW variety. And you want to stop looking, but you're also trying to figure out exactly what it is you're looking at, and even though some part of you knows it's going to scar your delicate psyche, maybe forever, you stare for just a second or two too long.

That's how this feels. I watch on in soundless horror as Harmony leans in and presses her lips to Wes's temple. His eyes dart up to mine.

I turn so my back is fully toward them, my heart racing. "Poor guy," I echo unconvincingly, my heart in my throat.

When Lyle asked Grady and me to be extras on a date, I obviously realized there was a chance that it might be a date that Wes was on, but I figured, what were the odds? Harmony was one of four Mountainettes, and each of them still had six contestants, so with all those variables in place, what was the likelihood that the one date I'd end up on would be with Wes . . . ? And, okay, this is starting to sound like a really weird SAT question, but the point is, I'd like to go home now, please.

Only, Harmony will think it's extremely strange if I suddenly leave. She was so excited when she saw me sitting here in the bakery earlier. "Nina!" she'd squealed. "Here for moral support. Oh, I love you! Thank you! Thank you!" Leaning in close, she'd whispered conspiratorially, "Confidential bestie-cousin secret? I think the guy I chose for this date is my front-runner."

Harmony is the kind of person who thinks she's in love every time she talks to a new guy, but I knew she must really like whoever this contestant was since she didn't even seem to clock Grady sitting with me at the table. And normally, Harmony would notice. There's more than one reason I've kept Grady away from my family, and part of it definitely has to do with the potential awkwardness of my cousin deciding she's in love with him at first sight.

Not only is Grady handsome, but he also sings and plays guitar, which has always been Harmony's kryptonite. Luckily—or so I'd thought at the time—she seemed too distracted by her impending date to take any notice of Grady, so I thought I'd just be able to catch up with my friend in peace, no awkwardness involved.

Stupid, naive Nina of five minutes ago. How little you knew about life.

"Everything all right?" Grady asks, pulling me back into the moment.

I look down to see I've torn the paper napkin in front of me into nervous shreds.

"Good. Fine. Great!" In hindsight, it might've been more convincing if I hadn't said those three words right on top of each other.

Maybe I'll get lucky. Maybe Wes will be concussed or something, and the date will be canceled. At the thought, I immediately feel bad, because I don't want him to be seriously injured . . . but how serious is a concussion, anyway? Just a really mild one, preferably?

"All right, people," Lyle calls out. "They're about to come inside and start filming. I know it's going to be really difficult not to watch what's going on, but try to pretend like it's just a normal day and you're unaware of the cameras."

So the date is going to proceed. That's good, because it means Wes doesn't have a serious head injury. I'm already repenting that I wished that on him at all. Because it's fine! We can't be together, and he has a job he needs to do, and I can't betray my family. So. It's fine. I'll focus my attention on Grady and pretend nothing is happening behind me.

When I look up at Grady again, his forehead is creased. "You sure you're okay? You look all . . . squirrely."

I'm not entirely sure what that means, but I know it means I'm making a face of someone who isn't fine, which is dumb because I am. Fine, that is. I make a concerted effort to relax my expression. "Tell me more about the expo you're going to." I raise an eyebrow at him. "Does that mean you've finally decided to go through with the pub?"

He shrugs. "Eh, I dunno. An Irish guy opening a pub. Is it too cliché?"

For as long as I've known him, Grady has been talking about his pub. Planning for his pub. Scouting just the right location for his pub. He has the seed money for it, but he seems reluctant to commit. A part of me wonders if it isn't the Irish stereotype, but something else that's holding him back. Then again, a business is a big investment, so maybe he's just making sure this is the right path for him.

"Just don't fall in love with Knoxville and decide you're going to leave Chicago." I meant for it to sound like a joke, and I hope my voice doesn't betray too much emotion at the statement.

Grady's face softens. He nudges me with his knee under the table. "I'm not goin' anywhere." His eyes move to something just over my shoulder, and he frowns. "Ermmm . . ."

I start to glance behind me, before reminding myself that under no circumstances am I going to look at that part of the bakery during this "date." "What?" A terrible thought strikes me. "Are they kissing?" I whisper.

"Noooo." Grady drags out the word longer than necessary his brow furrowed in confusion. "Do you know that fella or something?"

Blank face. Blank face! "Why?" I ask as innocently as I can.

"He keeps staring over here. I swear, he just glared at me for smiling at you."

Despite myself, I look over my shoulder. Wes and Harmony are seated at a table a few feet away. They seem to be talking and laughing, but sure enough, after just a few seconds, like he can't help himself, Wes darts his eyes over to us. Seeing us both watching him, he looks quickly away again.

"He's probably just nervous," I hedge.

"Sure," Grady returns, sounding unconvinced. "I always stare at pretty girls when I'm nervous, too. Really calms me right down."

I glare at him coolly to show that I'm not impressed. "Your dry Irish wit is not appreciated right now, thank you very much."

"Hmm," is all Grady says in return.

I wait until he's taking a sip of his water, and therefore hopefully won't notice, before I glance back over my shoulder to see if Wes is still looking at me. His leg is jackhammering like crazy under the table, but at least for the moment, he's smiling and nodding at whatever Harmony's saying. My stomach twists at the sight.

Pretend, I remind myself. *It's just pretend.* Although . . . is it? When Wes and I met, he was pretending to be someone he wasn't, and we developed real feelings. *I* developed real feelings, anyway. My gaze darts back and forth between Harmony and Wes. It's hard to know what I'm supposed to feel. Jealousy, that he might actually start to like Harmony. Worry for Harmony, if he's only using her. Frustration, that once again I've been sidelined, watching everyone else get to live their lives while I just wait around to be useful.

Then, as if drawn to me like a magnet, Wes's eyes snap up to mine. I hurriedly twist back around in my chair and find Grady watching me with a knowing expression. "Hmmmmmmmm," he says, drawing it out longer this time.

"Oh, hush, you," I tell him.

Lyle's voice cuts through the room. "Hang on just a moment, lovebirds!" he tells Wes and Harmony, before addressing everyone in the bakery all together. "The director wants to get some shots of just the two leads, so we need to clear out the room so we can fit in some additional equipment."

The seasoned extras in the room seem to understand what that means, and they all rise to leave. I rise after them, willing myself with all the strength I can muster not to look over at Wes and Harmony again.

Grady stands. "Are you off for the day, then?" he asks me. "You wanna go grab a bite?"

Because the room is already significantly less full of people and noise, I wonder if his question carried over to Wes. And I wonder even more what he'll think about overhearing that—a man asking me out for a meal. *He* doesn't know that Grady is just a friend. To the ignorant ear, it might sound almost date-like.

Except, no! I'm not wondering what Wes thinks about any of that. I don't care. It's nothing to me. Nothing, I say!

"Sure," I tell Grady. "That sounds great."

Lyle crosses over to us before we can go. "Sorry to get you in and out of here so quickly. It's usually a longer process, but the bakery is on a tight schedule." He gives me a meaningful look. "And I just heard Perry might be stopping by on set, so it might be a good time to take off."

Ah, yes. The man who's trying to fire me. I nod to show Lyle I understand. "Got it. We'll get out of your way."

"I'm gonna run to the jacks before they kick us out of here for good," Grady tells me, motioning toward the bathrooms near the back of the room.

While I wait for him, I watch the production crew as they begin the difficult task of trying to figure out how to fit in the second camera. It looks like this might take a while. I move myself up against the wall to take up as little space as possible.

Despite my better judgment, I cast my eyes around the room, searching for . . . *nobody*. I am definitely not looking for anybody in particular or wondering what he's doing or if he's gazing into Harmony's eyes adoringly or giving her that crinkly smile of his that makes my heart skip a beat every time. I am definitely not doing that because it would be stupid and pointless and definitely, definitely not something I would do.

The front door to the bakery opens with the jingle of a bell, and the sound pulls me from my spiral. A man I don't recognize enters. He is oozing with tan, white-toothed, vaguely plastic-looking Hollywood smarm, and my hackles instinctively rise, even though it takes my brain another moment to connect the pieces of whom he must be.

"Perry!" Lyle calls out loudly. Too loudly, really, but he obviously wants to make sure I've heard him. "What a pleasant surprise. What are you doing here?"

Shoot! When Lyle said he might be stopping by set, I thought he meant *later*, not within moments. Grady is still in the bathroom, and I can't just leave him behind; even if I could, Perry is standing right next to the front door, so I can't exactly make a fast escape. I have no idea if he knows what I look like, but if he does, and he catches me here, that will be the end of working in the wardrobe department. No more laughing with Deja over the latest bizarre costume we're supposed to piece together in less than a day. No more singing show tunes with Lyle on our way to set. No more seeing Wes, full stop.

With my back to the wall, I slowly slide along it until I reach a door. I have no idea where this door goes, but it will at the very least take me into another room. Maybe I can hide out until Perry leaves.

Luckily there's still so much commotion going on—between the crew setting up for the next shot and Lyle loudly laughing at something Perry said, probably to distract him from seeing my quick escape—that no one seems to notice as I open the door and slip inside.

Oh! It's a pantry. A big, beautiful, well-stocked pantry. I'm not much of a baker, but Helen would be absolutely ecstatic if she had a pantry this nice. It's also dark and cool and quiet, and I'm all alone. I let out a deep breath, relieved—

Until the door opens, and someone quickly slips inside. My heart freezes, more out of surprise than real fear. There's no way Perry followed me into a closet, right?

But as my eyes adjust, my heart picks up speed again. Nope. It definitely isn't Perry in the pantry with me.

It's Wes.

Chapter 25
Nina

For a moment, we just stare at each other. From where he's standing with his back to the door, there's about four feet between us, but somehow it feels like no space at all. My body once again—you guessed it—freezes. There are about a million things I want to do right now, but I'm waiting, holding my breath, to see what he does.

Wes just continues to stare at me, though. His hand is splayed out on the door, fingers pressing against the wood, like he can't quite trust himself to move and needs to keep himself anchored there. His eyes are so intensely green right now. I feel like they could burn a hole through me if I let him keep looking at me like that.

It occurs to me all at once that I'm going to have to be the one to break the silence, even though he followed *me* into the room. That doesn't feel fair. But then again, none of this has felt fair. Him coming back into my life like this. Almost close enough to touch, but so very far away.

"What are you doing?" I ask him quietly. My voice is an annoying combination of breathlessness and another, more unfamiliar quality that for once, I don't bother to obscure from my tone—irritation.

It's enough to make Wes blink out of his stupor, finally breaking that too-intense, too-long stare. "Uh. I . . ." He clearly did not plan this out and has no idea what to say.

On another day, I might have found this charming, might have even taken some hope in it. But right now, today? It just annoys me further. "You shouldn't be in here. Someone might notice—"

"FBI," Wes blurts unconvincingly.

I raise an eyebrow at him. "FBI?"

Credit where credit is due, I guess, because he commits to the bit. "FBI business. We need to check the ID of your companion, make sure he isn't a security threat."

The sigh that escapes my throat happens completely without my permission. But once it does, I realize it is the only appropriate response to this situation. "Wes. Come on. This is . . . you can't do this."

"Can't do what?"

"This!" It comes out firmer, louder, than I meant it to. Wes glances at the closed door behind him, so I lower my voice, but I hold on to my aggravation. I am so very sick of pushing it down, pretending like it's anything else. "I've done every-thing you've asked me to do. I've answered your questions. I've kept your secret. I've lied to my family. I've stood by and watched while you—"

Looked at Harmony the way you used to look at me. Use her like you used me. I bite off the words, still not able to say them, even though my body is shaking with anger. Determinedly, I hold his gaze, wanting him to see, to know, just what all of this has cost me. "You don't get to corner me in empty rooms," I finish. I realize that I'm shaking. "And you certainly don't get to play the jealous boyfriend."

I wait for him to deny it, but he doesn't. He clenches his jaw, like he's biting back something he shouldn't say. A muscle ticks in his cheek. We are staring at each other again, and the room is so full of unspoken things, it feels like I might drown in them.

"I can't—" he starts.

I'm desperate to know where that sentence ends, but before it does, the door starts opening behind him. Wes moves just in time so it doesn't knock him over, flattening his back against the wall behind the door, obscuring himself from whoever's entering on the other side.

It's Lyle. Lyle's head, to be more precise, poking through the gap in the open doorway. "Nina. Coast is clear. You can come out now."

So much has happened in the past two minutes that I honestly forgot why I came in here in the first place. Perry. He must be gone now. I do my best to smile at Lyle, nodding. "Okay. Thanks."

I hesitate. This conversation, whatever is happening here with Wes, doesn't feel like it's over, but Lyle is clearly waiting for me to follow, and I can't think of a single excuse why I shouldn't.

It's probably for the best anyway, I realize as I slide my gaze back to Wes's, just for a moment. The air between us is so charged it feels like the room might implode if I stay here any longer. As I walk past him—still not close enough to touch, but close enough that we could touch if we both reached out our arms just a little bit more—it feels like I'm on fire.

Once I'm back in the bakery, I can't run outside fast enough.

I round the corner of the building, away from the crowds of people who've gathered to watch the filming. Once I'm out of sight, I take in a few deep breaths. Maybe I should quit the show. Maybe I should pretend that I'm sick. Maybe I should try to find some excuse to go back to Chicago. Uncle Aaron won't like it, but he *really* wouldn't like it if he knew all the secrets I've been keeping.

Someone clears his throat behind me.

For one heart-stopping moment, I think that it might be Wes, but when I turn around, it's Grady who's followed after me. He eyes the expression on my face. It must give away everything that I'm feeling, because he sighs deeply. "All right, Nina," he says, "out with it. What's going on?"

Chapter 26
Nina

I wait until we're far away from the bakery, walking along one of the more secluded trails around the Lodge, before I tell Grady the whole story. "Nate isn't Nate," I reveal. "He's Wes, and I knew him from before the show. Well, when I knew him before, his name was Cass."

"O-kay." Grady furrows his brow as he tries to follow along.

I've never tried explaining this to anyone before. It's a lot more difficult than I thought it would be. "He was in prison then. And we fell in love—" When I say it out loud, it sounds too presumptuous, because Wes never admitted his feelings in so many words, did he? So I quickly amend, "Well, *I* fell in love with him. Who I thought he was, anyway. Which is maybe who he still is? I'm not sure. Anyway, there were mutual feelings there. I think. We were in prison, so it's not like we had a lot of time to talk about it."

Grady's eyebrows arch up a notch. "You were in prison?"

"No, I was still a postulant," I explain.

He blinks at me.

I guess I need to clarify that more, but those aren't the important details. "He was undercover at the time. But I didn't know that. And I fell in love with him. And we made out."

More rapid blinks from Grady. "While he was in prison?"

The more I try to explain this, the more completely bananas it sounds. I wish we were texting right now instead of talking out loud. I'd have the perfect GIF for it —the grimacing one, with the blonde girl in the pink sweatshirt. "Yeah. But that's not the worst part of it."

"There's more?" Grady asks, sounding aghast.

"Don't worry," I reassure him. "I can't actually tell you the rest." There's the whole *confidential* part of being an FBI informant, after all. Even though I haven't been assigned to do anything yet, Morrie was very clear that I can't say anything to *anyone*.

Grady lets out a low, frustrated sound that I've never heard him make before. "Nina," he says through gritted teeth. "You can't just say 'I have a big secret' and then say, 'Sorry, you don't get to hear it!' That's just . . . mean."

I can tell Grady is genuinely frustrated with me. I don't like that feeling. Grady has *never* been frustrated with me before. He's been my handsome Irish big brother/cheerleader since the day we met. I don't want him to change his mind about me . . .

And maybe I have some unpacking and deconstructing to do around the panic I feel when anyone is irritated with me for any reason. That can wait, though. For now, I just want Grady to stop looking at me like he's angry. Or worse . . . disappointed.

At the look of sheer panic on my face, Grady's expression softens. He sighs, taking me by the shoulders. "Are you safe? Can you at least tell me that much?"

I consider the question honestly. "Kind of."

Another growly noise from Grady, which I can tell he's doing his best to bite back. He takes in a steadying breath. "Is there any version of the truth you can tell me without breaking any promises?"

Ooh, that's . . . interesting. There's a difference between blurting out the entire truth to somebody and giving them pieces to connect the dots for themselves, isn't there?

Treading carefully, I begin. "I used to know Wes before, under very different circumstances. And it was a big surprise to see him here again. Especially since he's going by another name now. Which is different from his actual name." I raise my eyebrows meaningfully at him.

"'Kay." Grady nods slowly. I don't know if he's entirely with me yet, but at the very least, he doesn't sound completely lost.

Buoyed by even that little success, I continue. "And things are extra complicated because there's someone I know who might potentially be a criminal."

"Your uncle," Grady says without missing a beat.

Whoa. He got there extremely quickly. I blink at him in surprise, then do my best to still my features so no trace of emotion leaks through. "I cannot confirm nor deny that guess."

Grady nods to himself, clearly set in his own deduction.

That's not my fault! He got there on his own. "And if things go according to plan, then that person I know might go to prison. For a really long time. And that might be a good thing. And so I should probably let it happen. But other people also might get caught in the middle." At the thought of Harmony, I swallow hard. "Not legally so much as emotionally. Someone might even get their heart broken—"

"You," Grady says.

It's not a question. I stare at him, at first taken aback, then for some reason furious that he should jump to this conclusion. "Why would you say that? That's not . . . No. You don't know what you're talking about."

Anger is such an unfamiliar emotion for me that I feel out of breath. I never let myself get mad. I'll go to all the other deep, dark, bad places. Sad. Scared. Broken. But somehow anger has always felt more dangerous. Somehow, even if I've never put it into so many words, I've understood that if I ever let myself go down that rabbit hole, if I ever let myself get truly, viscerally angry about everything that's happened to me . . . I might never stop.

"Haven't you been listening?" I demand, and now I'm the one who's frustrated with him. Ha! How does he like that? Not a lot, I bet. Feeling like you've let someone down is a terrible feeling. And, okay, the rational part of me knows Grady isn't letting me down, that he's trying to help me, but the person I really wish I could unleash all my anger on is too scary and possibly a federal criminal and not *here*.

Grady looks at me like he understands all of this somehow. "Yeah. I've been listening. Seems to me like you're worrying about everyone else and not nearly enough about yourself. As usual."

That is just so . . . not true. He clearly wasn't listening if that's the conclusion he's reached. Without knowing what else to do with these feelings, I stick out my tongue at him and blow a raspberry. A loud, very unladylike one.

Then, unexpectedly, I burst into tears.

"You mad wee thing." Grady takes me in his arms, letting me cry into his shirt.

It's a cry I didn't know I needed, but now that I've started, I realize that it's been building up inside of me for a very long time. Since my parents died. Since I went to live with Uncle Aaron and Aunt Hope.

Since the moment I first saw Wes on set. Realizing Cass was never real. Watching Wes look at Harmony the way he used to look at me.

When I'm not so much a waterfall as a sprinkler, I sniffle and try to pull away, embarrassed that I've imposed on Grady for this long. To my relief, he doesn't let me go quite yet. It's been so long since someone offered me unconditional physical comfort. My uncle and aunt aren't really touchy-feely people, and by extension, neither is their family. I try to put on such a brave face for my friends, they probably don't know just how much I needed this. When I lost my parents, I missed the obvious things about them first. Their love. Their kindness. The time we spent together as a family, the fun things we did together, the good food and laughter. Our traditions. Our home. It wasn't until much later that I realized the only people who consistently touch you throughout your day is your family. Hugs. Kisses on the forehead. Tickles. Leaning against each other on the couch to watch television. Holding hands when you walk down the street. When you lose those core people in your life, you lose those easy, unweighted touches. And once that's gone, it's like you stop being connected to anyone else.

I lost that when I lost my parents. But maybe now I've found it again, with my chosen big brother.

Lifting my chin, I do my best to give him a watery smile. "Thanks. I'm okay. It's just been . . . a lot to process on my own."

"I'm sure it has been." Grady gives me a meaningful look. "But you don't have to do it alone. I'm here. And you know Helen and Matilda would do anything for you. Kimo and Thad, too."

I do. I do know that. And I realize how lucky I am to have them, I shouldn't take it for granted. But I also don't want to ask them for more than they can give. I don't want to be a burden.

"I'll be fine," I tell him, taking a step back. This time he lets me go, but I regret moving right away. He would have held me longer. *Why can't I just let him hold me longer?* I'm too worried he'll get annoyed with me, that he'll think I'm asking too much of him. "It'll all be fine."

And it will be. I'll ask Deja if I can work on the costumes back at the Lodge and not spend so much time on set. If I don't have to see Wes and Harmony falling in love, maybe it won't hurt so much.

Grady is still giving me that look, like he doesn't quite believe me. He seems to war with himself for a moment before holding his hands up in the air. "Listen, tell me to fuck off if I'm out of line, but for what it's worth . . . love can be messy. It's almost never convenient, and it sure as hell doesn't ask if it's a good time for it. You might think it's not worth it, that you can live without it, that someone else'll come along that makes you feel the way they do. That you'll get over it. But in my experience? You don't. Not completely."

Experience? What experience? Grady's never even hinted to me before about a romantic past, and for the first time, it occurs to me that he might have just as complicated a history as I do.

As if Grady senses he might have inadvertently given too much away, he barrels on before I can ponder it too long. "You've loved this fella for years already. That tells me it probably isn't gonna change just by wishing it will. So now you have to decide what's the bigger gamble: making a mess to be with him, or making yourself a mess by living without him."

The words hang in the air for a long moment. I hear what he's saying, I do. But I'm not someone who can just throw herself into a choice. I have to think about things, weigh out all the consequences in my mind. I need time to be alone with my thoughts. Ideally working on a project with my hands that lets my mind wander. Not for the first time, I desperately wish I had my sewing machine with me.

As if sensing my need for some space, Grady lets out a slightly too-loud sigh, signaling an obvious topic change. "Jesus. Scratch the food. I think I need a drink more." He offers me a smile. "Don't suppose there's a pub around here."

I cast my mind over the various places I've seen around town. "There's a place called the Pink Pony. Do you think that could be a pub?"

Grady pulls a face at me before he can catch himself. "Umm . . ." He seems to be struggling with the right words before he finally shakes his head. "Nah. Just forget it."

We turn around and start back toward the hotel. "There's a diner that makes really good pie," I offer him as an alternative.

"Ah, now. There's an idea. Let's get some pie . . ."

Chapter 27
Wes

My mind is still reeling from my "date" with Harmony and everything that happened. I know I should be strategizing, piecing together what Harmony and I talked about—which was mainly her love of the color pink, her affinity for macarons because "they're the cutest," and her love of missionary work, especially in really beautiful and exotic foreign countries. I should be figuring out how to use any of these tidbits of information to continue building the connection between us.

Instead, like an idiot, I can't stop thinking about Nina. Seeing her sitting in the bakery with that random handsome man, smiling at him, doing that thing where she tilts her head to the side and self-consciously tucks her hair behind her ear . . . Watching all of it unfold had driven me so crazy I couldn't help it. When I saw her slip into the pantry, I had to follow after her.

Now that encounter plays on a loop over and over in my mind. Nina's surprise at seeing me, the unexpected anger. It was a different side to her, one I've never seen before. I feel ashamed for putting her in that position, for cornering her and forcing her to call me out on my bullshit. She was right. I shouldn't have followed her. I shouldn't have asked her about the guy. I shouldn't have made any of this more complicated than it needs to be. Shame coils in my stomach at just how callous and careless I've been.

But . . .

But.

It's not always a conscious choice. Maybe that sounds like a cop-out. It probably is. But when she's in the room, I have to look at her. I tell myself not to, but my eyes are drawn to her. There's this pull in my body to be near her, even if we're not saying anything to each other, even if we're not touching or interacting in any way. Wherever Nina is, it feels like I belong there, too. And even though my brain is telling me it's a bad idea, it's *wrong*, in my heart, my gut, and everywhere else that counts, it's being apart from her that feels wrong.

All I want to do is go back to the cabin and regroup. Unfortunately, I have to film something called "confessionals" first. It'll be just me and the camera, and I'm supposed to talk about my impressions of the scene we just filmed. I'm going to have to stare at a camera and describe everything I'm feeling for Harmony. Everything *Nate R.* is feeling for Harmony, to be precise, because what I feel and what I want doesn't matter right now. As usual.

It all sounds awesome and like I'm not going to hate it at all. Not even a little.

The crew sets up in an empty patch of forest close to the cabin. It's supposed to look like I'm talking to the camera, but I'm really talking to Morrie, who's just beyond the camera lens and asking me questions. I've been told that he'll be edited out of the shots, so it will just look like I'm spontaneously proclaiming my love for Harmony.

People like to watch this sort of thing, apparently. Personally, it's not really my jam. I had to watch a lot of reality dating shows to prepare for this mission. A *lot*. And while all the drama can sometimes be entertaining, think of how much more entertaining these shows could be with *swords*. Just saying.

Once we're all set up, Morrie seats me on a stump directly in front of the camera. I stare uneasily down its lens. Usually when we're filming, we're encouraged to act like the camera isn't there, so it feels strange to suddenly address it directly—almost like it's the elephant in the room you've been pretending not to notice, and then suddenly you're having a conversation with it. Chatting about the weather and asking about its summer travel plans.

I glance slightly over to the left to see that both Morrie and the cameraman are watching me expectantly. "So I'm just supposed to talk about my feelings?" I ask.

"Sure. Why don't you start by telling us what you thought when you first saw Harmony," Morrie prompts.

Well, at least on that, I can be totally honest. "When I first saw Harmony, I thought, 'Oh shit, I'm gonna have to think of something clever to say on camera,'" I quip back.

I think that this will get at least a mild chuckle out of Morrie, but he just rolls his eyes at me. "Try it again, but something more romantic this time, please? This is a dating show, *Nate R.*" He emphasizes the fake name, I guess to remind me of whom I'm supposed to be right now.

Let me think. Nate R. Nate R . . . . He's from Tennessee! He loves football. He loves cornbread. Geez, why did I make my own backstory so generic? I really should have given this guy more flavor. Back when I first started going under-cover, I had whole notebooks full of details about my characters' personalities, likes and dislikes, habits and relationships. But each time I've had to do it, it's felt less and less like I'm playing a role and more and more like I'm losing myself to these other identities.

I take in a deep breath and try again. "When I first saw Harmony, I thought, 'Holy smokes. She sure is the prettiest gal I've ever seen.'" I lean into the Tennessee drawl a bit, hoping it will fill in the gaps for Nate R.'s lack of a personality.

Morrie gives me a look that tells me I'm really not pulling this off. "Better," he acknowledges begrudgingly, "but still not totally what we're looking for. We're playing into a romantic fantasy here. Channel your inner Nicholas Sparks, or whatever."

I don't have much of a frame of reference for romance novels, truth be told. My idea of peak romance is the speech Han Solo gives to Princess Leia in *The Empire Strikes Back* about her liking him because he's a scoundrel—try topping that, Nicholas Sparks! But I guess I can try to channel my own favorite heroes who have a romantic side. What did Kvothe think when he saw Denna for the first time . . . ? "When I first saw Harmony," I try again, "it felt like the universe was holding its breath."

Okay, maybe it's not the most original line, and maybe it doesn't make complete sense, but at least I get an encouraging nod from Morrie. "How does she make you feel?" he prompts again.

The trouble is that as nice as Harmony is—and she *is* nice, and bubbly, and full of energy, and even pretty funny sometimes—whenever I try to summon up more than friendly feelings, I'm hit with this wall.

So instead, I do what I know I'm not supposed to do. I open the door I'm supposed to keep locked.

I think about Nina.

"She makes me feel . . . aware when she's around," I say, treading carefully so I won't reveal too much of whom I'm talking about.

This seems to be more of what Morrie's looking for, because he motions with his hands to suggest that I should continue.

"You know that feeling when someone walks into a room, and all of your senses hone in on them? Wherever they are, at all times. Whatever they're doing. Even if you're not looking at them. It's like your entire body wakes up. Every feeling is that much stronger. And when you talk to her, every word counts. It holds that much more weight. Because it's not just a conversation. It's the two of you learning each other for the first time. Memorizing a story that you want to remember forever. Seeing how your souls might fit together." I laugh under my breath. "And eye contact? Come on. Forget about it. You can say so much more in just one glance than with an entire sonnet, when you look into the eyes of the woman you've been waiting for your whole life."

I swallow and pull myself back into the moment where I'm supposed to be. Here on *Mountain Man*. As Nate R.

"That's how I feel about . . . Harmony," I manage to tag on, even though the words taste like chalk in my mouth.

Because the truth is, I can lie about so many things. But this is the one thing I can't pretend away, no matter how hard I try.

I loved Nina when we first met, and I still love her now. And I can't pretend that isn't true. I can't pretend she isn't who I want.

I can't pretend anymore.

Chapter 28
Nina

That night, I lay awake in bed, staring up at the ceiling. It's been a long couple of days. My body is tired. I have an early call time on set tomorrow, so I'm desperate to get some sleep. But my brain is not cooperating. It keeps running over memories, snagging on all the emotional peaks and valleys of the day.

(*Wes.*)

It was so wonderful spending time with Lyle and having a life-changing conversation about beliefs that I'm still thinking about hours later.

(*Wes.*)

And seeing Grady made me feel centered again. Getting to be near someone who really understands me and believes in me, who's been my calm in the storm for so long, has helped me to feel recharged in a way I haven't since arriving at Green Valley.

(*Wes.*)

Finding out that Perry is lurking around set and wants to get me fired has definitely added in some new complications, but I've also felt really heartened knowing that Lyle and Sienna and Rae seem so invested in keeping me around, even if—

Lissa Sharpe

(Wes. Wes. Wes. Wes!)

Fine! Stupid brain. I finally relent and allow my thoughts to wander to where they've been pulled to like a magnet all day. Wes. The agony of seeing him sitting with Harmony, smiling and laughing. Harmony, who doesn't deserve this, not any of it. I try to latch onto that feeling, but I'm yanked back to him again before I can drift too far. I'm thinking of us together in the pantry, and his eyes—those clear green eyes—the look in them I can't quite define. The way he awakened something in me, an emotion so strong I couldn't keep it contained. *Anger.* I snapped at him! Me, Nina Delgado. I haven't raised my voice to anyone . . . ever, maybe? Some part of me worries I ought to feel contrite for it, but I don't. It was so very freeing to say what I was really feeling. To not hide behind forced smiles or silence.

And even though anger isn't a particularly positive emotion, for some reason it feels significant to me that I was able to feel that way with him. Now that my irritation has died down, I think it might be important that Wes was the first person to bring that out of me. Because you have to feel safe with someone to let yourself be honest, really honest. You have to trust that they'll see all the sides of you and won't recoil.

Strangely, I think I do trust him. Maybe that's foolish of me. I don't know him. Do I? I *knew* him once, or I thought I did. I've been telling myself that the person I knew then can't be the same one I know now. But what if . . . what if the same man who quoted naughty Bible verses to get me to laugh is the same man who let me see how ticklish he was because he could see I was uncomfortable and wanted to lighten the mood? And what if the man who doodled my face over and over on Bible pamphlets is the same man who couldn't stop himself from following me into a pantry, who just watched me with that *look* in his eyes while I snapped at him.

Longing, I realize. I think that look might have been longing.

I press my pillow over my face, using it to muffle my scream of frustration.

As if in response to my cry, someone knocks on my window.

I freeze, certain I must be imagining things that aren't there, because our suite is on the fourth floor. But then I hear it again. *Tap, tap, tap.*

When I look over at the darkened window, my heart lurches at the sight of Wes's face pressing against the glass. I rush over to open it. "What are you doing?" I hiss.

His face looks alarmingly pale. "I had to talk to you."

Perplexed, I search behind him, wondering if I misremembered a tree being right outside my window. But there's nothing there. "How did you get up here?"

Peering out further, I can see that there's nothing keeping him aloft except for a slim ledge that he's precariously balanced on and a fierce grip he's maintaining on the window frame.

My heart instinctively jolts with fear. What is this crazy man doing, and why is he doing it outside my window?

Before I can find a way to politely phrase that question, he clears his throat. "I'd kinda prefer to have this conversation inside," he says tightly.

I obligingly back away to give him space to enter. When he pushes his head and shoulders through the window opening, I dither on whether I should grab his arms and help pull him through, but before I can decide, he's managed to hoist himself into the room, hitting the floor with a dull thud.

My eyes instinctively check the door to my room is still closed as I listen for any sound of someone waking up, coming to investigate the noise. Uncle Aaron would be so disappointed if he found a man in my room late at night. Then again, Uncle Aaron is likely an embezzler, so maybe he shouldn't be casting any stones.

Luckily, the rest of the suite remains silent, so I hurry to Wes, who is still catching his breath on the floor. "Are you all right?" I rub his shoulder in what I hope is a comforting manner. I might've hesitated more to touch him if he weren't visibly shaking.

Wes closes his eyes, inhaling a few deep breaths. "I went through one of the empty rooms on this floor and made my way over on the ledge. Saw it in a movie once." He cracks one eye to look up at me. "Turns out, it's much harder than it looks."

He sounds so genuinely frazzled. And I'm sure it was very, very scary—only, he's safe now, so I can't stop imagining him clutching onto the wall like a spider monkey. A giggle escapes me before I can catch it. I cover my mouth, but it's too late.

He opens his other eye and tilts his head at me. "Are you *laughing* at my near-death experience?"

"I'm sorry." I try to press my lips together so they'll behave, but I feel them twitching under his scrutiny. "You just sound so . . . *distressed*."

His lips tug into a begrudging smile. "My mortal terror is funny to you?"

"A little." I don't realize my hand has wandered from his shoulder to smooth down his arm until he glances at it. I hastily pull my hand away, leaning back so I'm resting on the balls of my feet. Then I remember I'm in my pajamas, and even though they're in no way sexy or revealing, they're my *pajamas*. They're what I wear to bed. I hurriedly cross my arms to cover myself. "Is there a particular reason you're climbing buildings to find my room?"

Wes sits up, facing me. "There was just some official FBI business I had to talk to you about."

That sounds ominous. "Official FBI business?" I echo worriedly.

Wes nods, wetting his lips. I wait for him to tell me what it is, but he just stares at me, brow furrowed. "Wes?" I prompt.

He blinks. "Um, well. The business is . . ." He swallows. "I had to see you."

Oh. Something inside of me melts. Despite my better judgment, I feel myself flushing with pleasure. He came for me? He had to see *me*? I feel like I might be dreaming; this, it's too much what I've been hoping to hear him say.

Even so, I try to keep my expression firm. Despite what I've been grappling with, nothing has really changed. He might not remember that in this moment, but he will soon. And when he does, it's going to break my heart. "*Wes*. This is not a good idea."

"You're right," he agrees quickly, too quickly. Then tilts his head at me, looking somehow both wounded and genuinely perplexed. "Why not, exactly?"

"I don't know," I admit, because it's very hard to remain lucid when he's here in my room, gazing at me with those beautiful green eyes. I've never seen a color quite like it before. Like a lovely, clear pool on a warm, sun-dappled day. After a moment, though, the many, many reasons we can't be together come crashing back to me. I press my own eyes shut so I won't have to look at him as I say it. "My family. The show. The FBI investigation."

"Oh, that." His tone is light, but it's obviously forced. Cracking my eyes open again, because apparently I'm a masochist, I can see he feels the weight of it all, too, as he gazes at me over the few feet separating us. "What if I . . . don't care?"

"You do care," I remind him gently.

He leans toward me, only slightly, but in my postage-stamp-sized room, it significantly closes the gap between us. "What if I care *more* about you? What if I never stopped thinking about you? What if I don't want to have to pretend that I don't feel this?"

All the air in my lungs leaves in a whoosh. My gaze darts between his eyes and his lips, not quite sure where to land. "Wes," I say again, and I know I ought to say more, but I can't seem to make myself.

All my life, I've been taught to put everyone else first, to put my own needs last, and I know I ought to do that now, too. But something about Wes makes that impossible. I want him, and I've always wanted him, all to myself. Just for me.

Mine.

Slowly, slowly, Wes leans forward. One hand comes to rest on my waist. The other cups the side of my face. He waits for a moment, and I know he's giving me the chance to spook, to run, but I don't. My heart is pounding, my body is shaking, but I remain in place, waiting. I'm not quite brave enough to close the gap between us, but I am brave enough to stay still so he can.

When his lips touch mine, it feels as good, as right, as it ever did. I guess Wes is my very own time machine, because suddenly it's like no time has passed since that other kiss, underneath a table in a prison library, our bodies pressed together so tight I could feel his heartbeat dancing with mine. Somehow, amazingly, it's even more dangerous for us to be together now than it was then—with only a thin hotel wall between us and the rest of my family, and the weight of an entire FBI investigation looming over us.

For so long, I told myself I was so weak, so sinful, for kissing him that first time. But now it's starting to feel like I was wrong, not in the action but in the regret, because I'm responding to him just as readily as before. My pulse pounds. My skin tingles. There is nothing else in the world except for where he's touching me, nothing but his heart and mine.

I'm immediately lost in the sensation, the warmth of his lips and the solid press of his body against mine. That magnetic pull tugging me toward him every time we're near each other only intensifies with our lips moving together. When he slides his tongue against mine in a slow, sinuous movement, my mind erases any thought except *more, more.* I need to be closer to him. I need more of him. All of him.

I'm not aware of us moving until my back presses up against the wall. Wes uses this additional support to shift our bodies, silently urging me to climb higher. I open to him willingly and eagerly, wrapping my legs around his waist, feeling his grunt of pleasure as he pushes up against me. He's hard, pressing into me, and I am already getting wet and pulsing with need through my layers of clothing. His groan makes me tighten instinctively, and when he thrusts up against me, I gasp into his mouth.

It ought to be ridiculous, the two of us grinding against each other frantically, still fully clothed. But our mutual need is too strong. It ought to feel shameful. It *is* shameful. I'm proving everything my uncle has said about me right. I'm taking what isn't mine.

Only this time, it is mine. Wes is mine. And it doesn't *feel* wrong. How could it be wrong if it feels so right?

After a few moments, he's the one to pull away, breathing heavily as he rests his forehead against mine. My heart is racing, and it's a struggle not to chase his lips with mine, not to demand more, *more.* It feels like there could never be enough of us.

His eyes gaze intently into mine, the connection even more charged than usual at such a close proximity. "We can leave, tonight. Together."

"What about your investigation?" It's not really a question, more of a reminder. I know this isn't just a job for him. He must *believe* in what he's doing to put his life on pause and pretend to be someone else for days, weeks, months at a time. And I can't be responsible for asking him to throw that all away.

"I don't care about the investigation," he says quickly. Too quickly.

I pull back so I can give him a look. I can't help it—he sounds so much like a petulant child, and it's obvious he doesn't really mean that. "Sure, Jan," I tell him.

I wasn't trying to be funny, but the conversation was heading to such a dark, tense place that I think we're both relieved for the reprieve. He laughs, and I laugh quietly with him as he shakes his head at me. "Jan?"

He clearly has no idea what I'm referencing. "You know, the GIF? I think it's from one of those *Brady Bunch* movies." At his blank expression, I do my best to mimic the actress's skeptical expression. "Sure, Jan," I repeat. "It was a popular GIF for a long time!"

He shrugs. "I guess I'm not much of a GIF-fer."

"Why not?" I'm genuinely perplexed. GIFs are amazing! They're a much easier way to relay what you're feeling, rather than trying to put it into words. Words can be tricky, but images convey so much more. "They're so convenient. There's a GIF for every situation, you know."

Wes is still smiling, but it has a tinge of sadness to it. "Oh, yeah? What's the GIF for this situation—two people who want to be together but can't because of circumstances?"

His words send a heavy stone sinking to the bottom of my gut. Still, I do my best to consider his question seriously. "Probably the guy with the backpack lying down on the floor in despair."

We consider one another for a long moment. Wes reaches up to brush some of the hair out of my face. "What do we do, Nina?"

"I don't know," I admit.

I want to be the brave heroine in a fairy tale, the kind who would be willing to do anything for true love. But in real life, it all feels so much more complicated. I don't want Wes to jeopardize his career for me, and despite what he's saying now, I know that the investigation matters. To him and to me, both.

If Wes stays involved, though, that will mean more standing by and watching him with Harmony. I worry about what that will do to me. To him. To *her*. Harmony has always been a flirt, but what if she starts to really fall for him? What if it's like what happened with my cousin Miriam all over again?

The thought sinks like lead to the pit of my stomach. I can't let myself dwell on it anymore without feeling physically ill.

Now I'm the one who's wavering. How can the investigation be a good thing if it has the potential to hurt so many people?

"Will you tell me what Uncle Aaron has done?" I ask him. I know finding out all the sordid details won't give us a solution to our problem, but maybe it will help me to understand, really understand, why Wes is doing what he's doing. And maybe that will make all of this easier. "Morrie explained that he's been siphoning money from the churches—but how does he get away with it?"

Wes searches my gaze. "Are you sure you want to know all of this?"

"I need to know," I tell him, quietly but firmly.

Running a hand over his face, Wes sighs. "Your uncle's MO seems to be setting up a second-in-command everywhere he goes, someone he very publicly positions as his right-hand man or woman. On the surface, it probably seems to most people like your uncle is the face of the church, and this other person is in charge of the operations—and that might be true, mostly. But your uncle oversees all of the paperwork and expenditures. He doesn't take any large amount at once, just quietly skims off the top here, sets up a fake charity to receive donations there. Then, when questions start getting asked, he makes a very public plan to leave town to start a church elsewhere. But he leaves enough of a fake paper trail behind him that if anyone starts to ask questions, it makes it seem like his second is the one who's been committing the crimes." He shrugs. "Sometimes they take the fall. Other times, no one seems to have noticed—or someone covers up the tracks to prevent a scandal."

I take a moment, processing all of this. I think of Richard Moore, Sally Jasper, Rodney Tuttle, and others who are too far back for me to remember well. They were like members of our family once, so entwined with Uncle Aaron that it felt like they'd always been part of our lives. I don't know why I never thought it was strange that we never heard much from those people after we left, despite how close we'd been. Most of them were kinder to me than my uncle and aunt ever were. Understanding what happened to them—how they were lied to, cheated, tricked, all because they wanted to believe in something bigger and better than themselves—makes my stomach churn. Abusing someone's trust, making them believe they're the ones at fault, because of greed or to cover up your own despicable actions . . . it's hard to think of anything worse you could do to another human being.

I should know, I realize with a sinking heart. Isn't that exactly what Uncle Aaron has been doing to me for almost my entire life?

How much Aunt Hope is wrapped up in all of this, I'm not sure. It's hard to imagine that she could be completely in the dark, but it's also hard to imagine that she would intentionally do this to someone like Sally, who would laugh with us in the kitchen while we made Christmas cookies. And what about some of my older cousins? The thought makes me uneasy. Are any of them complicit? Miriam? Elijah?

Harmony?

We won't know the answers, of course, unless Wes and Morrie are successful with this operation. "Why don't you just arrest Uncle Aaron if you know all of this?" I wonder aloud.

Wes shakes his head. "Not enough evidence. He's guilty. We know he's guilty. We have witnesses who can testify to that much, but he's just too good at covering his trail. We need something concrete to be able to put him away."

It doesn't escape my attention, the way Wes is already grouping himself back into that *we* who's going to bring Uncle Aaron to justice. He might claim that he can walk away from this investigation, but he clearly can't, at least not without giving up some part of himself.

Sighing, I look up at the ceiling. *A little help here?* I ask silently. *What am I supposed to do?*

To Wes, I pose another question altogether. "What are you hoping to get from seducing Harmony?"

He winces at the word choice but obviously can't argue with it; that's exactly what he's come here to do. "Access to Aaron Miller. Obviously, ideally, I could get a confession out of him directly. That would be the express-lane version, which unfortunately isn't very likely."

"And the slower version?" I prompt, sensing he's not telling me something.

Wes takes in a steadying breath. Uh-oh. That doesn't seem like a good sign. "I win Harmony's trust during the show. We continue to date afterward. Then over time, I gain Aaron's trust, and he either takes me seriously enough as Harmony's boyfriend that he invites me into the family business, or I potentially become his next fall guy. Either way, I get access to documentation that we can use to indict him."

I process that, slowly, and now it's my turn to wince. Wes isn't spelling things out, but I can read between the lines of what that would mean. Weeks, months, maybe even years of pretending to date Harmony. Kissing her, holding her hand. Having sex with her, probably. Bonding. The thought of it is physically painful, a heavy ache in my heart.

At what point would pretending become reality? Could you really spend so much time intimately with a person without developing feelings? I suppose it's possible. But that outcome seems almost worse, somehow. To have to go through the motions of love, without any real love behind it—and to manipulate someone else into feeling those things, all the while knowing you aren't being sincere. I hate the thought of it for both of them. No one deserves to have their emotions played with that way.

And . . . I guess if I'm being selfish, I can admit I also hate the thought of it for me, too. Because it will be torture to watch all of that play out, unable to say anything, unable to protect Harmony. Unable to be with Wes.

As if sensing the direction of my thoughts, Wes speaks up quietly. "I know it's ugly—infiltrating people's lives that way. Lying straight to their faces. Using their trust in you and manipulating it to get what you want." His voice grows heavy with bitterness, and I see true self-loathing in the darkening of his eyes and the grim set of his jaw. "Believe me, it's not my first choice. But you haven't spoken to the victims. You haven't seen how whole families have been destroyed, reputations lost, innocent people imprisoned and shunned by their communities for things they didn't do. If there was another way . . ."

"What if there is?" The words leave my mouth before they're a fully formed thought, but as soon as I speak them, they begin coming to life in my mind.

Wes sighs. "It's not a good idea. You're technically an informant, but it wasn't planned. You haven't been properly trained or vetted—"

"So train me! Vet me!" I speak as forcefully as I can while still being *very* aware of the thin walls, my family close by. "You want to get close to Uncle Aaron, right? Be part of the family?" I motion to myself. "That's me. I'm there already."

"Nina . . ." He sighs and looks at me like I'm a bowl of ice cream but he's already over his sugar allowance for the week. Full of regret.

But I refuse to accept that. I refuse to let this be my life. I refuse to just sit by while Uncle Aaron takes one more thing from me. "Tell me what to look for. I'm already here. I'll look! And if we can find it before the show's over, you don't have to go through with the rest of it." Seeing doubt in his eyes, I hurry on, buoyed by my own momentum. "No, listen. I understand you'll still have to do your side of things, in case I'm unsuccessful. But if I am successful, you can self-eliminate from the show. People do that sort of thing all the time, don't they? You can make up some emergency for why you have to leave, and Harmony will still have other options around, and no one will get in too deep."

No one will fall in love, is what I mean. Not Harmony. Not Wes. I won't be betraying one of my cousins, again. And Wes and I will really be free to leave together, without the guilt of abandoning the investigation.

It's the perfect plan! Internally I'm that GIF of the two ladies from *Friends*, hopping up and down in excitement. And, okay, some of that excitement might be terror wearing a wig. But I can do this. I have to do this.

Wes still looks skeptical. "Do you think Aaron would confide in you?"

Some of my hope deflates, but I cling to the rest of it stubbornly, refusing to let that limp balloon of possibility go. "No. He kind of hates me."

It's the first time I've ever admitted that much out loud to anybody. I always thought it would hurt too much to say; I'm surprised at how freeing it feels to put the realization into words.

Wes reels back in a gratifying show of genuine surprise. "What? How is that possible? You're perfect."

It's said with such genuine feeling that I can't help but be touched. Then again, he always did see something special in me, even back before I could see it in myself. "They leave me here alone at the hotel suite all the time. I have access to his laptop, his iPad. If he's storing any evidence on there, I can find a way to get it to you."

"I don't know." Wes shakes his head, though I can see some of his initial cynicism is decreasing. His hesitation now is something else—reluctance, I think, to put me in danger. "You're a civilian. You shouldn't be getting involved."

"I'm an FBI informant," I remind him. "You've already pulled me into the investigation. You might as well put me to good use." I nudge him with my leg—the most PG touch of all time, but I feel extremely bold doing it, initiating this contact between us. He is warm and solid and *man,* and I savor the touch. "And besides, it'll mean I'll have to check in with you regularly to tell you what I've found. I won't be distracting you from your investigation then. I'll be participating."

A slow smile spreads across Wes's face, making that dimple of his pop in a way that makes my stomach feel like it's bouncing around a tumble dryer. "I guess that's true," he agrees slowly.

I grin back at him, unable to hide my excitement. Inside, I'm brimming with determination. This will work. It *has* to. Before Harmony gets too involved. Before Wes has to compromise too much of himself.

The sooner, the better.

Chapter 29
Wes

Even though I got only four hours of sleep, again, I'm grinning when the alarm goes off in the bunkhouse I'm sharing with a few of the other contestants. "Good morning, boys!" I shout to a chorus of groans. "Isn't it a great day to be alive?"

I don't think I've stopped smiling since I left Nina's room last night. All my dreams were happy. Of course they were happy; they were of her. Nothing much has changed with our situation, not really. We still have huge obstacles to overcome. We still have to hide our feelings for each other from everyone else.

But we don't have to hide them from one another anymore. And I can't put into words just what a relief that is. With one person, I can be completely and totally honest. With Nina, I can be completely and totally myself.

I'm still grinning as we sit down for breakfast. I must be acting just as obnoxious as I'm feeling right now because Kyle glowers at me from across the table. "Dude. We get it. You had a good date with Harmony. Stop rubbing it in our faces."

My smile falters, but only for a moment. Right. The Harmony of it all. If Morrie were here, he'd tell me I should be focused on using our connection on the date to make sure I get extra time with her in our group challenge today. If I'm going to win her trust enough to get access to her father, I have to use every moment we have together to the fullest.

I know a little something about that. When I first met Nina, we had only brief snippets of time together, little stolen moments. I took advantage of everything I had—drawings and notes and even Bible verses—to get her attention. I could use similar strategies with Harmony, I guess, but my gut clenches instinctively at the thought. It would feel like a betrayal to those memories with Nina.

No. I won't do it. There has to be another way.

But Kyle's words have had the desired effect. I'm no longer grinning as I shovel down my breakfast.

We're driven out to what appears to be the local high school's football field. Various stations have been set up around the grassy area, including what looks like a wood-chopping station, a rope course, and . . . holy Gandalf the Grey, is that an archery station?

My grin is back in full force as Morrie crosses the field to join me. He's already shaking his head before he's even reached me. "Get that dorky grin off your face, Ackerman."

"Are we doing an obstacle course?" I ask. "Is it full of nerd-tastic challenges that I, as a certified nerd, am uniquely prepared to conquer?"

It feels like the universe is finally shifting in my favor. Nina and I are on the same page. There's no coonskin cap in sight. And I can hit a bullseye in my sleep. Unless today's surprise twist is that I have compete in a banana hammock, this might be the first day of filming that I actually enjoy.

Morrie just continues shaking his head. "Don't pretend like you've been training for this stuff on purpose. You're just a dweeb who happened to luck out on a dumb TV show."

I ignore him. "I've been preparing my whole life for this," I whisper to myself, surveying the stations.

"Oh, brother," Morrie mutters behind me.

My good luck streak continues as the wardrobe ladies arrive and Nina is sent over to help out the guys on Team Harmony. Thankfully, our outfits are nothing too special today—flannel and jeans, the classic lumberjack look. Nina and the other wardrobe staff are basically just supervising and making sure we button and unbutton the right amount to achieve optimal sexiness.

I tell myself to play it cool as Nina approaches. There are too many people around who could overhear us for me to do otherwise. But I can't help myself from grinning ear to ear as her gaze slides shyly up to mine for the first time today. She tugs at the buttons on her cardigan like she needs something to do with her hands. "Do you have any questions about your costume?" she asks.

I glance over at the other guys in my group to make sure they aren't paying too close attention. They all seem more interested in studying the obstacle course and grousing about how difficult it's going to be. Still, I lower my voice as I look back at Nina. "Actually, I do have a really important question." I hold up my forearm to her, pointing to where the sleeve ends. "Is this sleeve length the sexiest showcase for my forearm, or should I roll it down one more time?" I turn down the cuff one rotation to demonstrate her options.

Nina presses her lips together to fight her smile. She does her best to match my serious tone. "Let me see it the other way again."

Silently, making my expression as stone-faced as possible, I roll the cuff back up.

Nina can't stop her giggles, and that makes me grin. She shakes her head at me, mildly reproving. "Definitely that length," she says. "Show off as much forearm as you can."

I arch my eyebrows suggestively. "So you think I should use my masculine wiles to try to win?"

Nina shrugs. "Sex sells," she tells me, completely straight-faced.

It's my turn to not quite catch my laughter. There is something wildly indecent about sweet, reserved Nina looking me dead in the eye and saying the word *sex*. My blood starts to thrum in my veins.

But, no, I remind myself. *We are surrounded by people, and I am Nate R. right now.* I clear my throat, deciding to steer the conversation into safer waters. "Well, luckily I won't need to rely on my slutty forearms alone today." I lean in closer, lowering my voice. "I happen to be pretty good at this stuff."

Nina's expression suggests she doesn't quite know how to react. "This stuff?" she echoes.

I motion toward the obstacle course. "Archery. Rope courses."

For the first time, it strikes me that Nina doesn't know anything about this side of me. It wasn't exactly the type of conversation that would've come up in prison. I realize I have no idea how she'll react—if, like Morrie, she'll think I'm a big loser and my obsession with escaping into fantasy worlds gives her the ick.

But after last night, I can't go back to putting up any kinds of walls with Nina. I need honesty and openness between us. So instead of downplaying my interest, like Morrie would no doubt beg me to do, I draw in a deep breath and take the plunge. "This is what I do in my free time. When I'm not filming reality shows." *Or going undercover for the FBI*, is the implied part of that statement that I hope she'll pick up on. "I'm sorta super into fantasy."

Nina's eyebrows lift in surprise. I can't read if it's good or bad surprise, but she's still smiling, so hopefully that's a positive sign. "Really?"

"Yeah. Basically, if it has swords or magic or elves, I'm down." But I realize that's underplaying it, so I admit, "I'm more than down. It's my favorite thing to do, to get lost inside another world."

Nina nods. I can tell she's really listening, really trying to understand. "What is it you like so much?"

I consider the question. "I think it's because the rules are so clear-cut? Right and wrong. Good and evil. And how good almost always overcomes evil in the end. The good people get what they deserve." I can't help adding, with a wink, "Plus, swords!"

Laughing quietly, Nina nods in understanding. "I haven't read too much fantasy," she tells me, "but I think I'd like that."

Feeling emboldened by my confessions and her openness to it, I decide to share one more thing that no one, except for Morrie, knows about me. Brutal honesty, right? "There's this channel on TikTok," I tell her. "*GeekOut*. You should check out some of the videos. See if you like them."

GeekOut is *my* channel, of course. Hopefully Nina can piece this together if she looks it up, despite the filters I use to disguise my face.

Nina nods, like she's taking what I'm saying super seriously. "*GeekOut*," she echoes. Maybe it's only my imagination, but it seems like she can tell I'm trying to share something important with her.

I grin again, for only the fiftieth time this morning, I think. "Yeah. Tell me what you think, when you get a chance."

Not long after, the contestants are called to the center of the field, where they film us receiving the obstacle course instructions from Chet Hodgkins. I'm only half paying attention, though. My eyes keep wandering, trying to spot Nina among the crew standing on the outskirts of the field, if she's still there.

Instead, my gaze snags on Harmony, standing only a few feet away from me with the other Mountainettes. While I've been looking for Nina, it's obvious *she's* been watching me. When my gaze meets hers, she grins and wiggles her fingers in a subtle wave.

Shit. I feel my own smile falter as the ice-cold bucket of reality is dumped back onto me. Right. Harmony. I recover quickly and smile back at her with a wink. Frankly, the gesture makes me feel gross, but Nate R. is a winker, so what can you do?

Luckily, if Chet Hodgkins's instructions are anything to go by, today will be more about the competition and less about flirting and conversing with the women. I'll just have to make Harmony think I'm doing well at the obstacle course for her benefit, and hopefully that will make her feel closer to me.

(*Gross. Gross. Gross. I hate it.*)

I push the thought from my mind as we gather for the first part of the competition—the rope course. From here, we'll go on to the wood-chopping station, where we'll have to successfully split a log in half before we can move on to the final station, archery. Whoever can land a bullseye first wins.

It'll be like taking candy from a baby. A hungry, angry baby. (Name that reference!)

What any of this has to do with being a mountain man or falling in love, I have no idea, but I'm not going to look a gift horse in the mouth.

I focus all my attention on the task ahead as we line up to begin the rope course. "On your marks," Chet Hodgkins calls out. "Get set—go!"

As has been established, the other guys are bigger and stronger than me. But that isn't necessarily an advantage on a rope course. My lightness and agility mean I can move faster to grab onto the first rope, and that my body isn't as heavy as I pull myself up.

By the time I reach the top of the rope-climbing tower, I'm already a few seconds ahead of the guy behind me, Everett. I tune him out, going to my happy mental place—the score from the BBC's *Robin Hood* by Andy Price (a criminally under-rated action/adventure soundtrack, if I may be so bold).

The wood-chopping obstacle is more difficult for two reasons: The first is, although I'm adept enough with an axe, I don't have the same strength as some of the other guys to split a log cleanly in half. The second is, it takes all of my willpower not to scream, *And my axe!* the entire time I'm hacking away at my log. Thus, Everett and a guy named Will both gain some ground on me there.

But I more than make up for it once we get to archery. This is my moment. This is the thing I was put on this earth to do. As the other guys scramble to notch their arrows, I easily slide mine into position, take aim, and shoot it at the target.

Bullseye.

That's right, ladies. I might not be the biggest guy here. I might not have to shop in the Big and Tall section, and okay, I might be five eleven and three-quarters, not a clean six feet, but I can notch an arrow like nobody's business.

I hope Nina saw my moment of victory. As dorky as my skill set might be, I hope wherever she is, she's proud that I'm her man. I resist the urge to search for Nina in the crowd, aware that the cameras are on me and everyone's watching.

Instead, I seek out a safer option in the sea of faces—Morrie. I grin at him ecstatically. He just shakes his head at me. *Loser,* he mouths, but I know he's proud of me, somewhere deep, deep, *deep* down inside.

Chapter 30
Wes

While the production crew sets up the next shot, Morrie pulls me aside to film a confessional. "Try not to gloat too much," he mutters. "We don't want you to look like a dork *and* a sore winner."

Another producer, whose name I've now confirmed *is* Lyle, coaches me on the type of sound bites they're looking for today. "Tell us about how it felt to be victorious, but try to tie it in with Harmony. How you did it all for her, or how you hope she noticed. That sort of thing. Don't be afraid to get too cheesy. Reality TV is a dairy-friendly environment."

I'll try to rely on the trick I used last time, thinking of Nina while I'm talking about Harmony. That definitely strayed into extra-cheesy territory, but it was all from the heart, so it didn't feel quite so skeevy.

It seems like Morrie is thinking about the last confessional, too, since he gives me a pointed look. "Don't worry about Wes. He puts the cheese in cheeseball."

I widen my eyes at Morrie, who definitely just called me the wrong name. "Nate," I correct him through gritted teeth.

Morrie's eyes widen back at me, and he grimaces. *Sorry*, he mouths.

Luckily Lyle seems to be distracted by something on my outfit. "The shirt is sitting on you kinda funny after all that running and climbing and whatnot." He turns, calling out, "Can we get someone from wardrobe over here? Oh, Nina! Can you come fix his shirt, Wild Card?"

Wild Card? Although I'm intrigued by the nickname, I'm immediately distracted as Nina approaches. Something in the set of her chin tells me she's going to try her best to remain professional throughout this entire exchange and not let on that she knows me. It's pretty freaking adorable, honestly.

I'm the seasoned FBI agent here, so I should be the one making sure no one clocks that we know each other—especially with Lyle and the cameraman observing this entire exchange, not to mention recording it. But I was always that kid—you know, the one whose mom told him, "don't push that button" and he had to try it, at least one time, just to see what it would do.

I really want to push Nina's buttons. All of them. I want to find out what each one does.

Ignoring Morrie's warning look, I give Nina a polite smile as she approaches. "Hey, Nina, right?" As if she hasn't been the person helping me with my outfits all week, or like I hadn't just heard Lyle call her name. It might be overkill, but if we're supposed to be strangers, I'm going to play up the fact that we're strangers. Hence, pretending I can't confidently recall her name.

Nina narrows her eyes at me, just a little. It's probably not something anyone else would notice, but I had a long time in prison to study each and every one of her expressions and learn exactly what they mean. And this one means she's amused at my dastardly subterfuge but trying not to let on that she finds me impossibly funny and charming. Or something along those lines. "That's right," she hedges.

"Did you see me win that obstacle challenge?" I ask her. "Pretty cool, huh?"

She doesn't answer me, just busies herself with adjusting my shirt, smoothing the flat part of her palm down over the creases. I let her do her work for a moment, enjoying watching her up close—the sweet slope of her cheek and the little upturn of her nose and the slight parting of her lips as she concentrates. Then abruptly, I shiver and let out a short but loud whoo. She jumps, and it makes me grin, as does the reprimanding look she gives me. "Ticklish," I tell her.

Nina ignores that as she gives my shirt one last tug. She's smiling, though. God, I love her smile. "Better?" she asks Lyle, turning to gauge his reaction.

He tilts his head, studying me, then nods. "Much better."

Nina glances at me one last time before turning to leave. I can't let her get away that easily, though. "Oh, Nina!"

She stops, looking warily amused as she waits to see what stunt I'll pull next. "Yes?"

I glance over at Lyle. Luckily, he's giving some quick instructions to the cameraman, so I decide to take my chance.

I turn back to her. "When I was coming into town, I heard a lot of rumors that there've been some break-ins at the Lodge. You might want to make sure your door is locked." I meet her gaze meaningfully. "Check the window, too, to see if it's locked."

I let the words linger in the air for a moment, hoping she'll pick up what I'm putting down. *I'll come by again tonight. Keep the window unlocked.*

Nina nods, just slightly. Enough for only me to see. "I definitely will—"

"There you are!"

A bright, sunny voice cuts through our exchange. I recognize it immediately, and I can tell by the look on Nina's face that she does, too.

Harmony.

Turning in surprise, I see Harmony approaching, beaming as she throws herself into my arms for an embrace. Over her shoulder, I see Lyle frantically motion to the cameraman. "Are we rolling?" he hisses.

I turn my focus back to Harmony as she pulls away long enough to kiss my cheek. *Don't look at Nina,* I school myself mentally. *Don't look at Nina.* Instead, I do my best to give Harmony an easy smile. "Hey, you. What are you doing over here?" I glance toward the producers. "Is this allowed?"

Harmony swats my chest playfully. "I'm a Mountainette. I make my own rules." She casts a cheeky look directly at the camera. "Isn't that right?"

"That's right!" Lyle calls to her, then motions for us to keep going.

I look down at Harmony's expectant face. I need to do something to be in the moment, be in character, but knowing that Nina is standing two feet away makes my mind go completely blank. I don't know how to pretend to be anything but who I really am in front of her. That's always the way it's been—even back when we met, when I was supposed to be Cass, a smooth-talking, hardened criminal.

Whenever she was around, I could only be cheeseball Wes, so besotted with a pair of beautiful dark eyes that I couldn't think straight.

"Did you see me win?" I ask finally.

Harmony nods enthusiastically. "That was so . . . unexpected, Nate. Where did you learn to do all of those things, like shooting a bullseye on the first try?"

Yeah . . . I guess I didn't really think through how to explain that. I shrug. "Beginner's luck, I guess."

A slightly awkward pause follows, then lengthens as I try to think of something to say. I struggle to find Nate R., the guy who's meant to be completely twitterpated with Harmony. She's looking at me expectantly, so I clear my throat. "And I hoped you were watching. I wanted to impress you."

Harmony squeezes my arm, smiling coyly up at me. "Well, it worked."

I hate this. I hate having to do this in front of Nina. Instinctively, I start to look over at her before quickly correcting myself—but it's too late. Harmony follows my gaze, glancing behind her at her cousin. "Nina. Can you give us some privacy, please?"

I let myself peek at Nina just long enough to see the way her expression changes, the way she visibly withdraws when only moments ago she was so open and happy. Pain flashes through her eyes, too quick to notice if you weren't looking carefully.

"Of course." She retreats toward where the rest of the production crew is congregating. You'd never know looking at her that she's anything but fine if it weren't for the way she's clenching her fists. Tight. Too tight.

She's going to hurt herself doing that. I swallow, hard, as I wrench my gaze away from Nina and back to Harmony.

It takes everything in me not to run after her.

<h1 style="text-align:center">Chapter 31</h1>
<h1 style="text-align:center">Nina</h1>

Wes and Harmony are still flirting in front of the camera. I try to focus on literally anything else, but my eyes keep snagging back on them. If that wasn't bad enough, Deja let me in on the secret that the winner of the obstacle course is going on a really romantic hot-air balloon ride with his Mountainette of choice, so that should be fun to watch. If by fun, you mean excruciating.

Why couldn't Wes have been investigating any of the other Mountainettes? It still would have been uncomfortable to watch him pretend to flirt with another woman, but at least I wouldn't have to simultaneously worry about her being heartbroken once the truth comes out.

No, that isn't true. No matter who the woman was, I would feel bad that she's being put in this position. The whole thing is so ugly and sordid and messy.

It doesn't feel that way when Wes and I are alone together, though. What we have feels so genuine and sweet and good. So far we've been able to block out all the other noise around us, but what happens when it gets too loud? What happens when it starts to drown out everything that's real?

I'm not going to think about that now. And I'm definitely not going to watch Harmony and Wes flirting with each other. My plan is to ask Deja if I can stay at the wardrobe department headquarters at Donner Lodge from now on. I'll work on the dresses for the upcoming masquerade ball so I don't have to see so much of what's going on during filming.

But Deja's busy talking to one of the producers, so I have to bide my time until I can get her go-ahead to return to the hotel.

In the meantime, I decide to distract myself with one of Wes's videos. Sorry, one of *GeekOut*'s videos. I admit, I was taken aback when Wes told me how much he loved all things fantasy. It's not that I have anything against fantasy, per se, it just doesn't really match with the way Wes usually presents himself.

But seeing him in that obstacle course today, I had the feeling that I was watching him in his true element. He was so confident and sure of himself. I'd never thought of shooting a bow and arrow as being particularly attractive (even if I did always weirdly have a thing for the cartoon fox version of *Robin Hood*—don't judge), but seeing Wes do it? I understood for the first time what Harmony was feeling all those years ago, showing me pictures and video clips of her favorite celebrity crushes. It felt *swoonworthy*.

Using my FBI phone, I download TikTok and create a hasty user profile so I can search for Wes's channel. I'm not allowed to have TikTok on my own phone, and even if I did, I'd probably have to show my aunt and uncle my user history, like they make my teenage cousins do. Honestly, the FBI is probably monitoring my phone usage less than Uncle Aaron is.

Finding Wes's channel, I'm surprised by how many views he has. I click on one of the top videos, in which Wes, dressed like Indiana Jones, demonstrates how to replicate some of his whip tricks. There's a black mask filter covering most of his face, but I can still see the sparkle in his pale green eyes and his cheeky grin. He's happy in a way that I've rarely witnessed before. Wes is a cheerful, upbeat guy overall, but here, he really looks *joyful*.

It's ironic that whenever he's undercover, being Cass or Nate R. or whoever else, he's dressed to blend in, he's hiding who he truly is. Here, in these videos, when he's wearing an obvious costume and mask, he seems the most like his true self.

And for some reason, the video is really, really working for me. On paper, it doesn't sound like something super attractive—a grown man dressed in a costume to look like a film character and demonstrating a technique for a talent that isn't remotely useful anywhere outside of a Renaissance faire. But whether it's Wes's confidence, or his obvious enjoyment of the subject matter, or the way the muscles in his forearms move while he cracks that whip, I find myself getting unexpectedly flushed.

Judging by the comments, apparently I am not alone. **Whip me any time daddy**, one user writes—and, oh, wow, that's one of the tamer ones . . .

I scroll to another video. This time Wes is wearing trousers and a tunic cinched with a belt. He's holding a sword and demonstrating the best grip and foot movements and such before he goes into a full, one-sided replication of a fight scene from *The Princess Bride*. Then he overlays the video with one of him acting out the other side of the fight, so it looks like he's fighting himself but in a slightly varied costume. He's so graceful, so limber—

"Is that the hot nerd? The one who replicates all the movie stunts?"

I jump at the sound of Deja's voice. I hadn't heard her coming up behind me. Quickly, I exit the screen. She likely wouldn't be able to tell he's "Nate R." because of the digital masks he wears, but it still feels like too close a call, and I can feel my heart pounding. I don't want to share this thing that Wes has given to me. I want to keep it as my own.

"I don't know," I return vaguely, then quickly change the subject. "Do you need me anymore here, or do you mind if I go back and work on the dresses . . . ?"

<hr>

After Deja gives me the go-ahead to leave, I search for Lyle to see if there's any chance he's heading back to the hotel and can give me a ride. Instead, I'm sidelined by Harmony, who looks thrilled to see me—unlike earlier, when she sent me away so I wouldn't be in the shot of her and Wes flirting.

She doesn't know, I remind myself, wanting to be rid of this unwarranted resentment I feel toward her. So I do my best to match her enthusiasm about how the day is going, but that seems wrong, too, like I'm helping to lure her into a trap.

I hate this.

"Did you see my man and his moves?" Harmony gushes. She fans herself dramatically. "I'm not usually into the whole nerd schtick, but I can see why it's a thing. There's something about a super attractive man doing something really dorky—"

My defensiveness rises up immediately. "It's not dorky. It's just a unique skill set."

Harmony looks taken aback, and it's no surprise why. I don't usually argue with her, or with anyone. Blinking, she corrects herself. "O-kay. I only meant they're pretty useless things to know how to do in this day and age. But it was kinda hot, right?"

Luckily, Harmony doesn't really need me to reply. As long as I nod along in agreement, she can use me as her sounding board and vent whatever it is she's feeling. I play along numbly.

"My producer told me we're doing a hot-air balloon next," she gushes, oblivious to my silence, which feels so thundering to me. "So romantic, right?"

I force myself to nod along. "Mm-hmm."

Harmony smiles to herself, twirling her hair. "He hasn't kissed me yet. I'm not sure why. I think he's trying to be a gentleman? But I'm going to make sure he knows the hot-air balloon will be the perfect place for him to finally ravish me with his lips. Maybe some tongue."

I think I'm going to throw up.

Harmony levels her gaze on me, seeming to really see me for the first time in this conversation. "Don't tell Daddy. I know he'll see it when it airs, but hopefully by then Nate and I will be engaged, so all can be forgiven."

I can feel my heart pounding in my ears, unfortunately not loud enough to drown out her words. *Engaged.* That's where this is all going. Unless . . .

"Hey, do you know Uncle Aaron's password?" I ask her, trying to keep my voice as innocent as possible, as if the thought just randomly occurred to me. "He asked me to download some hymns for him, but I'm locked out."

It's not a totally implausible excuse, but it's also not a great one. Although I get tasked with all kinds of random chores for my family, Uncle Aaron has never, ever asked me to access anything on his computer. Luckily, Harmony seems so distracted by her daydreams about making out with my boyfriend, she doesn't question me on my attempt to break into her father's laptop so I can investigate him for the FBI. (What is my life?!)

"Matthew seven underscore fifteen," Harmony tells me distractedly. "His favorite Bible verse."

My heart is racing for a different reason now. Could it really be that easy to unravel Uncle Aaron, and bring all this horrible pretending and betraying to an end?

There's only one way to find out.

Chapter 32
Nina

Later, when I make it back to my family's hotel suite, I'm surprised to find the rooms empty. There's no note from my uncle or aunt. No text messages either.

Based on the hour, I'm guessing they went out to dinner? My stomach rumbles as the thought crosses my mind. Something delicious and warm and nutritiously filling sounds amazing. But I don't want to get my hopes up anticipating they might bring something back for me.

Instead, I grab a granola bar, then check my watch. It's a little after seven. They could still be out for a while.

I should check Uncle Aaron's computer.

The moment the thought pops into my mind, I break out into a cold sweat. Sure, I'd asked Harmony for the password with the intention of using it, but the plan felt vague and distant this morning. Now, with an empty hotel suite and access to Uncle Aaron's computer, the possibility has swiftly become a reality.

Shoot.

Reminding myself that Uncle Aaron is a liar and has hurt people, lots of people, I approach his room with a firmer resolve. I'm doing this to help Wes, yes, but I'm also doing it for all the people Uncle Aaron has hurt. I'm doing it for *me*, for the little girl who just needed someone to love her but instead got trampled again and again and again. *No one deserves to feel that way.* The reminder, repeated like a mantra, carries me the rest of the way.

Even though the hotel suite is so silent I know no one else could be here, I hesitate outside the closed door to Uncle Aaron's room, knocking once, then again. Silence. "Uncle Aaron? Aunt Hope?" More silence. I knock one last time to be certain no one's there.

Then I enter the room.

It's the biggest room in the suite, with a king bed, a small sofa, a walk-in closet, a bureau, a desk, and an en suite bathroom. Despite the size, I zero in almost immediately on Uncle Aaron's laptop on the desk.

Holy guacamole. A part of me was hoping it would be hidden, so I'd have to report back to Morrie that I'd tried and failed, oh well, can't be helped, back to square one. (*Cowardice.*)

I try to summon up the mental image of one of my favorite inspirational GIFs. Maybe Walt Disney, telling me if I can dream it, I can do it? I don't know if trespassing into someone's private computer files was exactly what Mr. Disney had in mind, but it does make me feel more resolved.

WWHTMKGL&DD, I remind myself sternly.

Then I open Uncle Aaron's laptop and type in the password.

To my astonishment, it works. I know it shouldn't be surprising that his own daughter knows his password, especially since he and Harmony are so close, but some part of me was expecting an alarm to go off. Uncle Aaron to come bursting out of the closet. God to strike me dead.

Instead, I stare at the computer screen, wondering how to get started. It may be surprising to learn I've never broken into someone's computer for the FBI before. Where does one hide proof of illegal wrongdoings? Without any better ideas, I click on the Documents folder.

Most of the file names seem pretty mundane. Then again, I have no idea what I'm looking for. But none of them are labeled anything like "Super Shady Business Deals" or "Illegal Things I've Done." I guess that may have been hoping for too much, but it sure would have made my job a lot easier. Very inconsiderate of Uncle Aaron not to mark his white-collar criminal activities more clearly.

If that internal dialogue isn't clue enough, I am not very good at this whole being-an-FBI-informant thing. I'm halfway determined to inform Wes and Morrie that this was a mistake, I'm clearly useless, when I see something strange. Near the bottom of the files list is an unmarked folder. When I click on it, I jump as the computer emits a trill, my heart racing from the unexpected sound. A message box pops up, demanding a password to proceed.

Look, I'm no special agent, or mastermind criminal for that matter, but it seems to me if I'd committed a crime I didn't want anyone to know about, I'd hide it in a folder with its own secret password.

With shaking hands, I type in the same one I used to log in to the computer. The laptop emits another trill, this one sounding mildly disapproving. **Incorrect password,** the message box reads.

I have no way to know what another password might be. It could be anything, from another Bible verse to one of his favorite hymns to something completely random. If I try too many incorrect options, I worry the computer might lock me out—or worse, send an alert to Uncle Aaron that someone's trying to access this content.

Reaching into my pocket, I pull out the flash drive Morrie gave me just in case I found anything. I insert it into the laptop and begin downloading the folder, checking my watch anxiously. Knowing my family, it won't be too much longer until they get back. Uncle Aaron believes it's a bad idea to be out past eight o'clock, unless in service of the Lord. I'm actually not sure why. Presumably because the devil works in darkness? Or maybe he just gets sleepy after eight. I can't really judge him for that. For other things, sure, but not for that.

While I wait for the file to finish processing, I cross over to the window and glance down at my view of the front entrance below . . .

Just in time to see Uncle Aaron, Aunt Hope, and my three younger cousins walk through the front entrance of the Lodge and into the lobby.

No, no, no, no, no! I race over to the laptop, checking on the progress of the file. Only 78 percent completed. My mind races. Should I abandon the download and cover my tracks? I don't know when I'll get another chance to access Uncle Aaron's computer, though. Normally I'm left home alone more often than anyone else in the family, but on this trip, I'm almost never in the suite without somebody else there.

I have to take this chance. Don't I?

WWHTMKGL&DD.

I run through all the calculations of how long it will take my family to arrive at our suites. Maybe the elevator will stall. Maybe someone will chat with them for a moment at the front desk.

I check the progress of the download again: 84 percent. It's moving pretty quickly, but will it be fast enough?

I pace the room, jumping at every noise, certain it's my family coming into the suite. I shamelessly chew on my nails, even though Uncle Aaron always says it's a disgusting, unladylike habit. Then again, if he catches me breaking into his laptop and copying files for the FBI, my nails will be the least of his worries. So at least there's that.

Ninety-six percent. Just another 4 percent and I'll be in the clear . . .

This time when I hear a sound, it really is the door to the suite opening. I freeze. Shoot. No, we're past that now. *Shit!* It's too late for me to leave the room without anyone noticing. I can hear my family out in the main room, talking loud enough for me to hear their voices but not what they're saying.

One hundred percent. I hastily remove the flash drive, close out all the files, and shut the laptop screen. The top of the computer is warm from use. Uncle Aaron will know someone's been using it if he touches it in the next few minutes, but I can't worry about that now. I have to get out of here without raising any alarms about why I was in the room. But how—

The door to the bedroom starts to open. I dart into the bathroom, grab something off the counter, and come back out just as Uncle Aaron walks in.

He stiffens at the sight of me. "Antonina. What are you doing in here?" His tone is harsh, reprimanding, with none of the surface-level charm he uses to schmooze new parishioners or important people he wants to impress. He wrote me off a long time ago as not being someone whose good opinion he feels the need to concern himself with.

I do my best to smile, like he doesn't make it obvious every time he speaks to me just how much he hates me. "Sorry! We need more toilet paper in the other bathroom so I thought I'd check to see if they gave you any extra in here." I hold up the roll in my hand. "Do you mind?"

Don't look at the laptop, Nina, I tell myself sternly. *Keep smiling. Don't look at the laptop!* Somehow, I manage to obey myself, even though my guilty eyes keep wanting to stray from my uncle's piercing gaze.

"Fine." Uncle Aaron waves me out of the room with a dismissive gesture.

I don't wait for him to say anything else. Scrambling toward the door, I stop only when Uncle Aaron's voice reaches me. "Antonina?"

It feels like someone is playing ping-pong with my heart. Swallowing, I turn back to face Uncle Aaron. "Yes?"

He stands in the darkened room, face shrouded in shadow, so I can't see his expression. Even so, I'm sure he's somehow figured out what I'm doing. He knows. How does he know?

"Harmony's producer informed us we'll be meeting her final contestants this week."

It's so far from what I'm expecting him to say that for a long moment, I can only stare at him. "Oh?" I say finally, when it becomes clear he's waiting for a response.

"It probably goes without saying," Uncle Aaron continues, in that same calm, quiet voice, "that you won't be joining us for those meetings."

They shouldn't hurt me this way—these cold, detached words coming from a man I no longer like or respect—but they still hit me like a blow. And they were intended to. It would take so little effort for Uncle Aaron to include me, or even to explain things in a way that wouldn't devastate me. Thinking back on it, I can recall so many times when these little slights were delivered in exactly the right manner to wound and humiliate me.

Uncle Aaron is not a good person. I hopefully have proof of that right now, on the flash drive that's concealed in my skirt pocket. But I still don't understand why he goes out of his way to harm me. I still don't understand what's so horrible about me that he just can't bring himself to love me.

Once again, the silence stretches out until I realize I'm supposed to respond. That must be part of the pleasure for Uncle Aaron in these exercises in humiliation—watching me receive the verbal injury, watching me try my best to pretend it doesn't hurt. These types of interactions have happened so many times, they're what have formed the core of our relationship. But this time? This time I won't give him the satisfaction.

I'm not sure if Uncle Aaron can see me any better than I can see him in this darkened room. Nevertheless, I raise my chin and do my best to keep my expression as calm and unfazed as possible. "Then why bother saying it?" I challenge him.

Before he can answer, I turn and leave the room. I don't want to give him a chance to land another blow. I don't know if I'll be able to withstand it. My hands are shaking, my heart thundering in my ears, as I flee to the safety of my room.

Once I'm there, I turn the flash drive over in my hands. I don't know what exactly it is that I've downloaded. Maybe it's nothing. Or maybe what I have here might be enough to bring Uncle Aaron to justice, to bring resolution to all the people he's hurt and cheated and even destroyed along the way.

Maybe what I have here might be enough to end Wes's time undercover, so we can stop tricking Harmony, and he and I can finally be together.

Maybe what I have here might be enough to destroy my family.

I truly don't know what the best outcome would be. I don't know what to hope for as I take out my phone and type Morrie a quick message. **I think I might have found something . . .**

I don't add what I'd like to, because Morrie's already informed me that he doesn't understand or appreciate my GIFs. But if I were going to include one, I know exactly which one it would be.

Nervous Sheldon Cooper blowing into a paper bag

Chapter 33
Wes

This time when I scale the wall outside of Nina's room, I'm better prepared. I know which grooves in the bricks to fit my feet into for best balance, and I know to wear pants with some give so I can contort my body as needed. I've also brought a backpack full of supplies to ensure we have a romantic, fun night. I don't want Nina to think I'm only coming to visit her because I expect something to happen between us physically—although, if I'm being honest, I've definitely been daydreaming about all of the possibilities. But if she wants to take things slow, which is totally fine, I've packed supplies for a fun date night: board games, wine, plastic cups, snacks. Plus I put together a playlist with some of my favorite romantic scores that we can listen to together.

Some heroes wear capes. This one wears a backpack.

When I reach the window, I tap lightly on the pane with my fingertips. "Nina?" I whisper. "It's me."

Hopefully I don't have to elaborate too much on "it's me"—unless she has a bunch of guys climbing up to her window for nighttime visits . . . in which case, there's probably a few conversations we'll need to have.

A moment later, the window opens from the inside. I shimmy off the backpack and drop it into the room before climbing through myself.

This time I don't squeal like a tiny piglet in distress or land in a heap on the floor, so I'll count that as a win for my sexy manhood. Looking up, I see Nina is pacing the small length of the room, chewing on the end of her thumb. Uh-oh. In an instant, I'm on my feet, forgetting about the backpack o' fun. "Did something happen?"

Nina's eyes snap to mine, like she's only now registering that I'm there. She stops pacing, meeting my gaze. "You bet your bottom dollar something happened."

It's such an unexpectedly old-fashioned statement that even though I'm genuinely worried about her, I have to bite back a laugh. "What do you mean?"

"Uncle Aaron caught me in his room." Alarm must flash across my face, because Nina waves her hand. "It's fine. I made him think I was there for toilet paper."

Okay . . . I'm curious about that one, but it really seems like she's on a roll (no pun intended), and I don't want to interrupt her. Plus, two sisters, a mom, and four aunts have deeply instilled in me that sometimes a woman just needs you to shut up and listen. So I'm shutting up. I'm listening.

"Then he was rude to me," she continues. Her voice is low but thrumming with intensity; I can't quite shake the feeling she's recounting this all out loud for herself as much as for me. "So I was rude back."

My eyebrows arch in surprise. *Rude* is not exactly a word I'd ever use to describe Nina, but I can see this is a big deal for her. The FBI-agent part of my brain can't help but worry that this might somehow interfere with the investigation, but the part of me that cares about Nina tells it to shut the hell up, this is important. "Good," I tell her, nodding along to show my enthusiasm. "What'd you say to him?"

"He told me that it goes without saying I wouldn't be coming along to film with the family. So I told him, 'Then why bother saying it?'" she informs me, unable to hold back the triumphant smile that blossoms across her face.

Oh. I was expecting something a bit more dramatic, like that she'd told him he should go fuck himself—which, for the record, he would totally deserve. Her response feels very benign in comparison. But she looks so happy, and I don't want to do anything to dampen that. We can work on her trash talk some other time. "Yeah, you did," I encourage her, holding my hand up for a high five.

Still grinning, Nina claps my hand. She's pretty short, so she has to hop up to reach me, which is pretty darn adorable.

"I think I might have found something, too. On Uncle Aaron. I'll give the flash drive to Morrie tomorrow when I see him on set. It's password protected, so he's going to try to find someone who can hack it as soon as possible."

"Whoa!" This time I don't have to dial up any enthusiasm. That's amazing news. "Nina, you're a badass."

She grins at me. "I know!" Some of her excitement dims. "They came home unexpectedly, so I didn't get to look around more. I only had time to add the one file."

"That's okay," I reassure her. "You did great."

She really did. Most informants never have to do anything as risky as what she did tonight; they just check in with us and report on things they've seen or heard. Nina went out of her way to stick her neck on the line. But I shouldn't have expected any less. That's all part of what makes Nina so amazing; you might write her off because of how quiet and unassuming she can be, but it's all just an act to cover up how incredible she is. She's brave and selfless and smart. My woman has *layers*.

I catch myself a moment later, still grinning at her like a cheeseball. Luckily Nina seems too distracted to notice. She's chewing on the end of her thumb again, her eyes distant like she's trying to remember something. "If you want, I can tell you the names of some of the other files I saw, in case you want me to go back and look at them another time."

Check her out—she's gone spying one time and now she's Sydney Bristow. "Sure," I tell her. "Maybe write everything down while it's still fresh in your memory . . ."

I search the room for something she can write in. Finding nothing, I remember that I have my notebook in my backpack. I pull it out quickly, flipping through the pages to find a blank one.

Nina reaches out, stopping my hand. "What's that?"

I've inadvertently stopped on one of my sketches of Ryko, an original character I invented. He's a fantasy/steampunk hybrid—a conman, a gambler, a sword-fighter, a martial arts master, and an expert shot. Oh, and he may or may not bear a striking resemblance to yours truly if I walked around in a really cool tunic and duster and Indiana Jones–inspired hat.

Feeling myself begin to flush, I try to hurriedly flip past it. "Uh, whoops. That's nothing, just some doodling—"

Nina takes the notebook from me before I can fully turn away. "It's amazing," she says quietly, holding the book in her lap so she can study the page. "I love the chain mail."

I run an embarrassed hand through my hair, watching her expression as she looks at the drawing more closely. "I don't think I got the shading quite right on that one," I can't help but tell her, because it's always so awkward to have someone look at my work. I instinctively feel the need to apologize for it.

Nina gives me a look, like she's on to me and my self-deprecating ways, before turning her concentration back to the page. "He carries a sword *and* a gun?"

I run another sweep of my hand through my hair, letting out a nervous laugh. This is excruciatingly awkward—having to talk about the drawings I've never shown to anybody before. I feel more exposed than when I was in the tiny red underwear a few days ago. "I know that might seem anachronistic, but he's a time traveler. So he's an expert on several forms of deadly combat, throughout various time periods and cultures."

Nina considers this for a moment. "Kind of like a warrior Doctor Who?"

I think I just fell even more in love with her. A grin stretches across my face, unencumbered now by any awkwardness. "Yeah. Exactly. A warrior Doctor Who."

Nina beams at me, then looks back down at the drawing. "Do you have any more?"

Before I can stop her, she begins flipping the pages—backward, toward my other drawings, instead of forward toward the blank pages. I resist the strong, instinctive urge to snatch the book out of her hands, because Nina is smiling again, and who am I to stand in the way of that?

"This character goes on all kinds of adventures," she observes as she moves through the pages. She peers up at me through her long dark lashes. "He looks familiar."

"Yeeaaah." I draw out the word, trying to gather up my courage before I decide to bite the bullet. "His name is Ryko. He's sorta based on me."

Nina pretends to be surprised. "You don't say."

I shake my head before continuing, half wincing through my mortification. "Sometimes I daydream about turning *GeekOut* into more of an original show. Like, not just replicating the action sequences from other movies and TV shows, but writing my own character and stories." Seeing the way she nods along, clearly interested, I find myself continuing. "It would still be a show where people could workout with the character in fun, nerdy-inspired ways. But there would be a plot. Side stories. Maybe even a choose-your-own adventure element, where there would be different follow-up videos based on the outcomes the audience chose."

Even though these ideas have been percolating in my imagination for years, I haven't told them to anyone before. I've never even hinted at them as a possibility. Too late, I realize how much it would crush me if Nina doesn't like them. Laughing awkwardly, I try to backpedal. "I mean, they're just dumb daydreams . . ."

Nina doesn't look like she hates the idea, though. She's nodding thoughtfully. "What other characters would be in the show?"

Oof. That's a whole other can of worms. "Um . . ." I try to stall as she begins flipping through the pages again.

I know the exact moment she reaches *that* page. "Oh," she says quietly.

Most of the other images have been different ideas for Ryko—adventures he can go on, battles he can fight, costumes he can wear. Most of the images in my sketch pad are pure fantasy, not drawn from anything in real life.

But Princess Annais definitely drew on some familiar inspiration.

My book is full of dozens of sketches of her. Princess Annais, small and graceful and regal and beautiful. So beautiful, with her big dark eyes and her sad, wistful face. In some of my sketches, she's wearing elegant gowns, pulled entirely from my imagination. Ball gowns for masquerades and dances. Fierce cloaks and crowns for when she is sitting on her throne. Tunics and head scarves for when she is disguising herself as a peasant, moving throughout the city.

And, uh, maybe one where she is wearing very little—nothing but a small, little scrap of fabric, worn like a loincloth, sitting low on her hip bones and just barely skirting the skin at the tops of her thighs. Underneath a headdress of pine needles and leaves and wildflowers, her long dark hair is worn loose and unbound, covering her breasts, but just barely.

"That's when she goes to live among the forest people," I stammer to explain. "She has to adopt their customs and cultures for diplomatic reasons . . ."

I trail off, because yep, it's just a thinly veiled excuse I used to justify sketching Nina's beautiful body. To put to paper the delicate lines and soft curves that have haunted my imagination.

Nina was the girl of my dreams for so long . . . and only my dreams. After she stopped coming to Bible study, I truly thought I'd never see her again. So it didn't feel weird to create a character who bears more than a passing resemblance to her and to draw her again and again and again. I wanted to keep her with me, if only as a figment of my imagination. At the time, it felt like a romantic tribute to the woman I'd loved and lost.

Now that I'm here in the room with her, though, watching her look at these sketches, it kinda feels like I'm a creep who just wanted to draw her practically naked.

I clear my throat, scratching the back of my neck as I scramble to find something to say to justify this. I got nothing. "So. The thing is . . ."

Nina surprises me by cutting me off. She is looking at me from underneath her fringe of dark lashes, her head still bowed. "Is this how you see me?" she asks, the ghost of a smile tugging at the corner of her lips.

All elements combined—the tiny smile, the dark and sultry gaze—create a startlingly sexy expression, especially since I was expecting her to be disgusted with me, and it sends my blood thrumming through my veins. "Um," I stammer, "I mean, yeah. Yes. Not always but definitely sometimes. Yes."

Yeesh. That was bad. I try to remember the guy who was nicknamed Cassanova for his silver tongue. Some of that sweet-talking ability has to still be there somewhere inside of me. Swallowing, I regroup. "What I mean to say is, when I tried to imagine the most beautiful woman in the world, it was always you. So that's how I had to draw her."

One moment Nina is watching me, still clutching my notebook tightly in her hands. The next she's tackling me, pushing me down so I'm prone on the small bed. Her soft body presses into mine as her fingers tangle in my hair, her warm lips slanting over mine.

Nina. This woman drives me absolutely crazy. You couldn't picture a more innocent-looking person, with her cardigans and long skirts and the way she barely makes eye contact. But there's no slow acceleration with her. It's zero to one hundred in a matter of seconds, and I'm just the lucky idiot trying to hold on for dear life.

We tangle together, our hands starting out in G-rated places—hers in my hair, mine on her waist—but there's nothing suitable for young children in the way our bodies seek each other out for as much contact as possible. I don't want any part of me to not be touching her. Legs, arms, torsos. Her neck. I need to find a way to touch that soft, soft neck—

Nina presses her pelvis against mine, and all other thoughts instantly flee my mind. I should be embarrassed at how eagerly my cock stirs to immediate and full attention with even the briefest contact, but I'm too overcome with need. More. *More.* To be inside her would be the sweetest homecoming.

With a gasp, Nina wrenches her mouth from mine. "I can't. I can't."

All the wild want and need clouding every other function of my mind and body immediately dissipates. It's like there's a switch for my libido, and those words uttered in Nina's soft, panicked voice flick it to off. Hands in the air, I wrench back from her so dramatically that I smack my head against the wall.

For a panicked moment, we both freeze, listening to see if anyone is going to come check on us. After a minute, we relax again, exchanging guilty smiles.

Nina covers her mouth, clearly doing her best not to smile at my pain. "Are you okay?" she whispers.

It sounded worse than it was; I'm more embarrassed than hurt. But my dumb, hormone-addled brain turns to mush at her obvious concern for me. "Are *you* okay?" I turn it back to her. "Did I . . . scare you?"

Nina uncovers her mouth, shaking her head decisively. "No. I'm sorry. I just . . . I don't want to move too quickly. I'm sorry. Is that okay?"

The uncertainty in her voice breaks my heart, honestly. I get a peek into what her life must be like, if asking for even the most basic respect for her consent sends her into an anxiety spiral.

I sit up so I'm no longer prone on the bed but leaning on my elbows, the better to make eye contact with her and really make my point, I hope. "You don't need to apologize. I only ever want to do what you want to do, too."

Nina flushes, her eyes darting down to my cock, which is still quite obviously tenting my jeans. She bites her lip. *Dammit, Nina.* I'm a consent king, but I'm no saint, and even if I'd never do anything she doesn't want to do, drawing attention to her lips in conjunction with my cock is going to get my imagination all kinds of excited.

Luckily, Nina starts speaking so I have something important to focus on other than the Dread Pirate Roberts. (Still not answering any questions about that nickname.) "It's not that I don't want to. I want to do . . . pretty much all of the things with you. You're a temptation for me."

I . . . don't quite know how to read that. My groin has all kinds of feelings, knowing that Nina wants me as much as I want her. But that word—*temptation*. It carries some very negative connotations. I tread carefully, not wanting her to spook or overreact, but also wanting to be certain we're on the same page. "So . . . being with me would be a sin?"

I don't feel that way. I've never felt that way about sex, and I especially wouldn't about sex with Nina. Taking pleasure in each other, making her feel good, showing her how much I care about her without words—none of that feels like it should be wrong to me.

But if Nina feels that way . . . if anything we do would cause her guilt or shame, it doesn't seem like that can be the foundation for anything but misery. We might need to rethink if we can be together.

To my relief, Nina shakes her head vehemently. "No. That's not what I mean. It's more like, I find it really, really hard to resist you."

Oh. I wrap my head around that. Okay, I think I can get on board with that concept. I can't quite catch the smile that tugs at my lips, the little waggle of my eyebrows. "Well, I have been told I look irresistible in a coonskin cap."

Nina laughs, but her expression sobers again quickly. "I just worry about getting carried away before we're really ready. Before *I'm* really ready."

I swallow, hard, searching for the right words to communicate just how important it is to me that she feels ready and safe. "You're the boss," I tell her. "You set the pace. Where you lead, I will follow."

Am I just quoting the *Gilmore Girls* theme song now? Maybe. (Hey, I have two sisters and an appreciation for quick and witty banter. I've definitely watched more than my fair share of the adventures of Lorelai and Rory, even if the show would be better with some crossbows. Just saying.) The point being, I want Nina to feel comfortable knowing that she is calling all the shots with our physical relationship.

Nina takes a moment to process this idea. Then she smiles, one of her sweet little Nina smiles that feels like a real victory earn. "I'm the boss?" she murmurs back, arching one eyebrow.

"O captain, my captain," I confirm, and am rewarded with an even bigger smile. I feel like I'm king of the world.

Yep, I've read Keats, too. *I'm a complex guy, sweetheart.* (Name that quote!)

Taking Nina in my arms, I kiss the top of her head and let my body relax as she snuggles against me. "We're in no rush," I promise her.

This time, I'm determined, we'll get things right.

Chapter 34
Nina

The next morning, I'm relieved when Deja asks me to stay behind at the Lodge to work on dresses for the masquerade ball instead of going to set with her. Today of all days, I don't want to be on set. The Mountainettes will be narrowing down their final three contestants at the Axing Ceremony, and if Wes goes through, it means he and Harmony will only be getting closer and closer. I know he'll only be doing what he needs to do, and what we've both agreed to do moving forward, but it's still not something I especially want to see. I've never been one to pick at my scabs; I prefer to hide all my injuries under Band-Aids and pretend they aren't there until they've healed, thank you very much.

Emotionally, this feels pretty much the same. If I don't have to see it, maybe I can pretend it isn't happening.

Before Deja leaves for set, I help her gather together the items they'll need for the shoot. "Thanks for letting me work on the dresses," I tell her as we move about the room. "I know all the costumes are important, but the pretty, shiny ones are my favorite."

Deja laughs. "Tell me about it. I have a bougie soul. When other kids were talking about their favorite superheroes at school, I wouldn't shut up about my favorite outfits at the Met Gala."

I laugh. "Me too! I used to sneak onto the library computers so I could look up all the outfits afterward."

Too late, I realize what I've suggested without saying it—that at home I would have been forbidden from doing something even as innocuous as looking up images from a major world event. Uncle Aaron and Aunt Hope think anything to do with celebrities or fashion is worldly and sinful, after all.

I tense, bracing myself for Deja's judgment—or worse, the familiar pitying look.

Instead, she appraises me, tilting her head to the side. "What are you doing after this show?"

That wasn't where I expected the conversation to go, so I blink at her in surprise. "What do you mean?"

"Do you have another job lined up after this?" The answer must be obvious on my face, because she explains, "Most of us move from show to show, or sometimes film sets if we can get the work."

My curiosity piques. "Can you make a living out of doing that?"

She laughs ruefully. "Not a great one, but it's enough to get by. Most of us aren't really in it for the money." She shrugs. "You're a good worker. I bet you could do it. If you ever make it out to Hollywood, you should look me up. I'll definitely let you know if there's a spot for you, whatever I'm working on."

The offer takes me by surprise. This whole time I thought I was only here because Sienna and Rae took pity on me. I guess that's how it started, but apparently whatever I've been doing was enough to impress Deja. She's a nice person but definitely no-nonsense. She wouldn't offer me this if she didn't really mean it.

My first impulse is to tell her that of course it can't happen. Uncle Aaron and Aunt Hope would never let me. Then again . . . if all goes according to plan, I won't be living with them anymore after this. I won't be spending most of my time running their errands and doing their household chores. I'll be . . . free.

The thought sends something warm blooming through my chest. It feels like hope. "Thank you," I tell her, unable to contain my smile. "I'll definitely take you up on that . . ."

Second to Nun

The only downside of spending all day working on the dresses by myself is that it gives me lots of time to think. I worry, of course, about what might be happening on set, but surprisingly, it doesn't take up as much of my mental space as I thought it would.

Instead, I can't stop thinking about last night with Wes.

The feeling of his warm, lean body pressing into mine. His soft, full-lipped kisses. The way each touch, each caress, each press of our body stoked a fire inside of me. No one has ever made me feel what Wes does so effortlessly. It's like all the voices in my head, telling me how sinful I am, are temporarily silenced by the pleasure, the *need*, he awakens in me.

I meant what I said when I told Wes he was my temptation, even though I know he didn't love hearing that. And I understand why. It isn't completely the right word for what he makes me feel. Temptation sounds like something inherently wrong and bad, and that's not what I feel when I'm with Wes. I feel powerless to resist him; but conversely, I also feel stronger, more in control of my life than I've ever been. When he told me I would be in charge of setting the pace for our physical relationship, I was grateful. Overwhelmed. No one has ever given me authority over my own choices before.

My whole life, I've been taught that sexual feelings are sinful outside of marriage. But how can it be a sin, to feel loved, cherished, respected, adored, and wanted?

Maybe this is one of those areas of my life I need to reconstruct. I know there are things from my foundation in faith I want to keep, that I don't want to destroy wholly. But in truth, I think there might be much more I want to get rid of.

(*Ingratitude.*)

Like *that*. That voice in my head that tells me everything I do is sinful and chides me for even the smallest of mistakes.

The voice that sounds a lot like Uncle Aaron's.

I know we should all strive to be the best we can be, to try to be as close to perfect as we can. But seeking perfection can be a daunting way to live. Sometimes, I want to sleep past six a.m. and not feel like I'm wasting God's gift of the day. Sometimes I don't want to busy myself with a dozen different tasks and have a never-ending to-do list I'm supposed to accomplish so I won't be idle; sometimes I just want to be lazy and do *nothing*.

I like fashion. I know it's frivolous and that Uncle Aaron would probably say it's vain, but I like beautiful clothes, and the way they can help people be their most beautiful selves. I like the artistry in putting together an outfit or a costume, and how just a simple swathe of material can completely change how we see a person.

I like how being near Wes makes my heart race. I like how he makes my body feel like it's waking up and paying attention. I liked finding that drawing he made of me and knowing he sees me as a sensual and seductive woman. I liked touching him, and kissing him. I didn't like the shame that came afterward, but I enjoyed the sensations in the moment, the closeness, the *being* with him.

I think I might want to do it again. I think I might want to do *more*.

The thought sends my body into full awareness.

The revelation startles me, frightens me. It feels like something I shouldn't admit out loud. And yet, once I think the words, I realize they're true. Sex *is* something that I want to explore. With Wes, specifically. With Wes *only*. There's no one else I've ever wanted to be close to like I want to be close with him.

The same pulsing, thrumming need I felt last night begins to build low in my belly. But I'm at work, nowhere near Wes, and this is not the right time or place to let my fantasies get the best of me. I should focus my energy on the beautiful dresses I'm sewing tiny sequins into to make them look even more magical under the bright filming lights. Harmony's is pink, of course. She's going to look absolutely beautiful in it—

As she dances with Wes, molds her body against his, kisses his soft, full lips.

Pressing my eyes shut, I take in a few deep breaths to center myself. Clearly, I'm going to need a distraction to get through today. My two modes seem to be either anxious or horny, and neither one is an especially productive way to work.

A sudden thought strikes me. Matilda has been raving to me about audiobooks ever since she discovered them half a year ago or so. I've never been much of a fan, since Uncle Aaron would only let us listen to the Bible or books with a central Christian theme, and both of those options usually just make my mind wander. But maybe, here on my own, away from my family, I might be able to try something new . . .

I pull out my phone and send a quick text to Helen.

Hey, this is really random, and it's okay if you're too busy, but I was wondering if maybe you might have some recommendations for some books for me to listen to?

A moment later, I add: **Specifically maybe books with some fantasy in them?** Wes seems to love those kinds of stories; it might give us something else to talk about in our nightly clandestine meetings.

Another moment of internal conflict follows before I tag on: **Maybe even books that have some kissing scenes? And other things like that . . .**

I almost delete the last text, but before I can second-guess myself, I send it off. Maybe listening to "spicy" books will be good practice for me. Maybe this will be a good way for me to decide whether I'm really ready to explore my physical relationship with Wes, or if I just got carried away with how nice it was to kiss him last night. But I figure if I'm the captain steering the boat, I better know which direction I want to go.

I expect it to be a while before Helen can get back to me. She's busy planning her wedding and doing all her day-to-day tasks in the library. So I'm surprised when I hear an almost automatic ping.

Yes, yes, yes!!! Helen writes back, with about a thousand more exclamation points.

I realize too late that I've just unleashed a particularly ravenous beast. As the old proverb goes, never ask a librarian for a book recommendation unless you're ready for at least a dozen to come your way.

Helen not only sends me a list of books, she also sends me links to the audiobook versions, tells me which ones are available on Libby and/or Hoopla (since I have very limited income, she knows this is how I get most of my books), and gives me detailed descriptions of what she enjoys about each of them. Some of them... honestly, I'm feeling flushed just reading the descriptions. People write about these things? I'm not one to judge, but I guess I never realized so many women fantasized about having sex with big colorful aliens. And until today, I definitely had no idea what "reverse harem" was. When I saw a book cover with a woman and a bunch of men, I assumed it was about a girl and all her brothers. After reading the description, I discovered I was very, *very* wrong.

After perusing the list, I send Helen a GIF of a panda bear covering its face with its paws. Hopefully this succinctly conveys to her that even though I'm thankful for the recommendations, I'd probably feel overwhelmed by anything else at this point. At least, that's what the GIF conveys to me.

I look at Helen's list again. I worry these are all going to be too advanced for my first ever romance novel. But after a few minutes, I find one that doesn't look quite as racy as the rest of them. It's a simple story about a peasant (Theera) who doesn't realize she's a princess, and the assassin (Khorum) who takes her under his wing to help her reclaim her kingdom. The guy on the cover looks a bit like Wes, which may or may not be why I choose it. (Spoiler: It totally is.) The fact that he's shirtless and making sultry bedroom eyes makes me flush with nervous anticipation, but I remind myself that the book will be on my phone, where no one else can see it.

That resolved, I check out the audiobook, then play it through my earbuds as I continue my work. For quite a while, the storyline seems like a normal fantasy plot, one that I quickly become invested in. As I cut and trim and pin and stitch, I get lost in the monotony of the motions, and my mind carries me away in the story that's unfolding. I start to really care about Khorum and Theera, like they're actual people who I get to follow as they fall in love.

There's nothing better than watching two people fall in love, is there? That's why fairy tales have been popular for so long. That's why people like these reality dating shows so much. There are so many awful things in the world, so many things designed to make you feel trampled and small. Love does the oppo- site, though. It makes you feel big, too big to be contained in one mortal body. It makes you feel seen. Maybe that's why across cultures, throughout history, the incredible miracle of falling in love is the story we keep telling again and again.

The time flies by quickly, and I'm lost in the magical kingdom of Onestia and the growing feelings between these two characters. It's a really beautiful story of self-discovery, learning to overcome adversity. Growing, changing, coming together. *That's the thing that a lot of people don't realize about romance*, I consider as I continue working. It's not just about the obvious parts—the kissing and the beau- tiful people and whatnot. It's about two people, who on paper seem like they shouldn't work together, realizing how much they have in common. Realizing how much they *need* each other. It's actually really sweet when you—

Then the first love scene begins.

Even though I can't see myself, I'm positive my ears are bright red. I keep glancing around the room to make sure no one can accidentally overhear what's playing through my earbuds, even though I have the volume on so low, *I* can barely hear the details. Nevertheless, I feel my body flush as the narrator's husky voice goes into long and lengthy detail about what exactly is happening—who's touching what and making what noise and who's putting what where. What exactly each character is feeling as it's happening.

The amount of detail honestly shocks and astonishes me. Not necessarily in a bad way. I've heard Helen read some of her stories out loud before, and those had almost as much description. But there's something more intimate about listening to these types of details in an audiobook. Like it's a secret the book and I are sharing together. Me, Khorum, and Theera. I feel as though I'm right there with them.

And then, to my surprise, I start to wish that what's happening in the scene was happening to me. And it all gets confusing, because a part of me feels like this *should* be shameful. I should have the strength to turn off the audiobook and put it away and never listen to it again.

But I also can't help but admit that I'm enjoying what I'm hearing. And that I'm desperate to know what happens next.

It doesn't take long before I realize that I won't be able to finish the audiobook before my shift is over. I know I won't be able to wait until tomorrow to hear what happens next, but I also know that I'll be too ashamed to listen to this type of story while I'm in the hotel suite with Uncle Aaron and Aunt Hope. The thought of somebody stumbling across the book—one of my cousins picking up my phone, or the app glitching and playing a chapter out loud for some reason— sends me into anticipatory spirals of anxiety and shame.

Luckily, I figure out that I can play the book on almost twice the speed to make it go faster. If I keep it up at this pace, then I might just be able to finish the story before I leave at the end of the day.

As the next few hours pass, I work in a frenzy, sewing on sequin after sequin until my fingers begin to blister, as all the while I am swept away in the romance of the fantastical kingdom. By the time I get to the end of my shift, and the end of the book, I've already downloaded the next two. Not as audiobooks this time, but as e-books I can read on my phone. It is still risky, since any one of my relatives could open my library app, but I figure it's safer than having something that could potentially play out loud and be overheard. Still, I vow to keep my phone with me at all times, just in case.

I don't know if Wes will be able to come to my room again tonight. It's got to be awfully risky for him to try to sneak away when he's already pretending to be someone he's not. Already putting his job at jeopardy, just to see me. But I find myself hoping very much that he'll be able to make it. He was on my mind the entire time I was listening to that story.

And I have a few things that I know now I really need to say to him.

Chapter 35
Wes

"Mountainettes," Chet Hodgkins announces in his ultrasmooth broadcaster voice, staring deeply into the camera's lens, "it's time to narrow down your contestants to your final three. These Mountain Men will be meeting your kinfolk and breaking bread with them."

We've reached another Axing Ceremony. In some ways, this is the one that will count the most. If Harmony chooses me, then I'll be meeting her family. I'll be meeting Aaron Miller. And sure, I doubt the guy will confess his white-collar crimes after chatting with me for an hour over dinner, but it will be first contact. My first chance to make an impression, to build a rapport with him.

Nate R. might be pretty boring in the personality department, but one thing I know about him for sure? He's great with parents. Respectful, deferential, trustworthy. The kind of guy you might want your daughter to marry. The kind of guy you might decide to take under your wing and bring into your shady family business.

I'm so close, I can taste it. Weirdly, it tastes like buffalo jerky—or maybe that's just because we had to eat half a pound of it in our last challenge before the Axing Ceremony, for reasons I'm not entirely clear on.

Of course, if Harmony doesn't choose me . . .

The heavily processed buffalo meat isn't the only thing curdling in my belly now. No. I can't let myself go there. Not now. Even if my thoughts have been full of Nina all day. Even if I dreamed about her all last night. Even if my heart feels empty when she isn't with me. Homesick.

Nate R. doesn't feel any of those things. Shaking my head, I do my best to clear my thoughts of anything but him and the mission I'm trying so desperately to fulfill.

Luckily, Harmony is the first Mountainette up to make her decision. One way or the other, I'll be put out of my misery sooner rather than later.

Harmony regards each of her four finalists—Everett, Kyle, Jake, and me—somehow managing to maintain a straight face even though tonight her outfit is almost as ridiculous as ours: a pink flannel dress, black boots, and a black beaver hat. For the record, we are each wearing overalls with no shirts underneath, a faux–fox face hat, and we're barefoot. I honestly am not entirely sure what weird mountain herbs Sienna Diaz and Raquel Ezra are smoking at this point, but this whole experience has been like a weird fever dream with banjos—and that's not even including the part where I reconnected with the nun I once met in prison.

"This journey has helped me grow so much," Harmony tells us. "For the first time, I feel as strong and steady as a mountain."

Keep a straight face, I remind myself. Nate R. would find this speech moving, not horribly cheesy.

"And I truly want to thank each of you for your role in that," she concludes, then turns to pick up the first ceremonial axe. "Everett—will you break bread with my kin?"

Beside me, Everett steps forward, taking the axe from Harmony. "I will," he tells her, before plunging the ceremonial axe into the love stump.

When he returns, Harmony regards us each in turn, her face solemn. "Jake," she says next.

I let out a breath as Jake goes forward to thrust his ceremonial axe into the heart-shaped stump. That leaves only one more axe for Harmony to give out. My heart is racing, my palms sweating, even though I still don't know what outcome I'm most hoping for. My entire body clenches as I wait to hear whose name Harmony will call.

After a long, dramatic pause, timed by the producers off-screen, Harmony is cued into picking up the third ceremonial axe. Another beat, before finally she says the name: "Nate R."

I'm so nervous that it takes my stupid brain a moment to catch up. That's me. I'm through to the final round. I'm going to meet Aaron Miller.

On shaking legs, I step forward, doing my best to smile my easy Nate R. smile as I stand before Harmony. "Nate R., will you break bread with my kin?" she asks.

"Absolutely." I grin broadly, like I don't have a care in the world.

I do, of course, but Nate R. doesn't. Nate R. wants this more than anything else he can imagine. Nate R. is all in.

As filming moves on to the next Mountainette, the remaining members of Team Harmony are ushered to a separate area away from the cameras. Everett and Jake are pulled to do their confessionals, leaving me with Harmony and her producer.

Harmony levels the other woman with a meaningful look. "Didn't you want to go check on the mics . . . ?" she asks her.

The producer nods way too vehemently for it to be convincing, unable to stop herself from glancing over at me. "Right. Of course. The mics . . ."

So, this obviously isn't about the mics. But I don't know that Nate R. would be self-aware enough to figure that out, so I pretend to be oblivious as the producer excuses herself to leave me and Harmony.

Alone.

My head swims. This is the first time we've really been alone together. No cameras on us. No producers shadowing us. There's a whole Axing Ceremony going on fifteen feet away, so no one's paying any attention to us. I wonder what it is that Harmony's so desperate to say to me.

I pretend to be oblivious to the situation for as long as I can, until Harmony clears her throat. We're standing so close that I can't pretend not to hear her. Forcing a smile, I turn to her. *You're Nate R.*, I remind myself harshly. *You like this girl.* "Wanted to get me alone pretty bad, huh?" I tease her with a wink.

I hate myself for all the winking. But what's done is done. And Harmony beams back at me; clearly she doesn't mind it so much. She coyly twirls a strand of her hair, smiling at me. "You know, you're my only contestant I haven't kissed yet."

Fuuuuuuuuuuck. It takes all of my self-control to keep my expression devoid of what I'm feeling right now. I'm blinking too much, but otherwise, I think I almost manage to pull it off. "Is that so?"

"You're meeting my family tomorrow," Harmony reminds me. "We're down to my final three. Don't you think it's time to pucker up? See if we have as much chemistry as I think we do?"

I feel sick to my stomach. It isn't Harmony's fault. If I were anyone else, if she was *someone* else in particular . . . But I can't help but think of Nina melting into my arms last night. She trusts me. I can't betray that.

Nate R. isn't betraying anyone, I try to remind myself, but it doesn't work this time. I can divorce myself from my own wants and needs in most things, but not this. Not from my own heart. It wants Nina, and only Nina.

"I'm waiting for engagement," I blurt out.

The words escape my mouth before I fully consider them, but now that they're out there, I realize I might be much smarter than I look. Even Morrie couldn't call me a complete idiot in this situation. Harmony's super religious. Thus, Nate R. is super religious. And sometimes, super religious people wait for physical steps in relationships (like kissing) until they've reached certain milestones (like engagement).

Holding my breath, I wait to see what Harmony's reaction will be. For a long moment, she stares at me blankly. Then blinking, stammering, she repeats, "To k-kiss?"

I nod, fully committed to this lie now. Drawing on the research I did into Aaron's church and ministry, I scramble to find the exact right phrasing that might sell this idea to her. "I know it's not conventional. But I made a promise to myself, and to God, that I would wait to share that gift with my future wife."

Is that coming on too strong? I never did much of the church thing growing up. We went on Easter and Christmas sometimes, but definitely not always. I feel like a total fraud trying to speak this language—which, hey, is fitting since I *am* a total fraud.

But something in the speech must ring true to Harmony, because she nods slowly, and I see her expression clearing as she absorbs the words. "That's certainly very . . ."

Wincing, I wait for her to finish that last sentence. Have I just shot myself in the foot? Is this thing over now?

". . . sweet." Harmony smiles at me, the lines in her face smoothing out so she's once again coy and adoring. "Your future wife is a very lucky woman."

I know I've pushed the boundaries far enough that I have to give her something back now. So, squashing down everything inside me that tells me I'm a liar and an asshole, I smile flirtatiously back at her. "I'm definitely very glad *you* think so." The strong implication there being that I want her to be my future wife.

Wrong. Wrong. This is all so wrong.

Harmony preens, clearly catching the subtext. "Can I kiss you on the cheek?"

"Of course." I tell my body not to tense as she leans into me, pressing her lips to the side of my face. Thankfully, I know Nina isn't here tonight, or else I don't know if I'd be able to keep myself from reacting more visibly.

When Harmony pulls back, I take her hand and squeeze it. "I can't wait to meet your family," I tell her.

At least that much is true, even if nothing else is.

Chapter 36
Wes

Come to the roof, I text Nina on her FBI burner phone. Somehow it feels safer that way; plus, it'll piss Morrie off if he finds out I was using it for this reason, so win-win.

I'm standing outside the Lodge, gazing up at the small window I know belongs to Nina. It feels hella romantic, even though I'm loath to make the inevitable *Romeo and Juliet* comparison. Romeo was kind of a doofus, and there's the whole thing where the play doesn't end so great for either of them. I want something better for Nina and me. I want to be . . . Flynn Rider. Here to set my girl free from her tower.

A moment later, a text chimes back from her.

Nina: I think you're forgetting the part where I'm not Spiderman?

I call her. She picks up before the first ring fully completes, her voice a hushed whisper. "Are you crazy?"

"We're in this beautiful place," I remind her, undeterred by her initial lack of enthusiasm for my incredible plan. "And I haven't gotten to see any of it with you."

There's a reason for that, of course. We can't exactly walk around town together. Someone from the show might see us. Someone from her *family* might see us, God forbid. And I know there are worse things than being cooped up in a hotel room with my lady fair, but knowing that Nina spends all her time either in a hotel suite or in the wardrobe room or on set has made me increasingly upset. There's a real magic to Green Valley, beyond just the ridiculously good-looking population. I want Nina to be able to experience it for herself.

From her pause, I sense she might be swayed, so I swoop in. "Sneak out of your family's suite. If anyone catches you, just tell them there's something going on with the show—a flannel emergency."

She huffs a laugh, and I can practically imagine her rolling her eyes at me. "Oh, of course, one of *those*."

"Then take the elevator to the top floor and find the staircase next to the ice machine. If you go up one more flight of stairs, there's a door marked Roof Access. I'll meet you there." Waiting for her response, I decide I might as well sweeten the deal. "And I have pie."

"I'll be there," she says quietly.

I'm grinning, even though I'm not entirely certain the pie wasn't more of a draw than me. Oh, well. As long as it gets her up there, where we can spend some time together, I'm happy.

As promised, I'm waiting for Nina once she makes it onto the roof. I'm guessing she had to work herself up to sneaking out, since she arrives a few minutes after me. It gave me time to spread out my picnic blanket and pop our champagne, so it was worth it.

I watch Nina as she takes in the sight—not just the picnic, but also the forest stretching out around us, the stars overhead, the moonlight glimmering off Bandit Lake. Her mouth falls open in what I hope is pleasant surprise.

I can't catch my goofy grin. There's something about Nina that makes me want to surprise her all the time. Good surprises only, of course. Anything that will make her smile. She deserves to smile much more than she does.

It takes me a moment to realize there's something . . . different about her tonight. My brain must be a bit sleep deprived because I spend way too long trying to figure out what it is.

Her hair has been freed from its usual long, neat braid, and combed into dark waves that reach almost all the way down to her waist. And she's wearing . . . a dress. I guess what she usually wears could technically be classified as dresses or skirt/blouse combos, usually a few sizes too big and covering up almost every part of her body so it's impossible to tell her shape underneath.

But this? This is a *dress*.

I don't know anything about dress types, but I can see her arms. Her beautiful brown, shapely legs. The material cinches in to show off her tiny waist, and the top of the dress is fitted to her body, scooping down to give the teeniest, tiniest hint of cleavage. On anyone else, I wouldn't look twice, but because it's Nina, and it's the tiniest hint of *her* cleavage, I have a hard time dragging my eyes away.

Swallowing, I lock my gaze on hers. "You look different," I manage dumbly.

Her dark eyes watch me closely. She tucks a strand of hair behind her ear. "Good different?"

"Beautiful."

It's a good word, but not nearly fitting for what I feel when I look at her. I want to call her my goddess and worship at her feet. I want to rhapsodize about her unearthly radiance. But I don't want to overwhelm her or spook her off—and anyway, as Morrie would doubtless tell me, it's probably better to ease into all the geekiness, little by little. Like trapping a frog in boiling water, but romantically.

Nina lights up, pleased by the praise, and she's so lovely it hurts. "I made it," she tells me shyly, smoothing her hands over the material.

"Shut the front door," I say. And not just because I'm trying to make her feel good—although that's something I always, always want to do, if it makes her this happy. But genuinely, the dress looks like something you'd see in the display window at a nice store, something a movie star would wear on a night out.

I could ask her why she doesn't dress this way all the time, if she's so good at making clothes like this, and she looks incredible. But the answer's obvious, isn't it? *Aaron Miller.* I've noticed that Harmony doesn't have to dress the same way as Nina. And from pictures I've seen in files of Nina's other cousins, they also don't have to dress like they're practically Amish. They all get to wear makeup and style their hair. But for some reason, Nina doesn't.

I've wondered for a while now why Aaron singles Nina out this way. Is it a control thing? A way to separate her from the rest of the family?

But bringing all of that up right now might dim the beautiful light shining from Nina's face, and I'd rather do just about anything than that.

So instead, I close the distance between us. Then, carefully, making sure I don't spook her, I reach out and admire the detailing on the hem of her skirt. I have no idea how it's made, but it looks intricate and pretty and like it obviously took a lot of time and effort. Running my thumb over the little bumps of thread, I smile up at her. "What a pretty costume."

To my surprise, Nina laughs—not in a mean-spirited way, but like she finds me hopeless and adorable. I can't help but laugh with her, even though I'm in the dark. God, I love it when she looks this happy. "What?"

"It's an outfit," she tells me, rolling her lip between her teeth. "Not a costume."

That thing she's doing with her lip is very, *very* distracting, but I wrench my eyes away from it to focus on the conversation at hand. "What's the difference?"

Nina furrows her brow, like this is the first time she's had to consider it. "A costume is something you wear to hide who you are," she decides finally. "An outfit is what you wear to reveal it."

I consider that for a moment. I think of all the different disguises I've worn, the different personas I've put on to distract anyone from seeing the real me. Then I think of the things I wear when I'm doing *GeekOut*, something that's just meant to bring me happiness. Arguably, those pieces of clothing—Legolas's ears, Jon Snow's cape—would be considered costumes by most people. But when I wear them, I feel the most like my true self. Maybe what I wear day-to-day is the real costume, then, and those chosen pieces of clothing I put on are my outfits.

"So what does this dress reveal to me about Nina?" I ask her, running the material between my index finger and thumb.

Nina flushes but seems to be taking the question seriously. "It's a classic silhouette, vintage inspired. It's simple but the more you look at it, the more you see." She searches my reaction.

I meet her gaze solemnly. "I want to see everything," I tell her.

Jedi's honor, I don't mean that to be an innuendo. I want to keep uncovering all the layers of Nina, to learn how to read each of her smiles. I'm in no rush for anything else, no matter how much I might want it. Delayed gratification is meant to be healthy for you, right?

So I'm surprised when Nina lets out a breathy moan and presses herself up against me—her body, her lips. Her fingers twining into my hair.

Surprised, but obviously not displeased. The Dread Pirate Roberts has been at alert from the moment I saw her in that dress, but I was trying to be a gentleman.

Screw that.

This is a pattern with Nina, I realize in the corner of my mind that's still capable of coherent thought as our tongues meet and tangle together. The way she lunges for me, so suddenly and so hungrily. It's like she's holding herself back as best she can, and all at once the dam breaks and she can't contain her desire anymore.

I eagerly respond, matching her fervor, using one hand to grab her hip and pull her in even closer to me. With the other, I let myself finally give in to the temptation I've been battling with all night and touch the smooth, soft skin of her legs under the fabric of her skirt. I skim my fingers over her knee, run my palm up the outside of one of her thighs. I stop just short of the swell of her perfect, round bottom, waiting for her cue to see if I can continue, as my pulse thrums in my ears.

Nina pulls back, and I release her immediately. To my relief, she isn't leaving, just fumbling with the zipper at the back of her dress. "Help," she pleads with me.

Whoa. Okay. That's what's happening now. I spring into action. After some more fumbling on my end, I manage to pull the zipper down. Nina sheds the dress like a skin she can't wait to get off her, standing so she can cast it aside, before turning back to face me.

She is so beautiful. I don't know how I'm expected to function like a normal human being when she is so perfect and sexy and lovely and standing right in front of me in only her panties and bra. I take in all the dips and curves of her. I've been imagining her for so long, I always wondered if I was just creating a fantasy, and now I realize that my imagination did not do her justice.

When I meet her gaze again, I find Nina watching me apprehensively. "I want to keep my underwear on."

I nod quickly. I want, *need*, to show her that no matter what happens tonight, I won't be disappointed. If she decides to stop right now, that's okay. If we end up only cuddling after this, that's fine. If she wants me to put on a clown mask, I'll for sure have some questions afterward, but I'll follow her lead. "You're the captain," I remind her, my voice rough with want.

Nina smiles at that, her shoulders relaxing. After a brief moment's hesitation, she steps back into my waiting embrace. I guide us carefully down onto the picnic blanket. *Thank God I brought a blanket.* I might just be the smartest man alive.

She is more measured now, less frantic, but no less intentional as she fits her body against mine.

I try to keep my own touch just as careful, to be cognizant to match the pace she's setting, even as my brain short-circuits at the sensation of my hands on her bare skin, so much warm, bare skin. I could spend all day, all night, just caressing it. Worshipping her. I don't know anyone more deserving of being worshipped.

As Nina settles into my embrace, the rhythm of her kisses begins to intensify, and I follow suit. When she turns her head to catch her breath, I trail my lips along her jaw, down her throat. The sound she makes will be etched into my memory forever. It's the sound I'll dredge back up the next time I take myself in hand, that moan of hopeless want, coupled with the memory of her soft and pliant against me.

Despite my best efforts to remain levelheaded, my pulse begins to spike as I lick and suck at the warm column of her throat and she moans again, squirming against me. The irrational impulse to bite down, to leave a telltale little red mark on her skin, begins to pound through my brain. Some inner caveman seems to have been unleashed inside of me, and I want to mark her, claim her, show everyone she's mine.

I can't. I won't. It would cause so much trouble. But I want to, desperately.

Unless . . .

"Lovely," I implore her quietly, "can I do this, but somewhere else?"

After a moment's hesitation, Nina nods. I pull back and rearrange us so she's lying on her back. Seeing her, splayed out and mussed and watching me with her dark, trusting, wanting eyes, I have to take a moment to regroup myself.

Then I lower my head so I can lick and suck and bite at the smooth inside of one of her thighs.

I'll just leave a teeny, tiny love mark. That's my plan, anyway. Dutifully I don't stray anywhere too close to the hem of her underwear, determined to respect her boundaries as I explore the softness of her skin.

But then Nina slides her fingers into my hair, gripping tightly, and she begins to rock her pelvis against the side of my face. She moans, that same frantic, almost hopeless sound as she seeks friction against her softness.

Oh, fuck. I don't want to push her boundaries, but my body responds immediately. Determination pulses through me—to quench that want, to give her whatever she needs, to make her feel as good as possible. Raising my head again, I search her face. "Nina?"

"*Wes.*" Her dark eyes lock on mine, wild with desire. She's still rocking her pelvis, searching for friction, for me, and the fact that I've pulled away even for a moment seems to have driven her close to desperation. "I want to . . ."

The words fade out, swallowed up in shyness, or maybe even shame. But this isn't one of those times when I can just let things go unsaid. I need to hear her say it. "What do you want, lovely?"

A long hesitation, in which I find myself holding my breath. *Nina,* I urge her silently. *Say it.*

"I want to come. Please."

Oh, hell yes. I'm so excited, my hands are shaking. I lower my head, but this time instead of focusing on her thighs, where I can already see a tiny, little red mark beginning to bloom on her skin, I take hold of her panties and wait for her nod of consent before I gently guide them over her hips, down her legs, and over her feet, casting them aside.

I've been dreaming of this pussy, of how soft and warm it would be, how good it would taste. It takes all of my self-restraint not to dive in tongue first. Instead I coax her to spread her legs, opening herself up to me. Oh, God. She is so perfect. So pretty and wet and waiting for me to help set her free.

I blow, softly, letting my breath tickle against her. Nina gasps, her hands finding my hair again and gripping on tight, frantically urging my face closer to her center. Fuck. She needs this. Still, I pace myself, trailing my fingers in light circles at the edge of her thighs, then letting my thumbs gently glide over her lips, spreading her open. I look up at her, over the length of her torso and the swell of her pretty, perfect breasts, and see her eyes dark and needy, her mouth open in soundless want.

Then I let myself go.

My tongue explores her every fold and crevice, mapping her terrain to my memory. Her hips snap up, seeking me out, a silent plea for more, and I give it to her, licking, sucking, swirling, until I reach the holy grail. When I begin to circle my tongue around her clit, Nina lets out a cry that is almost violent in its ecstasy. One of her legs loops over my shoulder, her heel digging into my back, spurring me on.

"Wes," she pants, her entire body tightening before she releases.

I soften the pressure of my tongue in response, not retreating fully, but gently coaxing out the remaining tremors of her pleasure. Fuck. That was so quick. I'm glad she finished, but I could have stayed here much, much longer, savoring each moment, each gasp, each thrust, each moan, for as long as possible.

But she's the captain, and I want this to be about *her* pleasure, not mine. So when Nina tugs me upward again, I take her in my arms, and kiss the top of her head, and hold her as she catches her breath, her heart pounding against me.

Chapter 37
Nina

I think I've been sewing the same stitch for the past five minutes. I keep catching myself doing it. I keep resolving to stop. But then my mind . . . wanders.

To last night. To Wes. His warm lips, his body moving against mine. My pulse spikes at the memory. I grip onto the fabric tighter. *Focus, Nina.* I *am* focusing, just on the wrong thing. His hands, touching me in secret, forbidden places. My teeth dig into my lower lip as my body flushes with heat. I'm remembering his soft breath against my thighs. And his tongue . . .

I've done it again, I realize, as I return to myself with a sharp, too-loud gasp. The same stitch. Shoot. Deja could fire me for this, and I wouldn't even blame her. The whole point of me staying back at the workshop was to make some headway on these masquerade dresses, and I haven't even finished the skirt I've been working on all day.

The way he looked at me last night in my pretty dress. The way his eyes lingered. Then how he looked at me *out* of my dress . . .

"Nina." A voice draws me back into the moment.

I blink at Deja in surprise. I can tell by the way she's looking at me that it likely wasn't the first time she said my name, either. "Hmm?" I ask, then shake my head. "Sorry, what?"

"I was telling you it's time to go home." Deja frowns at me, searching my expression. "Girl, are you okay? You look all . . . flushed."

I do my best to laugh as I ease myself up and out of my chair, abandoning the skirt for tomorrow. I'll be better able to focus then, after the family meet and greet is over. That's tonight. But I won't think about that. I'll remember Wes's promise to me last night, that he'll find me afterward and try to sneak me out of the hotel. Take me for a long drive, the windows down. Just the two of us. I wonder what he'll be wearing. I hope it's something that makes his eyes really stand out. They're such a beautiful green . . .

"Nina," Deja says again, bordering on irritated now. "Go home."

"Okay." The sooner I get home, the sooner I'll be able to go on my date with Wes. I'm so distracted by the thought that I miss the doorknob once, twice, before I manage to get it open. Then, smiling like an idiot to myself, I hurry up to the fourth floor.

I'd planned to make myself scarce once I got back to the hotel suite. Aunt Hope and the kids might've wanted my help getting camera-ready for the family meeting, so I thought I'd make myself useful, but otherwise I was going to hide in my room. If not, I suspected my excitement for tonight would be too obvious on my face. *Wes.* Being outside with him. Looking up at the stars. Holding his hand. Kissing and snuggling and . . . maybe more.

I couldn't wait.

Instead, when I step into the suite, I'm surprised to find my entire family, everyone who's here in Green Valley—sans Harmony—in the sitting area. They're already ready for the family meet and greet, even though that won't happen for another hour or so.

I stop in my tracks, taken aback by the sight of them all dressed up, looking at me solemnly. "What's going on?" A sudden, panic-filled thought struck me. "Is Harmony okay?" Maybe there was an accident on set. I can't think of any other reason why everyone would be looking at me this way. My gut tightens instinctively with fear. Something is wrong. Very, very wrong.

"Sit down," Aunt Hope instructs me tightly, motioning to a chair that's been positioned opposite the sofas where everyone else is sitting.

Second to Nun

Without meaning to, I glance over at Uncle Aaron. He is silent but watching me, and he has that look on his face that I've come to recognize well. He's about to teach me a lesson—and despite the somber expression on his face, I can see from the gleam in his eyes that he's really, really looking forward to doing it.

Oh, God.

Uncle Aaron knows. Somehow, he knows. About the undercover operation. Everything. I have to warn Wes. I have to do *something*.

Every instinct in my body is urging me to race for the door. But with Uncle Aaron watching me like that, any bravery I've managed to summon over the past few days deflates out of me like an old balloon. For so many years, he's been the one in charge, and I've been docile Nina, doing whatever he says. It's hard to shake that pattern, even after recognizing now that it's wrong.

Obediently I take a seat. My hands are shaking so badly in my lap that I clasp them together like I'm praying. Maybe I am. *Help me.*

As if taking my cue, Uncle Aaron finally speaks up. "Let's begin with prayer." We all bow our heads automatically, the most deeply ingrained instinct in the Miller household. "Lord, please guide us in holy paths. Please lead us away from temptation. Please save us when we have fallen so far from your grace."

I don't know if I've ever heard more ominous words spoken, especially when they're directed at me. This isn't the first time Uncle Aaron has preached at one of us directly through his supposed prayer to God, but the stakes are so high now. What does he know? Is it about Wes? Him being an undercover agent? Or what happened on the roof last night? Those memories are so special to me. What we experienced together was so tender, so *good*. But at the thought of Aaron knowing about them, berating me for them, I can feel the shame begin to creep in, distorting and tainting them into something I hardly recognize.

No. *No.* There is nothing shameful about what I did. I cling to that resolve, but it feels like a tiny buoy being tossed around in the waves during a storm.

"Forgive us for our weaknesses, Lord, and forgive us for our sins. Especially deceit and treachery. Making a mockery of the people who have given us welcome and shelter. Give us the strength to be transparent with our transgressions, and to ask the Lord for full forgiveness. Amen."

"Amen." I make myself say the word, even though it's chalky in my mouth. But it's possible Uncle Aaron doesn't really *know* anything, that he's just guessing.

And I refuse to do anything to allow him to point the finger of blame at me, even something as small as not properly closing off a prayer.

Silence stretches out for what feels like a very long time, though it's probably less than a minute. When I finally summon the courage to raise my gaze to Uncle Aaron's, he's watching me expectantly. "Anything you'd like to tell us, Antonina?"

The words are probably meant to be intimidating, but that last one—that formal use of my full name—gives me an unexpected surge of resolve. He doesn't know me. Not really. We've lived under the same roof for years, but we've been strangers that entire time. He couldn't tell you my favorite color or the foods I don't like or my hopes or dreams or what makes me laugh or anything even remotely important about me.

He's a stranger. Why should I give a single damn about what he thinks of me?

I cling onto that thought as I hold his gaze. It's easier said than done. My body still responds instinctively to him, my muscles tensing, my stomach roiling. Swallowing back the lump in my throat, I shake my head at him. "No."

The *no* clearly takes both him and Aunt Hope by surprise. I see the furtive look she casts his way. Uncle Aaron doesn't take his eyes off me, though. "Fine. Why don't we do some reading?"

The suggestion throws me for a loop, though I do my best not to let it show on my face. I'm so thrown off that when Uncle Aaron hands me some printed pages, I take them without question. My eyes scan the page, expecting some Bible verses that he will have selected to reprimand and shame me.

Instead, what I see sends bile shooting straight up to my throat.

Screenshots of the e-books I downloaded from the library—the ones with the sensual scenes in them. All my subterfuge to keep my uncle and aunt from noticing them was for nothing. They've been snooping through my things, looking for any reason to admonish me. And now they've found one.

Uncle Aaron—or, more likely, considering the amount of grunt work involved, Aunt Hope—has gone through the books and screenshotted some of the most lascivious passages. It must have taken some time to find all the naughtiest bits. Some distant, detached part of me half wonders if she enjoyed any of it. The books are well written, after all. They pack a strong emotional punch. Why shouldn't they be enjoyed?

Because people like Uncle Aaron want to make every pleasurable thing in life into a sin, that's why. Sex. Sugar. Beautiful dresses and silly reality shows. They want to use those things like battering rams to knock other people down and prove their own superiority.

"Read it," he instructs me now.

Startled, I look up at him again, making sure I'm understanding what he's asking me. He wants me to read this here, now, out loud, in front of my young cousins. He wants to humiliate me in front of them. And he wants to use me as an example to show them what will happen to them for experiencing completely normal, healthy feelings and urges.

Everything in me rebels against it. But if I don't? What will happen to me? I have nowhere else to go in Green Valley. Wes won't be able to break his cover, so I'll somehow have to find my way back to Chicago with no money, no phone (I'm sure my uncle will confiscate it if I refuse to give in to his commands). I'll be stuck.

Maybe I can appeal to his mercy. I force my hands to stay down at my sides, force my fingers to unclench. Try to appear meek and broken—just how he likes me best. "Please," I ask him quietly.

"Read it," Uncle Aaron orders me, and his voice is somehow both harsh and pleased. "Stand up."

After a moment's hesitation, I finally make myself rise to my feet, clutching the papers in my hands.

Before I can begin, Uncle Aaron addresses the rest of the room. "As you all know, children, we hold ourselves to very high standards in this family."

I'm not part of this family, I seethe silently. *Aren't you the one who's always reminding me of that?*

"So I was very disappointed when I received an alert on my phone that Antonina downloaded some books with highly questionable content. I thought to myself, these books must be work of high quality for my niece to so egregiously disobey our household rules. Why don't we let her read parts of them out loud to all of us, to see what we think? To see if they're worth exposing her soul to eternal damnation."

That's my cue, I guess. I grip the printed pages tightly in my hands, which are sweaty and shaking. Sick. I feel sick. But I don't know what else to do. "He grabbed the bodice of my dress in his hands . . ." I hesitate. Isaiah is *thirteen*. The twins are fifteen. This isn't right. Even if the words themselves aren't shameful, being forced to read them in front of children makes me ill.

"Read it, Antonina."

I'm sorry, I think to my cousins, before obediently continuing. ". . . and tears it open. My breasts come spilling out into the night air. He hungrily takes my nipple into his mouth, sucking as I . . . as I whimper and moan . . ."

I remove myself from the words as much as possible. I am just reading. I don't let myself fully comprehend what's written out on the page. I strip away any emotion and just read the words as blandly as possible. It isn't much of a rebellion, but it's as far as I can go without being censured.

Deconstruct this bullshit. I'm taking none of this with me when I go. I would rather burn down my entire house than keep any of this in it.

When I finish, the room is suffocatingly silent. No one will look at me. That's fine. I don't want to look at any of them either.

"Was it worth it, Antonina?" Uncle Aaron asks me.

I don't answer him, but that seems to be his desired response anyway. He doesn't want me to speak for myself. He wants me to wallow in my shame. I stare down at my lap and let him think my tears are from humiliation and not rage.

"Come on," Uncle Aaron instructs the rest of the family after a moment. "We have to get to the community center so I can give my sermon."

For all the times Uncle Aaron has berated me about making myself the center of attention, I can't help but notice that he's turned tonight into being about *his* sermon instead of the family meeting Harmony's potential future husband. *Hypocrite. Liar. Thief. User.* Now that the scales have fallen back, I can see Uncle Aaron for who he really is. *Abuser.*

"Antonina will stay here, of course," he continues. "So she can think about what she's done."

I sit quietly as they file out of the room. I'm afraid to move, afraid to breathe. I want him to think I'm broken, that I've been beaten back into submission. I want him to think that I'll spend the whole night crying here at the hotel.

But I won't. As soon as they leave, I'm going back to his room and getting onto his laptop.

I'm going to prove who he is, who he *really* is, once and for all.

Chapter 38
Nina

This time, I don't have to worry about being quiet or sneaky. As soon as my family leaves the suite, I make a beeline for Uncle Aaron's room. My blood is pumping hot with the shame of what just happened, but also something else. *Anger.* I am so, so angry about what he just did to me. About everything he's done to me.

If I were thinking more clearly, I might try to remind myself that there's still an active investigation happening that Wes is very much a part of. That I have nowhere to go if Uncle Aaron decides to kick me out. That I'm not supposed to go actively looking for evidence without Morrie or Wes giving me the go-ahead.

At the moment, it's hard to care. This fury has been building inside of me for years, maybe even since the first time I came to my uncle and aunt's home and they put me on parade for a bunch of strangers so they could fawn over how charitable they were for taking me in. And it continues to grow as I think about tonight—not just the way Uncle Aaron forced me to read aloud from my romance books, but all of it. I always knew that he and Aunt Hope had access to my phone, but I thought they just received notifications of my activity. I hadn't realized they could go into my apps, see what was on my screen.

The violation of my privacy makes me feel nauseated, and in no little part because I let it happen. Why? Why did I agree to have a parental control app on my phone like I'm a child? I'm not a child. I'm twenty-five years old! I should be able to read smutty books or get on social media or watch dumb YouTube videos or do whatever the hell I want, because it's *my* phone. Not theirs. I shouldn't have to use an FBI burner phone just to text my boyfriend for fear they'll see the messages and—

All at once, the truth hits me like a tidal wave, nearly knocking me off my feet. This whole trip, I've been wondering why I've heard so little from my friends. Then, when Grady visited, he told me he'd been texting me, but I'd never answered. With shaking hands, I pause my righteous quest for a moment to pull out my phone and search through my inbox.

There *were* messages from my friends, I realize. Lots of messages, that I *haven't* been responding to. Because they've all been marked as read, and the notifications must have been cleared from my phone while I was working. I read through some of them now:

Helen: I'm sure you're busy. Hopefully good things! Just let us know you're okay when you get a chance.

Matilda: Nina, this is urgent. Are you alive? I'm sending in a SWAT team.

Kimo: She is not sending in a SWAT team. But please let us know you're OK Peke

Kimo: I didn't mean for that last part to rhyme 😶

Grady: Nina's okay. I think. She might just need some time to process some things?

Thad doesn't say anything—he's not much of a texter—but I do notice there are some gaps in some of the conversations I've missed out on. Almost like . . . some messages have been deleted. If I were to guess, it's because my friends are saying things about my uncle and speculating about if he's holding me captive. (Matilda, most likely.)

I've always laughed off that idea when Matilda has made accusations like that in the past, but now I'm not so sure. How else would you describe this? He monitors my communication. He makes me follow his rules. He makes me work for him, doing all the household chores and extra labor. He controls what I eat, what I wear, how long I get to sleep, what I get to read, where I get to go, what I get to do with my time.

Second to Nun

I'm shaking with an odd mix of anger and pent-up energy, a scream building up inside of me that gets caught in my chest and won't come out. Storming toward the desk in Uncle Aaron and Aunt Hope's room, I slam doors behind me, knock over chairs, kick aside suitcases. The reckless gestures make me laugh, but in a way that isn't nice or even happy. *Burn it all down.* That's what I want. That's all I can do to quell this storm that's brewing inside of me, so it won't destroy me from the inside out.

This part of my story is done tonight. I refuse to let this be any part of who I am anymore.

Most of the drawers are empty, since it's a hotel desk, not Aaron's permanent workstation at home. What I do find is innocuous—a Bible (of course), a pad of paper with some notes scribbled down, some receipts that he's probably going to file once he gets home.

Then I see a folder, shoved into one of the lower drawers, all the way in the back.

Before I even open it, some part of me instinctively knows it's going to be important. When I open it, I'm expecting to find a bunch of files about Uncle Aaron, or maybe some church records.

Instead, the folder is all about me.

My birth certificate. My adoption records. My social security card. A detailed list of all of my expenses over the years—food, clothes, dentist appointments, etcetera. My passport—

My passport?

Cold floods through my body. I couldn't fly out to see Matilda and Kimo at Thanksgiving because I couldn't find my passport. That wouldn't have been a problem if my driver's license hadn't also expired earlier that month; I didn't bother to replace it right away because Uncle Aaron preferred for me to take public transportation to get around in Chicago, and Aunt Hope was keeping me busy preparing the hundreds of Thanksgiving care packages being offered by the church. Long story short, I was planning to renew my license once I got back from Hawai'i, and thought I would be fine flying with just the passport—until suddenly, the day before my trip, it was nowhere to be found. Uncle Aaron was there when I was frantically searching the entire house, desperate to locate it. And this entire time, he had it hidden away.

Why? Why pretend he was going to let me go, then hide my own passport away from me like I was a naughty child being punished?

Because he wanted to save face. Because he didn't want me to go, but he didn't want my friends to know he'd been the one to hold me back. Because even though the trip wouldn't have cost him any money, he didn't want to risk the chance that I'd leave and not come back. Because he'd decided long ago that I owed his family, so that meant they *owned* me in return.

"Fuck you," I whisper out loud. It's the first time I've ever, ever used that word, but God, do I mean it.

My resolve intensifies now. I have to find something, *something*, that can incriminate Uncle Aaron.

This time, when I open his laptop and type in his password, I don't bother carefully closing each file afterward. I don't care if he knows I was here, searching through his computer. In fact, I *want* him to know I've looked through all of his personal documents, all of his secret folders. Let him see what that feels like for a change.

Unfortunately, despite more tips from Morrie, I still don't really know how to make sense of a lot of the financial documents. Oh, well. I just open up Uncle Aaron's email and send Morrie anything that looks remotely important. I'll let him sort through all of that later.

We still don't know what's on the encrypted folder, so I leave that one alone, but I open other files at random, trying to find anything of interest. After what feels like rifling through hundreds of folders, I come across something interesting.

This particular folder seems to be full of voice memos. I click on one and am surprised to hear a voice I haven't heard in a long time: William Winthrop. He used to work for my uncle about fifteen years ago. I didn't interact with him much because he usually just came over to the house to speak to Aaron, but I do remember him having a gentle demeanor. He always smiled and looked into my eyes when he saw me. He remembered my name. That doesn't sound like much, I know, but so many people who came to visit Uncle Aaron would just follow his lead and pretend I wasn't there.

Curious, I continue listening.

"Is it legal?" William asks, sounding nervous.

"It's God's work," Uncle Aaron replies. *"We need to trust in His wisdom. His laws are not our laws, William. His ways are not our ways."*

"I understand, but—"

Uncle Aaron interrupts him, sounding irritated. *"I must have been mistaken. I thought I was working with a godly man."*

"You are! Aaron. You are. Just . . . let me wrap my head around it—"

I cut it off there. I don't need to hear anymore to know this will be important to Morrie. I send the clip to him, all the while wondering—why would Uncle Aaron keep a record of that conversation? Scanning over the folder, I see at least a dozen other voice memos, presumably all with similar types of content. Why hold on to things that could incriminate him as easily as any of the people with whom he was working?

Blackmail. Maybe I've been spending too much time with FBI agents now, but the answer comes to me pretty quickly. If any of his associates caught him embezzling, or tried to put a stop to anything he was doing, he had proof of their complicity, however reluctant or minor, to keep them quiet.

Disgusted, sad, enraged for these poor people who put so much blind trust into Aaron, I click on another of the voice files at random, dreading what I'm about to hear but hoping it might hold some further proof that will ensure Aaron pays for his crimes.

And I was right to dread it, I realize as the audio clip starts playing.

Because what I hear changes everything.

Chapter 39
Wes

As I approach the Green Valley Community Center with Morrie, I'm surprised to see how crowded the parking lot is. When the producers informed me they'd be filming my family meet and greet with Harmony at a community center, I thought maybe they'd blown all their budget on flannel and had to downsize. In my experience, community centers are usually heartfelt but ramshackle, rundown little places.

This place doesn't fit into that category, though. It's bustling and vibrant and feels like it might truly be the heart of the community.

I turn to Morrie, raising my eyebrows in surprise. "This place is hopping!"

"It's supposed to be the best-kept secret of Green Valley," he confides to me, like he's someone who's in the know about all the country's hot spots and he didn't just read this information on some blog.

(Don't let his exterior fool you. Morrie is a blog fiend. For all the guff he gives me about my obsessions, I've never seen someone get more excited about an alert from Medium.)

"Claire McClure got her start here, you know," Morrie adds, nodding at me meaningfully. No shade to whoever Claire McClure is, but unless she's in a bagpipe band or stars in a TV series with dragons in it, I'm pretty clueless about the wider world of celebrity.

Seeming deflated by my lack of enthusiasm, Morrie goes back into business mode. He motions to my ear, where a small earpiece is hidden. "Let's check it out one last time."

On the off chance that I somehow wind up alone with Aaron Miller, we're recording the conversation in case he says something incriminating. Hey, stranger things have happened, right? Just think about what Robert Durst admitted while he thought he was unmiked in the bathroom.

"Sure thing." I wait for Morrie to round the corner of the building before clearing my throat. "You still with me, Papa Bear?" I murmur.

Morrie's voice comes through on my end, sounding both clear and disarmingly close. "I'm begging you to stop calling me that."

"Mama Bear it is," I return without missing a beat. "Or would you prefer Baby Bear? I could shorten it just to Baby. Babe. Whatever makes you comfortable."

"Shut up, Ackerman," Morrie grumbles. "There's something seriously wrong with you . . ."

We approach the doors to the community center, and I exchange one last glance with Morrie as ourselves, before we become Nate R. and his producer, "Chris." This is a big moment. And looking at Morrie, I'm reminded that I'm not the only one who's been putting my life on hold to try and bring Aaron Miller to justice. For all our differences, I wouldn't trust anyone but Morrie to be here at my side.

I can tell Morrie is feeling something similar, even though he'd never admit it in a million years. Underneath all of his grumbling, he really does love me. Sweet little Baby Bear.

"You good?" Morrie asks.

My heart is racing. My hands are clammy. But I nod. "Yep. Let's do it . . ."

Morrie lets himself inside to alert the film crew we've arrived so they can get ready for the shot. After waiting a couple minutes as instructed, I step through.

It's difficult to ignore all the cameras in my face, along with all the people staring. Production crew, mostly, but there are also a ton of extras here tonight. Onlookers who will be making up the crowd, as well as some musicians up on stage. They're all Green Valley residents, from the look of them. I'll give you one guess how I can tell. In the crowd are a few faces I recognize, like Lyle and

Sienna and Rae and the woman from the bakery. I try my best to tune them out and to focus on—

Harmony approaches in a whirlwind of pink, nearly knocking me over with the exuberance of her embrace. I can't tell how much of this is put on for the cameras and how much is really her—but hey, I guess I'm not one to talk about being your true self. Pulling back, she squeals at the flowers I've brought along—one bouquet for her and one for her mother—and I get a better look at her outfit. She's wearing her trademark pink in the form of a pretty sundress, her long hair tied half up with a matching bright pink bow. A gold crucifix hangs prominently around her neck. She looks like Christian Barbie, if such a thing exists.

Good thing Nate R. is such a good Christian boy. I give what I hope is my easiest smile, aware of the cameras recording our interaction. "You're a vision," I tell her.

Harmony preens, faux shy. "Oh, you." She shoves me playfully, before glancing over her shoulder to where her family must be stationed. "Are you ready for this?"

"I've been looking forward to it," I say honestly. Because maybe after tonight, this will all soon be over. And then I can be with Nina.

She's not here tonight, thank goodness. It's going to be enough of a challenge putting on a show for Harmony's family, the cameras, the crowd, and Harmony herself, all while trying to make a good first impression on Aaron Miller. I don't know how I could possibly concentrate if I knew that Nina was observing the entire thing.

Harmony takes my hand, squeezing it as she guides me deeper into the gymnasium/auditorium. "My family can't wait to meet you . . ."

She takes me to her father first. This is the moment I've been waiting for, and I have to breathe through my nerves. Stay focused.

He sizes me up as I approach. His smile is camera-ready, wide but not especially warm. In his fifties, he's still a trim, handsome man, and with his all-American good looks and almost blindingly white smile, I can see why so many people have been so charmed by him.

But I don't think I'm imagining the hardness to him, too. Aaron Miller is very good at going through the motions of pretending to be approachable, but there's a wall up between us. "Nathaniel," he says, shaking my hand with a firm, too-tight grip. "Nice to meet you, young man."

It's a subtle move, but I clock it right away. The words sound nice enough, but that misuse of my name—Nathaniel instead of Nate—and the "young man" tagged on at the end are both designed to take me down a peg, put me in my place. Establish him as the top dog, the person I have to try and impress.

I do my best to mold myself into the person he so clearly wants me to be. Nate R. is eager to please, submissive. The kind of yes guy you might take under your wing if you were a shady criminal. "It's a pleasure to meet you, sir."

Aaron clearly likes the *sir* if his smirk is any indication. He gestures to the woman standing just behind him. "This is my beautiful wife, Hope."

Only after this introduction does Hope Miller step forward to greet me. I get the immediate sense that she doesn't do anything without Aaron's permission. Her smile is just as guarded as Aaron's as she reaches out to shake my hand.

"Very nice to meet you, ma'am," I say, handing her the bouquet I brought along for her.

I don't miss the quick glance she gives to Aaron, or the subtle nod he gives back, before she reaches forward to take the flowers. "Thank you. It's nice to meet you, Nathaniel."

After that, Aaron introduces me to each of Harmony's present siblings in turn: Isaiah, Merit, then Felicity. I'm surprised to note that Harmony's usually ebullient, vibrant personality seems muted in the presence of her father. It's not dimmed altogether, she's still her bright pink self, but like her mother, she seems to follow Aaron's cues carefully, not wanting to step out of line and draw his censure—or anger.

Once everyone has made their introductions, I look back to Aaron. It's a tactical move; I want to take every chance I can get to acknowledge him as the head of the household, since I know that will ingratiate me to him. "Your family is a credit to you, sir," I tell him.

Aaron reaches forward to squeeze my shoulder, too hard for it to be entirely friendly. Another assertion of dominance. "I look forward to hearing more about you and discussing your spiritual journey. But first"—he motions subtly toward the stage—"I have a few words to say."

Ah, yes, the price of Nina's internship on the show. Aaron somehow finagled his way into getting a few minutes of airtime for a short sermon. I do everything in my power to keep my distaste off my face. To look downright enraptured at the thought of getting to listen to Aaron Miller's bullshit.

I ought to win an Emmy for this performance. Best Undercover Agent on a Bonkers Reality Show.

As Aaron moves toward the stage, a man stops him by reaching out to shake his hand. Even from a few feet away, I can tell this isn't a Green Valley resident. He's all Hollywood, with his too-tan skin and too-white teeth and vaguely oily exterior. They converse deeply for a moment, gripping each other's hands in that way dudes who like to pretend they're macho alpha guys do.

Morrie must have noticed my interest from across the room. "Perry Seacrest. He works for the studio."

Ah, now I understand why those two are looking so chummy together. Two snake oil salesmen admiring each other's work. Nina told me about how this guy is trying to get her fired—yet another reason I'm glad she's not on set today.

After another moment of schmoozing, Aaron claps Perry on the shoulder, then breaks away, moving again toward the stage. One of the cameras focuses on him, but I can tell by the look on the cameraman's face that he's just as excited as I am to listen to what's about to follow.

Harmony squeezes my arm, leaning in closer to me. "Daddy really has a way with words," she murmurs, loud enough so only I can hear it. "And it will mean a lot to him if you can talk to him about what he has to say afterward."

She doesn't have to spell it out for me any clearer. The way to dear old daddy's heart is through flattery. That tracks with everything I've learned about Aaron Miller in my research. I smile back at her to show I understand, even if her tip is ultimately unneeded. I was already planning to pay very close attention to whatever he has to say.

Once Aaron reaches the microphone on stage, he waits for his cue from the producers to show they're ready to film. Then he breaks into a broad smile that's *almost* convincing. "My brothers and sisters in Christ. Welcome. My family and I feel so blessed to be here with you tonight."

I can feel the ripple of uncertainty in the crowd. If I had to guess, based on pure demographics, I'd assume most of the people here tonight are Christian. But it's also a public community center, and they probably aren't accustomed to such heavy-handed Christian sermonizing at their nondenominational gatherings.

One camera is still focused on Harmony and me, capturing our reactions, so I make sure to keep smiling, like I'm super enthusiastic to hear whatever it is Aaron has to say.

"One John, chapter one urges us to walk in the light and have fellowship with one another," Aaron continues in that polished, easy preacher voice of his. "And that's what I feel here tonight. Light. Warmth. Community. What a blessing it is to walk among others who are on the path of righteousness and to use our talents and our gifts to uplift each other. Can I get an amen?"

"Amen," someone from the crowd obliges.

Some of the crowd are warming to him. It's hard not to respond to his enthusiasm, his square-jawed charm. If I didn't know better, I might half believe his wholesome God-is-good act, because the words aren't all bad. Some of them might even be nice, if they didn't purposefully exclude anyone in the room who isn't Christian—and if they were sincere.

They aren't, though. That's the thing with Aaron. He isn't who he pretends to be.

Neither are you, a nagging voice in my head reminds me. It's the part of me that chafes against slipping into other people's lives, that loathes having to nod and agree when inside I'm rebelling against everything that's being said. It's all for the greater good, I know. But increasingly, it's becoming harder and harder to really feel that way. Stopping Aaron Miller is important. But being kept apart from Nina, having to pretend that she doesn't mean as much to me as she does, having to pretend to care for someone else . . . it doesn't feel right or good. It feels *wrong*.

"You know, one of the things I've always loved about the South—" Aaron stops abruptly, his eyes narrowing as he spots something in the crowd. Someone. For a moment, just a moment, his affable mask slips. "What are you doing here?" he blurts before clamping his mouth shut again—clearly irritated at himself for the slipup.

I turn to see who he's looking at. So does everyone else in the room.

It's . . . Nina.

My entire body tightens instinctively. *Nina's here.* Her presence is unexpected, and it's a problem, considering the show I'm going to have to put on tonight. But more to the point, it's a problem because of the way Aaron Miller is looking at her, the way his mask slipped, like he spotted a cockroach skittering across the floor instead of his niece. His beautiful, kind, smart, talented niece, who should never be made to feel less than, not by anybody.

"Be cool," Morrie tells me in my ear, as if he can read my thoughts. He doesn't have to. He can likely see what I'm feeling all over my face.

And so can the camera. I do my best to school my expression again, even though I can't help but let my eyes follow after Nina as she winds through the crowd.

At my side, Harmony grips my arm a little tighter. "I thought Daddy told her to stay home . . ." She sounds nervous, but also awed. It's obvious that no one, and especially not Nina, has ever dared to outright defy Aaron like this before.

And that's what Nina is. Defiant. The emotion radiates clearly in her body language as she cuts through the crowd. Aaron has started speaking again, sermonizing in his usual cadence, but almost nobody is listening to him; they're too focused on Nina and her determined march toward the stage.

An arm reaches out, stopping her. Perry. "Nina Delgado?" he asks her, looking pleased as punch with himself as he glances over at Sienna and Rae, who have also stopped watching Aaron onstage and wait, tensely, to see how this will unfold.

My gut clenches. He's finally caught her. Nina won't be able to lie; she just isn't very good at it, especially when she's called out so directly. She's going to get fired. I know how much the job means to her, what a lifeline it's been, and I preemptively ache for her.

To my surprise—and everyone else's, it seems—Nina just shrugs him off. "Yeah, I know. I'm off the show." She continues toward the stairs that will allow her access to the stage.

Even with one of the cameras still on my face, I can't help my jaw from dropping. What the hell is going on? Luckily, when I collect myself and glance over at Harmony, who clearly just overheard the same exchange, her expression is almost exactly the same. At least I'm not alone in being shocked by this turn of events.

By the time I turn back to Aaron, Nina has made it onto the stage. He's doing his best to pretend she isn't there, to keep speaking in his normal pandering tone, but his voice sounds strained, and it's clearly an effort.

She taps him on the shoulder. He ignores her. So she does it again, this time raising her voice loud enough to be picked up by the microphone.

"Hey. Hey! I have something to say."

Chapter 40
Nina

I've come to the community center charged on pure adrenaline, pure anger, pure rage. I hardly notice my family as I pass them, or Lyle, or Sienna, or Rae. Even Wes barely registers as a blip in my peripheral vision, I'm so focused on Uncle Aaron. It's time to finally hold him accountable. It's time for everyone to see who he truly is.

But the look he gives me when he finally turns to face me on the stage stops me cold. Uncle Aaron has never liked me. He's never been warm. He's never made any secret about the fact that he doesn't want me in his family. But this outright contempt in his eyes is something wholly new.

His face is turned away from the crowd and the cameras, back toward me, so only I can see him. Only I can see the way he's looking at me like I'm a disgusting little bug he wants to squash under his shoe.

Suddenly I'm seven years old again, trying to reach out and hold his hand in church, only for him to shake me off him and walk away. I'm fifteen, raising my arms and kneeling so he can check the modesty of my outfit, knowing he's doing so because he thinks I'm so inherently sinful that I must be trying to get away with something. I'm twenty-two, returning to his house after leaving my postulancy, seeing in his expression that I've just confirmed everything that he already thought was true.

I freeze.

I can't help it. I don't want to do it. I promised myself I wouldn't when I made the decision to come to the community center so I could confront him. *Never again,* I'd promised myself.

But old instincts die hard. For years, *years,* I've been trying to win Aaron's approval, capture even the tiniest morsel of his love. Even with everything I know now, it's hard to face him, knowing he's displeased with me.

Seeming to realize he's gained some ground, Aaron lowers his voice to a menacing whisper. "Get. Off. The. Stage."

I'm too frozen to do even that. If my flight instinct could kick in right about now, that would be helpful. For the first time, I become fully aware of all the lights, the cameras, and the people witnessing this moment. Desperately, I search the crowd for Wes, but the auditorium is too dark, the stage lights too bright, and it's impossible to pick him out.

No. If I'm going to overcome this, I can't wait for him to help me do it. *I* have to be the one to set myself free.

I think again of seven-year-old me. Fifteen-year-old me. Twenty-two-year-old me. It feels too daunting—impossible even—to face Uncle Aaron for myself. But for them? For the girl I was? For all the other people Uncle Aaron has hurt and will hurt if he keeps lying and cheating and charming his way through the world?

I have to.

Something shifts in me. I *have* to. Dragging my eyes away from the crowd, I focus my gaze again on Uncle Aaron. He must see that something in me has changed, too, because he takes a step back.

"I have something to say," I repeat. I'm not shouting this time. That isn't me. But my voice is firm. I won't falter this time.

Taking advantage of Aaron's changed position, I push in closer to the mic stand, talking hold of the microphone. If he wants it back, he's going to have to snatch it away from me—and the optics on that won't look good for him. Uncle Aaron has always cared so much about optics.

"I'm Aaron Miller's niece," I tell the crowd. My voice is so unexpectedly loud coming through the speakers that I instinctively flinch from the sound, but nevertheless, I force myself to keep going. "He and my aunt adopted me when I was a child."

I sense more than hear the uncertain murmur coming from the crowd. They don't know where this is going. They think this might be a nice story. It isn't.

"From the time I was a little girl, Aaron made me work to earn my keep. By the time I was a teenager, I'd taken over almost all of the household upkeep. I was a live-in housekeeper and nanny, but I never got paid. Instead, he kept a running tally of everything I ate, anything that was bought for me—toothpaste, deodorant, tampons."

I hold up the ledger that I took from the suite's desk; no one in the crowd will be able to see what's on it from this distance, of course, but I feel more confident knowing that I have proof in my hands. "Even when I became an adult, he held on to all my legal documents. My birth certificate. My social security card. A few months ago, my passport went missing, and I found out why when I looked through his desk tonight." I take it out of the folder and show it to them, too. "He was keeping this from me to make sure I couldn't leave without his permission. He wanted to control everything about me, from what I wore to what jobs I worked to what I ate."

As I've spoken, the outrage has started building up in me again. I'm almost grateful for it, because I know I won't freeze now. I've broken free. And I'll never go back in my cage again, not without a fight. "But that isn't the worst of it. Tonight I discovered that he's been using an app to monitor my text messages and screen mirror everything I look at on my phone."

A murmur of unease rises in the crowd. The picture they had of Aaron Miller in their mind is starting to rearrange. Good. But I'm not done yet. "And it gets even worse. Tonight I found a recording of a conversation I'm sure he never wanted me to hear."

I meet his gaze then because I want to see the look on his face once he realizes what I've unearthed. What truth I'm about to tell the world.

This isn't the only recorded conversation I found tonight, of course, and it isn't even the most inflammatory. There are some very legally questionable things I uncovered that I've already emailed to Morrie. But this one won't interfere with the investigation. It might not even affect him legally at all. It doesn't matter, though. This one is for me.

Aaron's face drains of all color. I feel the sweet satisfaction of it. He knows. I'm about to ruin the image of himself he's spent so many years building, and he knows it.

Ignoring the optics now, Aaron reaches forward, jerking the microphone stand away from me.

There's not much I can do about that; he's stronger than me. But I retreat across the stage, turning back to face the crowd and raising my voice to a shout. "When I was eighteen years old, a man who was a regular guest in our home told me he loved me, and I believed him."

I leave out the part where that man was my cousin Miriam's fiancé—not to protect myself, but to protect her. None of this is her fault. When she finds out, I want it to come from me, not from a television show.

"I'd never had a boyfriend before. Never been kissed. Never held hands with anybody." My voice is already raw from how loudly I'm shouting my truth out to the world. I feel a little unhinged, honestly, but in the best way possible. I wish my friends were here to see this. I know they would be so very proud of me. "So I was easy prey for him when he told me he was in love with me. When he pressured me into sleeping with him to prove I loved him, too."

The reflexive shame tries to wedge its way into my mind, but I force it back, unwilling to let it take hold of me. This isn't my shame. It's his. "Afterward, he made it seem like I was the one who initiated everything. He confessed to my uncle, and they both made me feel so . . ." For the first time my voice falters, but I push on. "Wrong. For doing something so normal. Something that came from what I thought was a place of love. It wasn't wrong." I'm saying this more for myself now than anyone listening. "I didn't do anything wrong. But they made me feel *so much* shame for it. Afterward, he got to go back to his life just like it had been before. And I was packed up and sent away, the horrible family secret. I've always felt so terrible about what I did. I convinced myself I must have misremembered things, that I must have been so much more sinful than I'd ever realized."

I reach into my cardigan pocket, withdrawing my phone. "But tonight I found a conversation between them that Uncle Aaron recorded."

Glancing over at him, I make sure he hasn't advanced on me. He hasn't, but his face is red and his shoulders are bunching up high, and I know it's only a matter of time before he snaps again. I have to act quickly.

"I think I'll let the rest speak for itself," I say, before I press play on the copy of the voice recording I sent to myself.

I've turned up my phone's speaker volume as loud as it can go, but without the microphone, it's still going to be hard for everyone to hear. Luckily the room is absolutely silent, all those faces in the crowd watching, listening.

"I understand the temptation." Uncle Aaron's voice comes through clearly. *"Believe me, I do. A lot of people like us who do missionary work in poverty-stricken countries develop—what's the phrase for it? Brown fever?"*

Ugly male laughter follows, from both him and Micah—Miriam's then fiancé and now husband. My stomach curdles all over again just listening to it. *"There's a lot going on under all those long, loose dresses,"* Micah confides, sounding clearly at ease about saying such objectifying things since he knows he's in good company.

"Why do you think I make her wear the long, loose dresses?" Uncle Aaron replies with another laugh. *"I could be in a lot of trouble otherwise. She's a very . . . well-developed girl."*

Bile rises in my throat. The way they say it, it puts all the blame on me, like I'm the reason these two adult men couldn't keep from sexualizing a girl who was barely eighteen.

"Take my advice, though," Aaron continues. *"I've gone down the same path. I was lured in by a beautiful face and a tempting body, and I made a wife out of her. We've made the best of things, but I've had to do a lot of work to keep her in check. A lot of work."*

I wonder what Aunt Hope is thinking, hearing that spoken out loud. It's hard to feel entirely sorry for her, since she always took Aaron's side, since she let him treat me like the family's dirty little secret all these years, but still. I wonder if after jumping through every single hoop he set out for her, time and time again, she's surprised to hear it still was never enough.

"You'd be much better off with a good, godly girl. A proper wife who knows her place." He's speaking about Miriam here, trying to urge Micah back to her, but I double-checked the recording to ensure he never mentions her by name. *"Have your fun with Antonina if you like. Bed her if you want. Get it out of your system. Then marry the right kind of girl."* He chuckles again. *"But you're still single now, aren't you? Might as well enjoy yourself—"*

I'm not sure why Aaron waited this long. Maybe he forgot just how bad this conversation actually was. Maybe he got a taste of what it feels like to be frozen in place, unable to move in a moment of crisis. But suddenly he's on me, his hand clamping down on my shoulder, wrenching me back so he can snatch the phone out of my hands.

It all happens so fast, I don't hear if the crowd reacts. I don't even know if I scream or try to pull away. All I'm aware of is one voice, cutting through the crowd.

"Get your fucking hands off her!"

Chapter 41
Wes

The next few minutes are completely surreal. Watching Nina stand up to Aaron and air out all his dirty laundry is so unexpected, and I am so fucking proud of her. Then pride morphs into outrage on her behalf as I listen to the story of how he basically pimped her out to some creep in his church, the audio recording of their conversation sending my blood boiling.

But none of that is anything compared to the moment Aaron lays his hands on her. Pure and blinding fury washes over me. I'm not thinking rationally. And I'm not thinking tactically. Tactically, I'm still Nate R., and even though Nina has just revealed some very incendiary things about Aaron's character, we still don't have the proof we need to file charges.

The second Aaron grabs her, though, I stop being Nate R. Nate R. is dead. There is no way in hell I can just stand by and watch that.

I don't realize what I've said out loud until several heads in the crowd swivel to stare at me. With what's going on onstage, it would have to be something pretty wild to draw away any attention from that spectacle. As soon as it clicks for me—that I've outed myself and Nina—it's hard to care, especially when he's still clutching her shoulder despite her best efforts to squirm away.

"Let her go!" I shout again, pushing my way toward the stage.

Luckily I'm not the only one moving. Someone closer to the stage throws their shoe at him. "Let go of her, asshole!" I recognize the voice as being Deja's.

Lyle gets onto the stage before me, shoving Aaron back and away from Nina. His normally affable features are twisted with outrage. "Big tough guy, huh, picking on a girl half your size? Why don't you try that with me?"

Aaron backs away, and Lyle uses his body as a physical barrier to keep him from getting any closer, so I'm able to move directly to Nina once I make it onto the stage myself. Shaking, she grips me tightly as soon as I get close. There are tears in her eyes, and the sight of them makes my gut clench. But I see, too, the way she keeps her chin up, even though she's clearly trying not to cry. I'm still buzzing with anger and adrenaline, yet I can't help but soften at the sight of that. She is so fucking strong, my Nina.

"I'm so proud of you," I tell her quietly, aware of the people still watching, the cameras still capturing all of this. It's starting to catch up to me, what I've just done, but I'm finding it hard to care. I keep my gaze locked onto hers. She's the only thing that matters in all of this.

Her eyes dart back and forth between mine, and I can see the pieces clicking into place for her, too. "What about the investigation?" she whispers, not wanting anyone to overhear her.

I don't care. I should care, but I don't. I cup her face in my hands. "I'm so proud of you," I tell her again.

"What the hell?" a voice calls out from the auditorium.

Harmony.

Even though I wish I could keep drowning out the rest of the world, the moment of reckoning is here. With a bracing sigh, I turn to face the crowd, angling my body between them and Nina. If there's going to be blowback from this, I want it to land on me, not her.

I hold up a hand to block out some of the stage lights. I can see Harmony, her face incredulous, her hands on her hips. Sienna and Raquel are farther back, both of them uncharacteristically discomposed: Sienna's mouth is open, and Raquel's eyebrows are up so high they're almost to her hairline.

Wincing, I seek out Morrie in the crowd. He is going to be so, so pissed. But to my surprise, he isn't even looking at me. He's texting something furiously into his phone—probably reporting me to Agent Decker, getting the paperwork started for my firing. God, it's going to be a lot of paperwork.

"What the hell?" Harmony repeats. I can't tell if she's really that outraged, or if she's just as flabbergasted as the rest of us.

"Harmony!" Aaron chides her from the stage. "Language."

I can't help but give him my most scathing look. After everything that was just revealed about him in these last few minutes, he still has the gall to chastise his daughter for (mildly) swearing. "Fuck off," I tell him, enjoying the look of astonishment on his face. He isn't used to being told off. Between Nina and Lyle and me, this is the third time it's happened tonight. I have a feeling, after the way Nina told her story, it won't be the last time.

Glancing back at Morrie again, I realize there's still a way I can salvage this. My position as one of Harmony's contestants is clearly over, but there's no reason anyone needs to connect this back to the FBI. Maybe they'll be able to send in an undercover agent another way, once the dust has settled. "It's true. I was one of Harmony's contestants—just a normal guy from Small Town, Tennessee . . ." That's probably laying it on too thick, but maybe people will think I'm just shell-shocked from having to make this confession on camera. "But I fell in love with her cousin."

Too late, I realize it's the first time I've used that word. *Love*. At least out loud. It wasn't exactly how I'd planned on sharing my feelings with Nina, but it's too late to take it back. And I don't want to. How could anyone see what she did on stage tonight, how fearlessly and ruthlessly honest and brave she was, and not be head over heels?

Her hand slips into mine. She gives it a squeeze.

I swallow back the lump in my throat. "So obviously, I'm going to have to leave the show now. I hope Nina will come with me." Far away from these lights, these cameras. Away from Aaron Miller. Somewhere quiet, just the two of us.

She squeezes my hand again.

From the way the crowd starts murmuring, I think maybe we've pulled it off. No one suspects that I'm anything but one of the contestants who fell in love with a member of the production crew. It can't be the first time it's happened on a show like this. Still gripping Nina's hand tightly, I glance over to make sure Lyle is keeping Aaron at bay, then start walking with her toward the stairs so we can make a quick and (hopefully) quiet exit.

"FBI!" Morrie shouts from the crowd.

Goddammit, Morrie, I was covering our tracks! Astonished that he would break cover this way, I stop to look at him.

Morrie is rushing toward the stage, brandishing his phone. "FBI!" he shouts again. "I have a warrant for Aaron Miller's arrest."

It's my turn for my jaw to drop. The crowd erupts in noise. Morrie's almost to the stage, but Aaron has started backing away, like he might try to run for it.

I guess it's time for me to finally drop my cover, too. "FBI!" I shout and make a beeline for him.

Sure enough, Aaron spooks and runs toward one of the backstage exits. He's pretty quick, but I'm younger and faster, and I have the added bonus of the classic *Mission: Impossible* theme song playing in my mind from all the times I've done speed-running training, trying to be as fast as Tom Cruise in his prime.

I take enormous pleasure in tackling Aaron Miller to the ground. Morrie joins me a moment later, slightly out of breath from all that running. (I bet he wished *he* trained with Lalo Schifrin's music now. Maybe he wouldn't be so winded.) "You wanna do the Miranda warning, or should I?"

"It would be my greatest honor," I return, pleased as punch. Aaron tries to wriggle out from underneath me, so I use my knee to pin him between his shoulder blades. "Aaron Miller, you have the right to remain silent. Anything you say can *and will* be used against you in a court of law . . ."

After the dust has settled and Aaron has been removed into custody with the help of local law enforcement (who, luckily, happened to be on-site—apparently the sheriff's deputy Jackson James always comes to these community center events), I check in quickly with Morrie in the parking lot. We'll need to follow after the police units shortly, but we have at least a few minutes to debrief.

"So what'd we get him on?" I ask. I assume something must have come up outside of our investigation here in Green Valley; maybe one of the witnesses was finally able to provide evidence.

"It was Nina," Morrie informs me. "She sent me a bunch of files from Aaron Miller's computer. I couldn't go through all of them while I was in the audience watching *that* shitshow unfold, but I heard enough to send it on to Agent Decker. Plus all that stuff Nina was saying onstage . . ." He shakes his head grimly.

My jaw clenches. I know what he means. All the controlling tactics Miller used on Nina—withholding wages, hiding her passport. Her situation was much, much worse than I realized. "Human trafficking?" I guess.

"Enough to make a solid argument for it, if Nina's willing to give a statement and present proof." We both know she will. Morrie continues, "And at least enough to use probable cause to search his computer. Decker was able to get through an emergency e-warrant while that soap opera was happening onstage."

He's not talking about the Aaron Miller stuff now; he's talking about me, making a fool of myself by rushing up onstage and shouting dramatically about the woman I love. Whatever. He can mock me all he wants. It was badass, and we both know it.

"It was a good strategy," Morrie adds. "Distracting everyone long enough to buy time for the warrant to come through."

He meets my gaze. He knows that wasn't what I was doing. And he also knows I almost blew my cover and wrecked the entire investigation.

He's giving me a gift. A lifeline. Honestly, I'm not sure I want it anymore. I'm not sure this life is for me. I want to help people, but I don't know if I can go on pretending.

But Morrie claiming my actions were motivated by strategy buys me some options. And it proves that deep, deep, *deep* down, he loves me just as much as I love him. If I thought he would accept a manly embrace, I would offer it, but instead I clap him on the shoulder. I can't resist needling him just a bit, though. "Thanks, Papa Bear."

He rolls his eyes at me, immediately moving away. "Ruin it. You always ruin it, man . . ."

With that all settled, I backtrack, overcome all at once with the need to find Nina, just to make sure she's all right, before I have to go down to the local jail. Aaron Miller is in custody, so I know she's physically safe, but I need to know she's okay—

Before I can make it even a few steps, I see her. She's standing outside the auditorium, waiting for me. I run to her, shamelessly, needing to be near her, and she runs to me.

We meet in the middle, half colliding against each other. I pick her up in my arms and hold her as tight as I can. I have to leave soon, I know, in just a few minutes; but I also know I don't want to leave her, not ever again.

"You did so good," I tell her. She doesn't even know the half of it yet. I can't wait to tell her how amazing she really was tonight and what she managed to accomplish. It's too complicated to explain, though, in the short amount of time we have, and I just want to hold her. I need to hold her. "You did so, so good."

She clings onto me just as tightly. She's so strong, but somehow she seems to need me as much as I need her. I don't know what I did to deserve her, in this life or any other, but I feel like the fucking luckiest man on the planet. I'm going to spend the rest of my life being the man she needs me to be.

Not Cass. Not Nate R. Just *me*.

Chapter 42
Nina

Before he leaves for the police station, Wes gives me his credit card so I can book a room at a hotel. I wish I could pay for it myself, but I don't have access to any money; the salaries for the various odd jobs I worked over the years always went toward paying back my debt to Uncle Aaron and Aunt Hope. Maybe now all that will change now that Aaron is in custody.

He's in custody. He's been arrested. Wes couldn't tell me much, but it's enough that the FBI thinks they can make a case against Aaron and get him sent to prison. His days of hurting people are over.

Over, but not forgotten. Now that the night's adrenaline has worn off, I feel shaky and exhausted. All I want to do is crawl into bed. I don't know what will come next, but hopefully Wes and I can figure it all out together. After he's finished with his business at the police station. And after I've had a chance to get some sleep.

Lyle—dear, sweet Lyle who jumped onstage to protect me from my uncle—offers to drive me to a hotel. I know staying at the Lodge would be more convenient, but it feels too close to my family, to my memories. I need some distance.

Unfortunately, there isn't much else in terms of lodging in Green Valley. "I can catch a bus up to Knoxville," I tell him. I'm sure he must be tired, too; and now that I've basically blown up his show, he's going to have a lot of work to do.

He looks at me like I've deeply offended him by making the suggestion. "Over my dead body," he says, and ushers me out to his car.

We're silent most of the drive. I know Lyle would let me talk to him if I wanted to, but I need time to process. To think. I stare out the window at the beautiful forest. I can't help but remember Harmony's excitement as we drove into town. *Harmony.* She's going to be absolutely devastated for so many reasons. Her father has been arrested. The show is over. Nate R. never existed, not really.

I'll think about that, and her, later. But for now, I give myself some space to think about myself. About what *I* went through tonight. About what I was able to accomplish.

Catching a glimpse of my own reflection in the car window, I give myself an encouraging nod. Somehow it helps, even though I'm only talking to myself. Maybe that's where it starts sometimes—silencing all those ugly outside voices. Maybe the first step is to be kind to myself, to show grace to myself, and to forgive myself for all the times I wasn't as strong as I wish I would have been.

No more freezing, I tell myself silently. *You can only move forward now.*

It's a start, at least.

Once I'm checked into a hotel in the suburbs just outside of Knoxville, Lyle makes sure I'm settled in before he heads back to Green Valley. Alone in the room, I take the opportunity to first delete the app my uncle and aunt have been using to track my activity, with the help from a handy YouTube tutorial to make sure I've severed the connection completely; then to message my friends and tell them what's happened, or as much as I can possibly explain over text.

It's late, and I don't expect to hear back until morning, so I'm surprised when my phone starts blowing up with replies. Most of them from Matilda.

Matilda: Nina, come home now!!!

Matilda: I just booked you a plane ticket.

Matilda: Never mind, I'm sending you a plane.

I don't know where to even begin to respond to all of that, so I send the GIF of the little boy who starts out laughing and then abruptly starts crying. That about sums up my mood right now.

After a few minutes of presumably talking his wife down, Kimo joins in:

Kimo: We'll come to you in the morning. I've set it up for everyone who can make it. You ok with that Peke?

After a moment, a few more chimes follow.

Grady: I'll be there.

Helen: We'll be there, too.

Thad is part of that we, obviously, but even *he* chimes in with a thumbs-up emoji. Coming from Thad, that's a pretty big deal. I feel honored.

I'm happy my friends are on their way. I'm excited for them to meet Wes, and for Wes to meet them. But I realize that before they get here, there are a few things I'll need to take care of.

Even though I know I don't need to, I write two letters—one to Harmony, and one to Aunt Hope. I know I could just text them, but somehow a text doesn't hold the same weight to it. I want them to have a physical letter, my handwriting, my words written out in permanent ink—something that isn't easy to delete or ignore.

I write to Harmony first, because for some reason, I feel like I have the most explaining to do to her.

Harmony, I know you probably don't want to hear from me now, or maybe ever again. I understand if you feel that way. I just want you to know, it was never my intention to hurt you. It's a long, complicated story, but I knew "Nate R." long before he was a contestant on the show. If you're interested, I can tell you more about it some time. But I don't want to try to justify hurting you, because I know I have, and I won't try to excuse that. Please know that I love you and that I'm here if you ever need me. Always.

Love,

Nina

. . .

Aunt Hope's letter is more complicated in many ways. Despite everything, I can't help but feel some residual guilt that I've destroyed her life as she knows it —or at least, I know that's how she'll see it. Never mind what Aaron Miller did to cause all of this. Aunt Hope has lived with her head buried in the sand for so long that she'll seek blame for the disruption of her peace, not for the actual cause of the rot in her family.

Some part of me still feels like I owe her for everything she did for me. But when I try to sit down and write a sympathetic letter to her, I find that I can't. So instead I write the things to her that I realize now I must have always wanted to say, but never felt brave enough to try—not even brave enough to think.

Aunt Hope, please know I never wanted to hurt you. If I could have protected you and the kids, I would have. But I can't help but wonder, why didn't you try to protect me, too? I was a child when I came to you. Did you really have no idea how many lives Aaron destroyed? Even if you didn't, you definitely knew about all the ways he alienated me from the rest of the family. You knew that he treated me more like a servant than a niece. You knew he took every opportunity possible to remind me of my place. I never asked for money, for nice things. I never wanted to take away anything from the rest of you. Why couldn't you have just loved me? Why did it always have to be conditional? Why did you make me earn everything I was given, all the tiny scraps that weren't nearly enough to make me feel safe or happy?

Despite how it might seem, this wasn't an act of revenge. In some ways I feel sorrier for you than anyone else. He took so much from you, maybe you didn't have anything left to give to me.

Nina

. . .

I don't expect to ever hear a reply from either one of them. But I realize in both cases, these were things I needed to say.

Life isn't a fairy tale. I know that now. There won't always be a tidy resolution. Wrongs won't always be righted. Some things might be left open-ended. But I think it's time, for the very first time, to take control of my own story.

Happy endings aren't just handed to you, after all. Not in the best stories, anyway. Sometimes you have to fight for them, to really earn your happily ever after.

I pull up Lyle's number and send him a quick message: **I know I destroyed the show. But I think I might know a way to save it . . .**

Chapter 43
Wes

By the time I make it up to Knoxville, it's already midmorning the next day. As usual, the paperwork and processing for the arrest took much longer than they make it seem like in the movies. God, I wish real life was more like the movies sometimes. For so many reasons. Lack of paperwork being close to the very top.

Nina texted me the address of the hotel and the room number she's staying in, so I know she's okay. But until I see her again, hold her in my arms, I'm uneasy and restless. I speed way faster than I should in the lumberjack truck that I "borrowed" from set (what? I'll give it back) and make pretty decent time, if I do say so myself.

The one consolation I had for how far away Nina has been from me this whole time is that she's also been far away from her family. I doubt any of them would do anything to her now that Aaron's been arrested, but sometimes people don't always respond rationally. Still, I've hated the thought of her being up here all alone.

So imagine my surprise when I near the hotel room and hear voices—multiple voices—sounding from inside.

Nina. I raise my hand to pound on the door, positive that I'm going to find the Miller family chewing Nina out for airing Aaron's dirty laundry, or worse. "Open up!"

Instead, when the door opens, I see Nina waiting for me. Just Nina. She must read the worry on my face because she smiles and nods at me. It's a certain, sure nod, like I'm the one who's just been through a life-changing, distressing incident and need to be reassured. "Everything's okay. Come inside . . ."

Too confused to do anything else, I follow her into the hotel room—where I find Lyle, Sienna Diaz, and Raquel Ezra waiting for us.

Seeing any of these people again was not on my bingo card for the foreseeable future, but Nina looks totally unfazed. Almost as if . . .

Ah, okay. Yep. Took me a moment, but I caught up eventually. Nina planned this entire thing, obviously. But why?

Nina takes my hand, which I squeeze gratefully, as she ushers me into the room. "You remember Nate R., whose real name is Wes. Say hi, Wes."

"Hi, Wes." My smartass mouth can't help but make a joke, even as I'm still completely baffled as to what is going on.

After everyone takes their respective seats, Sienna is the first to speak. "We were happy to get your text," she tells Nina.

Nina texted them? When? I'm really out of the loop here. I'd sort of assumed Nina and I would be personae non gratae with anyone from *Mountain Man* after basically demolishing their show. I'd even worried there might be a lawsuit.

"And we're very intrigued by your proposition," Raquel adds.

I really need to get out of the dark here. I don't like being the only person in the room who doesn't know what's going on. I'm usually the keeper of the secrets, not the person who has information withheld from him—and let me tell you, having tasted my own medicine, I am not a fan. "Anyone want to catch me up on what's going on here?"

Sienna's gaze is decidedly less warm as she looks over at me. "Ah, yes. The FBI agent who assured us he wouldn't destroy our show, then went on to—what was it he did again, Rae?"

"Destroyed our show," Raquel deadpans.

Ah, there's that hostility I was worried about. Reserved entirely for me. How fun. I clear my throat. "For the record, I would like to apologize for declaring my love for someone who wasn't one of your contestants. In public. On camera."

Raquel looked unimpressed by the apology. "Would you actually take any of it back?"

"No," I tell her honestly.

"Then don't apologize for it."

Fair enough. I look at Sienna, who shrugs. "Honestly, if we still wanted to make the show work, we could make it work. Declaring your love for the wrong person, revealing a secret double identity—that could all be reality TV gold, if that's still what we were interested in pursuing."

I hone in on that last part, both intrigued and confused. "You aren't still interested in doing the show . . . ?"

Sienna and Raquel exchange a look. Lyle clears his throat, speaking up for the first time. "Ms. Diaz and Ms. Ezra have decided that reality television is not where they would like their future creative endeavors to lie."

"It seemed like a good idea on paper," Sienna laments. "Filming something near home, being close to our families. Not having to leave for months at a time to shoot a project."

"Being behind the cameras for a change," Raquel adds.

"But after Perry got his oily paws on the production, the show was going downhill fast. He insisted on the next challenge being the women wrestling each other in the mud. In bikinis. Even though it was supposed to be the men competing for the women. So it made no sense, in addition to being completely sexist." Sienna stops, taking in a breath. It's clear this rant has been building for some time. "We were thinking of tanking it ourselves after that so it wouldn't be picked up past the pilot."

Raquel nods along with everything Sienna's saying. "Even before that, the show had its problems. It felt like most of the contestants just signed up to try to become famous. The only genuine connection that seemed to be forming was . . . well, you two."

"Us?" I look at Nina in surprise. "But Nina wasn't in any of the scenes, except for that time she was an extra in the background."

Lyle rolls his eyes theatrically. "Let me tell you a little something about how a reality show works, *Nate R.*" He says the fake name with more scorn than is necessary, in my opinion. But I *did* ruin the show that was his livelihood, so go off king, I guess. "The cameras are almost constantly rolling. Even when we aren't officially filming. You never know when you might catch a candid moment, a secret conversation." He levels me with a look. "Or two people falling in love when they aren't supposed to be."

Despite the weirdness of the situation, I can't help but smile as I look over at Nina. To know that some of those sweet moments of connection were captured on film, potentially memorialized forever . . . there are worse things I can imagine. "I guess I wasn't very good at pretending to not be in love with you," I tell her quietly.

"Atrocious," Lyle confirms. "Easily the worst acting I've ever seen in my life, and I got my start on *Killer Sexy Robots 4: The Thunderdome.*"

Okay, that's coming in a little hot, but again, I lost the man his livelihood, so I'll let it slide. I look back to Raquel and Sienna. "I guess it's nice you have that footage, but what does it matter if there's no show?"

"There's no *Mountain Man,*" Raquel corrects me. "But that doesn't mean we don't have a show."

She looks at Nina, as if waiting for her to fill in the blanks, and I realize yet again that I'm still a few steps behind. I look at my lady love questioningly. "What's going on?"

Nina takes in a deep breath, giving another one of her little nods to herself before plunging in. "I've messaged with Lyle about the possibility of turning the footage they already have of the *Mountain Man* show, plus some additional material, into a documentary. About us."

I stare at her, flabbergasted. "But . . . why? Who would watch that?"

No shade intended. I obviously love Nina, and I know I'm great, but I just don't see the appeal of watching two strangers falling in love with each other.

Immediately, though, I can tell this response was a mistake, since I seem to have simultaneously irritated Sienna, Raquel, and Lyle—three of the scariest people I've ever met. And again, I did time undercover in a prison.

"You obviously did not do the reality television homework that you were assigned to make sure you didn't ruin our show," Raquel tells me.

"And look how well that turned out," Sienna deadpans.

Lyle takes in a deep breath, clasping his hands together, like he's prepping himself to talk to a very dumb child. "So, reality television is one of the most watched forms of entertainment. Even when basically every other network television show is struggling to maintain an audience, reality TV still draws in millions of viewers each week. And within that category of reality TV, dating shows consistently draw in some of the highest ratings. You know why that is?"

I'm scared to even attempt an answer. "No?"

"Because people fucking love to watch other people fall in love," Lyle tells me. "Aside from being born and dying, it's one of the few shared human experiences across age and gender and cultural divides. We all love love."

"But we don't like to watch people *pretending* to fall in love," Sienna clarifies. "Which is why the rest of the show would, unfortunately, be such a bust if we tried to salvage any of it—even without the tacky mud wrestling. But the two of you . . ."

I look back to Nina, who is watching my expression carefully. "So you air a documentary about us and all's good. No suing us for breach of contract or anything?"

Raquel taps her chin. "Now there's an idea . . ."

Sienna elbows her, but she's laughing, which is hopefully a good sign.

My mind continues to whir over the possibilities. The plan was always for Nate R. to make an appearance on a high-profile show; that was a concession the FBI was willing to make. But for this documentary to work, I would need to appear on there as myself—Wes Ackerman, not Nate R. Even if the show somehow manages to fudge out all the parts where I'm an undercover FBI agent, the exposure would be much too high profile for me to go back to my job at the bureau afterward. My career with the FBI would be officially over.

I'm not sure that's such a bad thing, honestly. For all of my hopes and dreams about serving a bigger cause and helping people, since meeting Nina, this job has increasingly felt like the wrong fit for me. I do want to help people, but I don't want to spend all of my time facing the ugliest parts of the world. I want to do something that serves humankind, but also makes people happy. I want to make Nina happy. I don't want to put my life on the line anymore. I don't want to lose any more of myself by going undercover.

I just have no idea what else I can do.

As if reading my mind, Nina speaks up. "I've thought about the terms that Lyle sent over in the contract. I have some amendments I'd like made."

For the first time, Sienna, Raquel, and Lyle look taken aback, too. Ha! Seems like I'm not the only one in the dark anymore. "Okay," Lyle speaks up for the group. "Such as . . . ?"

"We'd be willing to forfeit syndication rights and a portion of our royalties in exchange for a small production team to help us film some exercise videos."

I look at Nina sharply, but she maintains her steady gaze on the three entertainment folk, who blink back at her in surprise. "Exercise videos?" Raquel repeats.

"They're called *GeekOut*," Nina explains. "They're workouts that cater to different fantasy fandoms. Wes has been making them for his TikTok feed for a few months. They've done good numbers, despite being relatively new and posted sporadically. With higher production quality—costuming department, lighting, sound—and access to distribution channels, I think they could really take off. Plus we have plans to integrate more of a role-playing aspect—to write original stories and characters and allow viewers the option of choosing between different outcomes."

Nina is honest to God pitching *GeekOut*—the *GeekOut* of my dreams, the one I never thought I'd have the time or funding to bring to life. And with the production power of Sienna Diaz and Raquel Ezra behind it, it might be something that could take off. Something we could make a living off doing.

I'm touched by her faith in me, but come on. That isn't something that real people get to do. You don't just get to pursue your passions and make money doing it.

I open my mouth to gently remind Nina of as much, but Sienna speaks up before I can. "Do you have any samples we can see?"

Nina hands over her phone, with one of the videos already pulled up. It's my "Fight Like Darth Maul" video, my most popular by far, where I demonstrate how to combat with a two-ended lightsaber. (Look, *The Phantom Menace* may have had its issues, but that fight scene with Qui-Gon Jinn—worth the price of admission.) Even knowing hundreds of thousands of people have watched the video already, it feels like a fresh new hell to sit in the room and watch three professional Hollywood producers critique my work.

To my surprise, all three of them are smiling by the end—even Lyle. "It's good," Sienna tells me. "It's aimed toward a clear audience. Simple, easy to grasp. And you're surprisingly funny."

Surprisingly? I feel like I should take that as an insult. I was Funny Guy, remember?! But I'm too happy they liked the video to care. (Much.) "Thank you."

Another glance is exchanged between Sienna and Raquel, before the latter speaks up. "We'd be willing to invest some money into this. Let our lawyer look over the contract, and we'll get back to you with some new terms."

I can't believe our luck. I want to say as much to Nina, but I don't want to jinx it. We'll save the happy dancing for when the producers have left the hotel room.

But to my surprise, Nina clears her throat. "Just two more terms I'd like to discuss."

My knee-jerk instinct is to tell her to hold her horses, we don't want to get ahead of ourselves or spook them off! But seeing the resolve on Nina's face, I check myself. She's gotten us this far. I trust her to make the right calls.

"I want Lyle to be involved in the *GeekOut* project, as the director," Nina says, and I clock the way his face lights up. "And I want to be in charge of the wardrobe department. Deja can oversee if she isn't too busy with her film projects and wants to earn a commission."

It's an incredibly smart call, I realize as soon as she's laid it all out. Nina is building herself a resume, so that if costume or fashion design is something she'd like to pursue in the future, she can show that she has a history of doing it at a professional level.

She's setting both of us up to platform this project into something we can do long term. Both of us, so we're able to pursue our dreams, and focus on ourselves, for the very first time.

Lyle looks to Sienna and Raquel for confirmation, doing his best to fight off a smile at the mini promotion he's been given, thanks to Nina's negotiating. "I think we can work with that," he says.

Finally, I manage to catch Nina's eye. Seeing the excitement there, I can't help but be enormously proud of her. I'll tell her in much more eloquent words as soon as we're alone, able to discuss it freely. But for now, I just give her a wink. *That's my girl,* I mouth to her.

"Those people really love you," I sum up for her as we cuddle together on the couch, once we're finally alone.

It won't last long. Her friends from Chicago are scheduled to arrive in less than an hour. Morrie's already messaged that he's going to need to debrief with Agent Decker and me later today. But for now . . . we're finally, finally alone. No camera crew. No family on the other side of the wall. Just the two of us.

It feels so good to hold her in my arms. Logically I know at some point I'm going to want to stretch, go to the bathroom, eat food, but right now that feels impossible. Right now I can't imagine being this perfectly content anywhere but right here.

"*Those people* recognized a good business deal," she corrects me. "It benefits them, too, if *GeekOut* takes off. And it will."

"And they'll be psyched about that," I add on for her, "because they love artistic fulfillment and money, but they *really* love you."

Nina avoids my gaze, tucking a strand of hair behind her ear. "Hmm. Do you want to get some sleep? You must be tired. Or food? We can order something."

I frown at her transparent attempt to change the subject. "I'm sorry. Are you being squirrely because I'm suggesting that people care about you? Because they obviously do. I'm not even reaching to draw that conclusion. Lyle's driven back and forth between Knoxville, like, ten times in the past two days. And Sienna and Raquel, two of the biggest movie stars in the world, basically just keep doing whatever it takes to get you to work with them."

"Mm-hmm." Nina still isn't quite looking at me.

"Nina." I take her by the chin, gently guiding her to look up at me. "Do you have a hard time acknowledging that people love you?"

Nina's flinch lets me know I've hit the nail on the head. "I know some people care about me." She hurries to defend them—as if it's their ability to love her that's in question here. "But love is a loaded word."

"And yet sometimes an accurate one," I remind her. "Again, let me reference by way of evidence all of your friends hopping on a plane and coming here to support you, no questions asked." Seeing that she still isn't quite buying it, I tentatively broach the subject we've both been avoiding these past few days.

"Just because your uncle made it his mission to make you feel unloved doesn't mean that he was right. I mean, I know I'm biased, but I think you're an extremely lovable person. Above average, even."

I'm making light of it with my tone, but it isn't light to me, not at all. I just don't want to scare Nina off by coming on too strong. She has no idea the effect she has on people, the quiet light and calm she brings with her everywhere she goes. Now that I've started, I can't stop trying to convince her. "I mean, how many people do you think just randomly get offered a job by two movie stars after meeting them for five minutes in a diner? How many people convince a jaded Hollywood producer like Lyle to hand over the keys to his car?" I reach out, tucking a loose strand of hair behind her ear. "How many nuns get an FBI agent posing as a convict to blow his cover because he can't stop thinking about her?"

Nina softens at that last example, though she still seems uncomfortable with the overall suggestion that so many people care about her. "At least three?" she guesses.

I shake my head at her. "Only one. Only *you*, Nina." My heart picks up speed as I realize the natural conclusion to this discussion. There's one sure way to prove to her that she isn't unlovable. "And just in case it isn't obvious, just so it isn't subtext anymore, just so we're totally on the same page, I want to make it totally clear that I'm in love with you. I think I have been for a long time. I don't think I ever stopped. And I know that I never will."

It's been implied so many times between us, especially in these last few days together. All of our plans for the future, as tentative as they might be, all hinge around each other. Wherever Nina goes, that's where I'm planning on being.

But this is the first time I'm saying it, out loud, to her directly—without an audience and a camera crew present. I need her to hear it. I need her to know she isn't unlovable. She's the farthest thing possible from that. I know firsthand, because I tried my best to stop loving her, and I couldn't manage it, even with all the odds stacked against us.

Nina's big, beautiful eyes glisten with emotion. "I love you, too," she tells me. "Still. Always."

Chapter 44
Nina

Four Months Later . . .

Filming has wrapped on the as-yet-untitled *Mountain Man* documentary, and for the last couple of weeks, Wes and I have been knee-deep in preparing for the *GeekOut* filming. We'll be doing a season of a YouTube show—thirteen episodes in total—that could potentially expand into more if it gains enough popularity. From what I've seen of Lyle's storyboards and Wes's ideas, coupled with Sienna and Rae's financial backing, I think it definitely will.

As if prepping for a show isn't busy enough, Wes and I have also been moving into our own place. We'll be staying in Michigan to be close to Wes's family, who have taken me in like one of their own; and luckily we're only about an hour's drive from Chicago, so I still see my friends for Pizookie night, and any other time I get to pop into town. Honestly, even though I'm technically farther away in distance than where I was living before with my family, I've gotten to see my friends way more often since moving—because now *I* get to choose where I go and who I spend my time with. What I eat. What I wear.

I'm trying to take it slowly, little by little. Small changes to test the waters and see how I feel. In some ways, it's been an overwhelming process, trying to decide what from my old life I want to keep, what I want to change, what I want to get rid of completely. *Construction, destruction, reconstruction.* I've started seeing a therapist, recommended by Helen's friend Sandra, and that's helped a lot.

But there have been some big changes, too. I don't keep a food journal anymore. Yesterday I ate French toast for breakfast *and* had ice cream in the afternoon, which is almost double the sugar allowance I used to be given for the whole week. Two days ago, it was a little warm, so I went outside in a tank top. My whole arms were showing! And . . . I watched *Bridgerton*. I know, c-raaaazy stuff.

Luckily, Wes has been beside me the whole way to help me navigate this new terrain. He is so agreeable with whatever I want to try. I never knew men could be that way—easygoing and kind and ready to talk and compromise and laugh and be silly. My whole life, being around men meant being on edge, being careful, treading lightly. But Wes seems to have truly taken to heart what he told me all those weeks ago. I'm the captain. I set the pace, and he happily follows my lead.

In most ways, it's absolutely wonderful.

In some ways, though, it's proven to be a problem. Well, one way, specifically.

Wes has been so gentle with me. Even though we've been living together for months now, we haven't slept together. We haven't even fooled around. There's been no touching of any bathing suit areas. We cuddle. We hold hands. We kiss, but it's the kind of kisses from the Hallmark movies that used to be some of the only programming I was allowed to watch—chaste and close-mouthed—not the kind that set your body on fire.

At first, honestly, that was what I needed. Time to process, time to heal. But now we seem to be in a holding pattern. Wes has never said as much, never even hinted at it, but I know he's waiting for me to take charge. To let him know I'm ready.

That's the problem with being the captain. Sometimes you have to lead, even if you aren't entirely sure how to.

Over the last couple weeks, I've started to feel ready again. I've been reading my romantasy books. And I haven't been subtle about it, either—I've left them around the apartment for Wes to find, all those covers with scantily clad men. Still, nothing. I've been watching *Bridgerton*, hello! If that isn't a sign that you're thinking about sex, I'm not sure what is.

Deep down, I know that Wes is right to hold off. If this is something I want, I'm going to have to learn to ask for it—directly, not passive-aggressively. I need to be able to own my desires and not treat them like something secret or shameful.

But literally nothing in my upbringing or my life thus far has prepared me to have this kind of conversation. It's like I'm fighting against all of my instincts, snuffing out that inner voice that tells me Wes will think less of me for having these urges or that I'm shameful for wanting these things.

Words have never been my strong suit. Luckily, I think I have an idea that will *show* Wes what I want, and that I'm finally ready.

When Wes walks into the living room, holding his phone up to me, a perplexed look on his face, I can't help but laugh. "What's this programmed onto my calendar?" My amusement seems to be contagious, because he's grinning, too. "'Meeting with wardrobe department.' I don't remember scheduling this."

"Hmm, some smart person must have linked our calendars." I rise from the couch, going up on my tiptoes to wrap my arms around his shoulders. He has to bend down to accommodate me—and the guy worried he was too short to be on *Mountain Man.* Ridiculous. "I know you've been busy, but I wanted to make sure we carve out some time for this. You don't have anything planned for the next couple hours."

"Smart." Wes gives me one of his sweet, quick kisses. "Why's my girl so smart?"

I pretend to consider it, then shrug. "You must have done something really good in your last life."

He considers it. "I'm pretty sure in my last life I was a Scotsman." Because of his unnatural love for bagpipes, he doesn't need to elaborate. I'm already well aware.

Now that it's time to implement my plan, I'm starting to get nervous. Maybe even second-guess myself. Do I really need to rock the boat? I'm pretty sure that's the number-one thing captains are taught *not* to do.

But I take a deep breath, steeling myself. "Why don't you sit on the couch? I'll show you a few of the pieces I've put together."

If Wes thinks it's strange that I'm going to model a bunch of costumes that are primarily meant for him and his character, he doesn't let on. Maybe he doesn't suspect anything. Him sitting on the couch as I show him different outfits has become such a regular part of our routine—as I experiment with new clothes and styles and fashions—that it might even seem normal to him.

I pause in the doorway, my heart racing. "Just one rule, okay? The costumes are all still a bit delicate, so don't touch anything. Just looking, okay? And you have to stay on the couch."

Wes makes a show of obediently sliding his hands underneath him and sitting on top of them. "Jedi's honor," he promises me.

I hurry to put on the first costume I've made. I *have* been hard at work making the different outfits Ryko will wear based on the challenges he'll be completing, but if everything goes as planned today, I won't be showing any of them to Wes.

Instead, I put on a dress I've made for myself, complete with a headdress and bracelets and boots. I check myself in the mirror to make sure everything is just right before going back out into the living room.

Wes smiles instinctively at the sight of me, then he straightens once he realizes what I'm wearing. I watch his eyes roving over me, the way he swallows, slow and hard.

"What do you think?" I ask, doing a twirl for him.

I copied my design from one of his many sketches of Princess Annais—the dream fantasy girl who bears more than a passing resemblance to me. She isn't going to be part of the *GeekOut* show—mostly because I have no interest in being an actress, nor in watching my boyfriend pretend to be in love with anyone else ever again—but I thought he might enjoy seeing her come to life. For his eyes only.

This costume isn't anything particularly outrageous, just a fitted emerald-colored dress that hugs my frame, but I can tell from the look on Wes's face that he really, really likes what he sees.

He starts to rise to his feet, but I hold out two hands, stopping him. "Wait! You aren't supposed to stand up, remember? And no touching. Just stay right there, on the couch."

Wes swallows again, his gaze traveling over my body once more before finding mine again. "What is this, Nina?"

"Do you like it?"

"I really, really like it." It might be just my imagination, but I think I see Wes's lap area start to twitch and . . . *expand*, for lack of a better term. That, coupled with the intense look in his pale green eyes, sends heat flaring through me. "Are you going to get any closer . . . ?"

"Not yet," I tease him, disappearing into the other room.

I know I could go to him right away, climb onto the couch with him, tell him he can touch me now, and I'd likely get what I want, what I've been waiting for. But I've had so much time to think about this moment, to plan it out in my head, that a part of me wants to get it exactly right. And, okay, yes, there are also more costumes I made that I want to show him.

So I make Wes sit and watch me as I try on more pieces, each one more revealing than the last. More cleavage. A higher slit up the leg. A shorter skirt.

By the time I come out in my last costume, there's no ambiguity whatsoever about whether Wes's lap is expanding. His cock juts up through the fabric of his gray sweatpants. Nevertheless, he's remained true to his promise to stay on the couch, hands underneath him, even though I can tell it's driving him crazy.

"Whoa," he gasps out when he sees what I'm wearing now.

It's the costume Annais wore for the forest people—the thinly disguised excuse for Wes to draw me practically naked. All I'm wearing is a slash of fabric for my skirt, a headdress—and nothing else. No shoes, no socks. No shirt, no bra. No underwear. Just like in his sketch, I've parted my long hair so it falls down on both sides of my chest, covering my breasts, but only just.

"Do you like this one?" I ask him directly. There's no need to pretend I'm doing anything other than what I am anymore. This is a full-on seduction.

My body spikes with pleasure as Wes squirms on the couch, his eyes raking over me, the muscles in his neck working overtime. "Nina. Come over here. *Please.*"

I bite my lip, pretending to consider it. "You'll keep your hands to yourself unless I tell you otherwise?" At his groan of protest, I remind him, "I *am* the captain, after all."

"O captain, my captain," he moans his agreement, even if it does sound completely anguished.

Slowly, I move toward him. My heart is pounding, both in excitement and some fear. Not because of Wes—I trust him completely, want him completely. But these are unchartered waters for me. Even though this won't be the first time I have sex, it will be the first time I do so fully consenting, fully choosing this for myself.

And I do. My body, already hopelessly excited by the situation, comes even further to life the closer I get to Wes. My breasts feel tight, heavy. My core throbs with heat. I come to a stop just short of touching him, loving the way he's looking at me, the way his body teems with almost tangible need. For me.

"Is this what you imagined?" I ask him. I turn in a slow circle to show him the full effect, and he groans again.

"Yes, lovely," he says. "Only better. So much better."

Smiling, heart thudding in my chest, I climb into his lap so that I'm straddling him. As I brush up against his cock, Wes groans, his head thudding against the back of the couch. "Fuck. Nina. Please. Let me touch you. I need to touch you."

I know. I feel it, too. I need him to be touching me. This was just supposed to be about me teasing him, playing with the control he's given me, but now that I'm here, almost naked, on top of him, feeling him buckling underneath me, trying so desperately to stay still for me—I realize something else has been at play, too. He told me I was the boss, that I was in charge. After everything that's happened to me, I think I needed to know, for certain, that this is true. That my body is mine. That I decide what course it takes.

Closing my eyes, I press my forehead to his. "Soon," I promise him quietly, then take a moment to catch my breath.

Wes seems to hear in my voice that this is no longer a game. He stills completely, waiting. Sweet, wonderful Wes. He's been waiting for me for so long. I know he'd wait for me forever, if I asked him to.

Still with our faces pressed close together, so I can't see his expression and he can't see mine, I tell him quietly, "I've started taking birth control."

I feel him twitch in surprise at that, before he goes still again. "Okay." I can tell he's trying his best to not put pressure on me, to not react too strongly. It would almost make me laugh, if my heart wasn't racing so fast.

"I can still get a condom, if you'd like," I continue. "Unless . . . ?"

"No, I'm fine without," he says quickly. "Whatever you want."

What I want is to feel him inside me, no barriers, as close as two people can be. "Wes," I whisper, "you can touch me now."

He moves so fast that I might fall off him. But he reaches out a quick arm to grab me and fasten me securely onto his lap. Then his hands are everywhere, everywhere, as if they can't quite decide where they most want to be. My hair, my back, my naked torso. Up my flimsy excuse for a skirt so he can take hold of my ass and pull me tighter against his still-clothed cock.

"Wes." I gasp at the friction this causes, then again when he leans forward and his mouth finds my nipple through my curtain of hair. "Wes!"

We rock against each other that way for a long, frantic moment, until it isn't enough anymore. "Take off your pants," I tell him, lifting up so he can do so.

He releases me just long enough to obey before reaching for me again—desperate, so desperate, to be touching me. He tries to slide a finger into me, but I push his hand away impatiently. "I don't need that. I'm ready."

I've *been* ready for weeks. I know it won't always be this way, but I'm so slick with pent-up want that I don't need any prepping. Lifting up again, I work together with Wes to position my entrance at the tip of his cock before sliding down.

Even with how aroused I am, it takes a moment of adjusting before I'm fully seated. Once I am, my gaze startles to his, finding him looking back at me, watching me, some fierce blend of want and love and need and lust in his eyes. "Fuck. *Nina.*"

I move. He moves. His hips thrust up encouragingly as I slide up and down his cock, my walls instinctively tightening around him. It's been a long time, for both of us. We both need it. I can see him, feel him, trying to hold back as I do the same, trying to prolong the pleasure as much as possible. His head falls against my chest, his tongue lavishing worship onto my breasts. One of his hands snakes between us, finding my sensitive, aching center and stroking, coaxing, caressing it as warm pressure builds in my core.

I'm the first to break, with a loud, urgent cry. Wes follows closely after me, fisting my hair, grabbing my ass, calling out my name like it's a prayer.

Afterward—when we've cleaned up, then unexpectedly gone for another round in the shower, then cleaned up again and climbed into the bed so we can spoon and snuggle—I brace myself, waiting for the onslaught of shame. My therapist told me it might still happen, that it could take some time to reprogram my responses. To reconstruct my relationship with my sexuality.

But at least this time, I don't hear any negative voice or feel any guilt or regret. All I feel is happiness—to be here with this man, so adored there's no room to doubt it, so desired I'm going to have a hard time walking straight tomorrow. To have found so much happiness after so many years of thorns, so thick that I'd long lost sight of any path that might lead me out of them.

Wes pulls me in tighter. "O captain, my captain," he murmurs into my hairline.

I giggle at the familiarity, the intimacy of the nickname, especially now that it's taken on a sexy new layer. "Yes?"

"I was just realizing . . . there's still another hour earmarked on my schedule for our meeting."

My smile blossoms on my face, a wild, untamable thing. "Yes?" I prompt him.

"Just so you know, for the record, you have my permission to come onboard any time you like."

From anyone else, it would be a line worthy of breaking up. From Wes, it makes me laugh so hard, I can feel the bed shaking. Rolling over to face him, I pretend to consider it. "Well, you know, we haven't christened the bed yet . . ."

Grinning, Wes leans down to close the distance between us.

Epilogue
BEKAH

"Stewie!" I call from the sofa as I turn up the volume on the telly. "Hurry up! It's starting!"

Poor, longsuffering Officer Stewart (Stewie for short—note, a nickname assigned by me, not suggested by him) trudges into the room. The man truly had no idea what he signed up for when he was given detail at my safe house. I'm not allowed to leave. I'm not allowed to scroll social media or post anything online. I'm not much of a reader, even less of a cook. My only current outlet is watching all of the reality television that we get access to on the basic government cable package we've been provided. Tight bastards didn't even splurge for streaming.

So far Stewart's suffered through three old seasons of *The Bachelorette* and more seasons than I'd care to admit of various *Housewives* spin-offs. Tonight, though, should be a special treat, and not just because I've made one of the few snacks I feel confident whipping up in the kitchen—Oreo popcorn.

"What is it this time?" Stewie asks as he takes the seat beside me on the sofa.

He can groan and complain all he wants about my telly choices. It's all just an act. I happen to know he got cross with me when he missed Rachel Lindsay's finale because Officer Mulligan (aka Mullie) was on duty the day I watched it.

"This show should be different," I tell him, handing him the bowl of popcorn, which he wordlessly takes. "It's called *Mountain Man*. Apparently, it was originally meant to be a reality show like all the others, but something big and dramatic happened on set, so they turned it into a documentary instead, showing all the behind-the-scenes rigamarole. Exciting, don't cha think?"

Stewie would never own up to it being exciting, of course—he's much too masculine and stoic to be able to admit that something as feminine as a dating show could be entertaining—but he's settled back into the sofa, not sitting up ramrod straight like when we first started watching our programs together, so I'll take that as a victory.

As the documentary begins, I'm immediately sucked into the wonky world of what would have been the *Mountain Man* show. "Aww, they should've followed through and made this. It's absolutely barmy! I love it!"

"Why are there so many axes?" Stewie wants to know.

"I dunno. Lumberjacks. Axes. It's a whole thing!" I shrug, powerless to explain the appeal of a flannel on a handsome bearded man. "Ask your wife about it. Maybe she can explain it better."

Stewie just scoffs. "Carly is not into lumberjacks." At my expression, though, he loses some of his certainty. "I think?"

I've never met Stewie's wife, of course, since she exists in that elusive world outside of the safe house, but I'd be willing to bet my last pint of Ben & Jerry's in the freezer that Carly has at least dabbled in some hot lumberjack Google browsing. Still, my job isn't to be the one to disenchant all of the Stewies of the world; let him still believe we women are simple, sweet folk who can orgasm from the tiniest bit of foreplay and definitely have never looked up monster erotica. (Not that I'm speaking from any personal experience or anything.)

"Nah, I'm sure she finds big, burly men who can chop wood repulsive," I lie. Probably unconvincingly, based off the side-eye Stewie gives me.

The documentary interrupts for an interview with the two movie stars who would have been the executive producers of the show, Sienna Diaz and Raquel Ezra. "Ooh, I love them!" I tell Stewie, both because I am eager for the shift in conversation topics, and because I genuinely adore both of those women. I'd give a kidney to either, if they needed it, that's the level of adoration I'm at. "Raquel is my style icon. And Sienna is my life icon. Or maybe reversed? It's impossible to choose."

"They look vaguely familiar." Stewie frowns as if genuinely trying to place two of the most famous women in the world.

God bless him. I resist the urge to patronizingly pat the side of his face, instead taking a long sip of my wine. In my experience, men don't like to be condescendingly patted. Shame, though, since the urge happens so very frequently.

"This scene was the first time we began to notice that one of our Mountain Men wasn't necessarily keeping his focus on the show," Raquel teases in the interview. "And if you watch some of this footage, I think you'll see what we saw . . ."

The documentary cuts to one of the *Mountain Man* scenes, which seems to have been set up as a date between one of the Mountainettes, Harmony, and her front-runner, whose name is, I think, Nate R. It's hard to remember the names of all the fellas, but I liked him ever since I saw him juggling and wearing that goofy coonskin cap. When you watch enough reality shows, you know it's genuinely refreshing to find someone who doesn't take themselves too seriously.

So far, Nate R. has appeared to be reciprocating Harmony's feelings pretty closely, but on this date—which takes place in a bakery—he seems distracted. His eyes keep darting over to a very pretty girl who's sitting a few tables over with a very handsome man with gorgeous dark hair—

I spit out the wine that's in my mouth. Yep. A genuine spit-take. That's really a thing, apparently. I never knew. I thought it was only something that happened in the movies. But here I am, so surprised the wine comes spewing out of my mouth. Shame—it was a pretty good one for being on discount. "Holy shit!"

Stewie seems to think I'm reacting to something dangerous. He's on his feet in an instant, one hand on his holster, the other reaching for his radio.

I wave him down before he can shoot anything again (RIP old coatrack), trying to deescalate the situation, even though my heart is racing. "No, no. It's fine. It's fine. I just—" As the man's face comes on screen again, I grab the remote and hit pause.

There. Slightly blurred, a few years older, still alarmingly handsome. Grady Kelley. I stare at his frozen face, surprised, then not surprised, by the way my heart lurches in response to him.

Stewie settles back again, looking between my expression and the screen. His response might be comical if I weren't still feeling like someone just pushed me off a high-speed train—emotionally speaking, that is. "You know that guy?"

Hah. That's a bit of an understatement, if ever I heard one. I fish around for the right words to explain what I was to Grady. What Grady was to me. "He used to be my . . ."

There are so many ways I could finish that sentence. I go with the one that is both the simplest and the most complicated. "My priest."

Well, not really *my* priest. I was never one of his parishioners.

But then again, he's always been *my priest*, in every other way that mattered.

To Be Continued . . .

Acknowledgments

As always, there are so many people to thank, I hardly know where to begin!

Thank you first and foremost to the amazing SmartyPants crew—Penny Reid, Fiona Fischer, Nicole McCurdy, Briana Ozor, M.E. Carter, and Julie Schrader. A book always takes a team of people to help become the best version of itself, but this book REALLY needed the whole team to become the story it was trying to be. My story is, thankfully, nowhere near as fraught as Nina's, but I was trying to tell a story that *is* very close to my heart, and having those outside perspectives helped me get over some of the hurdles that were holding me back. Thank you, thank you, to this wonderful team of editors and proofreaders—this book would not be what it is without you.

Thank you to my wonderfully supportive husband, Mike, and my littlest but biggest fan, J.

Thank you to the readers who have emailed and messaged me about Nina's story. It means so much that people were excited to read this and that you cared so much about this character.

Thanks to all of the fantastic soundtracks and composers out there who have inspired both Wes and me. This time through, Rachel Portman and the *Sisterhood of the Traveling Pants* 2 soundtrack were integral to capture the sound of Nina's heart.

And thank you for reading! If you enjoyed the book, I would truly love to hear from you. You can find all my info at www.lissasharpeauthor.com, where you can also sign up for my newsletter to get extra bonus material like playlists, dream casting, deleted scenes, etc.

About the Author

Lissa Sharpe is a mom, a wife, a teacher, a PhD, and an award-winning writer. She has written plays, screenplays, teleplays, short stories, songs, and now for the very first time, a romance novel. When she isn't having mental arguments with her characters, she is hanging out in the American South with her husband, son, and golden lab.

Find Lissa Sharpe online:
Facebook - https://www.facebook.com/profile.php?id=100095127281327
Twitter - https://twitter.com/AuthorLissaS
Instagram - https://www.instagram.com/lissasharpeauthor/
Pinterest - https://pin.it/1n38Ml7Vy
Website - lissasharpeauthor.wordpress.com
gmail- lissasharpeauthor@gmail.com
Newsletter: http://eepurl.com/iwYxdA

Find Smartypants Romance online:
Website: www.smartypantsromance.com
Facebook: www.facebook.com/smartypantsromance/
Goodreads: www.goodreads.com/smartypantsromance
Twitter: @smartypantsrom
Instagram: @smartypantsromance

Also by Lissa Sharpe

As Elizabeth Gilliland:
What Happened on Box Hill
The Portraits of Pemberley
Sly Jane Fairfax
Dear Prudent Elinor

As E. Gilliland:
Come One, Come All
Round and Round We Go

As Lissa Sharpe:
Nun Too Soon
Nun the Wiser
Second to Nun

Also by Smartypants Romance

Green Valley Chronicles
The Love at First Sight Series
Baking Me Crazy by Karla Sorensen (#1)
Batter of Wits by Karla Sorensen (#2)
Steal My Magnolia by Karla Sorensen (#3)
Worth the Wait by Karla Sorensen (#4)

Fighting For Love Series
Stud Muffin by Jiffy Kate (#1)
Beef Cake by Jiffy Kate (#2)
Eye Candy by Jiffy Kate (#3)
Knock Out by Jiffy Kate (#4)

The Donner Bakery Series
No Whisk, No Reward by Ellie Kay (#1)
Dough You Love Me? By Stacy Travis (#2)
Tough Cookie by Talia Hunter (#3)
Muffin But Trouble by Talia Hunter (#4)

Oh Brother! Series
Crime and Periodicals by Nora Everly (#1)
Carpentry and Cocktails by Nora Everly (#2)
Hotshot and Hospitality by Nora Everly (#3)
Architecture and Artistry by Nora Everly (#4)

Small Town Silver Fox Series
Love in Due Time by L.B. Dunbar (#1)
Love in Deed by L.B. Dunbar (#2)
Love in a Pickle by L.B. Dunbar (#3)

The Green Valley Library Series

Prose Before Bros by Cathy Yardley (#1)

Shelf Awareness by Katie Ashley (#2)

Dewey Belong Together by Ann Whynot (#3)

Checking You Out by Ann Whynot (#4)

Scorned Women's Society Series

My Bare Lady by Piper Sheldon (#1)

The Treble with Men by Piper Sheldon (#2)

The One That I Want by Piper Sheldon (#3)

Hopelessly Devoted by Piper Sheldon (#3.5)

It Takes a Woman by Piper Sheldon (#4)

Park Ranger Series

Happy Trail by Daisy Prescott (#1)

Stranger Ranger by Daisy Prescott (#2)

The Leffersbee Series

Been There Done That by Hope Ellis (#1)

Before and After You by Hope Ellis (#2)

The Higher Learning Series

Upsy Daisy by Chelsie Edwards (#1)

Green Valley Heroes Series

Forrest for the Trees by Kilby Blades (#1)

Parks and Provocation by Juliette Cross (#2)

Letter Late Than Never by Lauren Connolly (#3)

Peaches and Dreams by Juliette Cross (#4)

Young Buck by Kilby Blades (#5)

Package Makes Perfect by Lauren Connolly (#6)

All Fired Up by Allie Winters (#7)

Wild Goose Chase by Kilby Blades (#8)